MICHAEL GREATREX CONEY, who lives in Sidney, British Columbia, is a winner of the British SF Writers Association Award and the author of *Fang the Gnome, Brontomex, Cat Karina, The Celestial Steam Locomotive,* and *Gods of the Greataway,* as well as of several other novels and numerous short stories.

P9-CBV-133

KING
OF THE
SCEPTER'D
ISLE

Michael Greatrex Coney

A ROC BOOK

ROC
Published by the Penguin Group
Penguin Books USA Inc., 375 Hudson Street, New York, New York 10014, U.S.A.
Penguin Books Ltd, 27 Wrights Lane, London W8 5TZ, England
Penguin Books Australia Ltd, Ringwood, Victoria, Australia
Penguin Books Canada Ltd, 2801 John Street, Markham, Ontario, Canada L3R 1B4
Penguin Books (N.Z.) Ltd, 182-190 Wairau Road, Auckland 10, New Zealand

Penguin Books Ltd, Registered Offices: Harmondsworth, Middlesex, England

KING OF THE SCEPTER'D ISLE previously appeared
in an NAL Books hardcover edition.

First ROC printing, November, 1990
10 9 8 7 6 5 4 3 2 1

 Roc is a trademark of Penguin Books USA Inc.

Printed in the United States of America

BOOKS ARE AVAILABLE AT QUANTITY DISCOUNTS WHEN USED TO PROMOTE PRODUCTS
OR SERVICES. FOR INFORMATION PLEASE WRITE TO PREMIUM MARKETING DIVISION,
PENGUIN BOOKS USA INC., 375 HUDSON STREET, NEW YORK, NEW YORK 10014.

For Shanna, Ryan, Nicki, Mandy, Terry and David
with all my love

1
CASTLE CAMYLIARD

THE TWO GREATEST STORYTELLERS IN ALL ENGLAND came to Castle Camyliard late one autumn afternoon.

"He calls himself king," said Merlin.

"And why not?" Nyneve regarded the grim bulk of the castle in some awe. "It looks like the kind of place a king would live in. But not me. Not for any title." She was fifteen years old at that time, still learning about men but already beautiful enough to influence them.

The castle of this western land loomed dark and granite-faced from a breast of broken moorland. From its battlements the gray Atlantic could be seen on three sides, restless, sucking hungrily at the cliffs. North lay Wales, south lay France. Prisoner rocks struggled in the western sea, abandoned by the defeated land. Remains of a sunken Lyonesse could be seen all the way from Land's End to the Scilly Isles.

England lay to the east of the castle. There the Romans, with troubles at home, had been withdrawing their forces for many years. This made little difference to Camyliard. The Romans had never penetrated this far into Cornwall, and King Lodegrance reigned unchallenged.

"They've all started calling themselves king. Every little chief in England. Once the Romans move out, they get delusions of grandeur. Empty-headed peacocks, that's what they are. What we need is someone strong enough to unite them." A fine drizzle was falling and Nyneve was anxious to get on, but Merlin had shambled to a halt, gesturing with the willow twig he called a wand. "A leader of men!" he cried, addressing the empty moorland with shrill enthusiasm. "A man of courage and wisdom, with the strength of a lion and the gentleness of a deer."

"Have you ever seen stags in the rutting season?"

"A female deer, although manly in all other ways. To bring them all together in peace and understanding. A man like—"

"Like you, Merlin?" asked Nyneve skeptically.

"Like Arthur!"

A surprising change came over Nyneve. She flushed and said, "Yes."

"We will tell the people of Camyliard about Arthur!"

"Well, yes. That's what we're here for, remember? And this is about as far as we can get, thank the Lord. After Camyliard we head back home."

Merlin gazed resentfully at the sea beyond the castle. "These last few weeks have been a wonderful experience for you, Nyneve. I've protected you and fed you and sheltered you—"

"And tried to get in bed with me."

"—and given you the benefits of thousands of years of experience, and . . ." Her last remark filtered through to him and his voice grew petulant. "And all I've asked in return is a little friendship. A little daughterly affection. And what have I received?" He searched his ancient brain for the right word. "Rebuffment."

"Don't let's go into all that again. Come on, Merlin. I'm getting frozen to the marrow standing here. We've got another two miles to go, at least."

By the time they reached the castle it was getting dark. Lanterns cast a sickly yellow light on the wet walls and a cold sea breeze eddied around their ankles. The gulls were silent now, settling down for the night; and sleepy Camyliard goats uttered the occasional complaint from nearby barns.

A guard stepped clanking from the shadows. "Halt!"

"We *are* halted, for God's sake. Put that pointed thing down before you hurt someone. I'm Merlin."

A derisive laugh. "Oh, yes? Cast a spell, then."

"I will do as I choose. Now let us through. Nyneve and I have come to entertain the castle."

A sudden change came over the man. He didn't exactly spring to attention, but he was clearly impressed. "Nyneve? She's the storyteller. We've heard about her."

"And about me, clearly," said Merlin, piqued. "Now take us to the king."

King Lodegrance sat before a cavernous fireplace with his boots off, drinking wine. He was a short, thickset man with the dark hair of the Cornish Celt and a geography of lines on his face that suggested laughter, or cruelty, or both. In a deep chair opposite, his queen gazed at the flames, pale of face and hair, captured from Saxon forebears many years ago and never able to forget it. A handful of favored soldiers lolled about the chamber, attended by servants. A minstrel strummed a lonely air about a lost lass.

"For pity's sake stop that twanging," shouted the king. "The night's bad enough without your whining." Then he noticed the newcomers. "Come over here and let me look at you," he commanded. He examined the pair as they stood dripping onto the flagstones. "The girl's pretty enough. Clean her up and put some decent clothes on her. There's nothing we can do for the old man, though. By the Lord Jesus, I hope I never get that old. Feed him to the dogs. It's the kindest thing."

"I am Merlin!" cried the wizard, outraged.

"They are Nyneve and Merlin," said the guard. "You know, sire. The storytellers."

"Oh, yes. I'd heard they were heading this way. Well, you've come at the right time." The lines on his face arranged themselves into a grim smile. "Now we can hang that minstrel. And our daughter is sick. I understand you are some kind of a healer, Merlin. You will have a chance to practice your skills before you entertain us."

"Certainly," replied Merlin, trapped.

"Get them cleaned up, then," commanded the king.

Some time later Nyneve, bathed, scented, and dressed, was led into the king's presence again. His eyebrows lifted as he took in her black, lustrous hair, her heart-shaped face with its warm brown eyes, and her cuddlesome figure. They'd dressed her in one of the king's daughter's dresses, and it was apparent Nyneve was the more rounded of the two. In contrast was Merlin, with sacklike smock and bony ankles. "I trust my robes will soon be available," said the latter with a pathetic attempt at dignity.

"You look more entertaining like that," said the king. "But first you must see to my daughter."

The daughter, Gwen, was a pallid younger version of her mother, lost in a large bed. The bedchamber was vast and smoky, and as Merlin and Nyneve entered, a wad of soot flopped into the fireplace, discouraging the fire but offering compensation in the form of a rook's nest. The king accompanied them to the bedside.

"Work your miracles, Merlin."

Merlin took the girl's limp hand. Her eyes watched him with the docility of a heifer. Her face was thinner than Nyneve's, the jaw coming to a narrow point. "What seems to be the trouble?" Merlin asked her, hoping for an instant solution to his dilemma.

"That's for you to find out, Merlin," snapped the king. He swung around and left.

Merlin turned to Nyneve. "Rule number one is to ask the patient first," he said.

"The king wouldn't know that, not being a healer himself," said Nyneve mischievously.

Merlin laid a hand on the girl's forehead. "She has no fever." He took her wrist. "Her pulse is weak." He pulled down the bedclothes and gazed at the girl's half-clad breasts, seeking inspiration. He reached out a hand.

"Don't you dare!" snapped Gwen.

"I'm a healer. I'm accustomed to such things." His hand

hovered over her breast like a vulture, awaiting a sign of weakness.

"I think you're a filthy old man."

"You're right," said Nyneve. "He *is* a filthy old man."

Gwen smiled. "You're the first human being I've seen for months. Get this old fool out of here, will you, and let's talk."

Grumbling, Merlin departed. "He's all right, really," said Nyneve. "You just have to keep him at arm's length. It's his sister Avalona I'm frightened of. Or she may be his mother. I always forget—they're both so old."

"How old?" asked Gwen. "I've never seen anyone quite so old as him."

"Thousands of years, so he says. And I believe him, because he knows an awful lot. How old are you?"

"Seventeen. And you?"

"Fifteen. My name's Nyneve."

"Fifteen . . . ?" Gwen regarded her curiously. "You look much older. I mean, you don't *look* older, but you seem older. Where are you from?"

"Mara Zion, to the east. It's a village in a forest, not far from Castle Menheniot."

"You must have seen an awful lot of the world." Gwen looked sad. "I've seen nothing. I've never been farther than the beach in seventeen years."

"I've seen the greataway," said Nyneve, rather smugly.

"The greataway?"

"It's up in the sky. It's all of time and all of space, and it's huge. All the stars are in it, and Earth too. The stars are suns just like our sun, you know. Avalona took me into the greataway once. She showed me a god up there, called Starquin."

Gwen, baffled by all this, seized one solid fact. "God is called God."

"That's just what the Church tells you. Avalona says the Church doesn't know what it's talking about. Do the people in the village here believe in the Church and all that stuff?"

"I don't know. My father doesn't like me talking to the

villagers.'' Gwen sighed. ''He says I'm a princess and I should act like one. And that means not having friends in the village, apparently. I expect you have lots of friends in Mara Zion.''

''Not so many.'' Now it was Nyneve's turn for sadness. ''Since Avalona and Merlin took me into their cottage, I've lost touch with people. I sometimes see Tristan, our local chief, but that's about all. Except for the gnomes, of course. Avalona encourages me to be friends with the gnomes. She has some kind of a plan for them.''

''Gnomes? We call them piskeys around here. But how can you be friends with them? You can't even speak to them.''

''I can.'' Nyneve stood and walked across to a slit window. The hillside fell away to the unseen sea. The rain had ceased and the wet grass glittered silver in the light from the moons. In a rare coincidence, all three were full: Mighty Moon like a hard-edged coin, Misty Moon watery but still bright, and Maybe Moon a pallid shadow above the other two. Close by a rocky outcrop of granite she could see a ruddy glow. Tiny, shadowy figures sat around a wood fire. It was a gnomish tradition to meet at night and discuss the day's events. She'd seen such gatherings several times since leaving Mara Zion. It seemed the gnomes were becoming more visible all the time.

''As a matter of fact,'' Nyneve said, ''my best friend is a gnome called Fang.''

''That's a funny name for a gnome.''

''His real name's Will, but he killed a stoat and they renamed him Fang. It's an honor for a gnome to get a new name like that.''

''But how can you *talk* to him? We can't hear gnomes and they can't hear us. We can hardly see them.''

''There's a place in Mara Zion where the mushrooms grow in a circle. Avalona tells me it's because the gnomes' world and ours meet there like two bubbles touching. She said the atmospheres react and fix nitrogen in the soil— whatever the hell *that* means—and fertilize the mushrooms.

Anyway, I can step through into the gnomes' world whenever I feel like it.''

This didn't surprise Gwen, who already considered Nyneve to be omnipotent. ''What's it like in there?''

''Much like this world, except the humans look shadowy and you can't touch them. The gnomes call us giants, and they call our world the umbra.'' She chuckled. ''Sometimes I sit in the gnomes' world and spy on our people. I saw Tristan feeling a girl's tits once, but then she got frightened and ran away. What a bloody shame! Anyway, he's in Ireland visiting a woman called Iseult, whom he's sweet on.''

Gwen was enormously impressed with Nyneve's worldliness. ''Have you ever . . . made love, Nyneve?''

''Once. With Tristan just after Iseult left. He looked so unhappy and I wanted to cheer him up. It was nice. But then something happened and I haven't done it since.''

''What happened?''

''Oh . . .'' Nyneve flushed. ''It's ridiculous, really.''

''Go on!''

''Well, Merlin and I have been telling stories to the people in Mara Zion for a little while. Travelers have heard us and the word seems to have gotten around. And suddenly Avalona insisted we come to Land's End, telling stories on the way. I think she somehow has the idea we're going to change the whole human race. 'We are using the stories to make the world see sense,' '' she said, mimicking in a cracked voice. ''You see, the people in the stories are different from real people. They fight a lot, but when they've won, they don't gloat and kill their enemies. They let them go free. And they're funny about women too. They respect them, and if somebody insults a woman they beat the shit out of him. And they do one another favors, and they trust one another, and they go on quests that last for years. It's all kind of different, and fun.''

''But what does it have to do with you not fucking?'' It was Gwen's turn to flush as a forbidden word slipped out. She'd never talked like this before.

''Merlin and I have a kind of *talent*. When we tell the

stories, the audience *sees* them happening, in their minds. I can't explain it, but you'll see what I mean later on. This makes the stories seem very real to people. And they're very real to Merlin and I.

"The hero of the stories is Arthur. He's the best man that ever was. I know him so well, I dream about him every night, and I can see him and talk to him in my mind whenever I want to. Sometimes when my stepmother is being nasty, or I'm feeling bad about something, I slip my thoughts toward him and there he is, big and strong and gentle. To me he's *real*. I could never love anyone else."

Gwen's eyes were shining. "What a lovely story! How romantic you are, Nyneve!"

"Yes, aren't I." Nyneve noticed Gwen's heightened color. "You're looking better."

"All I need is someone to talk to. I've been going crazy all by myself in this castle, ever since Father caught me talking to Jacob in the village. And that was last spring. I've begged Father to send me away for a while—there are places where they send daughters of the gentry, and they learn all kinds of things and meet different people. But he says no. He says no to everything these days. He says there's too much unrest in England for me to travel. He says the Saxons are taking over, and he keeps worrying about someone called Vortigern. To hell with Vortigern, that's what I say. I want to see the world!"

"Maybe he'd let you come to Mara Zion sometime. You'd enjoy that. A girl can get into all kinds of trouble in Mara Zion. And I could introduce you to the gnomes."

"Oh, Nyneve. Would you have me there?"

"Of course." She regarded Gwen thoughtfully. "Are you going to listen to our story tonight?"

"Oh, yes!"

"Like I said, the stories are real. In a way, it'll be your chance to see something of the world. And it's a really exciting world, I can tell you. Get dressed, and let's go downstairs." She hesitated. "How would you like to be a part of the story yourself?"

"How do you mean?"

Nyneve grinned. "You'll see."

King Lodegrance regarded his daughter in amazement. "Merlin, you've worked a miracle. And I thought you were an old fraud."

"Old I may be," said Merlin with dignity, trying to conceal his equal amazement, "but fraud I am not. There's a strange magic in these ancient hands."

Gwen stood before them, fully dressed, a changed girl. "Nyneve says I can go and stay with her in Mara Zion for a while," she said.

Her father bit back an instant refusal. "We'll think about it," he said.

"We'd be happy to have her stay," said Nyneve.

"Let her go," said the queen. They were the first words she'd uttered all evening.

"No," he said automatically. Then, seeing the change in Gwen's expression, he said quickly, "Not at present. It's autumn now. I'm not having you spend the winter in some forest hovel. We'll talk about it in the spring."

She eyed him closely. "Are you just putting me off?"

He favored her with a rare smile. "No, Gwen. We'll really talk about it, and I'll make a few inquiries. And if I get the right answers, you can go."

"Father!" She threw her arms around his neck. Then she moved away a little, looking into his face. "Why? You hardly know Nyneve."

"Neither do you." He glanced at Nyneve, puzzled. "What the hell has come over me? Are you some kind of a witch?"

"Of course not. Merlin thinks he's a wizard, but I'm just a girl."

The queen said in flat tones, "Her witchcraft stems from her beauty. Any fool could see that, except my husband."

"Well, I think it's about time Gwen saw something of the world," said the king, "and she can't come to much harm in Mara Zion. It's only two days' ride away. Vortigern's never come that close—and if he did, Baron Menheniot's more than a match for him. They say there's a new fellow on the way up too. Name of Tristan. I daresay you've heard of him, Nyneve.''

"He has a magic sword," said Nyneve. "Merlin made it. It's called Excalibur. It's such a good sword that we use it in the stories."

"A sword with a name? That's not a bad idea." He glanced at his own weapon, leaning against the fireplace. "I think I'll call my sword Charles. Charles is a dignified kind of name. Anyway''—he recalled himself to the business at hand—"time's getting on. You people have a reputation as storytellers. So tell your story.''

He settled back in his chair, gulping wine and gazing expectantly at Nyneve.

She walked to the center of the chamber and looked around. "Here will be fine," she said after a moment. "And you bring that chair over and sit beside me, Merlin. I'll stand. We'll go over what we rehearsed last night, except I want to make one or two changes to my part. You don't have to worry about that.''

"Who's in charge of this story, that's what I'd like to know," grumbled Merlin, setting down his chair heavily and slumping into it. He still wore the washed-out smock, but he'd put on his conical hat to try to enhance his presence.

"This is the story we've been telling in Mara Zion," Nyneve told the audience. "Avalona and Merlin started it, and I joined in soon after. It's not like a normal story, because we've hardly invented any part of it ourselves. It just comes into our minds like a dream. It's a very real story and it follows its own path—we hardly guide it at all. It seems to have no end, although Avalona says it will finish thirty thousand years in the future.

"Sometimes I think it *is* real," she confided. "Avalona talks about happentracks—you know, other worlds near our world, like where the gnomes live—and I sometimes think the world of Arthur really exists on another happentrack very close to ours. Because sometimes we put real people into our stories, and they fit perfectly. And that tells me Arthur's world can't be far away. Tonight I want to put a real person in.'' She smiled at Gwen.

She brought her audience up-to-date on the saga as it had unfolded so far. She told them of King Uther Pendragon and his desire for the beautiful Igraine, and the underhanded way he got her into bed. She spoke of the birth of Arthur, then Merlin took over and described his part in teaching the boy. The audience listened attentively because the couple spoke so well; but this was ordinary storytelling, nothing more. Then Nyneve introduced the Sword in the Stone.

''When matins were over, the archbishop led his congregation out into the yard. Here was a marble block with an anvil in it, into which had been thrust a beautiful sword. Letters of gold were inscribed on the anvil:

WHOSO PULLETH OUTE THIS SWERD OF THIS STONE AND ANVYLD IS RIGHTWYS KYNGE BORNE OF ALL BRETAGNE.

That's what it said.''

And there was a sudden restlessness in her audience, and cries of astonishment.

''I can *see* it,'' said someone. ''By the Lord Jesus, I can *see* the Sword in the Stone!''

The chamber had become a theater. ''The nobles all tried to pull it out,'' cried Nyneve, and her audience saw a succession of grunting, sweating men laying hands on the handle, pulling, jerking, cursing, turning away in disgust. The men were real, with faces and hopes and families, and the audience knew all this. A murmur of wonder arose. This was better than a troupe of traveling players. It was better than anything they'd ever experienced before. It was also a little frightening.

''She's a witch,'' a voice cried.

"I don't care if she is!" shouted King Lodegrance. "Don't interrupt!"

Now Merlin took over, taking the part of the archbishop. "Nobody will ever move this sword," he cried. "You're all wasting your time. We will hold a tournament on New Year's Day to decide who will be king!"

And the audience saw winter close over the land, and they felt the Siberian winds blow.

The knights gathered for the tournament, helmeted, armored, and armed. Slipping easily into the part of Sir Kay, Merlin said, "Arthur, I've left my sword behind at our lodgings. Go and fetch it for me, there's a good fellow."

"Certainly, brother," said Nyneve.

She walked a few paces across the chamber, but her audience saw a young man walking through the streets of London. She stopped, and Arthur stopped. Before him was a marble slab with an anvil and a sword protruding from it.

"Then he caught sight of the sword stuck in the stone, and thought it was worth trying to pull it out. The marble slab sat in the churchyard under the trees, glowing in the January sunlight. There was a sound like angels singing. Arthur's hand tingled as he touched the sword."

Nyneve had told this part of the story before, so the words came easily, as did the visions. She felt her heart pounding as she said, "He took hold of the sword. He braced his foot against the rock. And then . . . he drew the sword out easily, as if it had been embedded in butter. For a while he stood with it in his hand."

The audience saw the sunlight on his auburn hair, and they heard the angels—which might have been birds—singing. And because they saw everything, felt everything, and knew everything, they knew he hadn't even seen the words on the anvil, and had no idea what a wonderful moment this was. He felt glad that he'd found a sword for Sir Kay, his foster brother; and that was all.

Arthur took the sword back to Sir Kay and the revelation took place, and the audience felt just as amazed as the characters in the story, even though they already knew it was *the* sword. They shared the emotions, they shared the joy. "So they crowned him king of all England," said Nyneve. "Nobody disputed him. It was right and proper."

Nyneve gave her audience a chance to relax, describing in words the subsequent events, giving them occasional glimpses of battles and tournaments, but saving the next big event for Gwen.

"A king should marry," said Merlin eventually. "England needs a queen. Tell me, Arthur, is there anyone you have in mind?"

The transition from narrative to action was smoothly done. Nyneve became Arthur in the audience's eyes, talking to an ancient magician of somehow greater stature than the real-life Merlin before them. That was one of the secrets of the story's appeal. Everybody was a little larger than life. "I love Guinevere," said Arthur, "the daughter of King Lodegrance of the land of Camyliard. She is far and away the most beautiful woman I've ever seen."

"That's good," said Merlin. "It saves me having to find someone for you. That kind of quest is doomed to failure before it starts. Now, I know you've made up your mind, but I have to tell you—Guinevere will cause you grief. The time will come when she'll fool around with a fellow called Lancelot. When that happens, don't say I didn't warn you."

"I'll take my chances," said Nyneve. "Go and break it to Lodegrance, Merlin, and bring Guinevere to me."

Then came the most amazing part of the performance, as though the audience hadn't had enough to marvel at. In their minds, they followed Merlin on a journey that culminated with the arrival at Camyliard and an audience with King Lodegrance. They saw Merlin walk into the same chamber in which he now sat. And they saw Lodegrance in their minds, and in reality at the same time.

And then: "This is my daughter Guinevere," said the vision of the king.

Into the chamber walked a fair, pale girl.

The real Gwen smiled, enchanted. "Bravo!" murmured the real Lodegrance.

"I can see why King Arthur is in love," said Merlin. "Your daughter is the fairest lady I have seen in all England."

"Thank you, Merlin. I find myself well satisfied with the match too. Arthur is a worthy man for Gwen's hand. Indeed, he could have all my lands, if he needed them. But he has enough land of his own, so I will give him something else."

"And what is that, Sire?"

"It is the Round Table, which Uther Pendragon gave me. It seats a hundred and fifty knights. I can let Arthur have a hundred knights to go with it, but I'm fifty short after beating off the Irish last autumn. I'm sure Arthur can raise the other fifty."

"Arthur will be highly pleased," said Merlin, and departed.

It took a fortnight to prepare for the departure of Guinevere and the hundred knights. The villagers set to work with a will, seamstresses working on Guinevere's wedding dress, ostlers preparing the horses and harness, carpenters dismantling the Round Table and loading it into carts. Meanwhile in the castle there was a fortnight of feasting and celebration, music and dancing, and Guinevere was the belle of the occasion.

By the time Guinevere and her escort departed, Nyneve's audience was as exhausted as if they'd danced for a fortnight themselves.

The storytellers fell silent. The images faded. The audience returned to the present, blinking like people coming in from the dark.

"That was amazing," said King Lodegrance.

"Wonderful," Gwen sighed.

"But I must tell you I never knew King Uther, if there was such a man; and I have no Round Table."

"It's just a story," said Nyneve, "I think. But it's had quite an effect on people. Tristan's based his whole behavior on it, and built a Round Table himself. Even Baron Menheniot's introduced the idea of chivalry to his court. With some difficulty, because they're a rough bunch of people. Anyway, it seems to be spreading around, the way Avalona hoped it would. Or,'' she said, correcting herself, ''the way Avalona *knew* it would. She knows everything.''

''Well . . .'' The king yawned and stretched thick arms. ''It's long past midnight. I must thank both of you for a very entertaining evening. You lived up to all the reports I'd heard.''

''Are you going to continue the story tomorrow night?'' asked Gwen.

''We must leave in the morning,'' said Merlin testily. It was well past his bedtime, and lack of sleep made him irritable.

''I'll tell you the rest when you come to Mara Zion, Gwen,'' said Nyneve.

She awakened the next morning to gray daylight and a tap on the door.

''Who's that?'' She'd bolted the door in case Merlin came shuffling into her chamber during the night, on the pretext of sleepwalking.

''It's me, Gwen. I've brought your clothes. They've been washed and dried.''

Nyneve unfastened the door. Gwen was dressed and, Nyneve was pleased to see, looking much brighter than yesterday. ''Come in. I think I must have overslept. Telling the story often does that to me.''

Gwen sat on the bed while Nyneve pulled on her clothes. ''The story. How does it end?''

''I told you. I don't know.'' In the cold light of day, Nyneve was beginning to regret her impulse in inviting this girl to Mara Zion. Without the lamplight to flatter her, Gwen had a vapid look. ''Last night was as far as the story's gotten so far,'' she explained, relenting.

''Do you suppose they really do get married?''

''I suppose so.''

''This Arthur. He's so *real*. I . . . I dreamed about him last night, Nyneve. He's very handsome, isn't he? It's dif-

ficult to believe he doesn't exist. I mean, how could everything be so *exact?*''

''I told you last night. I have a suspicion that it might be
a real world on a different happentrack.'' Looking out of
the window, Nyneve saw the tiny, half-seen figures of
gnomes flitting about their business. Obviously they had a
village here; some of their dwellings were probably under
the castle. The umbra: that was what the Mara Zion gnomes
called the shadowy worlds of other people. You could see
people in the umbra—just—but you couldn't hear them.
When she got back, she must ask her friend Fang. Apart
from her own world, had he ever glimpsed any other world
in the umbra—a world of chivalry and honor, peopled by
humans?

And if she could step through the fairy ring into Fang's world,
could she perhaps take a further step into Arthur's . . . ?

Suddenly she was impatient to get back to Mara Zion.

''Arthur—'' Gwen began.

''You'd better forget about Arthur,'' said Nyneve, more
sharply than she'd intended.

Gwen said, ''You're jealous, aren't you!''

2
WORLD-SHAKING EVENTS IN MARA ZION

In those far-off days the Roman Empire was menaced on all sides by barbarians. The Vandals, the Suevi, and the Burgundians had attacked Gaul in the early part of the century, and Alaric, King of the Visigoths, had besieged Rome itself. Small wonder that the Empire had begun to withdraw its troops from Britain.

In the Scepter'd Isle itself, the old ways were changing. Scottish, Pictish, and Anglo-Saxon raiders swept across the land, bringing new fears and new ways of life. Appeals to Rome fell on deaf ears. By the middle of the century the Great King, Vortigern, ruled most of England with the aid of Anglo-Saxon mercenaries. They held the Picts and Scots at bay, and some measure of prosperity returned to the land.

Then came the Saxon revolt in Kent, led by Hengist and Horsa. Vortigern's empire fell apart. The last remnants of civilized Roman rule came under siege as faction fought faction. Anglo-Saxon mercenaries fought for all sides, and many Britons fled to their hill forts, to the forests, and to the farthest corners of the land. The old aristocracy of Roman Britain struggled to unite against the mercenaries—but they lacked a leader. . . .

* * *

In a cottage in the forest of Mara Zion, an old woman explored the future.

Her two companions, Nyneve and Merlin, had been sent away for a month while Avalona pondered. Mara Zion was a small place in relation to the galaxy and the infinite great-away; but it was the place where she lived and worked. And she had a great Purpose that was incalculably more important than a handful of warring savages, because it affected every time and every place. She could not tolerate this local unrest. It would not be allowed to continue.

The seeds had been sown. The legend of Arthur—and so far it was no more than that—had spread across the country. Nyneve and Merlin had done a good job with the modicum of talent she'd supplied. It hadn't been difficult. Humans were credulous creatures, and in their minds an alternative world had been created: a world of chivalry and honor, yet a world of violence and bloodshed and death. A world where men would die for their king or their principles, and where their women would encourage them and bury them. A simple world where right conquered wrong. Camelot.

So now people were looking around for a strong leader to unite the factions, restore peace to the land, and hold it against invaders. A leader they could respect; a leader of principle; a just and honorable leader.

A leader like Arthur, for instance.

For the present time, and for a certain time of hideous danger in the far distant future, Arthur was the man Avalona and England needed.

But Arthur was two happentracks away.

Avalona examined the happentracks. On the nearest was an Earth that for a long time had been empty of animals. Then, thousands of years ago, a gentle space-faring race had seen it and sent down several exploratory parties of small bipeds. They were still there, tailoring their Earth for full-scale colonization.

And one happentrack beyond lay the world of Arthur, its history molded to suit Avalona's purposes. Underpopulated, simple, waiting to be put to her use.

Unusually, these two happentracks had not continued to diverge after the original branchings. Quite the opposite had happened. They had converged to the point that two of them could actually see each other, faintly. And all of them could see one another's moons. All that was required was the finishing touch.

Avalona concentrated. . . .

Two days' ride east of Castle Camyliard lay a stretch of rolling moorland topped by a pinnacle called Pentor. If you walked due south from the moor at the time of our story, you would pass through the forest of Mara Zion on your way to a cliff-girt beach. If you then picked your way over the rocks at the base of the western cliffs for a distance of perhaps two hundred yards, you would find a cave. If you looked closely at a point about a foot from the ground, where the limpet-encrusted rocks disappeared into the blackness within, you would see a pair of eyes. The eyes belonged to a gnome named Pong.

The time of the year was spring, several months after the journey of Nyneve and Merlin.

After a long and breathless wait, Pong emerged into full daylight.

He was of medium height as gnomes go, stockily built, his normally cheery face a mask of apprehension as his eyes darted this way and that. He wore heavy leather knee-length boots, into which were tucked thick linen pants of faded blue; a heavy, knitted black sweater with a roll neck; and on his head the traditional conical red cap was firmly jammed.

Pong looked like what he was: a sailorgnome with a secret dread. Poised for flight, he scanned the beach.

The subject of his dread was not in sight, however. He relaxed, stretched, smiled at the early-morning sunshine, sniffed the salt-laden air, savored the warm breeze on his face, and heard the scrunch of a footstep on the pebbles.

With a squeal of fright he whirled around and darted back into the cave.

A shelf ran along the west wall of the cave. Pong scrambled onto this, burrowed into a pile of blankets, drew his feet to his chest, and lay motionless. Soon he heard footsteps again, slightly louder than the beating of his heart. They echoed off the roof of the cave, approaching. In his terror, Pong fancied he could hear the chattering of giant mandibles, and the clicking of pincers limbering up for a grab.

"Hello?"

"Yah!" Pong let out an involuntary yell of horror.

"Is anybody there?"

"Yes. Certainly. Yes." It dawned on Pong that the voice was a gnomish one, rather than the roar of crustacean hunger that he'd imagined it to be. "Very much so," babbled Pong, sliding down from his shelf to greet the newcomer. "Welcome, welcome. My humble abode. Don't often get visitors. Lovely day."

"It certainly is." The two gnomes moved out into the sunlight and scrutinized each other.

Pong decided that this was the most pleasant gnome he'd ever clapped eyes on. The newcomer's boots were smeared with sheep dung, his pants worn and stained, his jacket ill-fitting, and his cap a curious color suggestive of decay. He had narrow, sneaky eyes and a bulbous nose. When compared to Pong's secret dread, however, he was a fine-looking figure of a gnome.

"You're a stranger to Mara Zion," said Pong.

The other held out his hand. "Bart o' Bodmin."

Pong returned the clammy grasp. "They call me Pong the Intrepid."

"Oh? Why?"

In later years Pong was to identify that as the moment when he first had misgivings about the character of Bart o' Bodmin. It was bad manners to question another gnome's name. Sometimes a name was hereditary, like Hal o' the Moor, whose ancestors had always lived at Pentor. Sometimes a name was earned, like Pong's friend Fang, who rid the forest of a fearsome beast. But once the name was bestowed, it stuck, and was carried into history by gnomish Memorizers. It was never challenged.

"I undertake perilous voyages on the seas," said Pong coldly, waving an arm at the sunny water. "What do *you* do?"

"I am a Memorizer."

"You're a long way from home. Shouldn't you be back at Bodmin, memorizing local history?"

"We're trying to get away from the concept of the parochial Memorizer, back in Bodmin," said Bart. "Gnomish history is more than a few scattered groups each going its own way. Gnomish history"—here his eyes took on a visionary gleam—"is an eternal and wondrous thing, spanning the galaxy. But gnomish history must be integrated, otherwise future historians will be not be able to make any sense of it. We must seek to portray the great sweep of our heritage, unified and glorious!"

"So you have a lot of traveling to do, Bart." Like all gnomes, Pong was proud of gnomish history. The immensity of Bart's mission deserved his respect. "Where's your rabbit? It will need feeding and watering."

"The bugger ran out on me," complained Bart. "And now I must continue on foot."

"I believe Jack o' the Warren has good riding rabbits," suggested Pong. "He lives in the forest."

"You must give me the directions," said Bart. "But meanwhile I need to rest." He sat down with his back to a rock. "Tell me about Mara Zion, Pong."

Something caused Pong to prevaricate. As Bart's narrow features squinted up at him, it seemed they had an almost ratlike appearance. "There's nothing I'd like better," he said, "but I have work to do. There is kelp to be cut, and the tide is right. I must launch the boat."

"A perilous voyage," said Bart thoughtfully, gazing at the sea. "Would you consider taking me along? I need to learn about Mara Zion customs."

Like most gnomes, Pong was a sociable fellow. Living in his isolated cave, however, he didn't often get visitors.

Occasionally a gnome would drop by to barter for edible seaweed. More often Fang would come, to bring him up-to-date on the latest happenings in gnomedom. But in general the sailorgnome's life was a lonely one, so he was not in the habit of turning away company.

"I'd be glad of your help." He cast a knowledgeable eye at the sea. "It looks as though it might blow up from the east, but the kelpbed's not far offshore. We can run for shelter if the weather worsens." He smiled at Bart, his earlier misgivings allayed. Sailing was a much less terrifying proposition when you had a crew on board.

Together they pushed out Pong's tiny craft. It was fashioned from birchbark pegged to a willow frame and had been known to carry as many as three gnomes in reasonable safety. It had been built by Pong's grandfather, Pew the Valiant, several hundred years ago. "We are a courageous breed," Pew had said, staring into Pong's eyes searchingly, "except for your father, who ran away inland soon after you were born, the coward. Look after the boat, Pong, and guard our way of life. It is your sacred trust, now that your father has deserted us." And then he had died, leaving the echo of his words in Pong's memory.

The boat was dry with lack of use, and consequently light. It wobbled alarmingly as Bart followed Pong aboard. Then Pong hoisted the tiny sail and they began to tack into the light onshore breeze.

Bart was watching the sky, a puzzled expression on his face. "What's all that stuff up there?" he asked.

"Stuff?"

"Silver stuff. Like clouds, only faster."

"Oh, that," said Pong carelessly. "That's just the umbra."

"The umbra?"

"Don't you have the umbra in Bodmin?"

"We have the umbra like you wouldn't believe! The Bodmin umbra is the talk of Cornwall. It's enough to rot your socks off. Giants live in it."

"They do here too. But the level of the sea is higher in

their world than ours. So what you see in the sky is the underside of their waves. You get used to it," Pong said offhandedly, aware that Bart was impressed by the peculiar sight. He scanned the shoreline. "Look, there's a giant now."

Against the solid background of the cliff, a spectral figure moved. Several times the height of a gnome, it climbed over rocks as insubstantial as itself. Once it jumped back as though avoiding a ghostly wave. It bent down, picking something up and putting it into a bag. Finally it walked up the beach and disappeared into the forest.

"A giantish woman," observed Bart. "They're much bigger in Bodmin."

"There's a school of thought in the forest," said Pong carefully, not wishing to appear stupid to this knowledge-able gnome, "that believes the umbra is getting closer."

"Funny you should say that. I can remember a time, oh, a couple of centuries ago, when you could hardly see the umbra at all. But these days"—Bart regarded the forest thoughtfully—"it's as though you could almost reach out and touch the giants."

"My friend Fang thinks the umbra will join our world soon. He knows a giant who can step from the umbra into gnomedom, just like that! Her name's Nyneve. Fang says she's very nice. It's a pity the other giants aren't like her, he says. But the Miggot—he takes care of the Sharan—he said it's the thin end of the wedge. He says before long our world will be full of giants, fighting and breeding! It'll be the end of gnomedom, the Miggot says."

If Pong had been more perceptive, he might have noticed a shrewd gleam in Bart's eyes at the mention of the Sharan. "The Miggot, eh?" Bart said thoughtfully. "Is he pretty much of a fool, this Miggot?"

"Oh, no, Bart. He's probably the cleverest gnome in Mara Zion. But for some reason he doesn't like Nyneve. Nyneve says the umbra is another world, just like ours. She says it's just a different . . . happentrack. That was the word she used, so Fang says."

Bart snorted. "It'll be a sticky end for your friend Fang, mark my words. It's a rash gnome who fools with giants."

The breeze fell away and the boat slid to a stop, barely rocking on the flat, bright sea. Pong had the strangest feeling that the world was waiting for something. The air felt electric, and the hairs of his beard seemed to prickle and come alive. The umbral waves thickened overhead, and an unexpected crackling made him jump. A bolt of lightning struck the sea half a mile away, raising a cloud of steam. Pong glanced at the sky fearfully. "Better get the mast down," he muttered.

Bart was leaning forward, in the process of fixing Pong with a penetrating stare. His eyebrows bristled compellingly. "But no matter how bad things get, Pong, my new friend," he said, "we need have no fear. The Gnome from the North will be with us."

"The . . . ?"

"The Gnome from the North. Our guardian and savior. Surely you remember the legend of the gnome who came from the north, dressed all in forest green, riding a rabbit white as snow?"

"Oh, *that* gnome," said Pong, baffled. "I think perhaps we should lower the sail. I don't like the look of this."

"When times were at their blackest, when gnomes were dying of plague and pestilence, when the crops failed and the very harvest mice turned savage, in rode the Gnome from the North, Pong."

"On a rabbit white as snow," repeated Pong absently, slackening the halyard. The sail came down with a rush, blanketing Bart.

"Exactly," continued the muffled voice. "'Follow me south, gnomes,' he said, and he led the gnomes out of their sorrow and despair, to a land where the rivers flowed with honey, and the trees were heavy with golden fruit."

"How could you keep yourself clean, if the rivers flowed with honey?" Pong jerked at the mast while lightning began to crackle closer. The umbral waves were like heavy clouds now, low and overpowering.

"It's a *legend*, Pong," shouted Bart irritably, trying to fight his way out from under the sail. "You must look for the meaning within yourself."

"There's a gnome in Mara Zion who says that kind of thing," said Pong, trying to sustain the conversation from politeness, meanwhile jerking the mast from its socket and laying it lengthwise along the gunwale. "We call him Spector the Thinking Gnome. Hardly anyone can understand him."

"Get me out from here!" shouted Bart.

"Sorry." Pong began to tug at the sail, and soon the flushed face of Bart emerged, moldy cap awry.

"I might have suffocated under there!"

"Not with the Gnome from the North watching over you."

Bart lurched forward and seized Pong by the front of his sweater. *"Never* joke about the Gnome from the North. Hard times are coming, Pong, believe me." He stared deeply into Pong's eyes. "Always remember the Gnome from the North will save us."

"The Gnome from the North," echoed Pong. It seemed the only thing to say. "Will he save *me*, Bart?"

"He'll save everybody. Provided you believe in him."

"I believe in him!" Pong dropped his voice. "Will he save me from the lopster, Bart?"

"The lopster?"

"It's a frightful monster that inhabits these parts. It's as big as a giant. Sometimes at night"—Pong whimpered at the memory—"I hear it sniffing around the cave. It's never found me yet, because I sleep on a ledge out of sight. But one day it will find me, Bart, and that's when I'm going to need the Gnome from the North."

"He will protect you, Pong, my friend."

"The lopster has two huge back legs and it can leap trees. Nobody stands a chance against it. Its body is plated with horny armor, and it has snappers to snap off your feet with. You know why I wear these thick boots? Because of the lopster."

"I know that, Pong," said Bart gently.

"Of course you do, because I've just told you."

"Let's not talk about the lopster, Pong. The Gnome from the North is watching over you at this very minute. Tell me about Mara Zion. This Fang, is he your leader?"

"Sort of. Our real leader is King Bison, because he's got the loudest voice. But Fang always takes charge when things get tough. Fang slew the daggertooth. Fang gave us the cry." Pong took up a paddle and began to propel the boat toward a place where kelp could be seen lying across the surface, brown and shiny.

"The cry?"

"Away, Thunderer!" shouted Pong, glad of an excuse to use the cry.

"What does it mean?"

"It doesn't mean anything. It's just what we shout sometimes. It makes us feel good. Spector says that's what counts. Our perception of the cry is more important than the cry itself, Spector says. Sometimes I wish I knew what the hell Spector was talking about," said Pong sadly. "I think Fang knows."

"And Bison," said Bart. "How does he feel when Fang takes charge?"

Pong considered the question carefully, and then said, "Relieved, I think. Elmera—she's the Miggot's wife—says Bison is not really leadership material. But, anyway, who needs leaders?"

A crafty smile played on Bart's lips, but Pong didn't notice. He was busy leaning over the side of the boat, slicing off kelp tips and stuffing them into a burlap bag. A light rain began to fall, developing quickly into a heavy downpour. The sun had disappeared and it had suddenly become dark. "Bugger it," muttered Pong. He hauled the bag over the gunwale and crawled under the shelter of the sail. Bart joined him. The two gnomes crouched side by side, staring at the weather. The rain was by now so heavy that they couldn't tell where the sky ended and the sea began. "There's a lot of water in the boat," observed Pong.

"Hadn't we better make for the shore?"

"Help me drape the sail over the edges of the boat," said Pong urgently. "It'll stop the rain from coming in."

But Bart had frozen into immobility. "Rain? It tastes salty to me, Pong." His voice was shrill.

Pong glanced at him and recognized the signs. He'd seen the same look on the face of King Bison when urgent action was required. Bart was paralyzed by the magnitude of the situation. He was not going to be any help. Pong crawled around the boat, pushing the edge of the sail over the gunwales and fastening it to cleats. The sail made an ill-shaped boat cover but it was better than nothing. Pong had often used it this way and had sewn loops onto it, to hook over the cleats. Entombed in the darkness under the sail, the gnomes huddled together. Pong could feel Bart shivering.

The boat began to toss wildly, throwing them about.

"Pong," said Bart after a while, "these voyages of yours. Have you ever met a storm like this before?"

"I could tell you tales of storms that would make your cap molt."

"Oh, that's all right, then. For a moment I thought this might be . . . unusual."

"Unusual? Hah!" Even to his own ears, Pong's careless laugh sounded more like a croak of despair. "This is nothing. A light chop, we sailors call it."

The canvas suddenly sagged under the weight of water, pressing down on their heads. Bart let out a squeak of fear. Pong forced his thoughts into a positive mold. Not for nothing, he thought proudly, was he called Pong the Intrepid. This would be a story to tell his grandchildren. *There we were*, he rehearsed, *alone on the surging waters. The mast had carried away, and Bart—my usually trusty mate from Bodmin—cowered in the bottom of the boat, utterly ungnomed by terror. And not surprisingly, for in all my years as a sailor, I had never—*

"Wah!" shouted Bart.

Pong and Bart were thrown into a heap as the boat heaved and seemed to rush upward as though rising to a mountainous wave. Water spurted in under the edges of the sail. *I won't be having any grandchildren*, thought Pong, and a strange calm came over him. *This is the end. It will be clean and quick. It's better than being eaten by the lopster. Good-bye, gnomedom. Good-bye, Fang my friend.* "Good-bye," he said aloud.

The violent motion abated to a gentle rocking. A brilliant light shone through the canvas, reflecting eerily off the water in the bottom of the boat, creating stars and halos around the wet planking. The gnomes stared at each other.

"You see the light?" said Pong. "It's the Great Grasshopper out there. Our time has come."

"I'm not prepared for the Great Grasshopper!"

"Compose yourself, Bart."

"I'm unworthy!" Bart babbled. "I'm not the gnome you thought I was, Pong. Oh, if only I could have my time again!"

Meanwhile Pong was unhooking the loops from the cleats. He threw the sail aside. "I'm ready!" he shouted fervently. No more would he be haunted by fear of the voracious lopster, by the necessity of living up to his name. All his troubles were over. He beamed at the sky.

The sky beamed back at him. A few puffy little clouds sidled slowly past the sun, as though scared of being evaporated. A passing gull, startled by Pong's yell, wheeled and squawked, releasing an elongated dropping that turned slowly end over end before splashing to the sea ten feet away.

At first glance, things looked surprisingly normal again.

Bart, by now curled into a fetal ball, was hurriedly repeating the Kikihuahua Examples in the hope of being granted a second chance. *"I will not kill any mortal creature. I will not work any malleable substance. I will not kindle the Wrath of Agni.* Oh, Great Grasshopper," Bart improvised, running out of traditional prayers, "I will not do any bloody thing at all, just so long as you spare me. I've been a treacherous and unworthy gnome!"

"It's all right, Bart," said Pong. "It's all right." The

cliffs were still there, and he could see the dark entrance to his cave. The forest stood behind Mara Zion beach, and the sea was still the sea, although dirtier than usual. Bubbles and muck rose to the surface as he watched.

But no mythical monster straddled the boat, inviting them to the Unknown.

Bart uncurled slightly and squinted up at Pong. "What do you mean, it's all right?"

"The Great Grasshopper hasn't come for us. It was a false alarm. I think it was just a tidal wave." In a way, thought Pong, it was quite disappointing. He unhooked the sail from the cleats and hoisted it.

Bart scrambled onto his seat and cast an eye over the cluttered waters. "Ah, yes," he said.

"All the same, we'd better get ashore and pull the boat well clear. Tidal waves rarely come in ones." Pong settled himself in the stern and set sail for the beach with a light wind behind him. "Everything's all right," he repeated for the benefit of Bart, who seemed to be shuddering excessively.

"Everything's all right," repeated Bart woodenly, ashen-faced.

"What did you mean, you're not the gnome I thought you were?" asked Pong.

"What?"

"A while ago. You said you were unworthy."

"Oh, that. A moment of humility, Pong. It pays to be humble when you're about to meet your Creator."

Pong was about to comment on the absence of the Gnome from the North in their hour of greatest need when, "Bart," he said urgently, "does the water seem kind of . . . *bright* to you?"

"No."

"That's because you're not used to being out on the sea. Usually it's quite dull compared to the land, because— Bart!" He pointed. "Look! The umbral waves have gone! That's the real sky up there!"

"So it is."

"But that's not. . . not *right*. What does it mean?"

"Listen to me, Pong, I don't care a bugger what it means. There's something about this boat that makes me sick to my stomach, and I'd be very glad if you got us ashore."

"The umbral waves are *always* up there. It's a fact of nature. Not many gnomes know that, not being sailors." Pong pondered on the phenomenon as they slid toward the beach. He felt an inexplicable dread, but he concealed it from Bart. Not for nothing was he known as Pong the Intrepid.

"Thank heavens," muttered Bart as they carried the boat up the beach and laid it beside the entrance to Pong's cave.

Pong did not share his companion's relief. His misgivings were mounting by the minute. "The sea," he said. "Look how far up the beach it's come."

"The tide's in, Pong. I thought you sailors knew all about tides."

"The tide never comes this high."

"Of course it does, Pong. There it is, see? That proves it."

"Come on, Bart. We must go and see Fang. There's something strange going on around here."

"I don't have a rabbit."

"Then we'll have to walk. It's only a couple of miles."

The gnomes made their way along the base of the cliff. Soon they reached another beach; and this time it was Bart who first noticed the change. "The trees, Pong. Look!"

Cliffs tend to be cliffs on whatever happentrack they exist. They do not differ perceptibly from one world to the next, except perhaps where a rock has fallen in one happentrack but is merely unstable in another.

But the umbra was always very noticeable in the forest. A tree, growing tall and straight in one happentrack, might never have existed in another, particularly if the branching of happentracks had occurred a long time ago.

For millennia past, the gnomes of Mara Zion had seen two forests. One they lived in. The other was a shadowy thing inhabited by giants, just a happentrack away but faintly visible nonetheless.

But now the shadows had disappeared and they saw one forest, one happentrack, one world.

"The umbra's gone here too," said Pong. "What does it mean?"

They found out soon enough.

"Hah! Piskeys!" came a roaring shout that seemed to vibrate through their very flesh. "I can see you!"

They swung around. A huge figure was scrambling clumsily down a cleft in the cliff. It jumped to the ground, and the beach shook. It ran swiftly toward them, with gigantic strides.

"Into the forest!" cried Pong.

Bart was already on his way, moving quickly with the characteristic gnomish scuttle. They darted into the undergrowth, Bart in the lead. Luckily they picked up a rabbit track almost immediately and followed it, hearing the crash of pursuit nearby.

"Come back here, you little piskeys! You can't get away from me." Heedless of obstacles, the giant plunged after them.

"North, Bart!" cried Pong. "Head north!"

"Which way is north?" Bart shouted over his shoulder, meanwhile rushing past a fork in the trail.

"The other way!"

Bart stopped abruptly. Pong crashed into him as he was in the act of turning. Bart grabbed Pong to steady himself. The sound of pursuit approached. Bart, paralyzed with fear, hugged Pong close.

"Let me go!" An appalling thought occurred to Pong. Bart was a spy, in the pay of the giants. That explained the shifty look. "Let me go, you bugger!" yelled Pong, prepared to sell his life dearly. Overbalancing, the gnomes toppled to the ground, grappling. It seemed to Pong that Bart's face wore an expression of cunning and ferocity.

Bart meanwhile had decided Pong had been trying to lead him into some kind of a trap. Throughout Cornwall, Mara

Zion gnomes were known to be untrustworthy and resentful of strangers. What better way to dispose of a stranger than to lure him into the hands of the giants? And here was Pong, pummeling him with his fists as they rolled in the dirt. "No way!" shouted Bart, rolling away, jumping to his feet and scampering along the path of his original choice, which led east. He was not surprised to hear Pong's footsteps close behind, and it seemed he could feel Pong's breath hot on his very neck.

In silence, the gnomes raced through the forest while the roars of giantish pursuit faded and finally ceased.

Pong ran in an agony of remorse. Belatedly, he'd recognized Bart's terror for what it was. How could he have been so mistrustful as to have suspected this excellent gnome from Bodmin? And now the frightened fellow was running along the path that led straight to the giants' village.

It was Pong's duty to save Bart. "Stop!" he shouted.

This caused Bart to put on more speed. "Go away!" he cried.

Despairing of making Bart see reason, Pong flung himself full length, grabbed Bart's legs, and brought him crashing to the ground. "You're heading for the giants' village, Bart," he explained breathlessly. "Don't you understand, they can *see* us now? It's all happened just like Fang said it would. We're living in the same world as the giants!"

Bart was silent.

Assuming the Bodmin gnome was having difficulty understanding what might be a local phenomenon, Pong continued, "It's been coming on for some time. The umbra seemed to be getting *clearer,* if you know what I mean. And then a few days ago, Fang actually *heard* two giants talking. But nobody would believe him, except me," said Pong proudly, "because I'm his friend. And possibly the Miggot believed him," he added in the interests of truth.

It seemed to Pong that some reply would have been in order, but Bart offered none. Had fear ungnomed him again? Pong stood, regarding the motionless figure in pity. "Buck up, Bart," he said.

Then he saw the rock under Bart's head, and the trickle of blood. "Oh, by the Sword of Agni," he whispered. "What have I done?"

He knelt beside Bart and gently lifted his head. The red cap was wet with blood around the rim. He eased it off and saw the ugly cut on Bart's forehead, near the hairline. The skin was darkening around the cut, and a lump was developing.

Pong replaced the cap. It would help to stanch the flow of blood. And in any case, it was a bad omen for Bart to be without his emblem of gnomehood. For a while Pong knelt there, consumed with guilt, then it occurred to him that this forest path was probably frequented by giants. He must get Bart out of sight. More, he must get Bart attended to.

Furthermore, he suddenly noticed a clump of cheesecups lurking at the side of the path, each plant taller than a gnome, waving menacingly. Their tubular flowers were a favorite haunt of the sluglike doodad—a particularly unpleasant gnomish creature. Doodads latched on to you and injected a fluid that turned you into a bag of soup. Then they sucked you dry. They had tremendous sucking capabilities, doodads did. Their skin was infinitely expandable. On Pong's list of gnomedom's most fearsome creatures, they ranked second only to the lopster.

And one was sticking its pale, blind face from a cheesecup now. The cup trembled as the doodad tensed itself for a leap.

Hastily Pong dragged Bart out of leaping range and into the bush. The horrible creature plopped to the ground and slid around for a moment or two, then climbed back up the stem, disappointed. Pong deliberated his next move.

Like most such settlements, Mara Zion gnomedom had its healer: a gnome called Wal o' the Bottle. Wal was the latest in a long line of hereditary healers, although some said the strain had weakened over the centuries. Certainly Bottle's patients rarely got better. But then they rarely got worse, gnomes having excellent constitutions. Pong was not

sure where Bottle lived, but Fang would know. Hoisting
Bart onto his back, he plodded back the way they'd come.

The pattern of forest paths seemed to have changed since
yesterday, with odd forks and intersections that Pong didn't
recall having seen before. Eventually, however, he came to
a familiar circle of mushrooms. Fang had once shown him
this place and told him it was some kind of a gateway between giantdom and gnomedom. Nyneve, the friendly giant, used it to get from one world to the other.

Having got his bearings, Pong walked on. Gnomes are
physically much stronger than humans in proportion to their
size, so Bart did not represent an undue burden. Before
long, Pong reached Fang's dwelling.

Except that Fang's dwelling wasn't there.

At first he thought he'd come to the wrong place.
Alarmed, he examined the nearby trees. They were not the
trees he remembered. In particular the giant lurch, beneath
whose roots Fang's home had nestled, was nowhere to be
seen. In fact, Pong realized, he hadn't seen a lurch tree
anywhere in the forest today.

And yet it *had* to be the place. There was a moss-clothed
granite boulder beside the path, facing south. He and Fang
had sat with their backs against it many times, enjoying the
sun through the trees. And the little stream where Fang
dipped his water flowed nearby, as before. But the lurch was
gone, and in its place stood an elm. He could see the dark
entrance to a cave where the roots of the elm clutched at
the ground, but it was not Fang's cave. As the dread began
to grow within him, he felt the ancient gnomish instinct to
crawl into the nearest hole. So he crawled among the roots
of the elm, dragging Bart after him. After a while, exhausted from the excitements of the day, he fell asleep.

When he awakened, it was dark and the forest was alive
with night sounds. A soft wind breathed into the cave,
bringing unfamiliar smells. Pong wished he was back home
where he knew the smells and could identify them. Any one
of these sudden warm whiffs could be a gnome-eating ani-

mal. Even the lopster was better than this. Shivering, he huddled up against Bart, who seemed to be breathing more easily.

Bart awakened with a start. "Is that you, Pong? What happened? I have a terrible headache."

"You tripped and hit your head on a rock."

"I did?" It seemed to Pong that Bart shot him a glance of the deepest suspicion; but it could have been the distorting effect of the moonlight slanting across the cave. "Where are we now?"

"I don't know," said Pong miserably. "Fang's home's gone. I've been thinking about it, and I don't think gnomedom exists anymore. The Miggot always said this was going to happen. We're in a different world, Bart. It's the giant's world, and I'm not sure there's any place for gnomes in it."

"You'd better go and take a look around!"

"In the middle of the night? It's dangerous out there, Bart!"

"On the contrary, it's safer. The giants will all be asleep."

Outvoted, Pong climbed to his feet and stumbled out into the moonlight. A short walk confirmed his suspicions. None of the nearby gnomish dwellings existed anymore. He visited the site of King Bison's home, and Clubfoot Trimble's, and the hollow log that the Mara Zion gnomes had used as a meeting place. Everything was changed. Not a gnome was in sight. Finally he climbed to the top of the western ridge, where the forest gave way to rocks and scrub, and looked across the valley. There had been a stream down there. The Princess of the Willow Tree, Fang's girl, had lived in a riverbank burrow. And farther south, where the meadows gave way to marsh, Fang's father, the Gooligog, had lurked in his unsavory tunnel. And now—

And now a wide expanse of water glittered strangely in the moonlight. The valley was a bay, and the gnomes' dwellings were drowned.

Strangest of all, there was only one moon in the sky,

hard-edged and brilliant. Misty Moon and Maybe Moon were gone. The night sky looked unfamiliar, unnatural.

And the gnomes themselves? It didn't bear thinking about. In tears, Pong stumbled back to the cave.

"Everybody's gone, Bart! Except the giants, and now they can see us, and before long they'll catch us. Do you know what they'll do then, Bart? They'll push spits through us and roast us. That's what giants do in Mara Zion."

"In Bodmin," said Bart, eyes wide with fear, "they lay metal plates on fires and make gnomes dance on them while they slowly fry from the feet up."

"Oh, how I wish the Gnome from the North would come!" wailed Pong.

"And then they sprinkle them with herbs, and pour wine on them, and season to taste."

"And snatch us up onto the back of his snow-white rabbit and ride off with us to a far better place than this!"

"I'm wondering if the situation hasn't gotten a bit beyond the powers of the Gnome from the North, Pong," said Bart.

"Nothing is beyond his powers," said the new convert piously. And it said much for his faith that, as the first faint light of morning chased away the moonlight, they heard the thumping gait of an approaching rabbit.

"Here he is!" shouted Pong, awakening from a light doze and jumping to his feet.

"Who's that?" came a shout. "Are there gnomes there?"

"It's Pong the Intrepid and Bart o' Bodmin! Take us!"

"Don't be silly. How can one rabbit carry three gnomes?"

Pong swung around to address Bart. "The Gnome from the North says he can't take us all. What's the answer to that, Bart?"

"The answer is that it's not the Gnome from the North, Pong."

Pong confronted the newcomer who jumped to the ground and advanced out of the gloom. "Jack! What's happened to gnomedom? Where is everyone?"

Jack o' the Warren was disheveled, his cap at a desperate

angle. "Everybody's been captured by the giants! The last I saw of them, they were being taken toward the Lake of Avalon by a giant called Galahad. I followed at a safe distance, then I thought I'd better come back and see if I could find anybody else. Who is this Bart o' Bodmin, anyway?"

Bart emerged from the cave, bowed gravely, and introduced himself. The gnomes clasped hands.

"What are we going to do now, Jack?" asked Pong.

"There's only one thing to do. We must go to the lake and try to rescue Fang and the others."

"From the giants?"

"We would be neglecting our duty if we didn't at least try."

"You're right." Pong concealed a gulp of fear by clearing his throat, then said, "Bring us two of your finest rabbits, Jack, and we'll be on our way." And surprisingly, his spirits began to rise at the thought of a new purpose.

"Rabbits?"

"To ride on. You have a string of good riding stock. I wouldn't go to anyone else for a rabbit."

Jack sighed. "I've given the matter a lot of thought, Pong, and I've decided I'm going to come clean. I'm going to tell one gnome the truth, and that gnome is you. I have to share the burden I've carried all these years, but it must go no further than you, Pong."

"But Bart's here. He'll share your burden too."

"That's all right, because Bart was never deceived by the bogus rabbits."

"What bogus rabbits are you talking about, Jack?"

"The rabbits I never had," said Jack o' the Warren sadly.

"But your string of riding rabbits was famous throughout gnomedom!" cried Pong.

"Their fame was undeserved. I never had any rabbits. I never kept them in a fenced compound safe from moondogs, and I never bred them, carefully selecting the fastest and strongest as instructed by the Miggot. It was all a big lie. Oh!" cried Jack happily. "You don't know how good it makes me feel, to tell someone this. I'm free at last. I'm going to tell people my rabbits disappeared along with gnomedom as we knew it, Pong, and I'm trusting you to do the same. And you, Bart.''

''Of course.'' Pong stared at Jack, bewildered. Another part of gnomedom was gone. The Warren string of riding rabbits had turned out to be a phantom existing only in the minds of gnomes. Was nothing real anymore? The riding rabbits were part of gnomish history. They had been committed to memory by the Gooligog, the gnomish Memorizer. The great Thunderer, Fang's rabbit who had been a leading figure in the Slaying of the Daggertooth, had supposedly been bred by Jack. Was Thunderer real, or was the whole episode of the Daggertooth another myth? ''What rabbits have we been riding all these years?'' he asked.

''When anyone's needed a rabbit, I've always given them my own. And then I've gone out and trapped one for myself, and trained it. Have you ever tried to train a rabbit? They don't *want* to be trained, you know. Not really. I bear many scars.''

''But . . . why?'' asked Pong helplessly. ''How did this all happen? Everybody thought you had rabbits.''

''No. It was my father who had rabbits.''

''But he bequeathed them to you, surely?''

''He never had the chance. When he got old and feeble, they overthrew him.''

''Overthrew him?''

''I never found out the full details. The day I went to discuss it with him, he was gone. His housemouse was sitting there alone, licking its lips. The rabbits had left a couple of days previously. So I never inherited the string.''

''But why did we all think you had?''

''It was that damned Miggot's fault.''

''I hardly think you can blame the Miggot for a fraud on this scale, Jack.''

''One day the Miggot said to me, 'How's Boots's cough?' Boots was one of my father's rabbits; a big, lazy fellow. And the Miggot stared down his nose at me with those terrible eyes of his. And I said, 'Fine.' That was all. Just

'Fine.' There was no intent to deceive. Perhaps I didn't want to soil the memory of my father. Perhaps I was scared of the Miggot and didn't want to get involved in lengthy explanations. 'Fine,' I said. And that single bloody word doomed me to a lifetime of falsehood.

"Because Bison said the next day, 'I hear Boots is better. That's good. And has Helen had her babies yet?' I was trapped. I told Bison that Helen had had six babies: three brown, two black, and a yellow one that had unfortunately been born with only three legs, but that I was keeping it because it wouldn't be able to survive in the outside world. And Bison said my sentiments were a credit to me.

"It grew from then on. Many's the time I almost told people that some dreadful disease had swept through the string, leaving no rabbit alive. But I didn't, because I knew they'd expect me to found another string, and I couldn't go through the effort of inventing a whole new bunch of rabbits when I'd gotten to know the existing ones so well. There was Loppy, who was fussy about eating dandelions. There was Chopper, a sad rabbit who'd been leader of the string until he was deposed by William, who smelled funny. There was—"

"That's all right, Jack. You don't have to tell us any more. We understand," said Pong.

"*I* don't understand," snapped Bart. "I've never heard of such weakness. And what is it about this Miggot that you're all frightened of, anyway?"

"You'll understand when you meet the Miggot," said Jack. "If you ever meet the Miggot. Well, thanks to the Miggot, we've got to walk all the way to the Lake of Avalon."

Pong thought it a little unfair to blame the Miggot for that, too, but he didn't say anything.

"And, anyway," said Jack quietly to Pong a short while later, "I'm better off without real rabbits. Have you ever watched rabbits together, Pong? They're filthy buggers. Utterly without shame. How my father could live with all that filth happening on his very doorstep, I'll never know!"

3

THE COMING OF ARTHUR

SO IT WAS THAT THE THREE GNOMES SAT ON A HILL-side overlooking the Lake of Avalon and witnessed the event that was to change the history of the world.

The sun was trying to shoulder its way through ragged clouds and a light mist felt its way along the shore. A large crowd of humans were leaving the beach, making their way slowly southeast where the moors descended into the forest of Mara Zion. A few were slumped on horseback. Others walked with bowed heads and dragging feet like a defeated team.

If they had looked back, they'd have seen a narrow, black boat sliding out of the mist and moving slowly toward the shore. Three people sat in the boat: an old woman dressed all in black, a man in gleaming armor, and a girl with a mass of dark hair.

"That's Nyneve," said Pong. "She's the friendly giant."

"Well, just don't call out to her," said Bart. "She's out-numbered down there."

"The old woman's Avalona," added Pong. "But who the man giant is I've no idea. I've never seen him in the umbra."

"He looks cleaner than your average giant," said Jack.

The boat was directly below the hillside on which the gnomes sat. They could see the occupants clearly as the bow scrunched onto the pebbles and the male giant jumped lightly ashore. He lifted the women out. First Avalona; and either the man was very strong or the woman was very light, because he plucked her from the boat with no more effort than plucking a blade of grass. Next Nyneve; and she was a solid, well-built girl. He held on to her longer, and kissed her as he set her on the beach.

"There you are, you see," said Jack. "Sex again. They never think of anything else. Next thing they'll be on the ground, pulling the clothes off each other."

"I don't think so," said Pong. "They hardly ever have sex when there's more than two of them present. It's like a giantish version of Hayle." Hayle was a gnomish custom. It recognized that certain topics of conversation—such as the foolish nature of gnomes from Hayle—could be very funny when discussed in a group of up to four gnomes, but in bad taste in larger gatherings.

The three giants stood there for a moment. The sun came out and the man's hair glowed an astonishingly bright red. He bent and removed his boots, then paddled back into the lake. The watchers heard him yell with anguish at the coldness of the water. For a while he seemed to be searching, stooped over and peering down as he waded farther from the shore. Then he uttered a cry, and his hand plunged into the water up to the shoulder.

He brought a sword to the surface. Staring at it, he regained the beach. He brandished it, and the sun sparkled from the wet, polished blade like a stab of lightning. He gave a joyful shout. The words carried clearly to the gnomes on the hillside.

"A man could have some fun with a sword like this!"

Bart groaned. "Just like all the giants. When it's not sex, it's fighting."

Pong wasn't so sure. "But there's something different about that giant. . . . Do you sense it, Jack?"

The keeper of bogus rabbits said wonderingly, "If I didn't know better, I'd say there was something *good* about him."

They watched while Avalona walked away alone, along

the beach. "Look there!" said Bart suddenly. "Aren't those gnomes? They'd better get out of sight of the giants!"

"Nyneve wouldn't hurt them." Pong watched as the giants knelt before the gnomes and a conversation took place. "Let's get over there and find out what's going on. I think that's Fang there, and some of the Mara Zion gnomes. It looks as though they're free again. We don't need to rescue them, after all," he said, relieved but a little disappointed.

"Hey, gnomes!" shouted Bart, but the group was too far away to hear. Then the giants stood and the gnomes scuttled off southward. "Too late," said Pong.

"Now what do we do?" asked Bart.

"Find something to eat," suggested Jack. "I think I saw some mushrooms back there."

A great leader had died.

A group of his followers rode despondently from the Lake of Avalon into the forest of Mara Zion. A fine rain sieved through the trees, sitting in little globules on those who kept their armor polished (such as Torre), and dribbling in rusty streams down those who did not (such as Palomides).

"What I'll never understand," Palomides said, breaking the silence at last, "is why you threw Tristan's sword into the lake, Torre. That was the act of a fool."

"He commanded me."

"A somewhat selfish command, if you don't mind my saying so."

"It was his deathbed wish." Torre began to get irritated. "Would you deny Tristan his deathbed wish?"

"If he behaves like a dog in the manger, yes. I could have used that sword myself. It would have been easy enough for you to have hidden it behind a bush. He was in no condition to know what was going on."

"He thought that an arm clad in white samite would rise from the lake, catch the sword, wave it three times, and draw it beneath the surface."

"And did an arm do these things?"

"Well, no," admitted Torre, "it didn't. I must say, I really didn't think it would."

He reined his mount to a shambling halt and the others followed suit. An important moment had come. The village was only a mile away, and it was necessary to come to terms with the situation before facing the women who had taken a different route home. The women would be viewing the death of the great Tristan from a sentimental standpoint. It was up to the men to take the practical view.

If they could agree upon what the practical view was.

Palomides spoke first. Sitting a little taller in his saddle and gazing from man to man, he said, "There is a new spirit abroad in the forest of Mara Zion."

They responded with cries of outrage. "How can you say that?" asked Governayle hotly. "Our leader is hardly cold yet. Have you no respect?"

"I didn't say it was a *better* spirit," said Palomides quickly, realizing he'd misjudged the mood of his audience. "I said it was a *new* spirit. A sadder spirit. We are downcast at the loss of our late, great leader. However, every cloud has its silver lining. Excalibur lies in shallow water."

"Will you stop talking about the sword!" shouted Torre.

"You'll be talking about the sword soon enough, when the Baron moves in and takes over."

There was a moment's thoughtful silence. "The Baron was at the funeral," somebody said. "He didn't seem unduly depressed."

"He was overjoyed," said Palomides. "Our strong man was dead. And remember, it was the Baron who killed him."

"I've been wondering about that," said Torre. "I thought Tristan was supposed to be invincible with the sword Excalibur in his hand. Yet the Baron defeated him."

"He was tricked into using a different sword, as I understand it," said Governayle sadly.

"He got carried away with the idea of his own omnipotence," said Palomides. "He'd begun to believe he was King Arthur himself, straight out of those stupid stories Nyneve tells. He was trying to make the stories come true! He saw himself as King Tristan of all England. That's why he started babbling on about the arm in white samite. Don't you remember, that was supposed to happen when King Arthur died? Well, it didn't happen to Tristan. He was no mythical king. He was just an ordinary mortal like us. A villager from Mara Zion. Do you know why he was always so eager to jump off his horse and fight on foot, man to man? Hemorrhoids.''

"You've gone too far, Ned," said Torre grimly. "Draw your sword!"

"Is that your answer to everything? My God, Torre, I—"

"Hush!" said Governayle. "Somebody's coming."

They became silent while the rain fell steadily, muffling the forest sounds. Then they heard it, too: the rhythmic jangle of a man in armor walking. Soon they could see him through the trees, approaching on a converging course from the west. Torre and Palomides urged their horses forward to a confluence of forest paths.

"Who is he?" asked Palomides.

"I'm damned if I know. He's a stranger around these parts."

The newcomer was unusually tall. His bearing was aristocratic, although, Torre guessed, he was still in his twenties. He wore no helmet and his hair was a fiery red. He saw them, paused, and smiled. The eyes were blue, the nose straight, the chin firm.

"I don't like the look of this fellow," whispered Palomides.

"Halt, stranger!" called Torre. "By what right do you walk the paths of our forest?"

The man looked surprised. "Do I need a right? The forest is free to everyone, surely? I'm just passing through. I mean no harm."

"Then why are you armed?" asked Palomides. "Is that a sword you're wearing, or am I seeing things?"

"It's a sword, true enough," admitted the stranger with

a disarming grin. "It's a hell of a sword. With this sword in my hand, I will never be defeated in battle, so I'm told. That's a lot more than you can say for your average sword."

The words were strangely familiar. Torre swung from his saddle and peered at the weapon. "Just draw that thing for a moment, will you? I'd like to take a closer look."

"And while I'm wearing the scabbard, I'll never be wounded," added the man, unsheathing the blade.

It glittered in the new sunlight like a polished mirror.

"By God!" shouted Ned Palomides. "It's Excalibur!"

"Excalibur!" echoed the men, urging their horses forward.

"You bastard!" said Palomides, sliding from his horse and drawing his own blade. "You've defiled the memory of Tristan! Excalibur was to have remained at the bottom of the Lake of Avalon until the end of Time! On guard!" He struck a hostile pose.

"Easy, Ned," warned Torre. "You know what Excalibur can do. And anyway, you were talking about shallow water yourself, only a moment ago."

"I am a Mara Zion man," said Palomides with dignity, "so I have more right to Excalibur than this carroty fool. Hand it over, fellow!"

"Don't try to make me," said the stranger quietly.

"God damn it!" blustered Palomides, thrusting clumsily. "You're in a lot of trouble, stranger!"

"Ned! Stop that!"

A young girl came running down the path, long black hair tossing down around her shoulders. Darkly beautiful, she wore an emerald-green dress with a leather belt. A murmur arose from the men. "It's Nyneve," somebody said. "Jesus Christ, she looks better every time I see her."

Palomides seemed to puff up at the sight of her. He swung mightily with his sword. His opponent stepped aside and allowed the blade to thud into a stout elm.

"I'd leave it there if I were you," said the stranger, watching Palomides trying to jerk the sword free.

"I'm . . . going . . . to get you, you bastard. Aha!" The

elm released the blade. Palomides, off-balance, sat down heavily.

"Stay there, Ned," said Nyneve, arriving breathlessly. "You don't want to get hurt, do you?"

"What's all this about, Nyneve?" asked Torre. "Who is this fellow?"

She smiled, savoring the moment. She looked into the blue eyes of the stranger, and the love in her own eyes was so naked that the men shifted and coughed in embarrassment.

"This fellow?" she said, her face glowing. "Oh, this fellow is Arthur."

After a while, time seemed to start moving again.

"Arthur?" echoed Torre. "What do you mean, Arthur?"

"That's his name."

"A coincidence, of course," said Governayle. "There must be dozens of Arthurs in Cornwall."

"I'm sure there are," said Nyneve sweetly. "But this is *the* Arthur."

"Let me get this straight," said Torre. "For a long time now, Nyneve, you've been telling us stories about a mythical crowd of people ruled by a fellow called King Arthur. And that's all they were—story-people. Certainly you managed to make the stories sound convincing. I could *see* the events in my own head while you were talking. King Arthur, the Knights of the Round Table, the battles, the tournaments—hell, Tristan was so impressed, he even had our own round table set up in the village. But it wasn't real. We always said that. It was just a dream. A great dream, but a dream nevertheless. Wasn't it?"

"It wasn't a dream, Torre."

"Not a dream?" There was an apprehensive murmur from the men. Arthur's empire had been vast and powerful. And although the principles of chivalry on which it was founded seemed sound, an awful lot of men had died upholding or opposing them. Nyneve's story-world had been a glorious and a violent one. It was fun, but they'd been secretly glad it wasn't real.

"It's true enough," Nyneve confirmed, "and this *is* Arthur."

"Pardon me," said Torre to the stranger, "but you look too young to be Arthur."

There was a muttering of agreement from the others. This man, although of handsome bearing, did not live up to the almost godlike image of the fictional Arthur. Probably nobody could have. The Mara Zion men scowled at the pretender, annoyed that anyone should try to detract from the glorious dream of Camelot. "The man's a bloody fraud," said Palomides. "He's fooled you, Nyneve. We should run him out of the forest."

Nyneve said quickly, "Let me explain it the way Merlin and Avalona explained it to me. You've heard of happentracks?"

"Happentracks?" They looked at her blankly.

"Different streams of time. Haven't you ever wondered what might have happened in the future if you'd done something differently today? Well, maybe there's another you somewhere in time, living another life because you *did* do that thing differently. According to Avalona, new happentracks are splitting off all the time. Whenever somebody makes an important choice, off branches a happentrack where they made a different decision. And that begins a whole new alternative world. See what I mean?"

"I think so," said Torre doubtfully. "But where *are* these happentracks?"

She waved a hand uncertainly, encompassing the men, the forest, the sky. "Everywhere. Right here. Avalona found Arthur and his people on a happentrack quite close to ours. She felt it might be useful to some mysterious purpose of hers—you know what she's like."

They nodded. They knew what Avalona was like: a black-clad figure, pale-faced, with eyes hard as stones, stalking silently around the forest on missions known only to herself. What they didn't know was how the young and vivacious Nyneve could bear to live with Avalona and her senile companion, Merlin.

"She thinks Arthur's happentrack branched off only a few centuries ago. So a lot of the people on that happentrack are the same as on this."

"You're trying to tell me there's a Palomides in Arthur's world?" asked Ned. "There's another me?"

"There was, I expect."

"Was?" Mara Zion people were nothing if not superstitious, and Nyneve's emphasis brought an expression of alarm to Ned's face.

"Well, Arthur's happentrack has rejoined ours. That kind of thing happens occasionally. So the other Ned and you are both the same person now."

"If that's the case," said Ned shrewdly, "I'd have a whole lot of new memories. But I don't. So you're talking nonsense."

"You wouldn't *know* you have new memories. They'd seem like old memories."

"Makes sense," said Governayle, coming to Nyneve's rescue. "But it doesn't explain why this fellow you call Arthur is so young. The Arthur in your stories must have been forty years old by the time he died."

"Avalona explained that. She said happentracks don't have to be simultaneous. Arthur's joined us in an earlier time in his life, that's all."

"But . . ." This was too much even for Torre. "If that was true, we'd know exactly what was going to happen to him, because you've told us in your stories. He's going to be the king of all England, and he's going to marry Guinevere, and all that stuff. But we could change all that right now, simply by killing him. So I'm with Ned for once, Nyneve. You're talking nonsense."

"But you won't kill him, Torre," said the girl quietly.

"But I could."

"But you won't."

They stared at each other. "By God, I will!" shouted

Torre, drawing his sword. Then he remembered and sheathed it. "He has Excalibur," he said heavily.

"Exactly."

"But if he didn't . . . ?"

"But he does. Don't worry about it, Torre. The time will come when you won't even dream of killing Arthur. And remember, the stories I told you all happened on a different happentrack. There's no reason why they should happen exactly the same on *this* happentrack."

And if they'd been astute enough, they'd have noticed her flush slightly. On *this* happentrack, she was determined, there would be no marriage to Guinevere. . . . "And then there are the gnomes," she said hastily. "At least I can prove *them*."

"The gnomes? What have they got to do with anything?"

"They were on a different happentrack too. Now they've joined us, just like Arthur. . . ."

"She shouldn't have said that," observed the Miggot of One.

"Why not?" asked Fang, whispering too. "We can hardly hide from the giants forever."

The two gnomes watched the humans from under a rhododendron. In recognition of their precarious situation they had left their scarlet caps at home and wore gray flat hats, brown jackets, and pants. This effectively blended with their surroundings but left them depressed. They stared miserably from the giants to each other, deposited by fate in a strange and violent happentrack. Their only friend among the giantish humans was Nyneve.

"Anyway," said the Miggot, "it's time we got back to the Sharan. She will shortly give birth."

The thought of attending the unicorn's labor did not appeal to Fang. "Do you really need me?"

"No," said the Miggot. "But it's your duty as leader of the Mara Zion gnomes."

"Am I still the leader?"

"Of course. Why not?"

"Well. . . ." said Fang diffidently, "I thought perhaps now things are settling down, Bison could take over again. I never felt comfortable about deposing him, actually, Miggot. I felt I'd been guilty of some sort of coup."

"Coup? I'd say Bison abdicated. He couldn't take the heat. As a leader, he's finished. A dead issue."

"Oh, all right, if you say so. I'll continue on a temporary basis, until Bison recovers his, uh, vitality."

"Come on," said the Miggot impatiently.

The gnomes wriggled carefully backward from under the bush; then scuttled away through the undergrowth. The paths were strange and they lost their way many times. By the time they reached the blasted oak where the rest of the Mara Zion gnomes had hidden themselves, it was mid-afternoon.

"I wish we'd chosen somewhere else for the camp," observed Fang as the blackened branches came into view through the surrounding, intact foliage.

"It's an excellent spot, Fang," said the Miggot, who had chosen it.

"Don't you think there's something . . . pessimistic about it? I mean, a *blasted oak?*"

"You've been listening to Spector too much," snapped the Miggot. "It's a tree, not a symbol. And the roots provide good cover."

"It's Fang and the Miggot!" came a joyful cry. "They're back!"

The gnomes rushed from concealment and greeted the pair, pumping their hands, slapping them on the back.

"Well done, Fang!" cried the Princess of the Willow Tree, hugging him tightly.

"The spirit of gnomedom is not dead," announced Spector the Thinking Gnome.

"So did you see Nyneve and Arthur? What did they say?" asked King Bison. "Did you arrange a suitable area of the forest for founding the new gnomedom? Has Arthur instructed the rest of the giants to let us live our lives in peace?" There was an unaccustomed acidity in Bison's voice. As the gnomes' recently deposed leader, he was beginning to feel the loss of authority.

"Well, not exactly," admitted Fang.

"Not exactly what?"

"Not exactly any of those things. We saw Nyneve and Arthur, yes. But a crowd of giants were there and things weren't going too well. It didn't seem wise to show ourselves."

"Not wise?" echoed the Gooligog, Fang's father and the Mara Zion Memorizer. "But up at the lake, Arthur assured us he would protect us! 'So long as I'm alive, no harm will come to you gnomes.' Those were his exact words. Are you saying Arthur lied?"

"No, Father. He meant what he said. The only trouble is, the other giants don't accept him."

"But he's Arthur! He's destined to be King of England, according to Nyneve. How can they not accept him?"

The Miggot helped Fang out. "Obviously there must be certain formalities before Arthur can sit on the throne."

"Formalities? Like what?"

"Like conquering the rest of England, you fool," snapped the Miggot, losing patience. "You know how giantish society works. It's not like gnomedom. Giants have to fight for what they get. You've seen them doing it often enough in the umbra."

"So what are we going to do?"

"What we intended to do. Rebuild gnomedom. We'll just have to exercise a little caution, that's all. We'll maintain a low profile until Arthur's influence spreads. Then we'll emerge triumphantly from hiding and take our rightful place as important members of the forest community."

"I'm damned if *I'll* go into hiding," said the Gooligog. "Gnomes have never hidden in my memory." The Gooligog's memory went back many thousands of years. "It's demeaning, expecting us to—"

A crashing in the bushes cut him short. He bolted for cover, ignoring the demeaning aspect for the sake of expediency. The rest of the gnomes followed, concealing themselves among the decaying roots of the oak. They waited fearfully as the snapping of twigs and the rustle of leaves came closer. "You see what I mean?" whispered the Gooligog to his companion in hiding.

"What's that you say?" yelled old Crotchet, who was deaf.

The forest fell suddenly silent. Then: "Is that gnomes?" came a shout.

The voice was a gnomish piping, rather than a giantish roar. "It is gnomes!" Fang shouted back. "Who is that?"

"It's Jack o' the Warren and Pong! And Bart o' Bodmin!"

The gnomes emerged from cover and greeted one another. Bart introduced himself. Such a meeting of gnomes would normally have been an occasion for feasting, but food was scarce and beer was nonexistent in this inhospitable new world. So the gnomes contented themselves with sitting around the base of the blasted oak and nibbling on raw mushrooms.

"Would it be safe to light a fire?" Pong asked after a while.

"Kindle the Wrath of Agni, you mean?" exclaimed Bart. "But that's against the Kikihuahua Examples! *I will not kill any mortal creature,*" he began to recite unctuously. *"I will not work any malleable substance. I will not kindle the Wrath of Agni. In this way I will take a step toward living in accord with my world and—"*

"Yes, we know all that stuff," said the Miggot impatiently. "And we don't kindle the Wrath of Agni. Broyle the Blaze does it for us. He's accepted eternal damnation. I see you're wearing a brass belt buckle. That's a malleable substance, wrought by the Accursed Gnomes. You're a bloody hypocrite, Bart o' Bodmin."

"We don't light fires in Bodmin," muttered Bart stubbornly.

"We do here," said Fang shortly, throwing sticks into a heap. There was something about Bart that he didn't quite like, and it worried him to see Pong fooled by this suspect gnome. "Kindle the Wrath of Agni, Broyle!"

"I . . . I don't have the sacred torch," said Broyle the Blaze unhappily. "Somehow it got left behind in our old world. Woe is me. I've betrayed the trust."

"You'll just have to light another torch," said the Miggot. "It's a small price to pay for the warmth and comfort of us gnomes."

Broyle began to tremble. "It's happened too often," he said. "Often I've forgotten to maintain the sacred torch because I've been contemplating, or sleeping, and I've had to kindle the Wrath of Agni all over again. I'm a disgrace to the Firelighters Guild, and one day Agni will strike me down with a bolt of lightning, you see if he doesn't!" He glanced at the sky. "That looks like a very black cumulus up there."

"Pull yourself together, gnome," snapped the Miggot.

"Is that how you do it?" asked Bart. "You have one gnome take on the responsibility, and he lights all fires from the same torch? Isn't that bending the Examples to suit your selfish purposes?"

"Broyle prays for forgiveness," said the Miggot. "And anyway, it's *kindling* the Wrath of Agni that's against the Examples. There's nothing wrong with *maintaining* the Wrath of Agni if someone else has kindled it for you. Broyle kindles the Wrath once, then lights everybody's fires with the sacred torch. At least, that's the principle of the thing. But the torch keeps going out."

"So what are we going to do?" asked Fang, regarding the pile of sticks.

"Oh, to hell with you, Broyle!" shouted the Miggot, losing patience as the firelighter shot another glance at the sky. "I'll light the bloody fire myself. I happen to have an example of the Wrath of Agni in the Sharan's new cave, to keep her warm," he informed the gathering at large, "and if that offends anyone, bugger them, that's what I say."

Everybody maintained a polite silence as the Miggot stumped off among the roots of the oak, to reappear with a blazing brand. He thrust it among the sticks. Flames spread, and the Miggot grunted in satisfaction.

"One thing I don't understand," said Pong, once they were seated before a cheerful blaze, "is how you gnomes escaped from the giants."

"It was the strangest thing," said Fang. "The giants captured us right after the happentracks joined, and took us to the Great Hall. We thought we were in big trouble. They had us dancing on the table. There was a fire nearby, and you know what *that* means."

The gnomes groaned. They knew what a giantish fire meant.

"And then, in came Nyneve. I doubt if she could have saved us by herself, but there was this giant Galahad with her. He seemed to have a strange power over the others. And a giant they call the Baron came, too, from over the other side of the moors. He told them to release us.

"Then Galahad took us to the Lake of Avalon and we watched Tristan's funeral, which was rather sad. But then this new giant came out of nowhere. Arthur. Nyneve introduced him to us. He seemed like a good giant. Then they left us and we made our way back."

"Where's Galahad now?"

"He vanished about the time Arthur appeared. It's a pity, because he'd have been a good giant to have on our side."

"He said something odd before he went," said the Miggot. "How did it go, Gooligog?"

" 'Happentracks are funny things. You and I, we don't quite coincide. You'll find out, one day when we meet again,' " quoted the Memorizer.

"So . . ." Bart looked around. "What do we do next?"

"We rebuild gnomedom," snapped the Miggot, who, like Fang, seemed to have taken a dislike to Bart.

"Right now?"

"Well," said the Miggot, "I have to attend to the Sharan. She's about to give birth. What the rest of you do is up to yourselves."

"Rather an inappropriate time to have your Sharan giving birth, isn't it?" said Bart.

"As a matter of fact",—the Miggot snarled, "it's an extremely appropriate time. She will be giving birth to digging creatures, and if there's any kind of creature we need right now, it's digging creatures. We'll call them moles."

"Why?"

The Miggot stepped close to Bart and stared down his long nose at him. There was a wart on the end of the Miggot's nose that acted like a gun sight, and the accuracy and penetrative power of his stare was famous throughout Mara Zion. Bart backed off, blinking. "Because that's what they are." The Miggot's voice was quiet, but it held a frightful menace—all the more so because gnomes are not normally menacing people.

"Of course," said Bart quickly. "Of course. May I witness the birth?"

Shortly afterward the Miggot, Fang, Bart, and Spector met the elfin Pan outside the Sharan's temporary quarters.

"The moles are born," Pan announced.

"Oh." The Miggot was disappointed. He liked to watch every detail of the Sharan's labor; it gave him a sense of achievement to see creatures emerge from her womb according to his specifications. The Sharan herself lay on her side, panting, her normally glossy silver coat dull and matted. Two moles sucked on her generous teats. As often happened with small creatures, they had emerged from the Sharan fully grown.

The Miggot eyed them critically. "Something's wrong. They're deformed. Now what shall we do?"

The Kikihuahua Examples forbade the killing of any living creature. The Miggot sometimes awakened in the middle of the night trembling, having dreamed of a forest populated by monsters of the Sharan's creating, which he could neither control nor dispose of.

"The moles are exactly according to specification," said Pan coldly.

"Why are they blind, then?"

Spector, sensing yet another clash between Pan and the Miggot, said quickly, "It's probably a protective measure to ensure our sympathy."

"It doesn't ensure *my* sympathy," snapped the Miggot, who believed in natural selection. "Far from it. It tells me they're unfit for survival."

"There was no mention of eyes in your specifications," insisted Pan.

"Why would I need to tell you about eyes? Every animal has eyes. There are some things we take for granted. How in hell can these moles see without eyes?"

"Perhaps they make a noise and receive the echo back, like moondogs," Fang suggested.

"Moondogs have big ears." The Miggot regarded the two moles in growing anger. "These things have no ears. They're little better than lumps of meat with claws." He stepped close to Pan, seized his ragged smock, and tried to stare furiously into the elf's eyes. Pan, however, overtopped him by several inches and was able to gaze loftily over his head.

"Let me run through your original request." Pan was enjoying the argument. For once he felt he was on firm ground. "You asked for a creature that would live underground, skilled in digging tunnels. You said it would make life much easier because suitable burrows for use as gnomish dwellings were always in short supply."

"In Bodmin," Bart could not resist saying, "we live above the ground in stone huts. It's healthy. It's clean."

"My cousin Hal lives in a stone hut," said the Miggot in tones of the utmost contempt, "and he certainly doesn't keep himself clean."

"In pursuance of my duty, I planted a telepathic scenario in the Sharan's mind," continued Pan, ignoring the interruption. "I gave her to understand she would soon be living on a world where the air was poisonous. The only salvation for her children lay underground, where oxygen-producing fungi grew. So she produced the most suitable children for that environment. Eyes and ears would be a disadvantage, because there's nothing down there to see or hear. But I'll warrant the moles have an excellent sense of smell, to sniff out their food.''

"What do they find to eat down there?'' asked Fang.

"Insects.''

"You mean . . . flesh? But isn't that against the Examples? We can't create flesh-eaters, can we? Surely the moles ought to eat grass, like rabbits do.''

"They're not going to find much grass underground, are they?'' Pan regarded Fang impatiently. ''And anyway, we have a precedent. Many generations ago, we created the shytes.'' He pointed out a group of untidy black birds waiting hopefully at the entrance to the cave. ''They're flesh-eaters to a bird.''

"The shytes were designed to keep the forest clean,'' said the Miggot. ''They feed on carrion. They do not eat live flesh. Fang is right. The moles contravene the Examples. You have twisted my specifications, Pan. This is a matter of the utmost gravity.''

As though alarmed by the Miggot's condemnation, the moles detached themselves from the teats and began to dig. The soil was light and sandy, and in no time they had disappeared.

"Stop them!'' shouted the Miggot.

"Too late,'' said Pan. ''They'll be all right. They're supreme in their environment.''

"They're the only animals *in* their environment, you fool. Now I'd like to get them back into ours. How can we put them to work if we can't find them?'' asked the Miggot, practical concerns overriding his conscientious objection to the creatures.

"You must follow them down their holes and lure them out with kindness. Kindness is in your nature, Miggot; you people are always telling me that. Gnomes are kind and good.''

"We could tie thongs to their hind legs,'' suggested Bart, "and drag them out whenever we wanted. And we could train them to dig where we needed, by chivvying them a bit.''

''Chivvying them?'' The other gnomes regarded him in mild alarm.

''A good poke up the backside with a sharp stick will work wonders.''

This evoked an image so similar to the gnomes' traditional fear of being roasted on skewers that the subject had to be changed at once. The gnomes hurried out of the cave, leaving the offensive words echoing behind. For once, the sight of the Gooligog emerging from the trees was welcome. He stamped irritably toward them, birds circling low over his head.

''If the shytes only feed on carrion, why are they following the Gooligog?'' asked Pan triumphantly.

''The Gooligog's time must be near,'' the Miggot explained. ''The stench of death is upon him.''

The Gooligog joined them, kicking aside a shyte that hopped before him like a pallbearer. ''This is a macabre situation, Miggot,'' he shouted, ''and I want something done about it. One of the bastards landed on my head this morning. By the Sword of Agni, they're worse than that bloody housemouse of mine!''

''I thought you'd come to terms with the housemouse, Father,'' said Fang. ''And anyway, wasn't he drowned when your burrow flooded out?''

''He escaped and followed me, the faithful bastard. He was with me last night.'' The shytes were not the only carrion-eating creatures in gnomedom. Elderly gnomes traditionally kept housemice in their dwellings, to clean up when they died. ''I saw him standing there in the moonlight, trembling,'' said the Gooligog. ''He's getting old too. I'm going to outlast the brute, mark my words. But not unless you call off these bloody shytes, Miggot. A while back I sat down under a tree to contemplate, and the buggers were all around me in an instant! Have you ever smelled a shyte's breath?'' He lashed out with a gnarled stick, catching a bird squarely in the rib cage and bowling it squawking across the clearing, shedding feathers.

"I don't think my father's going to die yet, Miggot," said Fang mildly. "He seems very spry to me. The shytes have got it wrong."

"They know," said Bart o' Bodmin wisely. "They know."

"The laws of nature," murmured Spector. "And the balance of life. The moles are born, the Memorizer dies."

"Well, I'm not dead yet," snapped the Gooligog, "and I'll thank you not to anticipate the happy event, Miggot. So where are these moles? People are getting impatient back in the forest."

"You see those holes?" The Miggot pointed. "That's where the moles are. You're welcome to go down and fetch them, Gooligog. Bart tells us kindness will bring them out."

"It would be unwise to follow a flesh-eating creature down its hole," Spector warned him. "I can visualize an occasion when it might not respond to kindness."

"Thongs are the only way," Bart agreed.

The ensuing discussion lasted until nightfall, by which time the gnomes had made their way back to the blasted oak. Probably the only practical suggestion came from Fang: "We could wait until the moles abandon their holes, and then move in."

"Rebuild gnomedom at the whim of burrowing animals?" cried Lady Duck. "What kind of credibility does that give us in the forest?"

"We must discuss priorities," said Spector the Thinking Gnome. "That would be the logical thing to do next, with only two moles. Then, when we've found a way to put the moles to work, we will have a plan of action all mapped out."

"It seems to me," said the Miggot, "that the first burrow to be dug should be some kind of community gathering place."

"Absolutely!" shouted Clubfoot.

There was a murmur of agreement and the gnomes found

themselves nodding at one another wisely. It was several seconds before the first screams of dissent were heard.

"Nonsense!" cried Elmera.

"Forget it, Miggot!" roared Lady Duck. "If you see rebuilding Tom Grog's disgusting drinking hole as a major priority, then you're a more selfish and stupid gnome than I thought. We need places to live, not stinking burrows where male gnomes drink themselves senseless!"

Tom Grog, a polite and pleasant gnome, said quickly, "You're welcome at the Disgusting anytime, Lady Duck. So is Elmera, even. If more females used my establishment, it would be a much happier place. It's hard for a gnome to be doing his job according to the rules of his guild, and yet find half of gnomedom against him."

"I never mentioned the Disgusting," said the Miggot, aggrieved. "By the Great Grasshopper, why does every discussion come back to beer?"

"That was what you meant," said Elmera. "I should know, Miggot. I've lived with you for countless years, God knows why. You don't fool me."

The discussion petered out without any decisions being reached, which was the norm for gnomish meetings. In gloomy silence, the gnomes prepared for another night in the open.

"Tomorrow," said the Miggot after a while, "Jack will furnish us with rabbits, and we'll seek out our dwelling sites. For myself, I prefer this spot." Lying on his back, he gazed up at the charred branches of the blasted oak. Shytes perched there, waiting for the Gooligog's eyes to close.

"The giants ate the rabbits," said Jack quickly.

They considered this disturbing news, then Lady Duck said, "If they could eat rabbits, they could eat anything."

"I have no fear," said Pong the Intrepid, "for the Gnome from the North will watch over me."

"Amen," murmured Bart o' Bodmin.

"The Gnome from the North," echoed Jack o' the Warren.

"You'll have to tell me all about this Gnome from the

North sometime,'' said King Bison, ''because right now I have plenty of fear. I could do with someone to watch over me too.''

One by one, the gnomes fell asleep.

4
THE SWORD IN THE ROCK

NORTH OF THE FOREST OF MARA ZION, PENTOR ROCK emerges jagged from the smooth dome of the moor like a hatching dinosaur. It is a bleak spot, where the winds blow unobstructed from the far side of the Atlantic. Sheep and ponies roam the sere grass, long-haired against the freezing winters, and when they face the wind, their coats stream flat against their bodies as though combed. When the snow falls heavily, as it does once every eleven years, most of the animals die. The children of the survivors grow just a little bit more hardy, as though Nature is trying to do better next time. Natural selection applies on the moor, and the Miggot of One would have approved.

One spring day in the year of our story, a gnome stood examining the base of the rock. Coincidentally, he was the cousin of the Miggot. His expression was gloomy and his attention was divided, because from time to time he would glance apprehensively over his shoulder.

"Hello, little gnome!"

"Aaargh!" The gnome wheeled around with a shout of terror.

The monstrous and unexpected apparition was clearly female. It was dressed in a long black cloak, black-haired and white-faced like a figure glimpsed by moonlight. The beauty of the face was unearthly.

"Don't be frightened." The voice was gentle. "I'm not

going to harm you. My name is Morgan le Fay. What's yours?''

"H-H-H . . ."

"Hector?"

"H-H-Hal. Hal o' the Moor."

"And what are you doing all alone at this windswept spot, Hal?"

"I'm looking for my cave."

"Is your cave hard to find?"

"Impossible, it seems," said Hal unhappily, encouraged by the friendly tones of the giant. "It was here a fortnight ago, before the flood. But then it disappeared. That horrible old giant they call Merlin crawled into it and took it with him somehow."

"Oh, Merlin!" Morgan le Fay laughed. "I've been wondering where he'd gotten to. So he's inside this rock, is he? I always knew something like that would happen to him."

"Well, I wish he'd come out, and let me have my dwelling back."

"I may be able to arrange that for you." She took a gold-capped wand from beneath her cloak and tapped on the rock. "Open, Pentor," she said. Nothing happened. The wind blew as before, whistling among the fissures of the rock. A few ponies ambled toward them, munching. "What's gone wrong here?" murmured Morgan.

"You need to do more than tap on it," Hal ventured. "You need a work party with hammers and chisels fashioned by the Accursed Gnomes. Gnomes are excellent stonemasons. We can make things from stone without disobeying the Kikihuahua Examples. Chipping at stone doesn't count as working a malleable substance. It's allowed. Anyway," said Hal quickly, realizing he was getting onto philosophical quicksands, "you need time and patience to break open a rock this size. You won't do it by tapping with a stick."

"This is a *wand*, you little fool." Morgan's disguise slipped for an instant.

"Well, it's obviously not a very good one."

She regarded him speculatively. There was a great temptation simply to put her foot on him and, with a grinding motion, fertilize the short grass. It would be an excusable act and probably for the ultimate good of life on Earth. But Morgan was a Dedo, or Finger of Starquin, and able to resist earthly temptations. "Tell me, Hal," she said sweetly, "exactly *how* Merlin got stuck in this rock."

"Well, he came up here with Nyneve. It was getting late and he wanted to rest. He crawled into the cave and tried to get Nyneve to go in there with him. She wouldn't. The moons were up and she wanted—"

"The moons? Of course! This all took place before the happentracks merged."

"There were three moons, then they became two."

"And Merlin disappeared just about the time one of the moons did?"

"That's right. He—"

"Be quiet, gnome. I have to think." And in the way that only Dedos could, she cast her mind into the past, seeing separate happentracks merge backward into a widening stream of flowing Time. She saw the grasses rise as the wind abated. She saw the sheep and ponies in ghostly multiplicity; the moor smudged with their possible courses and positions; all of them trotting backward, converging, becoming more solid. The sun was easy to backcast, as were the moons. The clouds and the rain she could divine by the soil and the plants. Morgan le Fay concentrated, slowed Time, and the sky darkened.

"The moons are back," whispered Hal. "What have you done?"

It was evening and the three moons he'd known all his life were back in the sky. Pentor Rock bulked huge and black before them. Two ghostly figures moved near the rock. Their lips moved, but Hal could hear no words. One of the figures—an old man with a long beard—dropped to his knees and crawled into a cave.

The air tingled with an electric tension, as though a thunderstorm were brewing.

"Now!" said Morgan, tapping the Rock with her wand.

Two moons winked out. Night turned into day. The figure standing beside the Rock disappeared.

"My dwelling!" cried Hal. The hole at the base of the Rock had returned. He ran forward.

"Wait," Morgan cautioned him. "All right, Merlin," she called. "You can come out now!"

Spluttering and grumbling, the ancient Paragon emerged from the cave. Surprisingly, another creature emerged at the same time: a beast of the most disgusting aspect, hairless with batlike ears. It bolted, snuffling, into the night.

"Can you imagine it?" Merlin expostulated. "Two weeks alone with that brute? The cave was so damned small that whatever way I set up the hibernation field, that stinking bastard was inside it with me. Why did you do this to me, Nyneve?"

He stood painfully, rubbing his legs and blinking. Then his eyes became accustomed to the daylight, and he stared. "It isn't Nyneve," he said.

"No, it's me, Merlin," said the Dedo. "Your sister, Morgan. Aren't you pleased to see me?"

The old Paragon's jaw had dropped slackly agape. He hitched it up and said quietly, "Perhaps I was better off in the cave, after all."

"If I hadn't come along, you'd have been in there for thirty thousand years. And according to my calculations, this rock would then be destroyed, and you along with it. Pull yourself together and take me to Avalona, you old fool. Terrible happenings are in the ifalong, and somehow they must be forestalled!"

Happentracks may branch and happentracks may join, but the little cottage deep in the forest of Mara Zion never changed. The slate roof was thick with moss, and the cracks in the stone walls were home to a hundred varieties of plant life. Insects dwelt in there, too, eating one another and any plants that took their fancy. They could make no impact on the timbers of the cottage, though. These were black with age and as hard as the stone itself. They spanned the interior and angled up to support the roof, where huge spiders prowled.

It was early evening when Nyneve pushed open the creaking door and entered. Avalona sat by the fireside in a high-backed chair, eyes closed as she rummaged through the ifalong in search of unsuitable happentracks. The fire had burned out hours before.

"We went to the village," said Nyneve.

After a long pause Avalona returned to the present. "What was the feeling there?"

"It was so frustrating! They simply refused to accept Arthur. Ned Palomides even challenged him, knowing Arthur wouldn't be so unfair as to draw Excalibur on him. The whole thing's a big joke to them. They will not acknowledge that he's the Arthur of the legends, traveled back in Time."

"I wouldn't expect them to. Why should they?"

"He's a great man, Avalona!"

"No man is great. Only Starquin is great."

"Well, Arthur's pretty damned good!"

"Give it time, Nyneve. The nearby ifalong is already decided. Arthur will be accepted and will become king of England."

"I wish I could see some sign of that happening. Just a glimmering of respect from those bloody peasants; that's all I ask."

"And what does Arthur ask?"

She shrugged in frustration. "Nothing, it seems. He's quite satisfied with things as they are."

"That's because he does not know the full extent of his destiny. To him it is nothing—just a story told by a young girl with a gift. He doesn't believe you any more than the villagers do. And that's the way it must be. Arthur's future must be allowed to develop naturally, and as time goes by you will find that the legend and the man become indistinguishable. By the time he is king, the existence of the legend will have lent an inevitability to events that will make his path much easier."

"And who will be queen?"

"Guinevere. You know that."

"Gwen from Camyliard? But that was just a part of the story!"

"If Arthur is to be king, then logic ought to tell you that Guinevere will be his queen."

Over my dead body, said Nyneve, but she said it to herself. "Can't Arthur stay here with us?" she asked. "It's cold at night in that tent of his. And it doesn't do much for his image in the village, living rough like that."

"He must be seen to be an ordinary human, free from supernatural influence. If he lives with us, he will become associated with us in the minds of the villagers."

"But he already has Excalibur. How supernatural can you get?"

"Excalibur is not supernatural. It simply spans two happentracks. Its user appears invincible because his doppelgänger in the other happentrack has already seen the blow coming, and has parried it. Excalibur operates slightly in advance of events on our happentrack, that's all."

"Oh. And I really thought it was magic."

"Magic is relative to knowledge, Nyneve. If you . . . Hush. What was that?"

The sound of voices came to them; one shrill, a reply in gruff, cracked tones.

"This is one happentrack I had not foreseen," said Avalona.

The door burst open.

"Morgan le Fay!" exclaimed Nyneve.

"And Merlin," said Merlin. "Thought you'd gotten rid of me, didn't you, Nyneve!"

"I had nothing to do with you getting trapped in that cave. It was a convergence of happentracks!"

"Oh, I'm sure it was. Pretty convenient convergence, if you ask me. I suppose you had nothing to do with the moondog that got trapped in there with me."

"Be quiet, you two," said Avalona coldly. "Morgan— why are you here?"

"Have you lost the knack of reading the ifalong?"

"I have not. I did not include you in my calculations."

"There's a lot of things you didn't include. Like the destruction of your Rock, the death of Starquin and all of us!"

"Yes, I foresaw that. I am working to prevent it from occurring."

"I don't see much in the way of preventive measures around here!"

"Calm yourself, Morgan. You are a Dedo."

"Emotions can be very satisfying. When things go wrong, it helps to stamp and scream and blame something. Then you can reassess the problem with a clear mind. But that's beside the point. The point is that your Rock will be destroyed in approximately thirty thousand Earth years from now, by humans, just at the time Starquin is approaching on the corresponding psetic line. That line will cease to exist—and Starquin with it. And you, Avalona. And I."

"It is my Rock and my problem, and I am dealing with it."

It was the nearest thing to irritation that Nyneve had ever heard in Avalona's voice. She watched in fascination as the two Dedos faced each other. Even Merlin was quiet, standing in a dark corner and watching events with apprehension.

"I see absolutely no sign of action at all!" Morgan said. "Humans will destroy your Rock, right? So the sensible precaution is to destroy the humans first. Yet they still exist. The countryside is alive with them. You even have gnomes now, it seems. Dirty little devils."

"I propose to eliminate the danger to Starquin with a minimum of adjustment to the ifalong, Morgan. There is little to be gained by rash and drastic action. Existing life-forms can be allowed to continue, where appropriate. Skillful manipulation is the correct course to follow."

"The dangers are too great."

"Not according to my calculations. If everything goes according to plan, Starquin—and ourselves—will continue to exist on 87.362 percent of happentracks at that point in the ifalong."

"If you eliminate the human factor, it will be one hundred percent!"

"It will not. Other dangers will arise."

"How do you know, if you haven't forecast the effects of an Earth free of humans?"

"Morgan, sit down. You, too, Merlin. Let's combine our skills instead of arguing. And let me remind you of the purpose of our existence."

Nyneve, forgotten by the immortals, sat quietly in her corner and listened with fascination and no little dread.

"I don't need you telling me our purpose. I need action," said Morgan le Fay. She was still standing, and her black clothes seemed to suck from the room what little light there was. Only her face was pale, waxen; her mouth a scarlet wound.

"When Starquin saw this planet," said Avalona, ignoring her remark, "he scanned the ifalong and foresaw the evolution of an intelligent race. So he sent down the Dedos to witness events. He was *interested*, Morgan. Our corporate entity is an inquisitive being. What else is there for him, except to become inquisitive about the Universe? He was interested in how the humans would develop, and in what would happen next. Intelligent life is rare.

"So we do *not* wipe it out in a moment of panic. That would remove the purpose of a few millennia of Starquin's existence. That would be an intolerable waste."

"If Starquin wants to know what happens to the humans," Merlin piped up, "all he has to do is scan the ifalong."

"Merlin," said Avalona in flat tones, "you are an old fool and you have outlived any usefulness you might once have had. I can foresee the time when it will be necessary to disincorporate you. I thought I had you safely out of the way for the next thirty thousand years, but now my sister has seen fit to release you. The ifalong has become complicated by your continued presence and by the arrival of my sister, and Starquin no longer has reliable data. Nobody has. The matter must be simplified."

"By eliminating the humans," said Morgan le Fay.

"By eliminating you and Merlin, perhaps," said Avalona.

The three immortals stared at each other. A hunting owl hooted once, and there was a tiny scream from outside. Some lives were cheap, others more durable.

"By eliminating *you,* perhaps!" screeched Merlin, emboldened by the presence of Morgan, whom he regarded as an ally. Then, terrified at what he'd said, he fell silent with his knuckles to his mouth, staring wide-eyed at the fire, toothless gums munching.

Morgan le Fay said, "This is silly human talk, Avalona. We both have Rocks to guard. For one of us to eliminate the other would mean deliberately provoking a failure of duty."

"But we must weigh the possible consequences of that against the known consequences of precipitate action against the humans."

"You will agree, though, that the ifalong is subject to different interpretations."

Avalona stared at her coldly. "I am never wrong."

"Wrong or right may not be the point."

And the discussion continued far into the night. Nyneve fell asleep in her chair, taking into her dreams a curious elation. Avalona was not perfect. Her omniscience had been challenged by one equally as great as she. The ifalong—the composite future of all happentracks—could be a matter of opinion. Little things could be changed. . . .

The plan came into her mind, full-grown, sometime during that night.

One fine morning a few weeks later, Governayle was riding through the forest on his way to the beach. Trotting beside him were his two dogs, Snapper and Sniffer. The young man sang softly to himself, happy because all appeared to be well in Mara Zion, and because he had arranged to meet Nancy Weaver in the dell at the back of the beach. Nancy was a big girl, well versed in the arts of love. The morning promised to be a pleasant one.

It was Sniffer who made the discovery.

Governayle was already thinking it had perhaps been a mistake to bring the dogs. He loved his animals dearly, but there was no doubt they could be a disadvantage at a lovers' tryst. Snapper and Sniffer were big and clumsy, and had a bad habit of treading all over anyone lying down and licking them.

And now Sniffer had disappeared into the bush, following some intriguing scent. Scents could occupy that dog for hours.

"Sniffer!" called Governayle, exasperated. The bush was thick hereabouts. He dismounted and plunged in pursuit.

A deer trail indicated the route the dog had taken. Governayle followed, bending low. Soon the trail widened into a clearing. It was an unknown place, bypassed by the well-worn paths to the beach. Two tall oaks shaded a rocky cliff.

"What on earth . . . ?" exclaimed Governayle.

Short grass grew in the clearing. The sunlight, striking through the leaves of the oak, tinted the grass a bright emerald. The sunlight fell also on a sword of crude workmanship, apparently embedded in a heavy black anvil. The anvil sat squarely on a large boulder.

In itself, the sight was so remarkable that Governayle missed the implications. He hurried forward and grasped the carved handle, which projected at chest height. He pulled, but the sword remained where it was. He walked around the boulder, examining it. It was approximately square, and marks of chisels could be seen on its surface. The anvil was an ordinary piece of blacksmith's equipment; there was one in the village just like it. Except that this anvil had a slot in the top, through which the sword passed. Governayle tried waggling the sword. It was a good fit in the slot, but not a tight one. He could rattle it from side to side, but he couldn't pull it out. He concluded that the tip was stuck in the boulder itself.

"Governayle!"

He wheeled around with an abashed smile, preparing to face Nancy's accusation that he enjoyed a mystery more than her loving. But it wasn't Nancy. This girl was more beautiful than Nancy, but she was also more aloof.

"Hello, Nyneve," he replied.

"What do you make of this, then?"

"I don't know what to make of it," he admitted. "It's a poorly made sword, but why would anyone want to stick it in this rock?"

"Well, obviously, it's the Sword in the Stone," said Nyneve with a hint of asperity.

"I can see it's a sword in a stone."

"No, I mean *the* Sword in *the* Stone. The sword that Arthur pulls out."

He stared at her. "Why would you think that?"

"Well, what else could it be?"

"Arthur's sword was just one of your stories, Nyneve. And a good one too. But why should you think this sword is connected with that one? This could be any old sword stuck in any old rock. For all I know, swords could be stuck in rocks all over England. It could be a secret part of the manufacturing process, to temper them."

Nyneve felt herself flush with irritation. After all her work of the past weeks, she'd expected a more positive reaction than this. "I wish you wouldn't keep calling it a rock. It's a stone. It's *the* Stone. Haven't you seen the inscription on it? Come on. Take a look around the other side."

Governayle followed her. Sure enough, there were words engraved in the anvil that he hadn't noticed previously. Nyneve read them aloud.

"WHOSO PULLETH OUTE THIS SWERD OF THIS STONE AND ANVYLD IS RIGHTWYS KYNGE BORNE OF ALL BRETAGNE."

"Is that what it says?"

"Can't you read?" An appalled suspicion grew in her.

"Not very well," he admitted. "Not well enough to read all that stuff, anyway."

"Can anyone in the village read?"

"Well, you used to live there before you moved in with

the old witch," he said, getting annoyed. "Did you see much reading going on?"

"I suppose not." Nyneve had been taught by Avalona. It had never occurred to her that the villagers might not be able to read the inscription. The legend had never mentioned this problem. In the legend, people had taken in the inscription at a glance and marveled. Governayle showed no sign of marveling. And yet, according to Avalona, that legend was a real event on a different happentrack. For an instant Nyneve had a weird feeling of disorientation. Was she creating the legend, or was she imitating it?

By mid-morning a small crowd had gathered around the sword in the stone. Torre was there, and Palomides, and other Mara Zion notables. They all gazed at the inscription uncomprehendingly.

"But that's just what *you* tell us, Nyneve," said Torre in reasonable tones, after Nyneve had read the words aloud for the tenth time. "And you seem to have a vested interest in this fellow Arthur's success. And come to think of it, we don't even have any proof his name is Arthur. Nobody knows him. His name could be Albert, for all we know. He could be deceiving us all."

"And for all we know," added Ned Palomides, "the inscription could read WHOSO PULLETH OUTE THIS SWERD OF THIS STONE AND ANVYLD SHOULD STRAIGHTWYS BE HANGED FROM YE CLOSEBYE OAKE."

"Or it could be directions for a new kind of pump." Torre eyed the sword critically. "Perhaps it's not meant to be a sword at all. Perhaps it's just a handle, to be pumped up and down." He tried to work the handle and failed. "And then again, perhaps not."

"Here comes Albert," said Palomides.

The pretender to the throne emerged from the forest, whistling cheerfully, hands in his pockets, his recently acquired lurcher Bull's-eye at his heels. Nyneve's heart leapt at the sight of him. Treacherously, and at the same moment, she found herself wishing he looked a little more kingly. Mounted on a white steed, perhaps, dressed in glittering chain mail and carrying a shield bearing a royal device. Clearly she needed to do some work on him.

"What's going on here, then?" he asked.

Palomides explained. "It's the Sword in the Stone, Arthur. This is your big moment. Pull the bugger out and you'll be king of England!"

Nyneve stepped quickly in front of Arthur. "Don't even try. This isn't the right time." He could ruin the whole plan. She should have taken him into her confidence, but she'd had the feeling he wouldn't go along with what she proposed. Sometimes Arthur's naïveté and honesty could be a drawback.

"If you say so, Nyneve." Arthur regarded the sword curiously.

Torre said, "It's not *that* sword, Arthur. It can't be. Pay no attention to Palomides, he's just pulling your leg. If it was the real Sword in the Stone, this would be London, and there'd be moonbeams shining on it and angels singing and all kinds of stuff like that. You'd hardly get the Sword in the Stone in some muddy little glade in Mara Zion."

"It *is* the real Sword," insisted Nyneve. "And one day Arthur will pull it out. But not now." She felt like crying. Everything had gone wrong. Governayle's discovery of the sword had been premature; she'd thought it was well hidden.

She was saved further explanations by the jingling arrival of Sir Mador de la Porte on splendid horseback. Despite an ignominious defeat by Tristan a few months previously, Sir Mador's career had progressed by leaps and bounds. Following the recent death of Tristan, he had been appointed Knight of the Southern Realm, which meant that he represented Baron Menheniot's interests in Mara Zion and neighboring settlements. He was not a popular figure with the villagers. They suspected he intended to exact a regular tribute from the village, and was only awaiting the right moment to do it.

"Whoa!" he roared to his horse. "What goes on here?" he asked.

They explained. Sir Mador had heard the legend of Arthur; furthermore, he could read. Dismounting, he examined the inscription, his lips moving silently. Then he examined the sword, assessing his chances. "Yes," he said at last. "It seems to be the right sword." He laid a huge, mailed hand on it and tugged. The Sword remained firmly in place.

"We've all tried," said Torre. "Nobody can pull it out."

"Arthur hasn't tried," said Palomides craftily.

Sir Mador swept Arthur with an imperious stare. "Ha, the stranger we've been hearing about. Try your luck, Pretender."

"I don't see why not," said Arthur, who'd been annoyed at being left out of things.

"No," said Nyneve.

Ignoring her, Arthur stepped up to the Sword. Despite their skepticism, the onlookers held their breath. There was certainly something deeply impressive about this tall figure that his simple peasant clothing could not conceal. And as Arthur laid his hand on the haft, the sun, which had been hiding behind a thick white cloud, chose that moment to emerge in all its glory. The dell came alive and Arthur was suddenly godlike, his hair a golden corona.

He pulled.

The sword remained firmly in place.

Bracing a foot against the anvil, he pulled again. A little bead of sweat trickled down his brow.

Nothing happened.

"Oh, bugger the thing!" he cried.

"I told you not to try," said Nyneve, tears in her eyes.

"Yes, it's all very well to say that *now*," Arthur began angrily. Then he became aware of his grinning audience, swung on his heel, and strode away into the forest, Bull's-eye slinking behind.

"That's the end of him," said Sir Mador. "His credibility is shot, if he ever had any. I hope we've seen the last of the pretenders out of Mara Zion. Tristan got his just desserts, and now Arthur's moment of glory is over, such as it was." He examined the faces of the villagers. "Which of you peasants will try next? You, Torre? No, I don't think so." He turned to Nyneve. "I must congratulate you on your plan. You laid the groundwork very well with those stories of yours. You had us all believing in King Arthur and his Knights of the Round Table, but when it came to picking your real-life Arthur, everything fell apart. Face it, Nyneve, nobody can live up to those stories. The Baron will get a laugh out of this."

During his short speech, a surprising change had come over his audience. "The Baron may laugh too soon," said Governayle.

"I didn't see *you* pulling the sword out, Sir Mador de la Porte!" said Torre angrily. "At least Arthur bears an honorable name. What bloody Porte are you Sir Mador de, anyway?"

"It is a hereditary title," explained Sir Mador with dignity, "and the location of the Porte is lost in antiquity. Some say it refers to the gates of heaven."

"Or perhaps the door to the privy. Whatever it is, it's French. And that's only a short step from being Irish!"

Surprisingly Sir Mador brushed the insult aside with a tolerant smile. "You should brush up on your geography, Torre. Meanwhile I'll ride to Menheniot and tell the Baron about the Sword in the Stone. Somewhere in Cornwall there may well be a man capable of pulling it out. But I don't think so. Anyway, it will give us the chance for a feast!"

Word of the existence of the Sword in the Stone spread quickly through the southwest of England and was greeted with huge excitement. The legend of Arthur was a popular one. The majority of the people lived under the rule of local landowners and dreamed of the day when a new and just leader would arise; dispossess the barons, earls, and dukes; give each peasant a plot of land; and protect their women-folk from licentious collectors of fealty. It was a beautiful dream, and the legend of Arthur put it into simple language.

And now a sword in a stone had appeared, in a magical

forest rumored to be inhabited by monsters, unicorns, and gnomes. It couldn't have happened in a better place.

The people flocked to Mara Zion. . . .

Tents hung from spreading branches and families camped under them. The status of a person was in inverse proportion to his distance from the Sword in the Stone, which was now covered by a purple pavilion. Around it stood the pavilions of the gentry, including Baron Menheniot. In a broad concentric circle outside hung the tents of the soldiers. Farther away, and spreading off fingerlike along the banks of the streams, were the peasants' tents. Food was prepared on a community basis, and a constant stream of supply carts rolled in from distant towns. Old acquaintances met for the first time in years, and children and dogs gamboled around their feet.

The gnomes stayed away, huddled in their new and partly completed dwellings.

"The amount of breeding going on in those tents boggles my mind," grumbled King Bison, just returned from a short foraging trip.

"Arthur will soon put a stop to that kind of nonsense!" cried Lady Duck confidently. "Mark my words, Bison, if Nyneve's scheme comes off, it'll be a great day for gnomedom!"

Nyneve herself had persuaded Arthur to set up camp as close to the Sword as possible, in preparation for the great moment when he would stride from his tent, grasp the haft, and, amid yells of astonishment and approbation, draw the Sword from the stone with a flourish.

"It didn't happen like that last time," said Arthur.

"The time was not ripe. The audience wasn't assembled, don't you see? If you'd pulled the Sword out in front of a handful of villagers and Sir Mador de la Thing, the news would have been suppressed." She regarded him speculatively. Should she tell him the truth? No. He was a painfully honest man, and would never agree to trickery. Sometimes she found herself wishing he were a little more ruthless in his pursuit of the Crown. . . .

A heavy body blundered into the tent, bulging the fabric. Someone uttered a hoarse yell. "I wish I was back on the other side of the forest with the gnomes," said Arthur gloomily. It was evening, and a light drizzle dampened the tent. Sounds of revelry came from all around.

"Your place is among the common people," Nyneve said, reproving him.

"Well, you can't get much more common than this." The tent was small, thrown over the branch of a sycamore, and weighted around with rocks. Broad leaves hung from the branch inside the tent. There was barely room for the two of them. Arthur lay with his back against the bole, and Nyneve sat opposite, her hands clasped around her knees. "Nyneve," said Arthur after a long silence, "I wish I knew what was going on. I wish I could remember something, *anything*, about my life before I woke up in that boat. You keep telling me I'm the reincarnation of some legend—and that I'm 'destined for greatness,' as you put it. Well, I've got to tell you this. I don't feel destined."

"What *do* you feel?"

"I feel kind of damp. The rain's trickling down the walls of this tent. And I feel like . . . like a pawn. Nothing at all like a king."

An overwhelming feeling of love and pity took hold of Nyneve as she watched him. Was it fair, what she was doing? He looked so unhappy, with water dribbling down the tree trunk behind him, bareheaded and barefooted, Bull's-eye shivering and stinking at his side. He was dressed in the green shirt and trousers he'd borrowed from the village. After all, he couldn't spend his days permanently encased in armor. . . . She straightened her legs so they lay one on either side of Arthur's outstretched right leg and leaned forward to bring her breasts into view under the loose blouse. *How do you seduce a future king?* she wondered. He'd never shown any sign of noticing she was a woman.

"Why don't you stop worrying about all that stuff for a while?" she said softly.

"Huh?" He raised his eyes to hers. "I wish I felt I belonged," he said.

She hitched herself forward so that her groin pressed against his foot. "Why don't you stop worrying?" she repeated, her voice a whisper.

He was regarding her in surprise, as though making some slow, radical reassessment of the situation. "Huh?"

"How does that feel?"

"What?"

"Your foot, silly."

"Oh. . . . Oh, God, Nyneve." His toes moved a fraction, and then were still, stiff.

"Listen, you must have known *something* before you woke up in that boat. Otherwise how could you speak the language?"

"It's not that." His foot had withdrawn an inch.

"What is it, then?"

"You're . . . so *young*. You've been looking after me. It would be wrong to . . . to take advantage of you."

She moved forward again, impatiently, trapping his foot between clenched thighs. "Who's taking advantage?" There was irritation in her voice. "Doesn't it occur to you that you're embarrassing me, sitting there rigid like a corpse? Is that chivalrous, to discomfit a lady in that way? Be honest, don't I have any effect on you? Yes or *no!*"

And on the word *no* she pushed her own foot into his crotch. When she felt the heated hardness, an uncontrollable shivering took hold of her. She seized his hand, pushed it down the front of her blouse, and pulled herself toward him. He uttered a murmur of protest as his hand became trapped in her clothes, then there was a tearing sound and their position became more comfortable.

"Oh, Nyneve," he said.

"There's this as well," she said. "Life isn't all worrying about one's destiny." And she sighed with happiness as she found he hadn't left all his instincts behind on his old happentrack.

When morning came, his arms were still around her and

she awakened slowly, deeply content. The rain had stopped and the tent glowed with sunlight. She disengaged herself gently, dressed, and made her way to a secluded stream where she bathed. The ice-cold water had never felt so good. When she arrived back at the tent, Arthur was dressed and chatting to a knot of villagers. He, too, seemed to have been rejuvenated by the night's events. When he saw her, he smiled, and made a point of drawing her into the group.

"The Baron's holding a tournament today," he told her, "but nobody from Mara Zion is taking part."

"With Tristan dead, there's not much point," Torre explained. "Sir Mador will carry all before him. I'm not giving him the satisfaction of putting me on my back."

"Tristan could stand up to Sir Mador, then?" asked Arthur.

"He used Excalibur," said Ned Palomides. "And come to think of it, you have Excalibur now." There was a sly grin on his face.

"Arthur has more important things to do than enter a stupid tournament," said Nyneve quickly.

"In the end," said Palomides, "Excalibur didn't do the late Tristan much good. There's always some kind of a catch with magic swords. If it *is* a magic sword. That remains to be proved."

"Arthur is *not* entering the bloody tournament, Ned!"

"What's he going to do, then? I'd have thought winning a tournament was an essential first step to becoming king of England. I take it you haven't given up that idea, Arthur?"

"There's a quicker way," said Nyneve. "Arthur is going to draw the Sword from the Stone."

The villagers exchanged amused glances. "Second time lucky, eh, Arthur?" somebody said. Palomides guffawed.

"Come on, Arthur," snapped Nyneve. "Let's go and see what's happening at the Stone. It's getting crowded around here."

It was even more crowded at the Stone. People had been lining up since the previous evening to try their luck, and

the queue straggled off into the trees. The hopeful ones were
not all men. Quite a few big, burly women were lined up,
no doubt recollecting legends of Queen Boadicea.

Baron Menheniot, Sir Mador de le Porte, and a group of
soldiers supervised operations, making sure none of the
hopefuls carried illegal aids such as crowbars. The pavilion
had been struck, and the Sword in the Stone stood revealed
in all its intriguing glory. Merlin was there, and Morgan le
Fay; and another woman, middle-aged and running to fat.

Sir Mador was arguing with a Gypsy who held a huge
brown dancing bear on a flimsy leash. "Bears are not allowed," he was saying.

The Gypsy, a sallow little man with a monkey's face,
said, "It says 'Whoso pulleth . . .' I can read, you know.
'Whoso'—that's anybody."

"This is ridiculous." Sir Mador was annoyed. "Bears
are powerful creatures. I don't deny the animal could probably pull the Sword from the stone. But what the hell would
that prove?"

"That he is king of England."

"A bear? What kind of qualifications does a bear have to
rule England? His sole requirement for pulling that sword
out is brute strength!"

"That's the sole requirement of anyone here."

Merlin's plump companion uttered a scream of laughter.
"I wondered when somebody would realize that! If we're
to be ruled by a brainless hulk, then let the bear try, Sir
Mador. He's as good as any man in that queue!"

Sir Mador gazed heavenward in frustration. "Only humans, Gypsy. Only humans."

"Take a look, sir." The Gypsy stabbed a gnarled finger
at the inscription. " 'Whoso pulleth . . .' Show me where
it says, 'Except bears.' "

"It's *implied*, you fool. Now get on the road again, or
whatever you people do!"

"We're staying to entertain the people," said the Gypsy
in dignified tones, "as we have the right to do. We are
Gypsies and we go where we please, and if you try to pre-

vent us, we'll put a curse on you. Let me see, it's Sir Mador, isn't it?'' And he screwed up his face, making a show of remembering the name. ''We Gypsies are citizens of the world, and woe betide he who tries to deny us free passage!''

''That animal is not a Gypsy.'' Sir Mador put his finger on the flaw in the other's argument. ''That animal is a bear. You may think *you* can go where you please, but the bear can't. Now get it out of here!''

He motioned to the soldiers, who seized the Gypsy and began to drag him away. The bear, however, objected to the attack and uttered a spine-chilling roar. The soldiers backed off hastily. The Gypsy raised a finger and pointed it at Sir Mador. Sir Mador swung around and strode rapidly away, assuming the power of a curse was inversely proportional to the distance between cursor and cursee. The soldiers stood by, bewildered.

''More power to your finger, Gypsy!'' shouted the fat lady. ''Mador always was a pompous ass!''

The Baron, who had been observing these events, sighed. ''There has to be an answer to this,'' he said. ''A fool like that Gypsy could turn the whole affair into a farce.'' He caught sight of the newcomers. ''Hello, Nyneve,'' he said. He'd met her some months previously when she'd entertained the castle with stories of King Arthur. ''Mador tells me you have a claimant to the throne here—named Arthur, oddly enough.'' He laughed. ''It wouldn't surprise you to know that most of the men in that queue are called Arthur too. Suddenly it seems to be a very popular name. Even a couple of the women are called Arthur, although that stretches my credulity.''

''Nyneve,'' Merlin interrupted, a crafty expression on his face, ''I'd like you to meet someone.'' He turned to the plump woman. ''This is Nyneve, my Lady,'' he said, ''handmaiden to my sister Avalona. And this is her friend Arthur, a recent arrival on the scene.'' Now his tone became positively gloating. ''And this, Nyneve, is Queen Margawse, wife of King Lot of Orkney.''

Margawse!

She felt her face whiten, and for a moment she thought she was going to be sick. Merlin was watching her intently. Margawse! According to legend, Arthur's aunt. And again according to legend, the woman on whom he got Mordred. *On whom he got Mordred*—what a weird expression! There was something biblical about it. And Mordred was to be Arthur's downfall.

Somehow or other, this happentrack had to be changed. . . .

5
THE VERTICAL KNIGHT

"**A**RE YOU ALL RIGHT, MY DEAR?" QUEEN MARgawse was concerned. She was almost a head shorter than Nyneve, with a jolly, kindly face. She looked like somebody's aunt. But not the kind of aunt that somebody would sleep with. Was this one of Merlin's peculiar tricks?

"I'm fine, thank you. I just felt a little dizzy for a moment. I haven't had breakfast yet." Nyneve stole a glance at Arthur. He was smiling at Queen Margawse in the pointless way one does when introduced to a stranger. There was no sign of lust in the smile, no concupiscent twinkle in his eye.

Was the legend wrong?

If it was wrong about this, it could be wrong about other things. Like Guinevere. And like Arthur becoming King of England. After all, this *was* a different happentrack. But Avalona had said Arthur was destined for greatness. . . .

Nyneve didn't know what to think.

"I think," said Morgan le Fay in her calm tones, quite unlike the dead voice of her sister, "that I will try for the sword myself, later today."

"What a woman!" said Merlin admiringly.

"When does the tournament start?" Nyneve asked the Baron quickly, feeling that if she didn't say *something*, she would start crying.

"Within the hour. My knights are at the village now,

preparing. It will not be so grand as our Menheniot tournaments but I trust you will find it entertaining.'' He smiled, offering his arm. ''Would you care to accompany me?''

After making sure the others intended to come, too, Nyneve agreed. They set off up the path in the direction of the village. Behind them, the crowd began to cheer as the bear tugged ineffectively at the Sword.

''Go to it, Arthur!'' shouted the Gypsy.

''Arthur! Arthur!'' roared the crowd.

''By God, Mador had better resolve that problem soon if he wants to take part in the tournament,'' observed the Baron grimly. ''That animal is making a laughingstock of us all. Perhaps it would be a good thing if he did pull the bloody sword out,'' he said, beginning to cheer up. ''Then we could crown him and have done with it. I could house him at Castle Menheniot and issue edicts on his behalf. I could rule the country through that bear.''

Nyneve glanced up at him. He was built like an oak; tall and gnarled, with long, strong limbs emerging from the trunk at appropriate places. His face was square, his brow heavy. He exuded an aura of power. Now he was smiling at his fanciful notion of a king bear. ''Why did you make an occasion of this?'' she asked curiously. ''The last thing a man like you would want is a king ruling over you, surely?''

He chuckled. ''A man like me? What do you know about men, young Nyneve?''

''Answer the question, old Baron.''

''Not so damned old that I can't appreciate a pretty girl, and a clever one too. You're right. The last thing I want is a united England. I'm very happy with my slice of it and I owe fealty to no man. But look what's happened now. The legend of Arthur—*your* legend, damn you—has spread far and wide. The idea of a ruler of all England is in every peasant's mind. It's become more than an idea; it's an ideal. And when peasants start thinking in terms of ideals, it means they're not satisfied with the way things are.

''Suddenly Camelot looks good to them. Nobody's poor in your stories. Nobody has to tend the animals or work the fields. And now—here's this Sword in the Stone. I don't know how it got there. It could have been there for centuries, perhaps since there *was* a local ruler called Arthur. I don't believe for one moment there's any magic attached to it.

"One thing I do believe: The Sword is going to stay stuck in the Stone. I've tried to pull it out and so has Mador, but we can't shift it. And neither can Arthur."

"Arthur hasn't tried yet," she lied.

"I mean Arthur the bear. And if he can't shift it, nobody can. So the bubble will burst. People will take it as a sign that nobody is meant to be King of all England, and that a divided country is in the natural order of things. The Arthur legend will be discredited, and we can go back to living like normal people again." He grinned at her. "You're a fine storyteller, Nyneve, but you can't change the natural course of events."

"We'll see about that, Baron Menheniot."

He regarded her thoughtfully. "How are your gnomes settling in?" he asked. "Isn't it the strangest thing, the way they suddenly appeared?"

"Happentracks," said Nyneve vaguely. Arthur was walking with Margawse, talking politely.

"I want to make sure everybody accepts them for what they are."

"And what's that?" Nyneve's tone was cold. The Baron's reputation was far from blameless in the matter of human or any other rights.

"People. Members of the forest community."

"That's the way they see themselves."

"And I want them to accept us for what *we* are. Bring them to the tournament, Nyneve."

"What? They won't like it. The gnomes are kind and good. They'll hate a tournament!"

The Baron gave a bark of laughter. "If we are to accept them, they must accept us. Our strengths and weaknesses, our goodness and badness. We're human and we're all different, and they must learn to live with us. Go on now!"

He slapped her on the buttocks, the way one might dismiss a horse. "Bring them to the village!"

By early afternoon the tournament was in noisy progress. Heavily armored knights on horseback clashed, and the earth heaved as they fell. Archers loosed singing arrows at straw butts and yelled their triumph or disappointment. Swordsmen swung their clumsy weapons mightily, smashing opponents to the ground by the sheer weight of their blows, rather than any nimble skill. A notable exception was Arthur—Nyneve's Arthur—who scorned the heavy armor and fought in leather jerkin, pants, and boots. Much quicker than his adversaries, he began to attract attention.

"Looks like a bit of a pansy, that Arthur of yours," grunted the Baron. Nyneve sat beside him on a raised platform shaded by bright fabric stretched between poles. On either side of them sat favored guests. The rear of the platform was hung with a thick tapestry that extended partway around the sides. This tended to obscure the view, and Nyneve asked the Baron about it. "I don't believe in leaving my rear unprotected," the Baron replied. "By the time anyone cuts their way through that cloth, I've got my sword out."

The gnomes sat on a table in front of the Baron. They watched the proceedings with little enjoyment and winced at any show of blood.

"Which of you little fellows is Fang?" asked the Baron.

Eight tiny caps bobbed, eight little faces turned to him. "Fang?" repeated Lady Duck. "What do you want with Fang?"

"Well, he's your leader, isn't he? I thought he'd be here. Nyneve's told me a lot about him."

"Fang is nominally our leader, yes," said Lady Duck stiffly. "On an interim basis. He is of imperfect character, though. Our traditional leader is King Bison. Show yourself, Bison."

Bison shot the Baron a terrified glance from behind the protective bulk of his wife.

"Bison is empowered to speak on behalf of us all," said Lady Duck.

"Speak then, King Bison," said the Baron good-naturedly.

"W-what shall I say?" The reluctant spokesman's voice quavered.

"Oh, anything. Tell me where Fang is."

"Fang? Fang? I don't know where Fang is. Why should I know where Fang is?" Whimpering with fright, Bison looked to the others for support.

"Fang is training the moles," said the Miggot firmly.

"The moles! The moles!" chorused the gnomes guiltily. "Training the moles!"

Rapidly losing interest in this aspect of gnomish culture, the Baron said, "What's imperfect about his character?"

They looked at each other, then the Miggot said, "Nothing."

Simultaneously the Gooligog said, "He's a rash young fool, that's what!"

Meanwhile Pong was explaining, "I'm not a gnome who goes in for touching people, but Fang—"

Spector said, "Leadership material manifests itself in many forms. For instance—"

Their views were cut short by Lady Duck's shout: "Fang is a sexual pervert!"

The embarrassing frankness of this statement stunned the other gnomes into silence and they quickly transferred their gaze to the tourney. Two mounted knights collided with frightening force, crashed to the ground, and lay motionless. The gnomes glanced rapidly here and there, seeking something nicer to look at. Nyneve found eight pairs of desperate eyes fixed on her.

"A gnomish sexual pervert?" repeated the Baron. "I thought you little people weren't interested in sex."

"Exactly!" cried Lady Duck. "I can't remember when Bison and I last performed our duty to the race. When was it, Bison?"

"I prefer not to think about it," muttered Bison.

"What about you?" The Baron suddenly realized that one of the gnomes had been silent up to this point. He was different from the others; his cap was a peculiarly unpleasant shade of brown. "What are your views on Fang?"

"I hardly know the gnome." His eyes were downcast, his manner shy.

"Scowl's a stranger," explained Lady Duck. She lowered her voice. "He's one of the Accursed Gnomes, you know."

"Accursed Gnomes?" Gnomish society was more complex than the Baron had realized. First the perverted Fang, and now this.

"The Accursed Gnomes sin against the sacred Examples, to their eternal shame."

"Examples?"

"The Kikihuahua Examples, which is the gnomish code of behavior bequeathed to us by our ancestors, the kikihuahuas." And as Lady Duck began to repeat the famous words the others joined in.

When the chant came to an end, Scowl alone continued. "Forgive us for our transgressions. We think we are right but we have no way of knowing. If we are wrong, we beg your forgiveness. Descendants, know that we tried in good faith."

"You hear that?" said Lady Duck. "We don't have to say that last part, because we don't transgress anything. But the Accursed Gnomes do, and their souls will rot in hell."

"Always provided that hell exists, of course," qualified Scowl. "It's a gamble we take. In all the travels of the kikihuahuas, hell has never been encountered. Or so our Memorizer tells us."

"He could be lying," said Spector. "Simply to put your minds at rest."

"Our Memorizer never puts our minds at rest. His personality is somewhat similar to your Gooligog, here."

"And what's that supposed to mean?" asked the Gooligog furiously.

"The Gooligog is no longer our Memorizer," said Spector, quick to sense the brewing of unpleasantness. "He has been deposed by his son, Fang. Replaced, I mean."

"Yes, but that doesn't mean he isn't a miserable bugger, all the same," Lady Duck pointed out. "And mark my words, Fang will go the same way!" She stared around at the gnomes triumphantly. "It's in his genes!"

The Baron tried to get the discussion back on track. "If it's such a risk," he asked Scowl, "why do you work malleable substances?"

"Somebody has to take the chance," said Scowl smugly.

"There's no sense in us all breaking the Examples," said Lady Duck. "So if a gnomish group needs, for instance . . ." She hesitated.

"To smooth out a rock wall," said the Miggot quickly.

"Or to repair a plowshare," said Spector.

"Or fashion a keel," piped up Pong.

". . . why, they call on the Accursed Gnomes," said Lady Duck, relieved. "And the evil is contained within a small group, instead of spreading throughout gnomedom like, uh, ivy." The others glanced at one another unhappily. The discussion was drifting into dangerous waters again.

"And will you always be Accursed, Scowl?" asked the Baron, amused.

"Until the end of Time," said Scowl happily. "Ours is a reprehensible way of life, but necessary. Without us, the gnomish species would have become extinct long ago."

"Their numbers are kept to a minimum," ventured Bison, "and we rarely visit their foundries. We deal with their traveling tinkers, like Scowl."

"We guard our secrets well," said Scowl. "And our foundries make the most abominable stink."

The discussion was interrupted by a roar of applause. Out on the field, Arthur held his sword high.

"Arthur's won the foot-combat event," Nyneve observed.

"Has he, now?" The Baron scanned the clearing thoughtfully. "What a clever fellow he is." The archery event had paused while the contestants gathered around Arthur to add their congratulations. "He's becoming quite the hero of the common people."

"Yes, isn't he."

The gnomes exchanged glances and relaxed, glad that they were no longer the focus of the Baron's attention. Arthur eased his way out of the crowd and ran lightly to the platform. He swept off his cap and bowed low. "My liege," he murmured.

"Sarcastic young jackass," muttered the Baron. Then, more loudly he said, "Come, join us. Find Arthur a seat at my side, Merlin."

This infuriated the old wizard because the places of honor on either side of the Baron were occupied by Nyneve and himself. If someone had to step down, he knew it wouldn't be Nyneve. "I would be delighted to offer you my place, Arthur," he snarled, but brightened almost immediately as he realized that this would place Arthur next to Queen Margawse, his legendary lover. He caught the anxious expression on Nyneve's face as the same notion occurred to her. Let the little minx stew for a while, he thought, and found himself a seat beside Morgan le Fay. "Hello, my dear," he said.

Morgan, lips parted, was watching a jouster who lay motionless on the short grass, blood seeping from the joints in his armor. She glanced at Merlin absently. "Oh, it's you. Do you have anything to drink in that bag of yours?"

"Potions, Morgan. The trappings of my calling."

"Oh, for God's sake." She resumed her scrutiny of the unconscious man.

Meanwhile the Baron was congratulating Arthur. "A most impressive performance. I should like to invite you to the castle, Arthur. You have the makings of a knight. Do you joust too?"

"No, he doesn't," said Nyneve quickly. On the tourney field, the ironclad figure of Sir Mador hurtled toward the hapless Bors de Ganis. Sir Mador's lance struck the other squarely in the chest, lifting him from the saddle and sending him crashing to the ground. "It's not fair," she said. "Sir Mador's lance is much longer than anyone else's."

"He has the strength to hold it, my dear. Many don't." The Baron turned back to Arthur. "How would you rate your chances against Sir Mador, Arthur?"

Arthur regarded the Baron steadily. "Better than most."

"So why don't you enter the joust?"

"I have no horse or lance. I had intended to compete with the archers."

"Come, now. Archery is for peasants. You strike me as a man born to greater things."

Arthur smiled. "So Nyneve tells me. All right, then. Give me the loan of a horse and a lance, and I'll compete."

"And armor," said Nyneve.

"I need no armor."

"Then you're a damned fool," said the Baron. "But a brave one. There's an injured man over there; it looks like Sir Bors de Ganis, another bloody Frenchman. You can use his equipment. He's in no condition to object."

"Shouldn't someone be attending to him?" asked Nyneve.

"The French believe God takes care of them. They need no mortal help."

"Don't be ridiculous!" snapped Nyneve.

The Baron glanced at her, grinning. "I suppose we should be thankful for small mercies. In the east, it's the Saxons who throw their weight about. At least the French have some dim idea of chivalry." He ordered his bugler to halt the proceedings. As the rasping note died away he shouted, "Is there a healer in the forest?"

Merlin, aggrieved, said, "I'm a healer. Everyone knows that."

"Then heal the Frenchman and be done with it, and let's get on with the tourney."

"Well, I can't do it just like *that*, you know. There must be a laying-on of hands. I must murmur the enchanted words."

"Then murmur them!"

"And the leeches." Merlin took a gourd from his bag and shook the contents onto the gnomes' table. The gnomes retreated as sluglike creatures milled around uncertainly, looking for something to suck. "I must apply the leeches."

"What on earth for?" The Baron regarded the creatures with distaste.

"To cleanse the evil humors from the body."

"Bors is a most pleasant fellow, for a Frenchman."

"That's a different kind of humor. You are not acquainted with the language of healing, Baron." As Arthur, accompanied by Nyneve, left to prepare for the tourney, Merlin and the Baron strolled over to the unconscious figure. Attendants had by now stripped Bors naked. Merlin placed the leeches at strategic points around the battered body. They began to suck, pulsing visibly. "You see?" said Merlin triumphantly.

"Erect a tent around him," said the Baron, noticing the rapt gaze of Morgan le Fay, still fixed on the patient. "Even a Frenchman is entitled to his dignity."

Meanwhile the gnomes were discussing Merlin's methods. "I suppose those *were* leeches, weren't they?" asked King Bison.

"Of course they were," said the Miggot sharply.

Bart, sensing a rift in the solidarity of Mara Zion gnomedom, asked, "What else could they be?"

"Well . . ." said King Bison. "Of course, happentracks have joined and we've crossed over into this new world. . . . And so *other things* could have crossed over. . . ."

"What kind of other things?"

"Doodads!" cried Elmera. "I believe you're right, Bison. They could have been doodads!"

"Doodads?"

"Horrible things." Elmera shuddered. "Another of the Miggot's mistakes. I've said it before and I'll say it again. A little knowledge is a dangerous thing. What do you have to say to *that*, Miggot?" She wheeled around on her husband.

"The doodads fill an ecological niche," said the Miggot

with dignity. "I was perfectly correct to create them. The niche existed, and I filled it."

"You didn't have to fill it with such horrible things."

"They bloody near killed the Sharan," said Bison reminiscently. "The moment they were born, they turned on her."

"The Sharan was never threatened. The doodad, handled properly, presents no danger to gnome or beast."

By now Bart was beside himself with impatience. "But what *are* doodads?"

"You might compare them to the butterfly," said the Miggot. "They feed on the seminal jelly of the cheesecup, and when the petal bowl of the plant is empty, they make their way to a female plant, and, er, fertilize it."

"Disgusting!" cried Lady Duck.

"Sex among animals and plants is perfectly acceptable," said the Miggot.

"Any mention of sex makes my blood run cold, Miggot, as well you know," Elmera put in. "And I'm not the only gnome who feels that way, thank God! Change the subject before I throw up, will you?"

"Arthur has mounted his horse," said Pong obligingly.

"By the Great Grasshopper, Pong," screeched Elmera, "you've gone too far! I *demand* . . . Oh. I see what you mean." Flushing, she turned her gaze to the tournament field.

At the eastern end of the clearing, Arthur sat easily on Sir Bors's roan gelding, wearing everyday clothes as though hacking casually through the forest. A temporary squire handed him a lance. Even this was a rustic thing, little better than a pole. Arthur smiled and couched it. Nyneve passed him her scarlet sash and he wound it around his forearm. To the west, Sir Mador closed his visor and settled his lance firmly into position. At the far side of the field, a ballista demonstration was halted, much to the relief of the villagers, who had been watching missiles pass closely over the roofs of their cottages. The archers, normally scornful of the highborn knights, paused too. All heads turned to the field of battle.

Ned Palomides grumbled, "I was just getting my eye in." Like the other Mara Zion archers, he had been faring badly in competition with the well-trained men from Menheniot village. "Why do we have to watch those posturing fools on their nags?"

"Arthur is jousting," Gawaine said.

"Arthur is jousting, Arthur is jousting!" mimicked Palomides, in falsetto. "And what's so bloody important about that?"

Gawaine laughed. "You have to admit archery's a piddling sport compared with jousting. There's something furtive about archery—the silent arrow, instead of the thunder of hooves and the honest, man-to-man collision."

"Well, anyway, Arthur will lose, just like we're losing. I don't see why we have to witness a further disgrace. Just look at the man! He's the most unlikely-looking jouster I've ever seen. He's practically stark naked! One thing you could say for the late Tristan—at least he dressed the part."

"I wish you wouldn't keep calling him the late Tristan, as though he were never on time," said Torre irritably. "And you're a fine one to talk about dressing for the part. You don't exactly cut a fine figure on horseback, Ned."

"It's the type of man that goes in for jousting that I object to. Once they get up on that bloody horse with a spear in their hand, they seem to think they're lords of creation. Tristan was just as bad as the rest."

For once Ned had the support of the majority, and there were grunts of agreement from the gathering. The archers had always felt as though they operated in the shadow of the jousters at these events, and resentment had been festering for a long time. The award for overall champion of the tournament went to the top jouster, and this, too, angered the archers.

Thus the scene was set for a peculiar occurrence that became the main topic of fireside discussions in Mara Zion and Menheniot during the coming months. . . .

Nyneve resumed her place on the platform. "I simply don't know what Arthur is thinking of," she said. "I tried to talk him out of it, but he wouldn't listen. Why is he doing this?"

"Jousters are the gentry," said the Baron simply.

"Arthur doesn't need to prove anything. He's our future king."

"He'll have to get past Sir Mador first."

Nyneve brightened a little. "We all know Sir Mador's a formidable opponent, Baron. But haven't you noticed luck just doesn't seem to be running his way these days?"

The Baron merely smiled and motioned to his bugler. The clear tones sang across the field.

The horsemen urged their mounts forward.

Immediately the effect of Sir Mador's equipment was apparent. His horse, so heavily armored that little more than hooves and ears were visible, lumbered heavily into a trot. Arthur's roan, however, leapt smoothly to the gallop, rapidly closing the gap. The opponents clashed like rams in the rutting season, then they were past each other, both still firmly seated, reining in their mounts and turning.

"Arthur's lance is broken!" cried Nyneve.

"I'm sure they can find him another," the Baron reassured her.

But it seemed that Arthur did not want a replacement. He waved away the lance offered by his squire and drew his sword. From the distant archers came the faint cry of "Excalibur!"

"Much better than a lance," said the Baron sarcastically. "According to legend, he is now unbeatable. Does he believe his own myth, Nyneve?"

Nyneve preserved an anxious silence as the contestants charged again. This time, however, Arthur's mount was noticeably slower. Thus it was that by the time they came within range of each other, Sir Mador had attained a full and irresistible gallop. The long lance probed swiftly toward Arthur. The tip, stained with the blood of a hundred opponents, pointed a sharp and deadly finger. Arthur raised Excalibur.

Nyneve closed her eyes.

Arthur twisted sideways in the saddle. The lance missed, brushing his jerkin. Excalibur swept down, striking the hardwood lance with the flat of the blade and deflecting it downward. Sir Mador lurched forward, off-balance. The opponents passed each other. Arthur reined in his gelding.

The tip of Sir Mador's weapon dug into the soft turf. His momentum carried him on, and he left the saddle, rising in a graceful arc at the end of his lance while the horse galloped from beneath him.

It would have brought the contest to a more seemly end if Sir Mador had then crashed to the sward in an untidy heap of flesh and iron. At least he could then have been carried off, honorably defeated. Some semblance of dignity would have been left to him. The name of Mador and his unidentified Porte would not have become the laughingstock of the west of Old England.

But Sir Mador's run of bad luck was destined to continue. As he rose into the air, the lance still gripped firmly between arm and hip, his velocity diminished. At the summit of his climb, all movement ceased. He hung there at the top of his lance, the tip buried firmly in the ground like a sapling recently planted.

''The bloody fool,'' snapped the Baron, rather unfairly.

Nyneve stifled a giggle.

''He puts me in mind of a toffee apple, somehow,'' observed Morgan le Fay.

''More like a monkey up a stick,'' grumbled the Baron.

''Why doesn't the poor man let go?'' asked Margawse.

''In all that armor? He'd come down like a ton of rocks. No, he'll have to wait for the soldiers to ease him down gently. Look, they're on their way now.'' A group of foot soldiers moved out onto the field with a noticeable lack of urgency. ''Mador needs to pay a little more attention to our image,'' said the Baron furiously, hearing laughter from the rescuers.

It was then that the inexplicable occurred.

The archers had been watching events quietly, not joining in the catcalls that had begun to emanate from the less responsible sections of the crowd. But now, as one man, they drew their bows and took careful aim.

A hail of arrows sped toward the perpendicular figure.

Yells of fear emanated from the encapsulated Sir Mador. Arrows clanged against his armor and he tried to curl himself into a ball like a threatened armadillo.

"What the hell are they playing at?" shouted the Baron. "Have they gone mad?" His gaze roamed furiously among his companions on the platform, seeking an answer to this mystery. "Why are they shooting at him?"

"I suspect it's just because he's there," suggested Morgan le Fay with a wicked smile.

"What do you mean, because he's there? What kind of a reason is that? This is war, for God's sake! I've half a mind to order my soldiers to return their fire!"

"The poor man," said Margawse. "Why doesn't somebody help him?"

Nyneve said, "I think it all has something to do with him being stuck on top of the pole. He's an irresistible target."

"Somebody gave a command." The Baron snarled. "That's what happened. Somebody gave a command and they all obeyed like mindless bloody sheep. By Christ, they're reloading. My own villagers are there too. They're drunk, that's what it is." His fevered mind snatched at another explanation. "They're all blind-stinking drunk!"

Another fusillade of arrows peppered Sir Mador.

"This has gone far enough!" The Baron's seat crashed backward as he sprang to his feet and strode onto the tourney field.

"Oh, dear," exclaimed Margawse. "The Baron's upset."

The Baron joined his soldiers around the lance. "Get him down!" he commanded. "Now! And you people"—he indicated the outer ring of grinning soldiery—"go and arrest the archers."

The second group departed, but the nearest men eyed the Baron uncertainly. "We can't reach him," one said. Sir Mador hung at least a yard beyond their upstretched hands.

"Come down, Mador, you bloody fool!" roared the Baron.

"It's . . . it's a long way!" came the muffled reply.

"Just let go. The men will break your fall!"

The men backed hastily away from the lance, and Sir Mador stayed where he was.

"Right," said the Baron grimly. "Fetch a halberd and we'll chop the bastard down."

"Perhaps he could undress up there, piece by piece," someone suggested. "Then when he finally lets go, he won't come down so hard. Maybe break an ankle, at worst."

"What's your name, fellow?"

"Herring, Sire."

The Baron, dark with rage, thrust his face close to Herring's. "I'll remember you, Herring. Meanwhile I'd like you to think of something. Just draw a little picture in what passes for your mind, Herring. Nothing too difficult. Just imagine Sir Mador in his underclothes at the top of that bloody pole. Go on, you stupid bastard. Use your imagination!"

Herring's closed expression changed slowly to one of doltish amusement. "Har, har," he said.

"You're beginning to understand, aren't you, Herring? The implications are dawning on you. Very funny, isn't it? There's something intrinsically amusing about Sir Mador, my right-hand man, perched half naked on top of a pole!"

Herring grinned happily. "There is that, Sire."

The others nodded agreement, chuckling.

"By the Lord Jesus Christ!" shouted the Baron, "I'm not taking any more of this. Push that bloody pole down, men, and to hell with Mador!"

"No!" shouted the treed knight as the lance began to sway beneath him.

"The ballista," said a quiet voice. "Roll the ballista over here and he can climb onto it."

Whirling around, the Baron found himself face-to-face with Arthur. "You! You're the cause of all this!"

"By accident, I assure you, Baron. Even so, I'm trying to make amends. If you maneuver the ballista next to Mador with the arm up, he can climb into the cup and you can lower him gently."

"He's right," yelled Herring excitedly. "Arthur's right!"

"Arthur! Arthur!" shouted the others, and the cry was taken up around the field. "Arthur!"

The Baron gave Arthur a venomous look. "Well said. Bring the ballista, men!"

The ballista arrived at the same time as the archers, a sheepish crowd of peasants in motley clothes. The soldiers, eager to make amends for their poor showing during the Mador crisis, jabbed them mercilessly into line before the Baron. They stood with heads bowed, avoiding his eyes.

"Right," said the Baron. "Who gave the order to fire at Sir Mador?"

They glanced at one another uncertainly. Nobody spoke.

"You!" snapped the Baron, picking on a slender young man who looked more intelligent than most. "Who gave the order?"

Governayle raised innocent eyes. "I can only assume it was the good Lord himself, sir. For myself, I heard no human voice. And yet I found my arm rising as though of its own accord, and my eye sighting along my arrow. I was aware of a huge body of men doing the same thing. It was an uplifting experience, giving me a sense of unity with nature, with the world around me. I aimed for the junction of helmet and neck, a vulnerable spot when the target is at a higher elevation than the archer. But I missed."

"Are you seriously trying to tell me that *God* made you do this thing?" The Baron stared at Governayle incredulously.

"There's no other explanation. Sir Mador has in some way offended the Almighty. This could also explain the run of bad luck that's plagued him since he left France."

The Baron continued to stare at Governayle, while his

lips began to twitch slightly. Then his gaze wandered upward, to see Mador climbing clumsily into the cup of the ballista. He shook his head. He placed his large, hairy-backed hands over his face and rubbed his eyes. When he regarded the villagers again, he looked suddenly tired. "It's been a long day," he said. "I don't want to waste time over this. There's the presentation to go through, and then we must go to the Stone. You, Smith." He addressed a Menheniot villager. "What in hell happened?"

"I don't rightly know, sir." There was an exalted look in Smith's eyes as he relived the event. "It was a strange and wonderful experience."

"I wish you were so coordinated in battle. Ah, Mador," he said, greeting the knight. "None the worse for your adventure, I hope?"

"No thanks to these murderous villains." Sir Mador carried his helmet. His face was flushed; little streams of sweat disappeared into his coarse beard like tributaries into a mangrove swamp. "With your permission I'll order the soldiers to march them to the castle. A bloody good flogging and a year or two in the dungeons will do wonders for their sense of loyalty."

"There is some cause for belief," said the Baron carefully, "that these men were the fortunate agents of Divine Intervention."

"They were what?"

"It is possible they were possessed by the Lord."

"What bloody lord, for Christ's sake? Are you telling me they were in the pay of someone?"

"You misunderstand me. I mean the Lord thy God."

"What in hell has God got against *me?*"

The Baron began to lose patience. "Will you stop asking questions, Mador? How else can you explain their action? No command was given. It was as though a Voice had spoken simultaneously into every man's mind."

"So what shall we do, canonize them? I've never heard such bloody nonsense in my life. They saw me up there, so they loosed off their bows. It's as simple as that. It was a moment of utter irresponsibility, illustrating the difference between peasants and gentlemen. Nothing more. And they must be punished for it. Give them into my hands, Baron.''

"You and I must talk in private, Mador. This is not the proper place for our conversation.'' The Baron began to walk away.

"What I have to say,'' shouted Mador, "the whole bloody world may hear, for all I care! You, Baron, are a pathetic weakling. You're not fit to govern a rabbit warren! You're scared of these peasants because there are so many of them. So you try to tell me the good Lord's against me.'' His expression was becoming crazed. He lowered his voice to a sinister whisper. "Well, let me tell you something. I'm a Frenchman. I happen to know God's on *my* side. Always has been, always will be. So what do you have to say to that, Baron Menheniot?''

The Baron replied coldly, "They shot at you because you looked like a prize idiot up there, Mador, and I don't blame them. Does that satisfy you? Now get off my land. Go back to France and your bloody Porte, wherever it is! I hereby strip you of your title of Knight of the Southern Realm. You're no knight for me!''

The departure of Mador brought the tournament to an end. The Baron resumed his seat on the platform for the prizegiving. Queen Margawse bestowed the prize on Arthur: a great shield ornamented with a complex coat of arms, and a moist kiss from her rather thick lips. Nyneve watched closely, but the kiss showed no sign of lengthening into a passionate embrace. The crackle of electricity was mercifully absent. Arthur lifted the shield and displayed it to the crowd.

"Arthur! Arthur!'' they roared. Then they rushed forward and seized him, and lifted him onto their shoulders. "To the Stone!'' someone cried. "Take him to the Stone!''

"The local hero,'' observed the Baron to Nyneve, with quiet sarcasm. "Well, there's nothing like a good anticlimax to knock a hero off his pedestal. You'll be coming to the Stone, of course, Nyneve? You won't want to miss this.''

She looked at him with wide-eyed innocence. "Didn't I tell you luck was on his side, Baron?"

"Well, I'm going to check the Sword first, just to make sure his luck doesn't get any assistance from his allies." His gaze traveled over her face, taking in the dark and lustrous hair, the bright eyes; and his expression changed. His gaze dropped to the round breasts pushing at the pleated bodice, and he said quietly, "You'll come to the castle with me afterward?"

"To tell you stories? We don't need stories anymore. We have a real Arthur."

"You know what I mean."

"Well, I don't know about *that*." She glanced at him mischievously. "My place is beside my lord Arthur, don't you think?"

"Come on." He drew her to her feet. "We don't want to miss the fun. Your place is with Arthur if he proves to be your lord by pulling the Sword from the Stone. But if he fails, you have no lord but me, Nyneve." He laughed and slapped her bottom playfully. "Get moving, minx. I'm an impatient man."

Accompanied by Queen Margawse, Morgan le Fay and other notables, they followed the crowd into the forest.

The story of Arthur and the Sword in the Stone has been told in many different ways—as many ways as there are happentracks, which are infinite. Many of the stories place the Stone in an ancient city such as London. Some—religions being influential in those days before real knowledge put a name to a God—set the Stone in a cathedral and fashioned it of polished black marble. And the Sword was a beautiful thing, as beautiful as Excalibur, polished and jeweled and glittering.

And the people are highborn and noble; and the Archbishop of Canterbury is there. There is a Sir Ector, and a Sir Kay, come to a great tournament attended by a multitude of knights and lords. And there is a small conceit inserted for the delight of the listeners: that Arthur came across the

Sword by accident (imagine that!) and drew it from the Stone without witnesses, and nobody believed him. So he did it again in front of the assembled notables. Then they knelt before him and called him King.

And it was Christmas.

Since there are infinite happentracks, it must have happened like that somewhere, somewhen. But that is not the way it happened here. On this happentrack it happened like this:

They gathered in a glade in the little-known forest of Mara Zion, a great mob of rough peasants with their yelling children and their jugs of beer and mead; and a failed bear. There was an Ector there, and a Kay, but somehow they had never achieved any eminence. The Stone was a roughly hewn chunk of granite and the Sword was a crude thing of hammered iron.

But to the onlookers the Sword was a thing of wonder, because they had all heard Nyneve relate the legend.

The Baron—the only person there who conceivably could be called a noble—stepped up to the Stone and laid his hands on the Sword. The crowd quieted, and adults shushed their children. The Baron spoke, and his exact words have been recreated by computer and entered into human history.

"Right, you fools, let's get this thing over with. Here's the Stone and this is the Sword." He braced his feet against the Stone and tugged vigorously. The Sword remained firmly fixed. "And if anyone can pull the sword out, they can be King of England and the rest of Europe, too, so far as I'm concerned. By now you've all had a try and failed, thanks be to the Lord. But now here's another pretender, another Arthur. He's better than most, I'll say that for him. Arthur!"

Arthur stepped forward, accompanied by Nyneve. "Good luck, Arthur!" cried Nyneve, and kissed him on the cheek.

"Arthur! Arthur!" shouted the crowd.

Arthur took hold of the Sword and drew it easily from the Stone.

The Baron's mouth dropped loosely agape. There was a

moment of total silence in the glade. Arthur lifted the Sword in both hands and held it over his head. Nyneve's tiny sigh was clearly audible.

Then the crowd went wild. They rushed forward, seized Arthur, and hoisted him shoulder-high. Nyneve found herself lifted, too, carried next to Arthur on a bobbing sea of heads. Somehow the Baron became airborne, too, waving his arms for support. Like a tidal bore, the mob surged through the forest.

"I thought they were supposed to kneel before me!" Arthur shouted to Nyneve.

"This is much more fun, isn't it?"

"How in hell did you do it?" the Baron yelled to Arthur.

He shrugged, ducking as he was borne beneath a low-branched oak. "Believe me, I'll never know!"

And the crowd bore them on, through the forest to the village, to a night when Menheniot and Mara Zion joined in celebration. The legends tell that England rejoiced, but the legends have been shaped by later technology. In truth, all this happened in a tiny corner of England, and the rest of the country had not the slightest idea what was going on.

6

A BLOODLESS COUP

FANG COULD TOUCH EVERY PART OF THE TINY ROCK-walled chamber from where he stood. Apart from a narrow thread of light coming from the roof, it was dark. A cool breeze blew, bringing with it a scent of ferns, moist soil, and mole droppings from the tunnel behind him, venting through the hole in the roof. It seemed to Fang there was another smell: of the hardworking and sweaty little people who had hollowed the chamber within this granite boulder. The smell of the Accursed Gnomes.

"Fang?"

"Is that you, Princess?"

She crawled from the tunnel into the chamber, breathless. "They're on their way. The Miggot just got back from the tournament." There wasn't much room, so she put her arms around him from behind.

They considered the situation in silence for a moment.

"How long have we got?" asked Fang eventually.

"Oh . . . probably long enough." The Princess's hands slid down to Fang's waist, and her fingers began deftly to unfasten his belt.

"Some of the gnomes have been looking at me strangely lately," said Fang hesitantly. "I've seen them doing it. And the women have a funny look in their eyes when they look at you, Princess."

"They're just jealous because I'm your girl, Fang. You're

112

a very attractive and distinguished gnome. And you're our leader. Step out of your pants, will you?''

"But the men look at me oddly too."

The Princess, busy peeling off her many layers of gnomish clothing, didn't reply.

"It's because of *this* kind of thing, I think," said Fang. "You have to admit we do *this* an awful lot. The other gnomes hardly ever do it. We're disgraceful and perverted gnomes, Princess, and the Great Grasshopper will punish us."

"Fortunately the Great Grasshopper can't see us."

"My father used to tell me his eyes were everywhere."

"Are you trying to tell me you don't *want* to do it?" asked the Princess with some asperity.

"I'm just saying that gnomedom doesn't approve, and since I'm gnomedom's leader, I should bow to the wishes of my followers. At least we should try to cut down on it."

"What's the use of being a leader, Fang, if you can't do as you like? And anyway, we're alone here. The others have no idea what we're doing."

"They can guess," said Fang sadly.

"But they'll guess, anyway, whether we do it or not."

It was a pity, thought Fang, that such a simple and enjoyable thing as sex could be the object of such disgust and condemnation. Not for the first time he wondered why this should be, and he remembered something the Princess once said to him. "I wonder if perhaps sex is naturally enjoyable, but our creators put a mental block in us and stopped us all from enjoying it. Because they were scared that if we did enjoy it, we'd fill the whole world with gnomes and there'd be no room for anything else." After a pause Fang said in relieved tones, "You're absolutely right, Princess. We're the victims of circumstance and the filthy minds of others. Now let me turn around slowly, darling. I don't want to bang my head on this thing in the roof."

"We must both be careful, Fang. After all, now that I'm preg—"

A roaring voice boomed through the chamber, cutting her

short. "Right, you fools, let's get this over with! Here's the Stone and this is the Sword!"

And the chamber shuddered, reverberating to the ringing clash of metal on rock.

"It's the Baron!" squeaked Fang. "By the Sword of Agni, this is it!"

"Stay calm, Fang. Oh, my God, what are we going to do?"

"W-wait. We haven't heard the signal yet!"

"I've forgotten what the signal is!"

"So have I! Oh, Princess, I've betrayed Nyneve's trust!"

Meanwhile the deep human voice had ceased, and with it the clash of metal. From a thousand throats the gnomes heard the cry of "Arthur! Arthur!"

"That's it!" cried Fang. "That's the signal! I have to pull out the peg!" He reached up and took hold of the end of the great Sword where it projected down into the chamber. There was a thick oak peg pushed through a hole near the end of the blade, to prevent the Sword being drawn from the Stone before its time. He tugged frantically at it. "I can't get it out! Oh, Princess, I can't shift it!"

"Twizzle it around a bit. It probably got a groove in it when the other giants tried to pull it out."

"Arthur! Arthur!"

"It's coming. . . . There! It's done. We've done it, Princess!"

And this time the metal sang as it slipped out of the groove in the Stone. A shaft of light replaced the blade in the chamber. Fang sank to the ground, spent. The Princess regarded him critically.

"Better get your pants on, Fang," she said. "Nyneve and the others will be expecting us."

"Oh, yes." Fang drew a deep breath and let it out in a shuddering sigh. "That's it, then. We've done it." His brow furrowed as he tried to recollect something. "What was that you said?"

"Get your pants on?"

"No, before that. Wait a moment." He riffled back

through his perfect memory. "You said, 'After all, now that I'm preg—' Then the Baron started shouting."

The Princess flushed. Though her genes often betrayed her, her upbringing had been normal for a gnome. "We're going to have a baby, Fang."

"We are?" He stared at her for a moment. "Are we really?"

"I'm sure we are, darling."

"How long have you been, uh, preg?"

"Probably since that first time in my old burrow. You were a very virile gnome that night, Fang."

Fang felt tears of joy stinging his eyes, so he grabbed the Princess and held her close, burying his face in her hair. A leader must not betray weakness. They stood like that for a long time, while the sounds of human presence drifted away from the Stone.

"What the hell is going on here?" rasped an unpleasant voice. "Why are you standing up against each other like that?"

"Hello, Miggot," said Fang. "We were just coming."

"It bloody well looks like it. We were wondering where the hell you were. Nyneve is waiting to thank you."

"Have the rest of the giants gone?"

"Yes, thank God. They're a noisy lot of buggers. And that tournament was a bloody nightmare. I tell you, Fang, we're going to have to keep clear of those giants. You've never seen anything like the fighting. And the blood." He shuddered. "Great cascades of it, pouring out of them. Oh, and Merlin put doodads on one of their people!"

"Why did he do that? Was it some kind of an enemy?"

"No, it was a friend, so far as I could see. But they were fighting their friends, anyway, so I suppose it makes sense. They're queer people, Fang!"

Fang and the Princess followed the Miggot down the long, twisting tunnel. Here and there they came across the remains of insects, still bloody. "The moles are obeying their instincts," observed the Miggot with satisfaction. "I think we can say they're successful. We'll have gnomedom rebuilt in no time.''

The tunnel rose sharply, and soon they were crawling out of a hole in a fern-clad bank. There was a ragged cheer. "Fang!" somebody cried. "Fang, Slayer of the Daggertooth, Deliverer of the gnomes from evil!"

"Fang! Fang!"

"Fang, Wallower in the Bed of Filth!" cried someone else.

"Who was that?" asked the Miggot sharply, staring at the twilit figures.

Spector spoke quickly. "A balance. Somebody is providing a balance. In fairness, all points of view must be heard. It is the gnomish way."

"What the hell are you talking about?" The Miggot scampered across the glade and seized the Thinking Gnome by his jacket. "You've said some stupid things in your time, Spector, but by Agni, that was the stupidest! This is a joyous occasion, you fool! It's a time for gnomes to rejoice together! Arthur, our protector, will take his place as king of the giants, all because of Fang here!"

"And Nyneve," said Elmera. "It was Nyneve's idea. Fang was merely the instrument. And by the way, what were he and that princess doing in there all this time? Ask yourselves that, gnomes!"

"Is it anybody's business what they were doing?" snapped the Miggot, letting go of Spector and swiveling to face his wife. He directed upon her a stare of potent venom, but she was accustomed to this and bounced it back at him.

"I thought so," she said smugly.

A thoughtful silence followed, during which the gnomes tried not to imagine what had been going on in the cavern. Finally there was a welcome diversion.

"Fang" came a voice from the sky. Nyneve knelt carefully, avoiding scuttling gnomes. "Thank you very much," she said simply. She held out her hand, and Fang stepped on it and was carried to her lips. She tipped his cap back and kissed him gently on the forehead. ''Thank you,'' she murmured again, and put him down.

''You see?'' hissed Elmera to Lady Duck. ''Even with giants!''

Nyneve said, ''I'd like to thank you all. You too, Scowl, for bringing your people to build the Stone. If there's any way I can help you anytime, just let me know. And Arthur will protect you against your enemies.''

''Is Arthur King of England now?'' asked Fang.

Nyneve laughed. ''No. That comes later. First he has to win all the nobles over. There's a lot of battles to be fought before Arthur will be king.''

''Why don't they just vote on it?''

''That's not the way we do things. A king isn't king because he's the most popular man in the country. It's because he's the strongest.''

''An excellent philosophy,'' said the Miggot approvingly. ''So Arthur will be staying around here for a while?''

''He's going to live in the village. The Mara Zion people have accepted him as their leader, and even the Baron's impressed with him. Oh, and he's said that if you gnomes would like to come and live in the village, there'll be a place for you. He thought you might be in danger, with no homes and a lot of strange creatures abroad in the forest.''

There was a murmur of interest from the gnomes, then Fang said diffidently, ''Thank Arthur very much, Nyneve, but we're really very happy where we are.''

Nyneve smiled. ''I told him you'd say that.'' She stood. ''Well, think about it. If you change your minds, let me know.'' She waved and was gone, leaving behind the scent of roses and an ominous silence.

At last Lady Duck said, ''Of course, it *would* save us the trouble of building new burrows.''

''We have the moles to do that,'' said the Miggot.

''What do *you* think, Bison?'' asked Lady Duck.

''It's not Bison's place to think,'' said the Miggot quickly. ''He is no longer our leader.''

''Well, *I* think—'' began Bison.

"What do you think, Bison?" The question came from more than one gnome.

Bison seemed to gain in stature, looking around him in gratification. "Well, *I* think—"

"Fang," muttered the Miggot urgently, "you're losing them. Now's the time for an inspirational speech!"

"Well, *I* think—"

"What do you think, Bison? What do you think?" The gnomes assumed—incorrectly—that Bison's hesitancy was a pregnant pause prior to the revelation of a master plan.

"*I* think," said Bison desperately, eyes darting here and there and finally making an emergency landing on Bart o' Bodmin. "*I* think we need have no fear, for the Gnome from the North will be with us. In our blackest hour he will ride in on a rabbit white as snow, gnomes."

"The Gnome from the North!" echoed the gnomes reverently.

"What the bloody hell are you all talking about?" shouted the Miggot. "The Gnome from the North is just some story of Bart's!"

"The Gnome from the North is as real as you or I, Miggot," responded Bart somberly, eyebrows bristling.

"And what's black about the hour? Things are looking pretty good!"

". . . and lead us to a land where the rivers flow with honey, and yet nevertheless it is possible to keep oneself clean," concluded Bison.

"In times of trouble," said Spector slowly, "the Gnome from the North is necessary."

"But we're not in trouble." Fang spoke at last, and to his relief he saw signs that the others were listening. Heads turned in his direction—although in the twilight it seemed to him that the eyes bore a blank and fervent look. "We've been offered a simple choice by Nyneve: Rebuild gnomedom, or go to live in the village with the giants. Either way we'll be protected. For myself, I think we should rebuild gnomedom and continue what we were put on Earth for. So really, I'm with Bison. But I don't see what the Gnome from the North has to do with anything.''

"True, Fang," said Bison eagerly, "True. But it's nice to know he's watching over us, isn't it?''

"I don't need him, Bison.''

"Well, *I* bloody well need him!'' cried Lady Duck. "And any gnome with a grain of common sense needs him too. We live in dangerous times! The forest is alive with predators we can't even guess at! The Gnome from the North is our guardian and savior.''

"It seems to me Arthur is our guardian and savior!'' said Fang.

"And what do you mean, continue what we were put on Earth for?'' asked Elmera hotly. "How can we be kind and good, and create life where it's needed, and all that stuff, when the forest is bursting at the seams with savage beasts hungry for the taste of gnome?''

"And then there's the lopster,'' put in Pong.

"Perhaps we should take up Nyneve's offer, after all,'' Old Crotchet said in a quavering voice. "I'm not as spry as I was.''

"Bugger the lopster,'' snapped the Miggot.

"Shut up, all of you!'' shouted Fang desperately. As the voices dwindled off into a reluctant silence, he cast around for inspiration and found it. "We have the Examples and we have our Duty. And I don't see any savage beasts around. We must get used to the ways of this new forest and the creatures in it. We must go quietly about our lives, watching and noting. We must learn how the creatures and the plants fit together into the greater scheme of things. And when we've done this, we must identify the places where new creatures are needed, and we must create them. It may take generations of gnomes to make this new Earth a perfect place, but we can do it! It's our duty! And speaking of duty, I have an announcement to make.'' He gazed around at his people, carried away by his own oratory, elated by the occasion and his news. "The Princess is preg!'' he shouted proudly. "I mean, pregnant!''

If he'd expected a roar of congratulation and the pounding of gnomish hands on his back, he was disappointed. The gnomes stared at him with peculiar expressions, then glanced at each other unhappily.

"I'm glad to hear it," said the Miggot quickly. "And speaking of creations, you all realize we'll have to keep the Sharan hidden from the giants. We mustn't even mention her name in front of them. If they get wind of the fact that we have an animal capable of creating any life-form we want, they'll grab her and use her for building giantish armies."

"The Sharan is a beautiful, wild thing placed in our care by our ancestors," objected his wife. "She has always roamed free as the wind."

"No, she bloody well hasn't. I've had to watch her like a hawk day and night, as well you know. The only time she's roamed free is when she's escaped!"

"Times have changed, Elmera," said Fang placatingly.

"And what about Pan?" asked Elmera, ignoring him.

"Yes, what about Pan?" shouted Lady Duck.

"Well, what about him?" asked the Miggot.

"Well, all I can say is," said Elmera, "that the whole situation is very unsatisfactory. There will have to be some changes around here, I can tell you!"

"Gird your loins, Bison," murmured Lady Duck. "Your time is coming!"

Bison looked anxious. "Why should I guard my loins? What's going to happen to me?"

"I said 'gird.' It's just an expression the giants use. It means get ready for the battle to come!"

"Battle?"

"For the leadership of gnomedom, Bison! The struggle for power!"

"I'm not at my best in that kind of situation, my dear."

"Fang is a spent force, Bison," whispered Lady Duck, nodding toward the current leader, who was trying to disentangle a misunderstanding between the Miggot and Clubfoot Trimble.

"If you say so, my dear."

"To the blasted oak!" bellowed Lady Duck.

This command so took the gnomes by surprise that conversation ceased abruptly. They looked at one another, then they looked at Lady Duck. They pondered the significance of the cry. "Why the blasted oak?" asked Pong eventually.

"Our traditional meeting place, of course!" She faced them, eyes blazing, Bison cowering at her side. "Mount your rabbits, gnomes!"

"Fang!" The Miggot bobbed up before Fang, narroweyed. "You know what this means, don't you?"

Fang regarded the glade. About thirty gnomes were clambering on their rabbits, uttering yells of enthusiasm. "To the blasted oak!" The cry echoed from many throats.

"Quite honestly, Miggot, it seems to mean we're going to the blasted oak. That's near where you live, isn't it? Why you live in such a gloomy place, I can't imagine."

"Because Elmera hates it, if you must know. But that's beside the point." The Miggot, through force of habit, grasped Fang's jacket and thrust his face close. "This is a coup, Fang. A coup!"

"A coup," repeated Fang, baffled. "A coup."

Jack o' the Warren, overhearing, said, "That's what the rabbits pulled on my father. A coup is a terrible thing."

Old Crotchet, who was too frail to ride, tottered near, grumbling. "The blasted oak is *not* our traditional meeting place. The hollow log is, but that's gone away. I never even *saw* the blasted oak until recently. Talk about tradition! Tradition means age, and respect. Tradition means knowing exactly where your place is in the scheme of things. There's no tradition about this place. It's too new. Tradition is memories and changing seasons and falling leaves and things returning to the good earth, like that dead badger I found outside my dwelling once. I could tell you things about tradition that would turn your stomach!"

"You mean coups," said Jack. "It's coups that turn your stomach, Crotchet. I never did find out what happened to my father."

"I wish I knew what you were all talking about," said Fang plaintively.

"In plain language," said the Miggot, "Lady Duck intends to depose you from your leadership, and put her husband in your place."

"Depose me?"

"Yes, depose you!" Now the Gooligog joined in, gloating. "Just like you deposed me from my post as Memorizer, you treacherous young fool. Now you'll know what it feels like!"

"Depose me? Why would she want to do that? Lady Duck is a friend of mine."

"She's also the husband of King Bison, who you deposed a little while back."

"The young bugger's drunk with power, that's his problem," muttered the Gooligog, wandering off in search of his rabbit.

"Oh, I see." Fang thought about this. "But surely the other gnomes wouldn't want this to happen. It was they who made me leader. Any deposing was quite accidental. I got the impression Bison was glad, anyway."

"Things have changed, Fang. The crisis is over. Bison can handle things. And Bison has normal urges."

"Urges? What kind of urges?"

Glancing over his shoulder, the Miggot whispered, "Normal sexual urges. Bison's sexual urges are well under control."

The remaining gnomes, appalled and disgusted at the turn the conversation had taken, drifted away. "There's nothing wrong with my urges," said Fang hotly. "Has it ever occurred to you, Miggot, that there might be something wrong with *your* urges?"

"Yes," said the Miggot surprisingly. "But then I'm accustomed to dealing with the Sharan and the business of birth and so on. I ask myself questions. I might say, 'What if . . . ?' And then I'll say, 'If that were so, then . . .' And following that, 'But supposing . . . ?' And then suddenly I'll say, 'A*ha!* '"

"My father began to talk to himself many years ago. It was the first sign."

The other gnomes had by now left, all except Lady Duck, who was advancing on them purposefully. "Fang! Miggot! It is essential that you attend the meeting!"

"What I'm trying to say is," muttered the Miggot urgently, "avoid giving the impression you're a gnome of robust appetites. Don't stand anywhere near the Princess. Don't look at her. It might be better to take a cold dip in the river before you appear before the meeting."

"You don't understand, Miggot," said Fang sadly. "But thank you for trying." And he followed the Miggot and Lady Duck across the glade to the remaining rabbits.

As he prepared to mount Thunderer, the Princess stepped out from the blackness of the undergrowth. "May I come with you, Fang?" she said in a small voice.

"Of course you can." He took her hand and pulled her up behind him. She put her arms around his waist and hugged him close. He was about to utter his famous cry that harked back to the Slaying of the Daggertooth but realized it was not appropriate. "Get going, Thunderer," he muttered.

The rabbit loped slowly along the dark path through the trees, as though affected by the gloom of its riders. After a while the Princess said, "Perhaps I should go away for a while. I never was a very popular gnome, and I'm afraid we both know why. I'm an embarrassment to you, Fang."

"We're staying together, Princess."

"But they're going to make Bison leader again! I know they are!"

"That's not important."

"Isn't it? Are you sure, Fang?"

He hauled on Thunderer's ears, pulling the rabbit to a halt, and twisted around to face her. "The only reason I became our leader was because nobody else knew what to do in a crisis. I don't know quite why it is, but I seem to think better when things are moving fast. Now we're going to rebuild gnomedom, and it'll be a slow business. Honestly, Princess, it would bore the pants off me to be in charge of all that, arguing with people, having to make all kinds of silly little rules and decisions, and having Elmera and the Miggot and my father complaining all the time.

"But one day things will go wrong again and I'll find myself in charge quite naturally, like the last time, without having to persuade people to vote for me or having to compete with someone I like, such as Bison."

"King Bison . . ." mused the Princess. "You're the real king, Fang. Remember what Nyneve said about Arthur? 'A king isn't king because he's the most popular man in the country. It's because he's the strongest.' " Unexpectedly she gave a little shriek of laughter. "King Fang," she intoned. "The words were almost made for each other."

Fang laughed, too, and kissed her. They clung together for a while. "Come on," he said at last. "We'd better not keep them waiting too long, or you know what they'll think."

When they reached the blasted oak, they found the others were already thinking it. Rows of gnomes sat on the blackened roots, and a large number of rabbits could be seen among the trees. It seemed that messengers had ridden the forest paths, rounding up most of the gnomes in Mara Zion. Broyle the Blaze had kindled the Wrath of Agni, and the merry dance of flames reflected from bright eyes and simple jewelry. There must have been almost a hundred gnomes there, being harangued by Lady Duck.

". . . wallowing in the responses of unnatural instincts and perverted flesh," she was shouting, amid groans of horror from the assembly. "Oh, it's you, Fang," she said more quietly. "Take a seat. You understand there's nothing personal in all this, of course."

"In all what?" asked Fang innocently.

"In my assassination of your character. It's expected on these occasions, and it rarely results in grudges being harbored. The main thing is to retain your dignity and not be goaded into retaliation."

"I don't have the heart to say anything against Bison."

"And then there is this Princess!" roared Lady Duck, satisfied. "We all know what *she* is. She is the spawn of two foul gnomes, infected with the poisons of the wild wart, who have since been banished to opposite reaches of the land!"

"Argh!" shouted the gnomes in disgust.

"Actually," said the Princess in clear tones, "they both went in the same direction."

"By the Great Grasshopper!" cried Lady Duck. "Is there no limit to their shame?"

The Miggot stamped forward, a squat, furious figure. "You all know me," he snarled, "and I'll bet none of you likes me. And that's fine, because I'm not too bloody fond of you, either. And why is that? Because you're fools, and I can't stand fools. You know what's happening here? You're being duped into dumping the best leader you ever had, and electing a failed has-been who's already proved he can't lead a rabbit to a dandelion!"

This was the first overt mention of the purpose of the meeting, and Lady Duck took it up. "Bison is fit and ready to take up any duties this gathering may entrust to him!" she cried. "Bison is a giant refreshed! Tell them, Bison!"

Bison's eye rolled like a spooked horse as he cast around for words suited to the occasion. "I am a giant refreshed!" he boomed finally. "That is not to say"—he dropped his voice to more normal tones—"a giant in the sense of a *human,* if you know what I mean. I wouldn't want you to think—"

The Miggot cut him short. "And all because of a minor disorder. In any other species, it wouldn't be looked on as a disorder at all!"

"*Minor* disorder, Miggot?" thundered Lady Duck.

"Fang's little sexual dysfunction. It—"

"Dysfunction? Dysfunction, you call it? He functions too bloody well, that's his problem!" screeched the Gooligog. "Filthy young bugger!"

"Do we blame Clubfoot for being clumsy?" yelled the

Miggot furiously. "Do we blame Lady Duck for her voice? Do we blame Pong for being intrepid?"

"Being intrepid is good, isn't it?" asked Bison, puzzled.

"Well, all right, then. Do we blame the Gooligog for his foul temper?"

"Of course we do!" cried Elmera. "The Gooligog is a pain in the ass, and his son is going the same way—mark my words!"

"Fang," said the Miggot wearily, "don't you have anything to say?"

"Not really, Miggot. I think they've made up their minds."

"Bison! Bison!" came the roar from a hundred throats.

"Bugger the lot of them, that's all I can say," muttered the Miggot.

It was dark and the forest leaves were rustling to a cold night wind by the time Nyneve arrived at the village. A huge pit fire had been lit the day before, and an ox (or to be honest, a cow recently savaged by wolves and deemed incurable) had been roasting for many hours. A noisy party was in progress, with beer and wine flowing freely from kegs set up on the other side of the green. The Baron's men were still there, getting to know the village girls to the obvious annoyance of Mara Zion's young men, but the inevitable fighting had not yet taken place.

Much to her relief, Nyneve caught sight of Margawse at a long table near the fire pit, attended by Baron Menheniot. It seemed her legendary charms had not captured Arthur. *The story must be wrong,* she thought. *And if this part is wrong, then perhaps the rest of it is just as unreliable. Including the part about Guinevere. . . .*

The same thought seemed to have occurred to the Baron. As Nyneve joined them, he asked Margawse, "Have the chivalry stories reached your part of the world yet, my lady?"

Margawse laughed, a jolly sound. "Oh, yes. I'm quite flattered. I never thought I'd be the kind of woman to play an important role in a saga! What a pity that kind of thing never happens in real life.''

"Nyneve invented the stories," said the Baron, grinning.

"I . . . I didn't exactly *invent* them," Nyneve said, stammering. "They just kind of *happened*. And I honestly don't know how you got into them, my lady. I thought most of the story-people were imaginary.''

"Nyneve's a witch," said the Baron with conviction.

"I'm just a village girl, really. My foster mother, Avalona, has the powers.''

"Where is that old hag, by the way?''

"At the cottage with Merlin, I expect.''

"I doubt it. Merlin's here, licking his wounds. I had the old fool thrashed, and he's lucky I didn't hang him.''

"You thrashed Merlin? But he has powers too!''

"Not strong enough to protect his back, I fear. You'd better take him home.''

"But what . . . what did he do?''

"You must ask him that. I don't want to talk about it.'' The recollection seemed to have put the Baron in a bad humor. "And if you run into Arthur, for God's sake pry him away from that Morgan woman. I've had a treaty drawn up between Menheniot and Mara Zion, and I need his mark on it. At least some good's come out of this day's work.''

"Arthur's with Morgan le Fay?'' A vague misgiving took hold of Nyneve. "Where did they go?''

"I don't know.'' The Baron eyed her speculatively, obviously regretting his obligations to Queen Margawse. "Well, if you must leave us . . . Ask Merlin. He should know everything, if he has the powers you credit him with.''

She found Merlin sitting under a tree at the edge of the forest, watching the festivities from a safe distance. He looked so disconsolate that she was moved to pity, and for a moment put aside her own worries. "Merlin! What happened?''

"That barbarian of a Baron had me whipped!''

"Why would he do a thing like that?''

The old Paragon snuffled miserably. "It wasn't my fault.

The circumstances were beyond my control. But he wouldn't listen." Rheumy old eyes met Nyneve's, then looked away again. "Sir Bors de Ganis died," he mumbled. "The Baron held me responsible."

"How terrible! How did it happen? I thought Sir Bors was just cut up a bit."

"He was. But the leeches killed him. You've no idea what a ghastly experience I had, Nyneve. Although," admitted Merlin, "it was probably worse for Bors. After I'd treated him I forgot about him for a while. The excitement of the tournament, you understand? When I finally went back to the tent we'd rigged around him, he was gone. Or at least, I thought he'd gone. It was getting dark, and my eyes aren't what they were. I'm getting old, Nyneve."

"You've been getting old for the last few thousand years," said Nyneve, becoming impatient. "Get on with the story, Merlin."

Sniffing, he resumed. "I noticed a kind of pale cloth on the ground, and I saw the outline of Bors under it. I thought somebody had put a sheet over him, to keep him warm. So I took hold of it and pulled." He groaned, shuddering. "But it wasn't a cloth. It was Bors himself—just his skin like a bag, with the bones rattling about inside. The leeches had sucked him dry!"

She stared at him. "How could leeches do that?"

"They must have injected him with some kind of solvent and let it sit for a while, then sucked all the nourishment out of him."

"You're thinking of spiders."

"They were leeches! You think I don't know the difference?"

"Perhaps they were something that looked very like leeches. Something from the gnomes' world. But even if they were, how could tiny little things like that suck a man dry?"

"Exactly what I asked myself!" said Merlin eagerly. "But then I thought of something else, and it made my blood run cold, I can tell you. Those leeches may have been tiny little things when I applied them to Bors, but they surely wouldn't be tiny little things anymore. They would be great big thriving things, their appetites whetted!''

He shivered at the memory. ''I've never moved so fast in my life. I got out of that tent and took a look at it from the outside. Then I saw them through the fabric, outlined against the firelight, huge blobbish things lurking under the tent roof and just waiting to drop on someone! Or so I thought at the time,'' he said gloomily.

''So what did you do?''

''I went to find the Baron, to warn him, for the good of the whole forest. I described what I'd seen. 'Those things are a danger to us all!' I told him. And he gave me a kind of funny look. I knew right away he didn't believe me, so I told the silly bugger to come and see for himself. But he was enjoying himself with Margawse and it took some time to get him away. And when we finally got back to the tent, we found the most ghastly thing!''

Squatting under his tree, he shot her a frightened glance. Nyneve felt a thoroughly reprehensible urge to laugh. ''Even . . . even more ghastly than the thing you found before?'' she managed to ask.

''Much more ghastly,'' Merlin assured her. ''The leeches had burst and fallen all over Sir Bors!''

''I expect it's nature's way of preserving a balance,'' said Nyneve. ''If they could keep growing indefinitely, they'd fill the world. There has to be a limit to everything.''

He looked at her suspiciously. ''All that is beside the point. What matters is that I'd told the Baron a very strange story, and when I tried to back it up, the evidence was gone. There was just the remains of Sir Bors smothered in a rich sauce, and I can tell you the Baron was very unhappy about it. 'What the bloody hell have you done to him, Merlin!' he shouted, and I didn't have any good answers. I told him I'd done everything I could for my patient and intended to return to the cottage, and he seemed to lose all control of himself. 'Soldiers!' he shouted. I tried to explain that violence was no solution to the problem.

" 'Can you think of a better solution?' he asked as the soldiers came running. I couldn't, so in all fairness I warned him that I had powers, and that his actions may come back to haunt him. 'I'll take that chance,' he said, laughing nastily. He was beyond reason, so I submitted reluctantly to his wishes. The rest," concluded Merlin miserably, "you know."

"What I don't know," said Nyneve, "is what's happened to Arthur."

"He went off with Morgan."

She tried to appear noncommittal. "Oh, yes, the Baron mentioned something about that. Did you happen to notice which way they went?"

"That Morgan," said Merlin enthusiastically, "she's quite a woman. Quite a Dedo, I should say. Different from Avalona. Between you and me, Nyneve, Avalona gives me the creeps, prowling around the forest and coming up behind a person suddenly, like Death itself. Morgan, now . . . she's different. You should have seen how she got Arthur!"

"What do you mean, 'got' Arthur?"

"Well, *you* know what I mean. He was talking to her quite normally, and then suddenly his face changed and his hands began to tremble. He kind of moved closer and was breathing heavily, and for a moment I thought he was going to jump her there and then! She'd put a spell on him, you see. But somehow he held off, and she led him away into the forest. Where they are now, and what they're up to, is anybody's guess!"

"But that's all wrong!" Nyneve found tears in her eyes and blinked them back furiously. "That *couldn't* happen. It was supposed to be Margawse, and then when it obviously wasn't going to be, I thought . . . I thought he was safe!"

"Nobody's safe with Morgan le Fay."

"But she's a Dedo! She's not human at all—she's a Finger of Starquin like Avalona! What possible reason could she have for . . . fooling around with Arthur? She doesn't have any feelings—does she?"

"Not unless it's in her interests to have them."

"And is it?"

He looked cunning—a most unpleasant sight in the firelight. "It may be. You know she and Avalona disagree about how to handle the next thirty thousand years? Well, I think this is all part of her plan to do things her way!"

"But why is she doing *this?* She's a Dedo and Arthur's a human! What . . . what does that mean?"

"It means whatever Morgan wants it to mean."

"What do *you* think that is, Merlin?"

'Well . . . Morgan intends *something* to come of this. To my knowledge a human and a Dedo have never mated. But Morgan's not your normal Dedo. I'd guess she intends to give birth sometime in the ifalong, and she wants to use some of Arthur's genes. I think she's going to produce something powerful and—how would you say it?—*evil*, something that can help her discredit Arthur and the idea of chivalry that Avalona's trying to put across, something rather like herself, only male. . . ."

"Mordred," whispered Nyneve.

They sat in silence. The music and laughter died away as one by one the revelers fell asleep. Somewhere in the forest something unthinkable was going on. Nyneve and Merlin, wakeful, sat under their tree. *At the moment of conception,* thought Nyneve, *something unique and recognizable ought to happen. Like an earthquake, or a shooting star.*

But the earth didn't move, and the sky was dark with clouds.

Merlin glanced at her craftily. "So there's no point in you running around after Arthur anymore," he said, touching her knee.

"It's too late. I love him." It seemed to Nyneve that the night would go on forever.

7

"THE IRISH ARE COMING!"

ONE MORNING THREE WEEKS LATER, PONG THE INtrepid was leaning over the gunwales of his birchbark boat, harvesting kelp. It was low tide and the flat, slippery strands lay along the surface, making his task easy. Grasping a strand, he pulled it into the boat until the kelp resisted, anchored by its roots to the seabed. Then he took his sailor's knife, fashioned by the Accursed Gnomes, and cut the strand off short. His new friend, Snout, pushed the boat to keep it in place. Snout was a dolphin from the giants' happentrack who seemed to have taken a liking to Pong and had gotten into the habit of helping with the harvesting.

The work was easier and safer at low tide. At high tide only the tips of the kelp showed at the surface, and Pong had to get a rope around them and haul the strands up bodily, roots and all.

And occasionally a baby lopster had been clinging to the roots.

Those had been terrifying moments. He'd let the kelp sink to the bottom and had sat there shivering, his gaze ranging fearfully over the sea. At the leap and splash of a fish he would scream. At any moment, Pong surmised, the monstrous form of *the* lopster—the grandfather of all baby lopsters—would emerge dripping from the surface and confront him furiously, towering over the boat. And then . . .

He heard a splash behind him and uttered an involuntary

yell of horror, dropping the kelp. His head snapped around. The water stretched, rippling toward France. Snout had caused the splash, frolicking. There was no lopster.

The lopster, he told himself, probably didn't exist in this new world. The creature had probably been canceled out by more favorable probabilities. Nyneve had tried to explain that to him. He'd made discreet inquiries elsewhere, and the giants had denied ever seeing such a creature.

The giants . . . For a moment Pong pondered the question of the giants. Though not a pleasant topic, it was infinitely preferable to the lopster.

The giants seemed friendly enough, though huge. But their size didn't bother him so much as their numbers. Already the world seethed with them, leaving precious little room for gnomes. How could any race allow itself to become so numerous?

Gnomes were not numerous. The structure of their society didn't allow it. Each gnome had a job to do. In Mara Zion gnomedom, Pong was the sailorgnome, Fang was the Memorizer, Elmera was the seamstress, Tom brewed the beer, Jack bred the rabbits, and so on. Occasionally there would be a supernumerary gnome; Fang had been one such, until he had taken over his father's Memorizer's duties. Young gnomes were often supernumerary, as were old gnomes; it was no disgrace. But the point was, every gnome had a job, or would have a job, or had had a job. Gnome communities were organized that way, everywhere. Loose guilds existed, and gnomes with the same jobs would exchange news and information by way of traveling gnomes. Occasionally a gnome would visit a nearby community and talk shop with his counterpart. Guild methods and secrets were fiercely guarded.

A few communities consisted of specialists such as the Accursed Gnomes, whose jobs could not be integrated conveniently into a normal community without causing distress.

And there were the unfortunate gnomes who, for one reason or another, didn't fit in anywhere. The Princess of the Willow Tree was one such. The circumstances of her birth were so shameful that she could never be accepted into any of the recognized guilds. She could only make herself useful in whatever ways she could.

Jobs were not necessarily passed from parent to child. At any one time there might be several children in a community, and any one of these could take up a job when an incumbent retired. Sometimes a pair of gnomes were unable to have children, and other gnomes would be obliged to bear additional children to step into the forthcoming vacancies. Usually, though, gnomes took on the jobs they were most familiar with—which was the job one of their parents had carried out.

As often happened on these occasions, Pong found himself thinking about his father, Poop the Craven, who had fled Mara Zion and never been heard of again. Why had Poop fled? Probably, thought Pong, because the lobster had risen from the depths and confronted him. And what was Poop doing now? No respectable gnomish community would allow him in; that was certain. Communities were carefully balanced. Although strangers were welcomed, it was fully understood that their stay would be temporary. Poop was probably leading a sad and nomadic existence.

Which brought Pong to Bart. How long did Bart intend to stay? He'd been in Mara Zion for four weeks now and showed no sign of moving on. He'd said he was a Memorizer; so how did Bodmin function without him?

Pong was a simple soul, friendly and tolerant as only a gnome can be; but it seemed he'd sometimes observed a crafty gleam in Bart's eyes. And that was not the kind of gleam one wanted to see in the eyes of an honest gnome. Another thing: Bart seemed to have a knack of befriending the more unsavory of Mara Zion's inhabitants, such as the Gooligog. Bart, decided Pong, was bad news. This was unfortunate, because Pong was responsible for introducing Bart to Mara Zion.

"Bugger it," Pong said to the wide ocean as he trimmed the kelp into bite-sized portions for gnomish cooking pots.

And the ocean, as though in reply, produced six black objects near the horizon. *Giantish boats*, thought Pong bitterly, remembering all the years he'd had the sea to himself. *Giantish boats coming this way, packed with giants all set to swell the forest population.*

He hoisted the sail and made speed for the shore. He could see banks of oars thrashing at the water, and sails straining full of wind. There was no point in sitting here in the path of those juggernauts. The boats had a warlike mien, even when viewed from this distance. *Probably Irish*, he thought resignedly, *looking forward to another battle.*

Irish!

What had Nyneve said the other day? "Pong, you have sharp eyes, and your cave is well placed. I want you to keep an eye on the horizon from time to time, and if you see any boats coming from the west, let me know immediately. We're expecting the Irish. They seem to have some kind of a grudge against us."

The little boat crunched onto the pebbles. Pong leapt ashore and dragged it up the beach. Possessed by a feeling of mild heroism, he ran to his cave. He would give the alarm. *The Irish are coming!* And Fang would commit it to memory at the monthly meeting, and it would go down in Mara Zion history: The Day Pong Saved King Arthur from the Irish Hosts.

"Away, Thunderer!" he cried enthusiastically as he entered his cave, full tilt.

Chit-chit-chit-chit! came an earsplitting reply from the rocky darkness.

"The lopster!" screamed Pong, feet plowing into the sand of the cave floor as he braked frantically.

Chit-chit-chit! Light reflected from a great triangular head from which sprouted armored feelers. They waved at him while the mandibles worked thoughtfully, limbering up for the taste of gnome. The head tilted and a huge eye scanned him with multifaceted impersonality.

"Oh, God!" screamed Pong, as his impetus took him sliding toward legs like peeled and jointed tree trunks. Full length, he scrabbled at the sand and at last succeeded in reversing direction. He shot out of the cave and scurried along the beach, dimly aware of a disappointed *chit-chit-chit* from behind. He untied his rabbit with fumbling fingers, leapt astride, and kicked it into a rocketing hop.

The cliff was a blurred wall to his left; the pebbles passed beneath the rabbit's flying feet in a broad gray streak. *From now on,* he thought desperately, *I will lead a good life. I will throw away my knife and cut kelp with a sharp rock. The firelighter will never enter my dwelling again. I will shiver through the winter with only blankets to keep me warm, and I will use no leather or skins, and it will be good for my soul. The house of Pong will be a monument to the Kikihuahua Examples.*

Blurred rocks changed to blurred trees as he entered the forest. The rabbit, receiving no direction from the paralyzed Pong, eventually lolloped to a halt at the woven willow fence of the new rabbit compound. Jack o' the Warren sat at the narrow entrance, eyes averted from a vigorously copulating pair of rabbits.

"Jack," said Pong casually, trying to sound like a gnome who had not been fleeing for his life. He had his name to maintain.

"Pong," replied Jack, brightening slightly.

"Would you have . . . such a thing as a flask of beer, Jack?"

"I thought you didn't believe in beer."

For a moment Pong debated telling Jack about the lopster. After all, Jack had confessed to the bogus rabbits, and Pong thought more of him for it. . . . Or did he?

No, decided Pong, he thought *less* of Jack. "It's been a hard ride," he said curtly.

Jack produced a flask and handed it up to Pong. Pong drank thirstily, and a glow of well-being began to spread from his stomach. He wondered why he'd never drunk beer before. He surveyed the compound with a benevolent eye. The two rabbits, their lust slaked, were munching their separate ways, but another couple was regarding each other with ear-waving interest.

"You have nerves of iron, Jack," said Pong kindly, as the rabbits began a preparatory nosing and shrugging.

"You get used to it," said Jack. "Provided you don't start thinking about what they're actually *doing*. I try to think of it as just another example of rabbity behavior, like eating. What could be more normal than eating?"

"Scratching," suggested Pong.

"I don't really think scratching is more normal than eating," said Jack seriously. "Eating is essential to survival."

"Scratching happens more often."

As if in support of Pong's argument, the rabbits moved apart and began to scratch. Jack regarded them in some irritation. Their various itches satisfied, they began to nibble at a clump of dandelions. "They lead a simple existence," he said tolerantly. "Eating, sleeping, and, er, filth."

"And scratching."

"Not a care in the world." Thoughtfully he said, "At least we haven't seen the woodypecker around the forest lately."

They rejoiced in silence over the absence of this garish and embarrassing bird, then Pong said, "I think it got left behind on our old happentrack."

"Long may it remain there."

Another silence followed while Pong began to feel that he'd forgotten something important. He worked his way back through his memory but the nightmare vision of the lopster dominated recent events to an overpowering extent. He skipped that and went straight to the moment he'd woken up. He'd washed and dressed and gone out to harvest kelp, the tide being low. Snout had been with him. The sea was calm, the horizon arched and even, and . . .

"The Irish are coming!" yelled Pong. "The Irish are coming!"

The results were not nearly so dramatic as he'd imagined. "You don't have to shout," Jack said, aggrieved.

"You don't understand! I've ridden nonstop from the beach to warn our friends the giants of the approaching peril!"

"Rabbits shouldn't be ridden so far nonstop," said Jack seriously. "Short bursts are what rabbits are built for. Short bursts with a rest in between. Perhaps a drink and maybe a few minutes grazing to restore the energy level. A good brushing"—Jack warmed to his theme—"will often work wonders for the exhausted rabbit. Get him into the shade. If necessary—"

"We must find Nyneve!"

"—fan his ears. The extremities are—"

"I'm going!" Pong kicked his mount hard—a time-honored method of overcoming exhaustion in rabbits—and like so many of the old remedies, it worked. The rabbit loped rapidly down the path, bearing Pong in the direction of Avalona's cottage.

During the short reign of the great Tristan, one problem had never been satisfactorily solved. In Tristan's Great Hall—a barnlike structure close by the village—three men were making yet another attempt.

"The purpose of the Round Table," said Arthur, "is to ensure that all knights are equal. The table has no head, therefore nobody can sit at it."

"All knights may be equal," said Torre, "but you are our leader. So what we really need is an oblong table with you sitting at the head."

"Or possibly," suggested Governayle, "a table in the form of an isosceles triangle with you sitting at the apex."

"That won't work," said Arthur. "The knights sitting nearest the apex will feel they are in some way favored."

"Well, aren't they?" asked Governayle. "I mean, if you don't favor Torre and I, for instance, why didn't you bring Palomides along to discuss this problem?"

Arthur found the implications of the question too complex, so he dismissed it brusquely. "Palomides is a jackass. Nevertheless, he is equal. Accept it. The table must be round, obviously; otherwise it wouldn't be the Round Table.''

"Tristan found he couldn't sit at the rim of a round table," said Torre, "because somebody would have to sit next to him, and they would be looked on as favored. He tried to get over the problem by cutting a hole in the middle of the table and sitting there. But that wasn't too successful, either, because he had to crawl through everybody's legs to get there, or walk over the table, which some people viewed as appalling manners, and inappropriate for a leader of men.''

"The Round Table became a liability," said Governayle. "And the women began to laugh, because we spent a lot of time discussing ways to make it work. Then one of the women suggested suspending Tristan from a harness and swinging him in a circle so that he kept passing before each person sitting at the Round Table. Unfortunately, by then we were all rather tired, and some people took her seriously.''

"*You* took her seriously," said Torre. "You said that Tristan could have a table suspended, too, swinging with him.''

Governayle flushed. "I don't remember that.''

"Yes, you do. You said that Tristan's food and wine would stay in place on his swinging table, because of some law of physics Merlin told you about.''

"Centrifugal force," muttered Governayle. "The table would tilt inward as it swung, and his plate and mug would stick to it.''

"There you are, you see. And then the women started to laugh, and we realized we were being made fun of. It was an embarrassing moment, and Tristan avoided using the Round Table after that. It had become discredited, and we didn't talk about it anymore.''

"The Round Table is a potent symbol of chivalry," said Arthur, "and it's a great shame that it should fall into disuse because of a few practical difficulties.''

"The women see it as a potent symbol of stupidity," said Torre.

"That will change. I propose to resurrect the Table." He thumped the heavy oak, raising a puff of dust. "But this time it will be constructed according to sound principles of engineering. Does the Great Hall have cellars?"

"It does. The stairs are against the north wall."

Arthur strode across the hall. Torre and Governayle followed, glancing at each other unhappily. The great Tristan, too, had sometimes become obsessed with appearances instead of victories. They remembered his famous speech following the Battle of Callington, when his forces were routed by the Welsh. "It matters not who won the battle," he had intoned from a makeshift platform on the village green, "it matters only who is *perceived* to have won."

And like many of Tristan's utterances, it had sounded pretty good at first hearing, and his men had cheered him resoundingly. But as the shouting died, a lone voice had called out, "But we are perceived to have *lost!*" And the men returned to reality with a jolt, and their wounds began to pain them again.

"I really think, Arthur," ventured Governayle, a reasonably sensible young man who lived in fear of being correctly identified as the Lone Voice at Callington, "that it would be better to forget the Round Table. It's brought us nothing but grief. We invested all kinds of time into building this place, and where has it gotten us?"

"I shall need a team of carpenters," said Arthur firmly, "and a team of horses. Make a note of that, Torre."

Torre, too, had been remembering Callington. The reason for their defeat had been apparent to all. Tristan, obsessed with the need for presenting a smart and disciplined appearance on the field of battle, had ordered his foot soldiers to burnish their armor and his cavalry to dubbin their saddles. The Welsh had attacked while both men and horses were undressed.

"You need a team of horses," he said, "and a team of carpenters. It shall be done."

"No, Torre," said Arthur patiently. "A team of carpenters and a team of horses."

"That's what I said."

"The sequence is important. A team of carpenters. Then—after a reasonable interval—a team of horses. And within the month," Arthur cried in ringing tones, "the Round Table shall live again!"

He had paused at the top of the cellar steps in order to deliver this pronouncement. The effect was spoiled somewhat by a crash as the main door flew open. Nyneve ran into the Great Hall, her black hair flying like a mane.

"Arthur! The Irish are coming! The Irish are coming!" She halted before them, breathless.

"The Irish?"

"Their ships are approaching the beach. I've alerted the men. They told me I'd find you here."

"It's Arthur's job to alert the men, Nyneve," said Torre sternly. "You've exceeded your authority."

"You did well, Nyneve," said Arthur reassuringly. "Do we propose to fight the Irish, or invite them to a feast?"

It was a good question. "By the time we find out," said Governayle thoughtfully, "it could be too late."

"Then obviously we should assume they've come to fight us, and act accordingly," said Torre. "Meet the bastards on the beach and hurl them back into the sea! Tristan did it once."

"Sometimes I feel I'm living in the shadow of Tristan," said Arthur sadly.

"Ambush them in the forest," said Governayle. "Lie in wait beside the path. Allow them to pass, then take them from the rear. As they turn, bring in a second force to attack their flank. That way we can wipe out every last man!"

"Won't they be expecting that?"

"No. They'll expect to take *us* by surprise. Nobody lives near the beach, you see. You get the most fearful cold winds funneling up the valley in the winter. So there's nobody to give the alarm. Who did give the alarm, by the way?"

"Pong," said Nyneve.

"That's the gnome who lives in the cliff cave, isn't it?" said Arthur. "Those little fellows are already proving their worth as allies. Size is no measure of courage."

Torre, a huge man, said, "Pong is reputed to be an unusually cowardly gnome. No doubt he fled from the Irish."

"He told me he fled from the lopster," said Nyneve. "But all this is beside the point, isn't it? You must get your armor on, Arthur. Your men will be waiting for you."

"I need no armor," said Arthur. "I have Excalibur."

"Excalibur!" shouted Torre enthusiastically.

"Come on, then!" said Nyneve.

Sometime later the forces of Mara Zion crouched in the undergrowth near the path to the village, Governayle's plan having prevailed. It was raining steadily, dribbling down the necks of the men and causing mutterings of discontent.

"There's fifty of us here getting wet," observed Palomides, "all because we've accepted the word of a frightened little bugger called Pong."

"He can't help his name," Torre pointed out.

"It's not his name I'm objecting to. It's his size. Never trust a small man, that's been my watchword, and it's served me in good stead."

"I'll grant you small men are often untrustworthy," said Torre, "but where you make your mistake, Ned, is in thinking of him as a man. He's not. He's a gnome. Different rules apply. For all you know, it's *big* gnomes that are untrustworthy."

"So maybe he *is* a big gnome. How can you tell unless you see a bunch of them all together?"

Arthur, crouched nearby, said, "This is not the kind of talk I like to hear from future knights. Remember this, and remember it well. All intelligent creatures are equal—men and gnomes, large and small. We must treat them all with equal respect and we must give them all the benefit of the doubt—until we find we're mistaken, of course. They are innocent until proven guilty."

"Why are we waiting here to kill the Irish, then?"

"The Irish are different," said Arthur.

Governayle helped him out. "For the purpose of this day's work, we may regard them as slightly subhuman. Unless, of course, they become our allies. That would put them on the side of God and everything that is right and just."

"Sometimes I don't know what the hell you people are talking about," complained Ned, baffled. "To me there are just two kinds of people. There are your enemies, who you kick in the teeth. And there are your allies, who you watch like a hawk. How can anyone change sides? It makes the whole concept of war meaningless."

"I've just remembered something," said Governayle. "The Irish *are* our allies."

"What!" Arthur rose slowly from concealment, shedding leaves and water.

"In the excitement we all forgot. In past years the Irish have certainly been our traditional enemies. That's how this misunderstanding has arisen. They made a habit of raiding the village and carrying off food and women."

"How did the village survive through the generations, with the women gone?" asked Arthur, interested.

"They took only the best-looking women. I'll say this for the Irish: They had good taste. All we were left with were the aged and infirm women, and a handful of younger ones who were not considered well favored. With these we bred. It was an intolerable burden, but we lacked a leader to organize us to counter it. Then came Tristan."

Palomides took the story up. "With Tristan as our leader, we defeated the Irish. But even the late Tristan had his shortcomings. Instead of executing the Irish forces to a man, he welcomed them as our allies, giving us something else to worry about. To cap it all, he took an Irishwoman, Iseult, as his wife. This had the effect of cementing the unhealthy relationship between Mara Zion and Ireland."

"So what you're saying," said Arthur slowly, "is that we've been waiting here to ambush our friends."

"You could put it like that," admitted Torre.

"It's a disgraceful situation."

"I would prefer to call it an honest misunderstanding, Arthur."

"We can't afford misunderstandings. I must be able to trust my lieutenants to give me accurate information. It would have been a terrible thing indeed, if we'd slaughtered our friends. If we are to bring chivalry to the world, we must practice it ourselves." His voice rose as he spoke, carrying to the rest of his force as they scrambled to their feet and gathered around him. "This is not a good start," he said.

The Irish chose that moment to attack.

The first sign that Arthur's force was under pressure came in the form of isolated shouts and the clash of metal from nearby. Then came a rising chorus of Gaelic yells of discovery: "Here's another one! By Christ, the forest's alive with them! Attack, men!"

"That sounds like our friends the Irish," observed Palomides nervously.

"There seems to be yet another misunderstanding," said Governayle.

Everybody looked at Arthur.

"Right, men," he said. "Fall back quickly to the junction of paths and regroup there. Governayle, Palomides, and Torre, come with me." He began to push his way through the undergrowth toward the sounds of battle. "Does anyone have some kind of a white flag?" he called over his shoulder.

Nobody had. The little group pushed on, Arthur in the lead. "This is where we need the dogs," whispered Governayle to Torre. "Dogs have a habit of running on ahead. You can get a very good idea of an enemy's frame of mind by the way he treats a dog appearing suddenly from the bush."

But they had no dogs, so it was without prior warning that they emerged into a clearing occupied by Irish soldiers.

"We come in peace," said Arthur quickly.

"That's bad luck for you," responded the Irish leader, a

large, heavily armored man, "because we don't. We come in anger. Our purpose is vengeance."

"Vengeance poisons the mind," said Arthur mildly. "It's a sickness that can corrupt every moment of your day. Of all human emotions, harboring a grudge is the most destructive. Far better to talk it out, to get it off your chest."

"That depends on the extent of the grudge," snapped the Irishman.

"Intelligent men do not think in terms of revenge."

"Actually, Arthur," Governayle said, breaking in, "intelligent men do. The capacity to harbor a grudge and act on it is what distinguishes us from animals. You don't get dogs, for instance, harboring grudges. Kick a dog and he'll forgive you within seconds. I know. I've tried it."

"The last time I kicked my dog," said Torre, "the bastard took a snap at me. I gave him a bloody good thrashing, I can tell you."

"Your dog's snap didn't constitute revenge. It was an instinctive reaction. The thrashing was revenge."

"It was a well-earned punishment, to teach him an important lesson."

"Did you feel better after doing it?"

"Of course I did."

"Then it was revenge," said Governayle.

"Exactly," said the Irishman, growing impatient with the discussion. "And we Irish want to feel better. Right now we feel bad. Reports have reached us that Iseult, the daughter of our king, is dead. She was entrusted to the care of your leader, Tristan, and he betrayed that trust, allowing her to be brutally slain. Men of Mara Zion, you have a lot to account for. Draw your swords!"

"Stay out of this," Arthur said to his men, abandoning hope of talking his way out of it. He drew Excalibur. "May I know who I am about to kill?" he asked politely.

"Marhaus," replied the big Irishman. Quickly he added, "I already know Torre and Governayle, and the donkey Palomides. But who are you? Shouldn't you put some armor on before you start waving that thing around?"

"My name is Arthur."

"That's a legendary name hereabouts. Can you live up to it?"

"We'll see, shall we?" The opponents stood at the ready. The Irish soldiers took the opportunity to seize the three men of Mara Zion and disarm them. The spectators formed a rough circle.

"Wait a moment!" shouted Palomides.

"Yes, donkey?"

"It wasn't us who killed Iseult; it was Baron Menheniot! He killed Tristan too. Tristan died trying to save Iseult's life! Or it may have been the other way around, I forget which. Somewhere there was heroism that day. Anyway, your quarrel is with the Baron, not us!"

The tip of Marhaus's sword dropped an inch. "Is this true?" he asked Torre.

"I wasn't there," the big man admitted, "otherwise I wouldn't have allowed it to happen. But that's the story as I heard it. Iseult was a brave and beautiful woman, and her death was a tragedy that affected us all. Mara Zion was in mourning for many months."

"Then came Arthur," said Palomides. "Not that Arthur wasn't very sorry about the whole thing as well," he added hastily. "But as I said, the guilt lies with that murderous Baron, who personally slew the daughter of the Irish king!"

"So what did you people do about it?"

"Why, we lodged a complaint, of course. We made our views felt, I can tell you. But the Baron is powerful and ruthless, so our options were limited."

Marhaus eyed Arthur and his men thoughtfully. "It seems we all have a grievance against this Baron. He killed your leader, and he killed our princess." Sheathing his sword, he turned to his followers, his mind made up. "We will join forces with the men of Mara Zion and march together against the Baron Menheniot!"

There was a roar of agreement. The Irish released Torre, Palomides, and Governayle and returned their swords. "We march!" shouted Marhaus.

"Wait a moment," said Arthur.

"What?"

"I concluded an agreement with the Baron less than a month ago. We are allies."

"Well, you'll just have to break your agreement, won't you?"

"I cannot do that. I gave my word."

Marhaus's sword was drawn again. "Is your word more important than your life?"

Excalibur flashed. "Yes."

"You're a damned fool, Arthur." Marhaus lunged. Arthur deflected the blade with an easy flick. Marhaus jumped back, avoiding the subsequent thrust by a hair's breadth. "Woof!" he exclaimed, eyeing Arthur with respect. His eyes narrowed. "That's Tristan's sword you've got there!"

"With this sword in my hand I will never be defeated in battle."

Marhaus nodded. An Irishman sprang from behind Arthur and snatched Excalibur from him. "That particular problem is disposed of," said Marhaus. "Now you have your last chance, Arthur. Join us against the Baron or be killed. The choice is yours."

"We choose an honorable death," stated Arthur firmly.

"Wait!" cried his three followers.

"Too late," said Marhaus. "Tie their wrists and ankles, men, and make them kneel before me. I will perform the execution personally."

Leather thongs were produced, and Arthur, Governayle, Torre, and Palomides were securely trussed and forced to their knees. Arthur remained silent throughout all this, but the others made their objections felt, particularly Palomides.

"I realize you're a donkey," said Marhaus, as the screaming began to get on his nerves, "but can't you at least try to die like a man? Follow the example of your leader. He shows no fear."

"That's because he imagines he's got a great future all mapped out for him," cried Palomides. "He probably thinks the rest of our forces will ride in and save him at the last moment. But I know they won't, you see. They're cowards to a man!''

"I admire courage," said Marhaus. "For that reason I would like to spare Arthur."

"No! Kill Arthur, spare us! We're on your side. Arthur's the one whose holding out against you!''

"Only because he's a man of honor. What do *you* have to say about all this, Arthur? Do you have any last words for mankind before your head rolls among last autumn's beech leaves?''

"Do it, Marhaus. My death on this single happentrack can have little consequence in the ifalong."

"You what? Is that some kind of witchcraft talk?"

"My apologies. Do what you feel you must."

"If you say so." Marhaus raised his sword. As if his intentions were not clear enough, he shouted, "Die, Cornishman!''

And there was a crashing in the undergrowth.

Marhaus, sword poised above his head, turned. A horseman burst into the clearing, scattering the spring rain from the leaves. He rode a white horse hung with scarlet tassels and wore a suit of silver armor. Behind him, as though drawn by a powerful and magnificent magnet, straggled the forces of Mara Zion on their assorted steeds.

"Saved!" shouted Palomides.

It became apparent that this was not necessarily true. The Silver Knight struck the sword from Marhaus's hand with a sweeping blow, but the Irish forces recovered quickly and a confusing battle commenced. The mounted men of Mara Zion found themselves at a disadvantage. The surrounding trees were dense, and the more maneuverable foot soldiers of the Irish were able to dart in and out of the forest at will, stabbing and thrusting. The horses, alarmed, bunched together in the clearing, stamping and neighing. Their riders were unable to get any swing behind their blows, for fear of decapitating their companions.

"Follow me!" Arthur said urgently. Still trussed hand

and foot, he rolled from under the horses' hooves, wriggled through the undergrowth, and found a place of comparative safety under a rocky overhang. Torre, Governayle, and Palomides followed him. They heard the clear tones of the Silver Knight call, "Dismount, men of Mara Zion!" Unable to assist the villagers, they watched the battle ebb and flow across the forest floor. Bull's-eye arrived and began to lick their faces.

Torre was struggling with his bonds, grumbling loudly when Governayle suddenly said, "Hush."

"Why?"

"I hear voices."

"That's not surprising with the forest full of soldiers."

"The voices of gnomes. Gnomes are on our side, Torre. Perhaps they can release us."

Faintly they heard a tiny voice cry, "Oh, no!"

"Woe is us!" cried another.

"Is that you, Fang?"

Silence for a moment, then two small faces peered cautiously around the edge of the rock. "It's Arthur," said Fang. "And Torre, and Governayle, and Palomides. And Arthur's dog."

"I can see that," snapped the Miggot of One. "And they're tied up, which isn't a bad thing."

"There's been a tragedy, Arthur," explained Fang, "and the Miggot is feeling bitter. Being the Miggot, he blames it on the whole giantish race. I've tried to point out to him that there are good giants and bad giants, but he won't listen to reason."

"Tom Grog is dead." The Miggot's face was contorted with grief and anger. "And the Disgusting is destroyed. It doesn't matter a bugger whether the culprit was a good giant or a bad giant. The point is, Tom was stepped on by a horse in the course of a battle between giants, which is exactly the kind of thing we were frightened of. I knew it would happen. But nobody would listen to me."

"We all listened to you, Miggot," Fang pointed out. "The problem was, we didn't know what to do about it."

"That's true," admitted the Miggot, remembering.

"I'm terribly sorry," said Arthur. "If there's anything I can do—"

"You can brew a fine dark ale in sufficient quantities to last gnomedom for one year," said the Miggot nastily. "And possibly a small quantity of stout for the females. And—"

"And a lager," said Fang.

"And a lager for the more active gnomes, who find the heavier beers tiring. And then there's the question of the damage to the Disgusting. We spent several weeks burrowing and furnishing the place to the most exacting specifications. And how can you compensate us for the loss of drinking time while the place is being rebuilt? That's what I'd like to know. And—"

"Let's be reasonable about this," said Palomides, becoming annoyed. "And in any case, it was probably an Irish horse."

"The Irish were all on foot," said the Miggot.

"That means Tom Grog was killed by a good giant," said Fang.

"It means there's no such thing as a good giant," said the Miggot. "And that's what I've said all along. Only gnomes are good, because we have the Examples to guide us. The very fact that you giants carry weapons is proof that evil lurks in your hearts."

"I don't know what to say," said Arthur unhappily. "Except that you'd better untie us before the Irish find us all here. I can only assure you that the Irish are even more evil than us."

The Miggot stood with folded arms and a stubborn expression, but Fang began to pluck at Torre's bonds. After a while he said, "I can't do it. The knots are too tight."

"I have my knife," said the Miggot, relenting.

"What knife is that?" asked Fang.

"The knife I carry."

"But knives are contrary to the Examples!"

"I pray constantly," replied the Miggot. "Now get out

of my way, Fang. This is not a time for scruples.'' He began to saw at Torre's bonds.

"It's all right for *Pong*,'' Fang found himself explaining to Arthur, "because the Guild of Sailorgnomes authorized knives long ago. And it's all right for the Accursed Gnomes, because they're beyond redemption, anyhow. But the Miggot? Why would the Miggot want to carry a knife around with him?''

"To cut the Sharan's umbilical cord,'' snapped the Miggot.

"But if that was all it was for, we could use some kind of a sacred knife and devise a ritual around it. We could utter prayers before using it, begging the forgiveness of our ancestors. And then we could put it away until next time. You don't need to carry it around with you, like a . . . like a giant.''

"You people really don't like metal things, do you?'' said Arthur, amused.

"With good reason.'' Fang told the salutary story of the Tin Mothers. "Long ago the kikihuahuas, our creators, lived on a world far away. You would have thought they were very civilized. They built huge spaceships and all kinds of machinery to take them all around the stars. They explored the greataway for a long time; but in the end they came back to their home planet. They were racially tired. They'd had enough of traveling and fighting and they wanted a rest. So they used their machines to make life easy for themselves. In the end they built the Tin Mothers.

"The Tin Mothers loved the kikihuahuas very much. They were built that way. They fed them, sheltered them, entertained them, and made sure they didn't come to any harm. And they discouraged the kikihuahuas from doing anything adventurous that might hurt them.

"A kikihuahua called Aoli saw the danger and gathered followers, and gradually they began to replace machinery with organic things. The Tin Mothers let them do it because it wasn't hurting anyone. Aoli's group grew, while the other members of his race became weak, lying in soft beds.

"Aoli's people became our first genetic engineers, and in the end they invented an organic way to get off their planet and away from the Tin Mothers, and fly through space again. The Tin Mothers watched them go, and wondered where the hell they'd gone wrong. So they went back to looking after the dying people. Aoli's people swore they would never kill, or light fires, or use metal, because those were the things that had almost exterminated their race. Aoli thought we should live in harmony with the elements instead of trying to bend them to our will. He invented the Kikihuahua Examples and we've tried to live by them ever since."

"That's a remarkable story, Fang. Do you think that kind of thing will happen to us humans?" asked Arthur.

"Of course it will. It'll happen to every intelligent species. I've talked it over with the Miggot, and he says it's an evolutionary inevitability. The Miggot often says things like that."

Meanwhile the Miggot had freed Torre and was cutting at Arthur's thongs. Torre began to untie Governayle. "I *do* need to carry the knife around," said the Miggot, "and the proof is right here. These are different times we're living in, Fang. Tougher times. We must adapt in order to survive. Nobody ever listened to me before, but they'll bloody well have to listen to me now. Are *you* listening to me, Fang?"

"Yes. Yes, of course, Miggot. Survival of the fittest. You've always said so."

"And do you agree with me?"

"Well, within reason, you know, Miggot."

"It would be a poor reflection on gnomekind if the only members of our species left on Earth in ten years' time were the Accursed Gnomes."

"Absolutely, Miggot."

"What about me?" asked Palomides, as the other humans stood, rubbing their hands to restore the circulation. The battle seemed to have moved south; a good sign, implying that the Irish were being driven toward the beach. Nobody else made a move to untie Palomides, so Arthur did it. Palomides got to his feet, grumbling. "We're missing all the action," he said.

"First of all we must do what we can for Tom Grog and the Disgusting," said Arthur firmly. "Show us, Fang."

Glumly Fang led them around the rock to a grassy glade heavily marked with hoofprints. One print was deeper than the others. The hoof had sunk in up to the fetlock, and the surrounding depression testified to the destruction of the Disgusting. "Look," said Fang.

At the bottom of the hoofprint could be seen the bloody remains of a gnome.

"Oh, God," muttered Arthur. He took a dagger from inside his boot and began to dig. It didn't take long. Soon the broken body of Tom Grog lay on the grass. Arthur took off his jerkin and laid it gently over the remains. He looked up at his men, tears in his eyes. "This must never happen again," he said. "Never."

"It was an accident," said Ned.

"We will not take the chance of such accidents. If we must fight, we will fight where we know there are no gnomes. I gave an undertaking to these people, and it seems I'm not fulfilling it." He stood, addressing the gnomes. "There are no words that can express my sorrow and regret. I can only tell you I will do everything in my power to make sure such a tragedy doesn't happen again. We will leave you now. I expect you will want to deal with Tom's remains in your own way." He saluted. "Come on, men."

An abashed party returned to the place where they'd left their horses. They mounted and rode south.

By the time they caught up with the battle, it was over. The Irish stood on the beach, a disconsolate rabble, eyeing the swords of Mara Zion nervously. "Now perhaps this time," said Palomides, "we will rid ourselves of these scum forever. The late Tristan spared them, but he was weak. You will prove a strong leader, I trust, Arthur."

"It was not my battle," said Arthur.

The Silver Knight was addressing the Irish. "Go now, and go in peace. If you come again, come in peace." His visor still covered his face, and the words had a compelling, echoing quality. "You will be welcome as allies. As enemies you will die. The choice will be yours, and we shall be ready for you."

Marhaus faced him. "We cannot be your allies so long as you are allies of the murderer, Baron Menheniot. But thank you all the same. We shall not come with warlike intentions again." He led the Irish into their boats.

Gawaine caught sight of Arthur's group and approached them excitedly. "You should have seen it!" he cried. "That Silver Knight fought like I've never seen a man fight. He inspired us all, and . . ." He hesitated. "Maybe we needed some inspiring at first. He took the Irish on single-handedly, more or less. So then we had to join in."

"How many are dead?" asked Arthur in flat tones.

"None that I know of. It was amazing. There was something about that Silver Knight that seemed to knock all the stuffing out of the Irish. After the first skirmish it was simply a question of chasing them to the beach."

The Silver Knight strode toward them and saluted Arthur. "I'm glad to have been of service."

"You're wounded." Now they could see that the forefinger of his right glove was missing at the tip. Blood seeped from behind the jointed metal.

"It's a pity," said the Silver Knight, with an odd kind of regret in his voice.

"Allow us to dress it." The women were emerging from the trees. "Nyneve," called Arthur. "Can you see to the Silver Knight's wound?"

"I fear it's too late," said the other, still in that strange tone. "My fingertip is lost forever."

"Well, yes, but at least we can stop you from bleeding to death."

"But you can't restore me to perfection."

"Avalona can heal the stump," said Nyneve. "I've seen her do that kind of thing." She bound the finger tightly with a narrow band of cloth. "Shall I take you to her?"

"I've heard of Avalona. She's the witch in the forest, isn't she? Yes, I'd like to see her."

Arthur said, "It was a fortunate chance for us that you came this way, sir. Where are you from?"

"Oh . . ." The other waved a hand vaguely. "East. South. Everywhere. I've traveled through many lands, and now I'm here. I don't know why, but this seems like my destination. I might almost say that something seemed to call me here. I have no idea where to go next."

"You're welcome to stay in the village."

"Thank you."

"Just one thing." Arthur regarded the Silver Knight curiously. "As a stranger to these parts, you came across two warring groups. How did you know which side to choose?"

The other pushed back his visor. His hair was fair, his eyes a penetrating blue, his mouth wide and smiling gently.

"Instinct," he said. "I am on the side of God and justice."

They watched in silence as Nyneve led him into the forest.

8

TOM GROG'S FUNERAL

FOUR PEOPLE IN HUMAN FORM SAT AT BREAKFAST THE following morning.

"What will you do now, Silver Knight?" asked Nyneve through a mouthful of gruel.

The other swallowed before speaking, and wiped his lips politely. "Call me Lancelot," he said, "since I'm not wearing my armor at present. As to your question, I'm going to accept Arthur's offer of accommodation in the village. There is much for me to do in Mara Zion." He smiled at them brilliantly. He wore a leather jerkin and pants, spotlessly clean.

"So it's Lancelot," Merlin said with a grunt. "I might have known."

"My fame has reached Mara Zion?"

"I was instrumental in spreading the word around," said the old Paragon. "Me and Nyneve, that is. You fulfill a legend in these parts, Lancelot. You—"

"That's enough, Merlin," said Avalona.

"I wasn't going to prophesy anything. I was just going to—"

"Don't. In any case, it is time you were leaving. The carriage is close by Penzance."

"How can you know that?"

"Merlin, if I say the carriage is close by Penzance, that's

156

where it is. Now get started on your journey or you'll miss it. You may take the mule."

"The mule? The mule? Have you any idea what it does for my standing in the village, riding a mule? Why the hell can't we ride horses like anyone else, that's what I'd like to know!"

"Mules are very hardy," said Lancelot quickly. "They're ideal for forest and moorland conditions. And they're sterile." He stood. "Thank you for healing my stump, Avalona. And for breakfast, beautiful Nyneve. Merlin, I'll accompany you on the first part of your journey. It looks like a fine day for a ride on the moors."

"Do you have to be so bloody positive about everything?" Grumbling, Merlin pulled on a filthy coat and shambled to the door. Lancelot followed, bowed to the women, and the two men left.

"He's a bit too good to be true," said Nyneve.

"He is what he is. We all are."

"Where are they going?"

"To Pentor. He is to meet a coach bringing Guinevere from Camyliard."

"What! Why didn't you tell me?"

"You could not have affected the issue."

"But why is she coming?" A sense of dread began to center around Nyneve's heart like a pain. "Why the hell do you have to bring her *here,* Avalona?"

"She is your friend. As I understand it, you invited her."

"Yes, but that was last year! That was before Arthur came! I would never have invited her if I'd known Arthur would be around. I threw out the invitation to be polite. You must have been in touch with her since." She stared at the Dedo furiously. "What's the real reason for her coming?"

"You already know that. You told the stories. She must take her place beside Arthur."

"But the stories don't have to come true in every detail!"

"The part of the story that deals with Arthur and Guinevere must come true. It is an essential part of my plan for the human race. Starquin must be saved from destruction. Would you challenge the plan, Nyneve?''

The cold eyes dwelt upon her and she shivered. ''No. I won't challenge the plan,'' she muttered. ''All the same, I thought things were going pretty well. . . .'' Catching another glance from Avalona, she fell silent. It was intolerable that Gwen should arrive when she and Arthur were getting along so well. But then again . . . She remembered the pale girl at Camyliard with the narrow, uninteresting face and the slightly vacant expression. Arthur wouldn't fall for a girl like that. She, Nyneve, would look pretty good in contrast. Perhaps she had nothing to worry about. She stood, pushing aside her unfinished gruel.

''I'm going to visit the gnomes. One of them was killed during the battle, and they're having a funeral. I must be there.''

''A gnome killed?'' For once Avalona seemed to be taken aback. ''Who was it?''

''Tom Grog, their innkeeper. It seems a horse stepped on his inn in the heat of battle. It was terribly bad luck.''

''Yes,'' said Avalona thoughtfully. ''We should never overlook the effect of chance on an otherwise well-organized happentrack. I didn't expect this. I must examine the ifalong to ensure the effects are not permanent. Leave me now, Nyneve.'' She closed her eyes in dismissal.

Soon afterward Nyneve, approaching the blasted oak, heard the drone of gnomish voices raised in dismal harmony. She found some three dozen gnomes sitting on exposed roots. Before them an open-weave basket lay on its side. Seven gnomes, all males, stood beside the basket. Their eyes were downcast, their shoulders slumped. From these seven came the harmonic drone.

A little apart from them, near the open end of the basket, stood Pong the Intrepid. He was peering inside. ''Oh, no!'' he cried, as though the body were metamorphosing into something unthinkable. ''Oh, no!''

King Bison, seeing Nyneve at the edge of the clearing,

left the group of seven and approached her. "Hello, Nyneve," he said in sepulchral tones.

"Hello, Bison. I feel really sorry about this. My people are responsible and I don't know what to do about it."

"Nobody except the Miggot blames you. It just happened," said Bison sadly. "When some people are much bigger than other people, somebody's bound to get stepped on. Tom Grog was the unlucky one. Just when we'd gotten the inn all built too. He was going to serve the first brew of new beer tonight. It just shows, doesn't it? You can't depend on anything in this new world of ours."

"Oh, no!" howled Pong.

"We have to make it up to you, Bison. There must be something we can do."

"It would be better if you told the villagers to stay away from gnomedom."

"I don't have that much influence over them, Bison. I could ask Avalona to do something, but you know what *she's* like. She'd say it would interfere with some essential happentrack."

"Maybe we should accept Arthur's offer and live in the village."

"Oh, no!" screamed Pong, staring into the basket, aghast.

"Is something horrible happening in there?" Nyneve asked.

"It's just part of the ceremony. Pong's the official crier, expressing grief."

"That seems an odd way to do it."

"We come from different cultures, Nyneve. What would a human shout if somebody died?"

Nyneve thought. "Well, he might shout 'Oh, no!' but that would be at first. When the initial shock had worn off, he would probably just keen."

"Keen?"

"Kind of a wailing noise. Or perhaps a whimper."

"We do that too. We have moaners. I'm part of the official moaning party today. But moaning gets automatic after a while, and we gnomes feel something more is required to reinforce the immediate grief. That's where the crier comes in. After all," Bison said sadly, "it's hardly ever that gnomes die. And when one dies by accident, that's dreadful. It's so . . . so *obvious*. There's a body, you see, all smashed up. Housemice take care of natural deaths, but this . . ." He shuddered. "We don't often see bodies. Pong's grief is real, you know. Every time he looks into that basket, he feels terrible."

"Even though he never drank beer himself," said the Gooligog, joining them. "You notice there are no women among the moaners?" His tone was indignant. "That's because they never really liked Tom. They say he led us astray with heady brews. I never liked Tom myself, as a matter of fact, but at least I can pay my respects in the proper manner."

Regrettably there were signs of a near celebration from the women as they chattered among themselves, paying scant attention to the moaners and the body. The hearty laugh of Lady Duck rang out, and Bison flushed in embarrassment. "They're making a mockery of the whole ceremony," he said. "My own wife too. We shall have to borrow your housemouse, Gooligog."

"You're going to set it on your wife? That's a little extreme, isn't it?"

Bison uttered a cluck of exasperation. "We have to dispose of Tom Grog, Gooligog. We can hardly leave him here, can we?" He waved an arm at the trees where rows of shytes perched with hunched shoulders, peering greedily down at the basket. Under other circumstances they would have been driven off by outraged gnomes, but on this occasion they were welcomed. Their drab feathers and strangled cries, conveying an impression of almost unbearable suffering, were considered particularly appropriate to a funeral. Food was occasionally tossed to them, to keep them there.

"Can't you use somebody else's mouse? I don't fancy leading that bastard through the forest. He took a snap at my leg the other day. Getting impatient, he is."

"That's precisely why we need him, Gooligog. He's *ready*, if you know what I mean. I don't mean you're *dying*, or anything like that. But your mouse—don't misunderstand me, Gooligog—always has an *anticipatory gleam* in his eye. He will have no difficulty disposing of the carcass, and it'll get him off your back for a while too."

"That's true," said the Gooligog, brightening. "I'll fetch him." He hobbled off into the forest. A small covey of shytes detached themselves from the branches and winged after him.

"The Gooligog's days are numbered," observed Bison with no discernible regret. "Fang is now our Memorizer, and the shytes are closing in. The birds sense it, you know."

"How do they know?" asked Nyneve.

"They can see a little way into the future. We bred them that way, thousands of years ago, to keep the forest clean. The Miggot tells me they get a picture in their mind of something lying motionless on the forest floor. So they wait around in that spot—and sure enough, before long something comes staggering along and falls down dead there. So they clean it up before it gets unpleasant. Unfortunately they're not good at distinguishing between death and sleep, particularly with old people. The Gooligog's woken up several times from a light doze and found them all over him, selecting the choicest parts. By the Great Grasshopper!" Bison paled suddenly. "I shall have to make a speech! The moaners are getting hoarse, and Pong seems to have wandered off somewhere. This is the time when the leader speaks of the virtues of the departed. I don't like making speeches."

"I thought you were good at it," said Nyneve, puzzled. "Everybody says that's why you're leader of the gnomes."

"They don't know the agony I go through." Bison groaned. "The self-doubt. The paralysis of the mind. The trembling knees. Above all the fear that a circling shyte will let go on me and I'll be laughed at. That's why I let Lady Duck do most of the talking."

He continued in this vein for a while. It became obvious

to Nyneve that he was playing for time. Eventually the Gooligog arrived with his housemouse on a leash, and Bison breathed a sigh of relief. "Good," he said. "It would be unseemly to utter the sacred words before the innkeeper has been properly dispatched."

"You could get Lady Duck to utter the words, Bison."

He shot Nyneve a look of disapproval and suddenly roared, "Pong!"

The intrepid one hurried out of the undergrowth. "Yes, Bison?"

"It's time to dispatch the deceased."

"Oh, yes." Well drilled, Pong took the leash and walked the housemouse to the basket. The housemouse, scenting carrion, pricked up his ears. Pong unleashed him and he bounded into the basket. There was a lengthy silence while the gnomes strained their ears.

"Oh, no!" cried Pong.

But it was not the traditional lament of the crier. It was a warning that something was going wrong. The head of the housemouse popped out of the basket. Fierce little eyes scanned the assembly. The gnomes backed off nervously.

Bison, safe under the protection of Nyneve, said, "The mouse seeks fresher meat."

The mouse made a scuttling run for its master. The Gooligog, with a skill born of a century of practice, delivered an accurate kick. The mouse rolled across the clearing, squealing. Nyneve stepped forward, seized it by the tail, and pushed it back into the basket, sealing it in with a nearby lid, apparently designed for the purpose.

Relieved that his work had been done for him, Pong turned to Bison. "It's time for your speech," he said.

"I need a beer."

"There is no beer. The innkeeper is dead and his inventory destroyed." Pong, the teetotaler, spoke with some satisfaction.

"By the Sword of Agni!" cried Bison, "gnomedom has come to a pretty pass. Never in gnomish memory has a leader been required to make a speech without beer."

"Speech! Speech!" shouted the women unkindly.

Bison glanced around with a hunted expression. "We're not all here yet!" he shouted back. "Fang should be here. I can't make a speech without my deputy!"

"Ah, Fang," said Clubfoot Trimble darkly.

"Find Fang!" roared Bison.

"He's probably still in bed with that woman of his," said Elmera.

"Oh, no!" shouted Pong, the words having become engraved on his behavioral patterns. "Not her!" he cried, to reassure himself his vocabulary was still intact.

"I saw Fang in the moonlight," stated Clubfoot Trimble.

"What about it?" asked Lady Duck.

"I saw Fang in the moonlight," Clubfoot repeated portentously, because the right question had not been asked. The gnomes had gotten into the habit of deliberately not asking him the right question, and it was beginning to annoy him. Since the death of his wife he had taken to lurking in damp parts of the forest, uttering gloomy prognostications. The gnomes were learning to ignore him.

"Has anyone seen the Miggot lately?" asked Bison, to change the subject.

"I saw him with Fang," said Clubfoot. "In the moonlight."

"All right, then," said Bison, exasperated. "What were they doing?"

Clubfoot paused for effect, then unleashed the words he'd been holding back delightedly for some time. "They were carrying a severed hand."

"Don't be disgusting," exclaimed Lady Duck. "I invoke Hayle!"

Her husband was interested, however. "What was the hand severed *from?*"

"The hand was severed from a giant's arm."

"Then it would have been too big to carry!" shouted Lady Duck in triumph.

"Well, a severed finger, then." Clubfoot backed down a degree.

"You're a liar!" cried Lady Duck, outraged by his persistence in this unwholesome topic. "A dirty liar!"

Clubfoot smiled cunningly. "Ask Fang. Ask the Miggot."

"Where *is* the Miggot?"

"He's busy," said Elmera. "And if he'd been wandering about in the moonlight, carrying fingers, I'd have known about it. There's precious little the Miggot can get away with, believe me."

Clubfoot subsided, muttering and discredited, his moment past. Bison, his courage restored by the exchanges, climbed onto a scorched stump. "Gnomes!" he shouted.

"Hush," the gnomes told one another. "Bison is going to make a speech."

"Gnomes!" roared Bison again, having had time to plan his approach. "This is our darkest hour!" The sun chose this moment to glide from behind a cloud, washing the clearing with brightness so that even the charred oak seemed to gleam with new life. "I mean," said Bison, "darkest in the sense of saddest. I don't mean dark as *such,* if you know what I mean. I mean dark in a metaphoric sense. Our darkest hour."

"Our darkest hour," came the sepulchral echo from a dozen male throats.

"So far as I'm concerned," came the clear voice of Elmera, "it's probably our brightest hour."

"It depends on the viewpoint," commented Spector. "Darkest or brightest, according to how you view the situation. The Miggot would agree with me, if he were here. We are fair and just in such matters. We are the gnomes. We are probably divided equally on the issue."

"I really don't think that's quite right, Spector," said Pong hesitantly. "The Miggot wouldn't think it was the brightest or the darkest, you know. He'd say it's an hour like any other hour, or any other minute, for that matter, and a gnome is dead, which is too bad, but then gnomes *do* die from time to time. That's what the Miggot would say."

"Thank God the Miggot isn't here," said somebody.

"Far better that he should be carrying severed hands. That's more his style."

"The Miggot is *not* carrying severed hands!" snapped Elmera. "He's attending to the Sharan, if you must know."

"So he hasn't even the decency to show up in our darkest hour?"

By now the phrase had begun to grip the imagination of the gnomes, and in the echoing drone of "our darkest hour" there were several female voices.

"The Miggot told me," shouted Elmera, forced for once into defending her husband, "that his work was of far greater importance to the future of gnomedom than the meaningless ritual surrounding the disposal of fleshy tissue. Those were his exact words, and for once I agree with him. *Anything* must be more important than this charade!"

"Hear, hear!" yelled Lady Duck.

"A revered figure in gnomedom has met his end in the most tragic manner imaginable!" roared Bison, taking on his wife at his peril. "And we who loved him have gathered to pay our last respects. Do you call that a charade?"

"He was stamped on by a bloody horse because he was too drunk to move!" Lady Duck retorted. "Do you call that tragic?"

"It could happen to any one of us!" Pop-eyed with fury, Bison stared around at his audience. "Any one of us. You, Clubfoot. You, Spector. Elmera. Pong. Me. Just one careless step by a giant and it's the Great Grasshopper for a gnome. Think of that. Think of that!"

It was a new Bison—a commanding, powerful Bison with a glittering eye—and they fell silent before him, even including Lady Duck. They glanced at each other, and they glanced fearfully into the trees. The forest was suddenly alien and threatening. A twig snapped somewhere, and somebody gave a little scream of fear.

"This," thundered Bison, "is our darkest hour!"

The twig snapped again. The sun went out and a cool breeze swept across the clearing; bringing, it seemed, the stench of Mankind. The leaves rustled, and the gnomes felt a steady thumping through the ground. They huddled together, eyeing the trees with dread.

Then bounding out of the shadows came a gnome dressed all in forest green, riding a rabbit white as snow. Smiling brilliantly, he waved a cheery hand.

"Greetings, gnomes of Mara Zion!" he called in ringing tones.

"We're saved!" cried Bart o' Bodmin. "It's the Gnome from the North!"

It had been hard work, dragging the severed finger through the forest, and unpleasant too. By the time Fang, the Princess, and the Miggot reached the Sharan's temporary quarters, it was daylight and they were limp from exhaustion and queasy with disgust. They threw themselves to the ground beside the Sharan. Pan had just finished giving her coat a thorough brushing and she was looking particularly beautiful, but the gnomes were not in the mood to appreciate this.

"I'd give anything for a beer," the Miggot said with a groan.

Pan, seizing his opportunity to be irritating, assumed a hearty demeanor. "Well, we have visitors, Sharan! This is our lucky day. And on such a fine morning too! And what's this I see? A severed finger? Tell me all about it, Miggot!"

As often happened, the Miggot's tiredness was banished by his temper. Struggling to his feet, he looked around for an easy victim, and his gaze lit upon an animal about the size of a fox, with gray, shaggy hair and a doleful expression. It watched him with doggy eyes.

"Who the hell do you think you're staring at!" shouted the Miggot. "Get out of my sight this minute!"

Shocked by the violence in the Miggot's tone, Fang said, "That's not a very nice way to talk to that poor creature, Miggot. It was obviously unhappy, and now you've made things worse for it. What was it, anyway? I don't remember seeing it around here before."

"It's been around for years. Mostly it keeps out of sight,

and no wonder. It's called the hangdog.'' The dank hindquarters of the miserable creature slunk behind a tree, and the forest glade seemed the better for its leaving.

"Did you create it?"

"Yes," said the Miggot curtly.

"What's it for?"

"It fulfills a need."

"Yes, and I'll tell you what need," broke in Pan mischievously. "It's a sop for the Miggot's ego. It—"

"Pan, I want you to visualize a scenario for the Sharan," the Miggot snarled. "That's what you're here for, isn't it? I want her to produce an offspring capable of passing for a giant. It must look like a giant and be as big as a giant but—and mark this carefully, Pan—it must think like a gnome. This is how it will survive. It will be so insufferably kind and good that it will appeal to what passes for decency in giants, so they will not harm it."

"It will be our representative in the giant's world," Fang put in, "and our protector. You see what we're getting at, Pan?"

"We don't trust that bugger Arthur," continued the Miggot. "His intentions may be good, but he's basically weak, and anyway, he's going to be so busy in the next few years he won't have time to look after us."

"I understand," said Pan. "You want a creature as big as a gnome but which thinks like a giant. Right?"

"Right," said the Miggot absently.

"I don't think that *was* right, Miggot," said the Princess tentatively. "I think Pan got it mixed up somehow."

"He'd better not, if he knows what's good for him." The Miggot directed his penetrating stare at Pan. "Big as a giant, thinks like a gnome."

"I've got it right," said Pan huffily. "And now the raw material. I see you've brought the giantish element, Miggot. What about the gnomish? A little slice from yourself, perhaps? It wouldn't be the first time you've contributed your genes to the Sharan's creation. Much more of this and we'll have a whole forestful of Miggots. Now there's a sobering thought.''

''Not this time. I don't have quite the right qualities, for which I'm truly thankful. We've talked it over, and we feel that the Princess is probably the most suitable person. What . . . er, gender of creature would that result in?''

''What sex is that finger?''

''Male.''

''In that case I can't tell you. Sex is a funny thing. Let me tell you a few things about sex.''

''No thanks.''

''The time may come when you wish I had.''

''Get on with it,'' snapped the Miggot. ''Create the scenario while we prepare the ingredients.'' He drew his controversial knife with a flourish. ''Princess! Come here.''

''I'd rather Fang did it, Miggot.''

''All we're talking about is a drop of blood.''

''All the same . . .''

''Oh, all right.'' Disappointed, the Miggot handed the knife to Fang.

When Fang took the knife to the Princess's hand, however, his own hand began to shake so much that Mara Zion was in danger of another amputation. ''I'll do it myself, Fang,'' said the Princess, and produced a little drop of blood which she squeezed onto the giant's finger. Meanwhile Pan had closed his eyes in concentration and the Sharan had assumed a faraway look, trembling a little as she received visions of the dangers for which she must prepare her offspring.

It was not a good time for an interruption, but at that moment there came a pattering along the forest path, and Spector the Thinking Gnome rode into the clearing. ''Here you are,'' he said.

''We're busy,'' said the Miggot.

''I'm sure you are. Aren't we all?'' Spector's burning eyes passed from the Miggot to Pan, to the Sharan, to the severed finger. His bushy eyebrows lowered, hooding his eyes as though to cut down visual input while his brain assessed the implications. "I have important news." The eyes snapped open again.

"Get on with it, then," said the Miggot.

Spector, a master of drama, considered spinning out the matter a little longer, but the Princess chose that moment to hand the knife back to the Miggot. The complex mind of the Thinking Gnome was able to read something peculiarly threatening into this act, and he said hastily, "The Gnome from the North has arrived."

"The Gnome from the North? That's just a story of Bart o' Bodmin's!"

"That's what I thought too. When the gnome arrived, I thought he was just your average stranger who happened to be riding a rabbit white as snow—I mean," Spector said, hastily correcting himself, "a white rabbit. Bart shouted that it was the Gnome from the North, but you know what Bart is. If the Gnome from the North didn't exist, he would have invented him. As a matter of fact," said Spector thoughtfully, "I thought he *had* invented him. Anyway, when we brought the stranger around, he insisted he *was* the Gnome from the North. And as Bart pointed out, he ought to know best."

"Brought him around?"

"His rabbit ran into the blasted oak and he hit his head. That's the trouble with albino rabbits; they have poor eyesight. He'd have been better off riding a rabbit black as night," mused Spector, "but the symbolism would have been wrong."

"But what did he say?" asked Fang curiously. "I mean, did he say, 'I am the Gnome from the North and I have come in your darkest hour to lead you to a land where . . .' and all that stuff?"

"Yes, what were his first words?" pursued the Miggot. "That's always important, a stranger's first words."

Spector thought. "I believe his first words were 'Greetings, gnomes of Mara Zion. Bugger it!' Then there was a heavy thud, and he said nothing else for quite a while."

"And later?"

"He groaned a few times, then he said, 'I am Drexel Poxy. They call me the Gnome from the North. This is your darkest hour? Leave everything to me.' "

"That's rather . . . presumptuous, isn't it?" said Fang. "How did the gnomes respond?"

"Bison said, 'Thank God.' But then Bison could visualize the weight of office being lifted from his shoulders. Lady Duck said, 'Who in hell calls you the Gnome from the North, anyway? I certainly don't, my good fellow!' Bart o' Bodmin kept shouting, 'We're saved, gnomes!' until it began to get on people's nerves, so the Gooligog pulled his cap down over his face. Elmera—"

"Yes, yes," said the Miggot testily. "What Fang wanted was a general impression. You don't have to demonstrate your memory to us, Spector."

"The general impression was that he was welcome. According to Bison, it *was* our darkest hour, and now here he was, just like Bart had foretold. They'd have welcomed your Cousin Hal at that moment, if he'd come riding in on a white rabbit."

"I don't understand why the white rabbit is so bloody important," said the Miggot. "White rabbits are genetically damaged, and the shytes tend to circle over them—a sure sign of an inferior beast."

"We had to fight the shytes off before we could bring Poxy and his rabbit around," agreed Spector. "They were on him in a flash. But you can't deny the symbolism, Miggot. White is good."

"White is the color a predator can see a mile off," objected the Miggot. "White is the color of doom, in my books. White is the color of dead flesh. Your father's been looking pretty damned white lately, by the way, Fang."

"He washes a lot. It's an obsession of his."

"Guilt," said Spector.

"About what? My father's never felt guilty about anything in his life. He's not the guilty type. Bart o' Bodmin's the guilty type. But Bart has quite a ruddy complexion. Probably because he's a moorland gnome, used to living in open spaces. I'm not too happy about Bart," said Fang boldly, "and I can well believe he has a guilty secret. But he hasn't washed since he nearly sank in Pong's boat. He said he never wanted to see or touch water again."

There was a somewhat startled silence. Spector's theories were not usually challenged in so forthright a manner.

The Miggot got the discussion back on track. "Drexel Poxy? There's something about that name I don't like. Mark my words, no good will come of this Gnome from the North!"

"I think he'll challenge Bison for leadership," said Spector.

"He doesn't have to challenge Bison. He just has to ask him to step aside."

"Exactly."

The gnomes looked at one another uneasily. The Sharan opened its eyes, snorted, and considered the giant's finger. The sun swiveled its shadows slowly across the glade.

It was a day of important events in Mara Zion. In years to come, Avalona was to speak of the nodal happentracks of that day. By evening the Sharan's unique organs had analyzed the genes of the finger. Drexel Poxy's headache had abated. Completing the significant branches of the happentrack, a carriage was drawing to a halt on the road south of Pentor Rock.

The coachman was alert and wary. He'd been expecting a suitable reception for Guinevere: a few knights and a couple of ladies' maids, and a carriage to take her on to Mara Zion.

But the pair at the roadside could well be highwaymen.

"We have no valuables!" he called, which was not the strict truth. Apart from Guinevere's jewelry, he carried gold for Castle Menheniot, being the pay for certain mercenaries. One of the strangers sat tall in his saddle, strong and well armed. The other, more reassuringly, presented no threat, being shrunken and ancient, straddling a moth-eaten mule and leading another that was even less prepossessing.

"That's beside the point," shouted Merlin irritably, having waited for several hours in the company of a knight whose pristine goodness was matched only by his supreme self-confidence. "We have come to meet Lady Guinevere!"

The carriage door swung open and Gwen looked out, hand clutching a scarlet cloak around her neck. "Oh, hello, Merlin," she said.

"My lady," murmured Lancelot, removing his hat with a sweeping gesture.

Merlin glanced at him in annoyance, then addressed the girl: "I have instructions to take you to Arthur."

A succession of expressions chased one another across the narrow face: surprise, doubt, puzzlement. "I thought I was to stay with Nyneve," she said. "Who is this Arthur you're talking about?"

"A local fellow," replied Merlin, at the same instant as Lancelot said, "The future King of England."

Lancelot's reply being the more promising, Gwen turned her attention to him. "You don't mean Arthur, as in the stories?" she asked.

"Yes. And you are Guinevere, as in the stories," he said, smiling. "And I am Lancelot."

After a long pause she said, "I don't think I want to come with you. Where's Nyneve? This is too strange for my taste."

"You needn't worry about *him*, Gwen," Merlin reassured her. "He's nothing like the legendary Lancelot. He's a real pain in the ass."

"I'm not worried about him." The blue eyes were troubled. "It's the whole thing that worries me. Are you trying to tell me I'm *that* Guinevere? How can I be? It was just a story, using the names of real people to make it more interesting, nothing more."

"But parts of it are beginning to come true," said Merlin. "A lot's happened since we were in Camyliard. You could be Queen of England, if all goes well."

"And if it doesn't go well, I could be burned at the stake."

"What is life without adventure?" said Lancelot.

"What is life without life?"

"It might never happen," said Merlin. "Nothing is working out exactly the way it's supposed to. You're supposed to fall instantly in love with this shining fool, for instance."

She regarded Lancelot steadily. "I feel nothing."

"You will," he said, smiling magnificently. "It will come."

"How much longer are you going to be talking down there?" shouted the coachman. "I have a schedule to keep. I should have been at Castle Menheniot by now!"

The sun lay low over the sea, gilding the panels of the carriage. A warm breeze brought the scent of wild roses, and somewhere a wolf cried. "This Arthur," said Guinevere, "what's he like?"

"Red-haired," said Merlin. "Tall. Good with a sword."

"Lacking in confidence, perhaps," said Lancelot judicially, "but not a bad fellow. His men seem to like him."

"Why isn't he here?"

"He was called away to put down a rebellion."

"I'm supposed to be a guest of Nyneve," said Gwen helplessly.

"Nyneve knows Arthur well," said Merlin. "Everything's arranged. A room is waiting for you at the Great Hall of Mara Zion."

"A Great Hall is a funny place to stay at, isn't it?"

"Arthur's castle is still under construction, my dear. Great empires must have small beginnings."

She regarded them both for a long moment, then some imp of mischief made her laugh aloud. "Is there room for me on that horse, Lancelot? I have no intention of arriving in Mara Zion on muleback!"

9

MIDSUMMER IN MARA ZION

As THE ROMAN CITIES DECLINED, THE BRITON WAR-lords set themselves up in the hills, prepared to fight against any invader, be he Pict, Irish, or Saxon. Many warlords renovated the Celtic Iron Age hill forts such as Cadbury, Glastonbury, and Badon, which had been lying unused since the Roman conquest. Others, such as King Lodegrance at Camyliard and Baron Menheniot, had always lived beyond direct Roman influence and merely strengthened their existing fortifications.

The Britons eyed one another with hostility from their forts, making frequent forays into their neighbors' territory and carrying off cattle, sheep, and women. They eyed the Saxons with even more hostility. These onetime mercenaries had settled in Kent and the southeast, and were spreading inexorably westward.

And just as inexorably, the legend of King Arthur and his Knights of the Round Table was spreading eastward.

Historians of later years would ponder over the curiously low birthrate of those years when humans and gnomes walked the English byways. For many years the population remained static. Kings fought kings, barons fought barons, and all fought the Saxons. If there was a truce, it would be for the purpose of uniting against the Picts, the Scots, the Irish, the Danes, or whoever else was lured by the green and fertile land.

Any male above the age of puberty and below the age of death might find himself a soldier at any moment, at the whim of his warlord. So far as women were concerned, a good man was hard to find—or any man, for that matter. All too often, they were either fighting or dead. Lonely spinsters abounded.

One such was Elaine, the beautiful woman of Trevarron Isle.

The Norman warriors had recently stopped by, landing on the island to capture sheep. They found a middle-aged couple who offered no resistance and were therefore speared amid laughter. Their daughter escaped and hid among a tumble of rocks at the eastern end of the island. Here a lone Norman found her. In the space of a day he gained her confidence because he seemed more gentle than the others. Then he left, leaving her unharmed but not untouched, swearing that he would return for her one day.

Elaine buried her parents and resumed her life, raising sheep and a few vegetables, occasionally sailing to the mainland to trade with the villagers of Mara Zion. In due course she became less mobile.

One midsummer day when the sun baked the rocks until they crackled, she lay in the shade panting, feeling the child kicking the walls of her belly. Around noon she saw a sail approaching from the north. Even as her heart gave a huge thump, she realized the craft was far too small to carry human cargo. Sighing, she climbed ponderously down to the sandy beach. The tiny boat grounded. Four gnomes stepped out, straightened their caps, and regarded her purposefully.

"Are you Elaine?" one asked.

"I am she."

"We are Pong the Intrepid, the Miggot of One, Spector the Thinking Gnome, and Fang."

"Isn't Fang anything?"

"He used to be our leader, but he was deposed. He has taken it well. There's no rancor in Fang."

"I'm so glad." Elaine knelt awkwardly before them. "So what brings you to my island?"

"We'd like to see your house," said the Miggot.

"Of course." She was pleased. "I don't often get visitors."

"Fang," Spector murmured, "she's—"

"I can see that. Avalona told Nyneve she would be. That's the point of the whole thing." Fang regarded Elaine sympathetically. "Lead the way but don't walk too fast, please."

"Of course."

The gnomes followed Elaine along the beach, then over rolling, close-cropped grass, past well-maintained fencing and neat vegetable patches, to a gray stone cottage staring sternly out to sea from under a heavy brow of thatch.

"Looks a bit gloomy, doesn't it?" observed Pong.

"That's what giants' dwellings look like. They have no feeling for the landscape," Spector told him. "They build anywhere it suits them."

But the interior was cool and cheerful, and the gnomes' spirits rose. A table wore a bright woven cloth, with a jug of lavender sprigs set in the center. The fire burned low, just enough to simmer a pot of aromatic stew. A chair by the window was covered with sheepskin, and beneath the second window was a newly built crib in which lay a knitted woolen blanket, dyed blue. The gnomes nodded at one another approvingly.

"What news is there from Mara Zion?" asked Elaine.

"The rabbit compound is complete," said Pong eagerly, "and Fang and the Princess are living near where Fang's old dwelling used to be. Clubfoot Trimble has been elected innkeeper. The moles built Bart o' Bodmin a burrow near the racetrack, and the Gnome from the North is living with him temporarily. The Gnome from the North talks of riding south."

"With luck he'll ride into the sea and that'll be the end of him," said the Miggot.

"I really can't understand why you're so impressed by this Drexel Poxy, Pong," said Fang.

"He came from the north, riding a rabbit white as snow."

"What's so good about that? I'm sure Jack o' the Warren could breed anyone a white rabbit, if they wanted one."

"But he came from the north," protested Pong.

Fang couldn't let that pass, either. "The north's over that way." He pointed. "Are you saying it's any better than *that* way? Or *that* way?"

Spector explained. "It's the *combination* that counts, Fang. Coming from the north on a white rabbit, don't you see?"

"No, I don't see, Spector, not really. Supposing I chose to ride into gnomedom from that direction, on a white rabbit Jack had lent me. Would Pong be so impressed?"

"Probably not. You don't represent the mystical."

"What's mystical about a gnome with a name like Drexel Poxy?" snapped the Miggot.

"I meant what *human* news is there from Mara Zion," said Elaine plaintively.

The gnomes remembered their manners. "Guinevere is living at the Great Hall," Fang told her, "and she and Arthur will be married in the autumn."

"Unless Lancelot gets her first," said the Miggot nastily.

"That's just a giantish rumor. Gnomes don't think that way, Miggot."

"Infidelity is a concept alien to gnomes," Spector remarked.

"That may be our bad luck," said the Miggot.

"*I* certainly can't understand infidelity," said Fang. "Anyway, Arthur and Guinevere are getting along very well, and Arthur is building a new Round Table in her honor, to be ready for the wedding. But Nyneve is terribly upset about the whole thing. She calls Guinevere a treacherous bitch. Nyneve loves Arthur, you see."

The Miggot recalled himself to the purpose of their visit and squinted up at Elaine. "You're not married. But you're pregnant. Where is the giant who fertilized you?"

Elaine flushed. "He's away in a ship. He'll be back soon."

"Do you think he'll be here for the birth?"

"I hope so. But even if he isn't, I'll have the baby to keep me company. It'll be a little part of him. Something to remind me of him, until he gets back." The flush had become a radiance, and the gnomes shuffled their feet in embarrassment. Most gnomes didn't think of other gnomes that way. Fang was an exception.

"Are you lonely here?" he asked.

"Sometimes," she admitted sadly. "But the baby will be here soon."

Later, as the gnomes sailed back to Mara Zion, Spector said, "At least you had the tact not to tell her the baby's going to die, Miggot."

They parted company when they arrived back at Mara Zion beach. Pong pulled his boat clear of the high-water mark and retired to his cave to recover from the terrors of the voyage. The Miggot rode northwest, to check on Pan and the Sharan. Spector rode northeast, to discuss death with the Gooligog. And Fang rode north, to talk to Jack o' the Warren about a slight lameness affecting Thunderer's left foreleg.

He found Jack peering through the woven osiers of the fence.

"Look at them! You see what they're doing?"

Fang looked. "They don't seem to be doing anything much. Just munching, the way rabbits usually do."

"They're leaning up against each other, Fang. They've paired off and they're leaning up against each other."

It was true. All over the enclosure the rabbits sat side by side, pressed against each other, heads close, as though exchanging confidential information.

"They're plotting something," said Jack. "History is repeating itself!"

"If they were plotting, they'd all be huddled in one big

mob"—Fang regarded the rabbits closely—"and every so often one of them would glance over its shoulder at you."

"Don't think I haven't seen them in a mob. It happens every time I feed them, and believe me, Fang, it makes my blood run cold. Oh, by the Sword of Agni," Jack lamented, "I wish we were back on the old happentrack in the days of the bogus rabbits. Nothing ever went wrong with the bogus rabbits. They never got sick, they never snapped at me, and they certainly never plotted against me. All I had to worry about was the occasional conversation with the Miggot. But now life's one long worry."

"They're not all plotting, Jack. Look over there. There's a pair lying head to tail."

"That's Standfast and Charger. They're the most stupid rabbits of the lot. They're probably wondering why they're not communicating. Oh, my God. They heard me. Look at that." His voice rose to a squeak of terror. The rabbits had all jumped apart—guiltily, it seemed, even to Fang—and were staring this way and that, ears waving attentively, heads high.

Then came a sound that froze the gnomes where they stood. A low snarl carried across the enclosure, followed by a single, sharp bark.

"A dog!" cried Jack.

They also heard the human voice that quite plainly followed the bark.

"Get them, Bruiser!"

The compound covered a ridge in the forest so that the far side was hidden from the gnomes' sight. The rabbits could see over the ridge, though. They bounded along, eyes rolling in terror. From somewhere came a squeal of pain and fear, and a dreadful snarling sound.

"What shall we do, Fang?"

"I don't know! Why ask me?"

"You're supposed to be a natural leader of gnomes!"

"Climb the tree!" Fang grabbed the lowest branch and hauled himself up.

"A tree!" Jack gasped, arriving breathless at the branch.

"What a good idea! I was looking for a hole. It's a gnomish thing to look for a hole in times of danger. But you have a more flexible mind, Fang." He stared down through the summer leaves of the oak, catching the occasional glimpse of a fleeing rabbit.

Then they saw the dog. It came over the top of the rise at a full run: a rawboned brown brute, jaws flecked with blood, ears laid back. It drove the rabbits before it, herding them down the slope toward the gnomes' tree.

Fang glimpsed the man and thought he recognized him.

The rabbits reached the narrow southwestern corner of the compound. Here the fence formed a cul-de-sac into which Jack drove rabbits he needed to examine, to treat or sell. The frightened creatures piled into the constriction, scrambling on top of one another into a packed, struggling mass.

The dog closed in.

It seized the outermost rabbit, gave it a single violent shake, and threw it aside. The rabbit lay twitching, dying.

"Good dog!"

The dog worked fast and efficiently. The rabbits couldn't escape, and one by one they were shaken and cast aside with broken necks, to die quickly. There was very little noise now. The dog was too busy to snarl. The rabbits would squeal once when they felt the jaws bite into their flesh, then the quick shake would paralyze them and they would die soundlessly. It was quite humane. In a short while they were all dead.

The man stooped and patted the dog. Then he picked up the two biggest rabbits. "Come, Bruiser!" he called, and strode off to be hidden by the intervening leaves. His heavy boots were quiet on the grass, then they crunched over rock. Finally the fence shook, and he was gone.

The gnomes sat on their branch, trembling and staring down at the dead rabbits.

"I didn't want this," said Jack, tears in his eyes. "I may have suspected them, but I swear by the Great Grasshopper, I didn't want this to happen."

"I know you didn't, Jack."

"We spent ages catching and taming those rabbits. Everybody helped. Nyneve and Torre built the fence for us."

They climbed down, crossed the enclosure, and came to a place where the fence was broken down. "This is where he climbed over," said Jack. "What shall we do now?"

"Build it up again and get hold of some more rabbits."

"What's the point? The giants will kill them all again."

"We'll have to report this to Arthur."

"That's tantamount to saying we can't look after ourselves!"

"All right," said Fang irritably, "you suggest something."

Jack scanned the enclosure, the broken fence, the dead rabbits. He looked at the trees. He looked at the sky. "We'll tell Bison," he said eventually.

"Yes. We'll tell Bison. And then we'll tell Arthur."

They found Bison sitting outside the entrance to his new dwelling. His eyes were closed, and the evening sun illuminated an expression of contentment on his face. A mug of beer stood on the grass beside him. An appetizing smell drifted out of the burrow; Lady Duck was preparing the evening meal.

"The giants have killed all the rabbits!" cried Jack, kicking him.

Bison opened one eye. "The what?"

"It was a deliberate attack. The rabbits are wiped out. Our means of transport has been taken away from us. The giants have immobilized us, and I think I know why!"

Bison opened both eyes. "That's terrible news. Although I still have my rabbit." He scanned the glade blearily. "And so have you two. I see them over there."

"But we have no replacements!"

"Do you need replacements right now?"

"We never know when we might need replacements! Fang told me Thunderer was limping."

"Slightly. He told me that too. He said Thunderer was favoring his right foreleg."

"Left."

"I'm sure he said right."

Jack appealed to the ex-leader. "Which leg did you say, Fang?"

"I said left, actually, but that isn't the—"

He was cut short by a thudding of paws as a rabbit white as snow bounded into the clearing. Drexel Poxy slid to the ground and eyed them expectantly. "Well?"

"Well, what, Poxy?" said Bison irritably. He was getting a little impatient with gnomes who wanted action from him at the time of the evening meal.

"Well . . . what's this meeting about?"

"Fang's rabbit Thunderer's right foreleg."

"Left, actually, but—"

"Is that all?" asked Poxy, puzzled.

"It's a serious matter," said Jack indignantly. "The slightest lameness in a rabbit can result in problems later on, if not properly treated."

"Thunderer is more than a rabbit. He's an institution," said Bison, drinking and wiping his lips. The gnomes nodded wisely, all except Drexel Poxy, who seemed dissatisfied and was about to say something when another rabbit hopped up. Spector dismounted. "The Gooligog accepted his destiny," he announced. "He is at peace."

"You mean, he's *dead?*" Fang cried, alarmed. Although he and his father had frequently been at loggerheads, he'd always hoped that one day there would be a reconciliation. He'd imagined the scene many times: the dank dwelling and the Gooligog smiling wanly up from a sweat-stained pillow. "Willie—I mean, Fang—forgive me. I've not always been the kind of father I'd like to have been." And Fang would hand him a mug of mulled beer, which the Gooligog would accept with trembling hands, spilling a few drops onto his nightgown. "You've been a good son to me, Fang." The next few words would be inaudible, because the Gooligog would choke on his beer and lie there coughing weakly, tears streaming down his ravaged cheeks. He would try to speak. "Hush, Father," Fang would say. "I understand."

And the sad hooting of an owl would drift into the burrow, and the faithful housemouse would be sitting at the foot of the bed, gazing at the Gooligog with liquid eyes, drooling.

"Dead?" asked Fang again, shocked and disappointed.

"He is composing himself."

"What do you mean, composing himself?" In Miggot-like fashion, Fang grabbed the Thinking Gnome by the lapels. "Composing himself for *what?*"

The Miggot himself arrived at that moment. "Nobody informed me of this meeting," he said, staring around accusingly. "What kind of leadership is this, Bison?"

"Composing himself for the inevitable, as must we all."

"We *all* must? I'm a couple of hundred years away from composing myself, Spector, you damned fool," said the Miggot, rapidly grasping the flow of conversation.

"All dead," said Jack sadly, recalling the original purpose of his visit. "Every one of them dead."

"Nobody's dead," said the Miggot firmly. "And if they were, it would be perfectly acceptable. Gnomes live, gnomes die. The young are strong, the middle-aged are clever, but the old are stupid and feeble and must be gotten rid of. Death is good. If it wasn't for death, we'd be knee-deep in senile gnomes, whimpering and babbling like the Gooligog. The same applies to all living creatures."

"It doesn't apply to the rabbits, Miggot. They were in the prime of life."

"That's why they're not dead, Jack."

"But they *are* dead, Miggot."

The Miggot eyed him closely. "By the Great Grasshopper, it's bad enough with Spector talking garbage. Don't you start, Jack."

Fang said loudly and clearly, "A giant and a dog broke into the rabbit enclosure this afternoon. They killed all the rabbits."

"I knew it," said Poxy. "It was bound to happen."

The other gnomes had been stunned into silence, but now a chorus of questions arose. "What giant? What dog? What do you mean, killed all the rabbits?" Others began to drift into the clearing, obeying that mysterious forest instinct that alerts gnomes when something interesting is afoot. "What enclosure? When? Why?"

Drexel Poxy leapt astride his steed, dominating the throng. "The giants have slaughtered our string of riding rabbits, just as I warned you they would. They have immobilized us!"

Bart o' Bodmin, newly arrived, cried, "The Gnome from the North speaks!"

The Gnome from the North speaks. . . . The words traveled from gnome to gnome, into the forest.

"He foretold it, and now it's come to pass!" yelled Bart. Gnomes nodded at one another. They should have listened to the Gnome from the North sooner. The Gnome from the North had mysterious powers. Everything he'd said was coming true.

"I don't remember Poxy foretelling anything," Fang remarked to the Miggot.

"Hush," somebody said. "The Gnome from the North is about to speak again."

"Fang's right!" shouted the Miggot. "That bastard never foretold a bloody thing!"

"Hush!" cried a score of voices.

"This is our darkest hour!" shouted Bart o' Bodmin.

"Our darkest hour," droned the gnomes obediently.

"Our darkest hour was weeks ago!" yelled the Miggot, purple with frustration. "What's gotten into you all? Our darkest hour was when Tom Grog got himself squashed and the beer ran out. We all agreed on that!"

"Our darkest hour!" roared Poxy in a voice worthy of Bison himself. "And it could have been prevented, because we were warned. The giants have reduced us to mere crawlers on the forest floor, little better than toads. Alas! Alas!"

"Alas!" cried the gnomes.

"But all is not lost!"

"Aha!" chorused the gnomes hopefully.

"What's happened to them?" asked Fang. "What's he doing to them?" Drexel Poxy seemed to have gained in

stature as he sat astride his white rabbit, holding his cap
aloft, exposing a balding, freckled pate and raking the
throng with blazing eyes.

"Mass hypnosis," said Spector, standing near. "It's a
giantish practice. I've never heard of it used on gnomes."

"Our salvation lies south!" bellowed Poxy, pointing with
his cap.

"South!" cried the gnomes.

"What's the answer, Spector?" asked Fang, alarmed.
"What shall we do?"

"South!" shouted Spector, eyes fixed raptly on the
Gnome from the North.

"Miggot?"

"I don't know." For once the feisty little gnome was at
a loss. "He's got them in the palm of his hand, Fang. He
seems to be able to do anything he wants with them."

"The Gnome from the North will lead us south," cried
Bart o' Bodmin, "as it was foretold!"

Help came unexpectedly.

"Like h-hell he will!" It was Bison, making his stand in
obedience to a ferocious prodding from Lady Duck.

"Do you defy the Gnome from the North?" asked Bart
incredulously.

Bison hung his head. Lady Duck shouldered him aside.
"You're damned right he does," she roared. "And you can
forget the Gnome from the North stuff too. His name's
Drexel Poxy, and that ought to tell you something. Look at
him! A dirty little gnome on a blind rabbit. When did he
last comb his beard? If you can call it a beard. It looks more
like trailing moss to me!"

Spector snapped out of his trance. "Look, there's a cock-
roach crawling in it!" he cried shrewdly.

The gnomes clustered close. "Where? Where?"

"The Gnome from the North is a friend and host to all
living creatures!" shouted Bart quickly.

Meanwhile Poxy was slapping at his beard. "Get that
bloody thing off me, Bart!"

"There is no roach, Drexel. It was irresponsible slander."

"Our rabbits are gone," shouted Poxy hastily, "and Tom Grog is dead. What next? How many murderous deeds must we suffer before we learn that giants and gnomes cannot live together in the forest. Huh? Huh?" Surreptitiously he clawed at his beard, convinced of a tickling sensation. "Don't think I'm blaming the giants. There are both good and bad among them. As is the case with all living creatures."

"It isn't the case with doodads, you fool!" called Lady Duck.

"There is a place for us all on this world: gnomes, giants, and doodads. Each has his niche. Our particular niche lies south, where the warm breezes blow in from the sea, where the land is soft and sandy, where there is no concealing undergrowth and gnomes and giants can see one another clearly and live together in safety and harmony and happiness!"

"Are you talking about the beach? You want us to live on the *beach?*"

"Well, yes, the beach," said Poxy in more normal tones. "I've talked to the giants, and they'll help us set up a nice little place there, and make sure we don't run short of anything, and so on. We'll all be looked after. We'll help them and they'll help us. Hand in hand"—he resumed his public voice—"gnomes and giants will march forward to a new tomorrow!"

"A new tomorrow!" echoed Bart. "Peace and plenty by the sea! The founding of a new gnomedom!"

"But we've only just founded *this* gnomedom," said Bison, puzzled.

"You founded it in the wrong place," said the Gnome from the North kindly. "It could happen to anyone. Fresh information is now available, and a new agreement has been reached with the giants."

"But shouldn't I have been the one to reach that agreement? I'm supposed to be our leader, aren't I?"

"I reached it on your behalf, Bison."

"Oh, that's all right, then. I'm sorry. For a moment I thought—"

"It's perfectly all right, Bison."

"Gather up your belongings, gnomes!" shouted Bart o' Bodmin. "Load up your rabbits and the Gnome from the North will lead you south!"

There was a noticeable hesitation. "You mean, right now?" somebody asked.

"The forest will tremble to the thud of rabbits' paws," shouted Poxy. "In ones and twos we will trickle along the byways, joining each other in a steady stream down the forest paths, uniting, mounting until a great flood of gnomes will escape from the darkness and dangers of the forest to begin a new life at the margin of the mighty ocean! South!"

"South!" came the answering cry from a fair number of gnomish throats. Yelling with excitement and anticipation, they hurried off into the forest.

About half the gathering remained. Drexel Poxy sat astride his rabbit, gazing inscrutably at Fang and the Princess of the Willow Tree, the Miggot of One and Elmera, King Bison and Lady Duck, Clubfoot Trimble, Spector the Thinking Gnome, Jack o' the Warren, Wal the Bottle, Broyle the Blaze, and some two dozen other gnomes standing unhappily in little groups. As the silence lengthened, the Gooligog emerged haltingly from the trees.

"What's going on?" he asked querulously. "Nobody told me there was a meeting."

"Are you joining us, Gooligog?" asked Poxy.

"Are *they* joining you?" the ex-Memorizer asked, pointing a skinny finger at the remaining gnomes.

"No."

"Then I'll join you," said the Gooligog. "Join you in what?" he asked, wondering what he'd let himself in for.

"In founding a new gnomedom. You will be our official Memorizer."

The Gooligog smiled a rare smile and left the clearing with a new spring in his step.

"And you, Jack," continued Poxy, "you have no rabbits now. Will you come with us? We can promise you a good life, and I have word that we shall have a new kind of animal for you to look after."

Jack shot a sheepish look at Fang. "A new animal? What does it do to you?"

"Nothing, Jack. This is a great and harmless animal called the tump. It has been in use in other gnomish settlements for generations, and we propose to bring it to Mara Zion. Well, not exactly bring it," he said, correcting himself, "because it moves very slowly and we haven't got forever. We will create it for you, Jack."

"With what?" asked the Miggot.

"With the Sharan, of course."

"I'm in charge of the Sharan."

Poxy eyed the sharp-nosed gnome. "Exactly."

"Well, I'm not coming with you to the beach. I'm staying here."

"You surprise me, Miggot. I'd always thought you were discontented with life in the forest."

"I'm a naturally discontented gnome," the Miggot snarled. "I don't need an object for my discontent. I'd be just as discontented at the beach as I am here. And I don't propose to move, now that I'm settled in at the blasted oak. There's something about the blasted oak that suits my simple requirements. I'm staying."

"Good for you, Miggot!" shouted Fang. There was a ragged cheer from the others.

Poxy scrutinized them coldly. "It is not right that the Sharan should be in the hands of an effete and dwindling group of gnomes. The Sharan is a symbol of gnomish progress and duty. She must be properly handled by gnomes who know which life-forms are required in this new world of ours. You must hand her over, Miggot."

"Absolutely not, Poxy."

There was a rumbling of agreement and Poxy suddenly became aware that he faced some thirty hostile gnomes. "Bugger you, then!" he cried. "You'll suffer for this!"

And so saying, he whirled his rabbit around and ran full tilt into an elm.

"Leave him there," said the Miggot. "We have more important matters to consider. We will reconvene at the blasted oak!"

"Shouldn't *I* have said that?" Bison asked Lady Duck privately. "I'm the one who's supposed to call meetings, surely?"

"Gnomedom has come to a pretty pass, Bison," his wife said unhappily.

10

WEDDING DAY

NYNEVE HEARD FOOTSTEPS ON THE FOREST PATH AND brushed away her tears impatiently. She would *not* show any signs of weakness on this particular day. Her misery gnawed at her heart like a hungry beast, unappeasable. Perhaps the answer lay in death. One day, when they found her body pale and lifeless in some lonely forest dell, they would be sorry. *He* would be sorry. He might even cry a little.

"Well, hello, Nyneve. Hello, hello!"

Merlin shuffled toward her, rubbing his hands together in that irritating fashion that always made her think he was limbering up to grab her. After the thousands of years he had lived, wasn't the flame of his libido due to flicker out?

"Go away, please, Merlin. I'm thinking."

"And crying, too, I'll be bound." He crept around her as she turned away, and peered up into her face. She was a good inch taller than he, but this hadn't prevented him from trying to overpower her in the past. "This is a sad day for you, young Nyneve. A day for thinking. A day for hard decisions. Forget him, Nyneve. He's let you down."

"He's . . ." She choked, then continued. "He's just ful-filling what he thinks is his destiny. And it's all my fault. I put Gwen in the story. And today he's going to marry her. And I love him more than anyone in the world. Oh, God!" She managed a laugh. "What a bloody stupid mess I've gotten myself into!"

He sidled closer. "I could make you happier."

"You!"

"You could close your eyes. Imagine it's him."

"That's disgusting! Don't you ever give up, Merlin?" She whirled around on him, eyes like hard black stones, and seized him by the throat. "I've a good mind to just squeeze the life out of you, you old goat. That'll make the world a better place, if not a happier one!"

He twisted away. "It's not natural," he shouted, "tormenting a man like this! How do you think I feel, seeing you around the cottage every day? It's enough to drive a man crazy, all this frustration!"

"Then turn yourself into a gnome. They think sex is horrible—and right now, so do I!"

"Well, I happen to enjoy it, what I remember of it. I'm happy to be a man. Or at least," he said, correcting himself, "a Paragon."

"According to Avalona, Paragons are perfect creatures, a part of Starquin just like Dedos."

"But in the male form." He leered. "With all that implies."

She stared at him furiously. The wedding would be in progress by now, and in due course Arthur and the vapid Gwen would be in bed together, romping happily between clean white sheets. How had she let this happen? She knew the legend, so she should have been ready for any blossoming romance between Arthur and Gwen. But all the talk had been of *Lancelot* and Guinevere, and somehow she'd been caught by surprise. She'd been busy with the gnomes and their problems, and Arthur had been rebuilding the Great Hall and the Round Table. And now this. A sudden wedding announcement, and Arthur unavailable for comment.

"To hell with all men!" she shouted. "To hell with Arthur!"

"That's better." He smiled at her, encouraged.

"And to hell with you too! You brought that little bitch into the forest!"

"Acting under Avalona's orders."

"You could have disobeyed them!"

"Just you try disobeying Avalona's orders sometime, my girl."

"Well, I'm not standing for it!" An idea was germinating in her mind, and it followed the course of the legend so closely, she could almost believe the seed had been planted by Avalona. "Get me a horse, Merlin!"

"I have no horse. I've always *wanted* a horse, but Avalona has seen fit to mount me on a mule. I can lend you a mule."

"For Christ's sake, Merlin, can you really see me riding into the wedding feast on a mule? I'd be the laughingstock of Mara Zion!"

His eyes widened. "You intend to fulfill the legend?"

"I can't see why the hell not. I mean to ruin that stupid wedding if it's the last thing I do. Now bring me a horse white as snow—I mean, a white horse. I've been talking to the gnomes too much lately. Bring me a white horse. At least do that much for me, and I'll be on my way."

"Nyneve, even if you were to remove your blouse for me, I couldn't bring you a white horse."

"I thought you had powers."

"I don't think anyone really has powers," the old Paragon said sadly. "Avalona is only clever, that's all. Everything has a logical explanation. I don't know where the magic has gone to. It's a shame."

"Bugger you then, Merlin!" she snapped. "I'll steal a horse. Everybody's at the bloody wedding, anyway. I'll steal a horse, and you'll see what I'll do next. I'll make sure that wedding is a bloody disaster, or my name's not Nyneve!"

She swung around and ran down the path, black hair flying like a mane.

Merlin watched her go. "You cunning old witch, Avalona," he muttered.

"Is that really you in there, Arthur?" whispered Gwen as she knelt beside the heavily armored figure. "Couldn't you raise the visor, perhaps?"

"It won't stay up," came the muffled reply. "I'm not going to risk it clanging shut in the middle of the ceremony. The Archbishop wouldn't like it."

"He doesn't look much of an Archbishop. His cassock looks borrowed, like your armor. It's too big for him."

"He's come all the way from Canterbury—Menheniot arranged it."

"Isn't Canterbury Saxon territory?"

"That explains the clothes. He was probably stripped and robbed on the journey, and had to borrow a cassock from a local priest. Robbers often strip people, so they tell me."

"A robber would need a strong stomach to strip that fellow. He could do with a damned good bath in holy waters."

"Have you never heard of an ecclesiastical smell?"

"And did you have to wear the armor? I like that green doublet better. It suits you, with your hair and everything."

"This is an official occasion," came the muffled reply. "I must be in uniform. Anyway, it's a bit late to start talking about doublets now. Start praying, Gwen. The Archbishop's about to begin."

The tiny chapel was packed with villagers and soldiers. One wall had been removed, allowing a view of the ceremony for a further crowd of several hundred gathered among the tombstones. The chapel roof sagged slightly as a result but was shored up with sturdy timbers. The congregation, sensing the approach of a historic moment, stilled.

"Dearly beloved," began the Archbishop in a thick French accent, "we are gathered here today . . ."

"I thought he was supposed to be the Archbishop of Canterbury," whispered Gwen. "He sounds more like the Archbishop of Calais, for God's sake."

"To join in 'oly matrimony . . ."

"Our Church has a strong French influence. Apparently the Archbishop wanted to conduct the ceremony in Latin, but the Baron talked sense into him."

"Thank heaven for small mercies. Not that it really matters what language he uses, as long as he gets it over with."

The Archbishop, sensing he was losing the attention of the young couple kneeling at his feet, raised his voice to a roar.

"The state of marriage, blessed . . ."

"Do I detect a certain irreverence in you, Gwen?"

"You could say that."

"That's nice. I have difficulty believing all this stuff myself." Arthur had raised his head and was squinting through his visor at the Archbishop. "Strange. He sounds quite normal when he shouts."

"Maybe that's why people always shout when they're talking to foreigners."

"No. That's not what I meant. I'd almost say he had a local accent."

Arthur regarded the Archbishop: a slim figure burdened by the enormity of his filthy cassock. The little cap hung over his ears as though dropped by a chance breeze, and his hair was a peculiar bluish shade, as though dipped in woad. The face was narrow, with a long jaw, but the skin was blurred with grime and streaked with crimson so that it was not possible to form an exact impression of the features.

"He looks as though he's crawled out from under a raspberry bush," said Gwen, echoing Arthur's thoughts.

"Arise," said the Archbishop testily.

Gwen rose gracefully to her feet but Arthur remained where he was, struggling under the weight of armor.

"Help him up!" snapped the Archbishop. "Are you trying to make a mockery of the whole ceremony?"

Torre, the best man, grasped the groom under the armpits and hauled him into an upright position. "Do you have the ring?" asked the Archbishop.

"I have the ring," said Torre.

Meanwhile Arthur had tugged off a gauntlet. "With this ring," he repeated after the Archbishop, "I thee wed." And he continued, faultlessly, to the end of his piece.

Tears glistened in Gwen's eyes as she repeated her vows in a low voice. Arthur watched her, holding his visor open with his free hand. The summer sun speared through the windows of the little chapel, pinning down the moment in time, fixing a nodal happentrack. Whatever else might have happened in the past, or might happen in the ifalong, Arthur *did* marry Guinevere, and for a while he loved her.

"Those whom God hath joined together," shouted the Archbishop, startling the bats from their day's sleep among the rafters, "let no man put asunder!

"And that means *you*, Lancelot, you slimy bastard," continued the Archbishop unexpectedly, pointing his finger at a startled figure halfway down the aisle, "because the good Lord knows full well what evil dwells within your heart!"

And so a most unusual ceremony came to an end, and the congregation surged in an unruly mob toward the horses.

Pan, the Miggot's elfin adversary, was a curious being. Neither man nor gnome, he had been fashioned by the kikihuahuas as a catalyst for the Sharan. He alone was able to communicate with her telepathically, but he did not always use this ability for the common good of the woodland creatures. All too often he was motivated by spite. On the morning of the wedding he suffered a typical fit of unpleasantness.

"What do you mean, I can't go to the feast?" he demanded.

"The invitation specified the gnomes of Mara Zion," replied the Miggot. "You don't qualify. You are neither gnome nor human. You are a lesser being. If you were as successful as the gnome species," he continued, holding up an imperious hand as Pan was about to object, "your kind would be more numerous. But you're not. There's only one. You represent an evolutionary dead end, Pan, and you may as well accept it with good grace."

"What's that got to do with not being invited to the wedding feast?"

"Well, you can't go, and that's all there is to it. Do your duty and look after the Sharan, and I'll be back in late evening. Drunk, I hope, so you'd better keep out of my way.''

He mounted his rabbit and rode off, leaving the sole member of a failed species fuming.

Pan sat beside a particularly charred root of the blasted oak all morning, his back turned to the Sharan, who grazed nearby. He wished all kinds of disaster on the principals at the wedding.

''Bugger them all!'' he shouted angrily.

Something of his frustration communicated itself to the Sharan, and she looked up, snorting nervously. Pan swung around and glared at her. ''And bugger you too!'' he yelled, directing a flash of mental hatred at her.

The Sharan began to trot to and fro, bleating.

Pan regarded her thoughtfully.

He'd goaded her into bolting before, and he could do it again. It caused people endless trouble when the Sharan bolted. And particularly now, when the happentracks had joined and the forest was alive with humans. And with everybody at the wedding, the Sharan could be many miles away before the Miggot got back. . . .

There used to be a dragon called Morble on the gnomes' old happentrack. He had been created by the Sharan as a familiar and a protector for Avalona and Merlin. He was a great and terrible creature. The Sharan had squealed with fright when he had emerged as a fearsome embryo from her womb, and she had refused to nurse him. The gnomes had kept him alive for fear of reprisals from Avalona, and as soon as he was able to fend for himself—which was surprisingly soon—they had released him into the forest.

Since the joining of happentracks, Morble had not been seen. It was thought that he was now living on a world of plants and trees where no other sentient creature existed that might cause a branching of happentracks. That way Avalona could find him whenever she wanted him.

But the Sharan did not know that. For all the Sharan knew, Morble could be emerging from the trees (and Pan directed the image at the Sharan) *right now, huge and hungry and*

*infuriated with the mother that had denied him comfort when
he most needed it. . . .*

With a bleat of terror the Sharan fled.

"Torre," said Arthur, "I have to talk to somebody. Sit
down and have a drink."

The Great Hall of Mara Zion was decked out with bunt-
ing and summer flowers, and the women of Mara Zion were
dressed to match, looking like ladies for once in their lives.
The Round Table, big enough to seat fifty ruffians pleased
to call themselves knights, was rapidly disappearing under
a steaming burden of platters. Meat there was in plenty:
roast beef, venison, lamb, pheasant, partridge—any unwary
forest creature that was not humanoid in form had been shot
during the past weeks and brought to the Great Hall to hang
and ripen for the wedding feast. The platters themselves
bore the crest of Menheniot. They were on loan for the day
and had been carefully counted.

Crazed by the sight and scent of so much food, the guests
trotted about the Great Hall like excited horses, chattering
and drinking, waiting for the signal to be seated. The
gnomes sat on a dais out of range of stamping feet, eyeing
their own vegetarian dishes hungrily. Beach gnomes and
forest gnomes sat at separate tables.

Beside the Round Table was the head table where Arthur
now sat, Bull's-eye at his feet, joined for the moment by
Torre. "What do you want to talk about?" asked the latter,
hoping that whatever it was, it wouldn't delay the eating too
long.

"All this." Arthur waved an arm at the gathering. "I
have mixed feelings, Torre. I feel at the mercy of events. I
don't know who I am or what I am. What do all these people
expect of me? Do they really think I'm going to fulfil Merlin's prophesies? I've been in the forest long enough to know
Merlin is little more than an old fool. And did he really
prophesy anything, or were he and Nyneve simply telling
stories around the countryside in return for board and lodg-
ing? Are we trying to act out a work of fiction like strolling

players? For God's sake, why does everyone take those stories so seriously?''

"You had to be there, Arthur. They were *real.* "

"If they were real, what am I? And what about this girl Guinevere? She's a stranger to me, Torre, and yet she's my wife.'' He stared moodily across the Great Hall at Gwen, a vision in blue and pale gray, talking to a group that included Gawaine and Lancelot. "And tonight I have to sleep with her."

"Not too onerous a task, I hope?"

"How do I know? I have no real feeling for her. She's pleasant to look at. Some men might think she was beautiful. And she's reasonably bright and easy to talk to. But when I'm alone with her, I don't feel any stirrings. Tonight could be a disaster, Torre. I don't want to let her down—or myself, for that matter."

"You're not the first new husband to feel like that. She's probably as nervous as you. Just eat plenty of meat and drink enough wine, but not too much." A flicker of curiosity crossed Torre's face. "Forgive my asking, Arthur . . . but have you ever bedded a woman?"

"I wish I knew."

"Have you ever *felt* like bedding one?"

"Yes, as a matter of fact I have."

"Might I ask who?"

"You might, but I'm not telling you." A vision of a young girl danced in Arthur's mind: dark where Gwen was fair; bouncy and sparkling where Gwen was quiet and reserved. "And there's another thing," he said hastily, before the thought could develop any further. "Has it ever occurred to you what people will say if Merlin's predictions don't come to pass? Here we are, a crowd of villagers in an overgrown barn, acting like knights and ladies. So how am I going to become king? I have no army; just you people. Sooner or later Mara Zion will get tired of waiting, and then what?"

"It is in the lap of the gods."

"I tell you, Torre, I'm in a tricky position." He glanced at a dark, smiling man in faultless dress, talking to a more roughly clad villager on the far side of the Great Hall. "What Menheniot must think of us, I don't know," he said unhappily. "I wish Governayle had been able to get here—he'd bring a touch of common sense to all this."

"What do you think of our wedding feast, Baron?" asked Ned Palomides. "Quite a good show for Mara Zion, eh?"

"A splendid occasion."

"And our new leader, Arthur. Somewhat different from the late Tristan, thanks be to the Lord."

Baron Menheniot frowned. "Tristan was a good man, as is Arthur. I regret having killed Tristan. It was a most unfortunate accident."

"But all that's forgotten now. Mara Zion and Menheniot are allies. We stand together against the Irish and the Saxons and anyone else stupid enough to pit themselves against us. And Mara Zion is strong with Arthur as its leader." Palomides shot the Baron a sly look. "It must be reassuring for you to have such a strong neighbor."

"You are quite a devious fellow, Palomides, do you know that?"

"So I've been told. I use my eyes and ears and I learn things. And I look ahead and plan." Palomides drank deeply from his mug, belched, and swayed toward the Baron. "As should Arthur, if he intends to be Ing of Kingland. Although somehow I don't think he will be. There are forces at work, Baron, forces to be reckoned with."

"Are there, now?" The Baron tried to move away, only to find a sweaty hand clasped around his forearm.

"Forces to be reckoned with," repeated Ned, pleased with the expression. "Are you with me or against me, Baron?"

Infuriated, Baron Menheniot snatched his arm free. "I am totally indifferent to you, Palomides," he said, walking away.

"Always remember I gave you the chance," Ned called after him.

The Baron, sighting the Archbishop nearby, approached.

"That was a convincing performance," he said quietly. "Although you got carried away toward the end."

"That Lancelot is a pain in the ass." The Archbishop glowered at the perfect knight, who was talking to Guinevere on the far side of the room.

"All the same, I think you should make your peace before you leave."

"Leave?" The Archbishop regarded the laden Round Table. "Who said anything about leaving?"

"It's hot in here. You're sweating. All that stuff's coming off your face and someone will recognize you any minute. Anyway, thanks for helping us out. When the real Archbishop failed to appear, I didn't know what we were going to do. I'd given my word to Arthur."

"You like Arthur, don't you?"

"I trust him. He's an honorable man. It's almost a pity the legend is all nonsense. He'd have made a better king than most. Come on, let's make peace with Lancelot. He has a lot of influence around here too."

"So do you think I look pretty, Lancelot?"

"Enchanting, my dear. Arthur is a very lucky man. Every man in the Great Hall wishes he were in Arthur's place."

"Including you?"

"Of course."

"You don't lie convincingly, Lancelot." She sighed. "Why does everybody suppose you and I to be lovers? Isn't it possible to be friends without climbing into bed together? You know whose fault this is, don't you? It's Nyneve's. Her stories were getting boring and she needed to spice them up a little."

"Has it ever occurred to you that she may have designs on Arthur?"

"Of course it's occurred to me. She once told me as much. But she doesn't stand a chance—I'll see to that. She's just a little village girl, but I'm to be Queen of England. I'll simply brush her aside. I'll have her burned at the stake for a witch, if need be," she added, warming to her theme.

"They tell me she has strange powers. She's going to need them."

"You can't have it both ways, my dear. Either her stories were pure invention, in which case it's unlikely you'll ever be Queen of England—or they are true prophesies, in which case Nyneve could be a very dangerous enemy."

"The only prophesy that's come true so far is that I married Arthur. And what a bloody fiasco that was, with Arthur and his armor and that weird Archbishop. No wonder the Church is in disrepute. How could he insult you in public like that, Lancelot?" She sighed. "And here he comes now, with the Baron. Try not to lose your temper."

"That's a thing I've never done, Gwen. Hello, there," he said easily. "This is indeed a distinguished gathering."

The Baron raised Gwen's hand to his lips. "You look beautiful, my dear," he said. "Marriage suits you." His smile was genuine, removing any hint of irony.

"Thank you, Baron Menheniot." She turned to the Archbishop. "And thank you for an admirable ceremony, considering the circumstances."

"The circumstances?" Alarm showed through the greasepaint.

"I understand you were robbed and stripped during your journey from London. What a terrible experience that must have been!"

"Appalling."

"Why do robbers strip people, do you suppose?"

"I . . . to steal their money belts, I think."

"And did they steal your money belt?" she pursued relentlessly.

"Yes. No. We members of the clergy have no worldly pelf."

"That's not what I hear about the Church."

"The Church may be rich, but its servants are poor. Our wealth lies in the next world."

"You have the ability to jump happentracks?" she asked innocently.

"I was referring to Paradise."

"Is it true nobody wears any clothes in Paradise, Archbishop?"

With a groan of despair the Archbishop put his head down and hurried away, cutting a swath through the revelers in his haste.

"Did I say something?" asked Gwen.

The Baron smiled. "Whatever it was, I'm sure his discomfiture is only temporary. Aha!" he exclaimed as a bell tolled. "I think that's the signal for us to be seated."

Conversations ceased. There was a murmur of anticipation as people turned to the Round Table. It was arranged that forty-eight favored guests would sit at the Table. The remaining guests, numbering several hundred, would sit at the smaller tables, on the stairs, on the floor, or anywhere else where they could find room for themselves and their plate.

Arthur stood at the head table, which was laid for two. Guinevere hurried to his side, calling greetings as she passed through the multitude.

The circular bench around the Round Table began to fill quickly. Suddenly there was a commotion. Merlin was on his feet, screeching and pointing.

"No! Nobody must sit in the Hot Seat!"

The Baron, who had been about to lower his muscular buttocks onto the bench, froze in mid-sit. Carved into the table before him were the words HOT SEAT.

"Why not, Merlin?" he asked, amused at the old wizard's frenzy.

"It means certain death!"

"That's a bit risky, isn't it? Why have the seat at all?"

"It's reserved for a knight who hasn't yet been born. He will shine like the rising sun above all other knights, and he will champion the oppressed."

"Whose oppressed will he champion?" asked the Baron, sitting down nevertheless. "Not *my* oppressed, I hope."

"He will champion the gnomes and will have the knowledge to lead them from the brink of disaster into a place of milk and honey."

"Sounds like a giant-sized Drexel Poxy to me," said the Miggot sourly, glancing at the table where the Gnome from the North and his followers sat.

"Shut up, Merlin!" shouted Gawaine. "We want to eat!"

"I'm just a messenger, that's all," grumbled Merlin, as others began to echo Gawaine's impatience. "Just carrying out Avalona's wishes, as usual. Sit in the bloody Hot Seat if you like, Baron. But don't say I didn't warn you."

Arthur struck the floor a sharp blow with a staff.

"Eat!" he cried.

And with a creak of heavy timbers the Round Table and its benchload of guests began to revolve.

Horses were in short supply on that momentous day. Nyneve tried the village first, where children were celebrating the absence of their elders. But the only mounts left were broken-down hacks, whose owners were ashamed to be seen riding them. The good horses had been taken to the chapel near Pentor. However, the sun was high in the sky, and the guests would by now be riding the forest trails southward toward the Great Hall less than a mile away. Nyneve took one last glance at the sorry group of nags and decided to walk it.

She reached the Great Hall at the same time as the first guests and withdrew among the trees to watch. After a while the bride and groom arrived in the carriage lent by Baron Menheniot for the occasion. They dismounted, smiling and waving. Arthur had changed out of his armor and wore a green doublet and black hose. Gwen wore a simple pale blue dress trimmed with gray lace. To Nyneve's prejudiced eye she looked particularly stupid. The guests cheered. Nyneve bit back a howl of anguish. More guests arrived, tethering their horses under the trees.

Nyneve sighted a big white stallion tossing its head and snorting in spirited fashion—an eminently suitable beast with which to disrupt a wedding feast. It was tethered to a beech a little apart from the other animals, probably because of its mettlesome nature. As the last guests filed into the Great Hall, Nyneve crept forward, unhitched the reins from a low bough, and mounted.

She rode quietly away, intending to kill time until the feast was in progress. The stallion moved gracefully, well under control. When she was safely out of earshot, she urged him into a gallop. Branches whipped past her face, sunlight alternated with flitting shadows, the wind cooled her face and lifted her hair, and her misery was soon transformed into exhilaration.

"Yaaah!" she yelled. The powerful back of the stallion surged beneath her, and for a moment the world looked good.

Then, unexpectedly, the horse shied.

Nyneve left the saddle, saw the ground rising to meet her, curled herself into a ball, and rolled. She came to rest with a thump against the bole of a tree and, blinking dizzily, saw the cause of her horse's sudden fright.

The Sharan trotted past, head down, drooling.

Nyneve hurried after her, the wedding feast forgotten for the moment. The Sharan must be caught and returned to gnomedom, quickly. If at all possible, she should be kept out of human view; Fang had warned Nyneve of the implications if the Sharan became a common sight around the forest.

"Let the giants think she's just an ordinary unicorn," the little man had said. "They don't expect to see unicorns very often. If they find out what the Sharan can do, they might start getting funny ideas. They're not so scrupulous about creation as the Miggot is."

And Nyneve knew Fang was right.

"Here, Sharan!" she called. The animal snorted and broke into a gallop. Nyneve ran for the stallion, threw herself into the saddle, and set off in pursuit. "Sharan!" she shouted desperately. Matters worsened as they burst from the trees and the Great Hall came into view. An excited barking broke out, and a pack of dogs joined the chase, snapping at the Sharan's heels. Terrified, the animal sped for the open door of the Great Hall.

* * *

"It's wonderful, Arthur," said Gwen. "How did you do it?"

The Round Table, with its great circular bench, rotated slowly past them; first one guest and then another would glance around, nod and smile, then abandon himself once more to gluttony. Arthur and Gwen sat at their separate table; therefore no knight could consider himself favored above others. Each had his turn in honored proximity to Arthur.

"The trick was more in keeping it secret." He laughed, tossing a beef rib to Bull's-eye. "The Table stands on an axle extending down into the cellar. It revolves in a box of tallow on the cellar floor."

"But what turns it?"

"A team of horses in the cellar. Four of them, harnessed to arms projecting from the axle. It's all very scientifically advanced. Even Merlin was impressed. He said Avalona couldn't have done better herself."

"I'm proud of you, Arthur," said Gwen, and she slipped her hand under the table and squeezed his thigh.

He regarded her, feeling a faint but welcome tingling in his loins. There was no doubt she was pretty today. And the blue dress revealed just enough of her breasts to intrigue a man without frightening him off.

"Lucky man, Arthur," called Baron Menheniot, swinging smoothly past.

"What's that?" exclaimed Gwen suddenly.

A commotion had broken out at the far end of the Great Hall. They heard shouting and the crash of breaking pottery. A table overturned, then an animal came dashing among the festive crowd: silver white and goat-sized, with a single golden horn projecting from its forehead. It was the horn more than anything else that had caused the uproar. The animal was singularly careless about where it was pointed.

Bull's-eye jumped up with a bark. The unicorn, which had been making for the head table, veered aside and bounded onto the Round Table, skidding among the platters and scattering them into the laps of the diners. Bull's-eye jumped up and attacked the unicorn viciously, snarling and leaping for the throat. The unicorn shook him off. Then the village dogs came pouring into the Hall in full cry, followed by a young girl on a white stallion.

"It's that little bitch Nyneve!" cried Gwen. "What the hell does she think she's playing at?"

People had jumped to their feet to catch the unicorn and control the dogs. Now they scattered as the stallion cantered up to the Round Table and, urged by Nyneve, climbed onto it to join the Sharan and a dozen dogs. The gnomes, anxious to protect the Sharan, began to slip between the diners and scramble onto the Table too.

"Get her down from there, Arthur," cried Gwen. "She's spoiling everything!"

Arthur gazed up at Nyneve, fascinated. She was wearing a man's white shirt with full sleeves. The front was trimmed with lace and carelessly buttoned; from where he sat, he caught a glimpse of the underside of one brown breast. Her leather skirt was short and her bare legs long, muscles tense as they gripped the flanks of her horse. She shook her hair away from her face, swinging it back in a rippling black wave, and stared arrogantly at her audience.

Stunned into silence, her audience stared back. The dogs stopped barking as they realized there was food all around them, free for the taking. Nyneve struck a dramatic pose, head back, one hand high. The audience held its breath, waiting for her to speak.

Nyneve came to her senses.

Suddenly she became aware of her situation. What in hell was she doing up here? The blur of faces became real people: Arthur, Guinevere, Pellinore, Palomides, Gawaine, Torre, all watching her, all registering every nuance of her behavior. Hundreds of people, each one storing a memory of her sitting on a stolen horse, standing on the remains of a ruined feast, half mad with jealousy and humiliation, revolving slowly as though on display. She would see this memory in the faces of those people from this moment on, whenever she met them in the forest. It would be there, haunting her, until every last one of them died.

Perhaps she should die first, and be free of them all. What a gesture that would be! They should remember her death rather than her disgrace. She dropped her hand to the dagger at her waist. Death for the love of Arthur! She would shout those words and insure herself a place in the legends of the land. The dagger was in her hand now, mere inches from her breast. Good-bye, Mara Zion! Good-bye, forest creatures. Good-bye, rabbits, gnomes, Fang! Her soft breast that hurt when men touched it too roughly, yet felt so good when the hands were kind. . . . Don't lose resolve! Now cut through that breast into the heart thumping beneath!

Now!

And the words! Shout the words!

Now . . .

Why was her hand trembling so? Why was her breast so sensitive, so painful? Why was her body suddenly so precious?

Why was she starting to cry?

Her hand dropped to her side. Through a mist of tears she saw people climbing onto the table, clawing for her.

"To hell with you all!" she said, sobbing. She clapped her heels into the flanks of the stallion and urged him into a standing jump from the table.

The structure emitted a groan and tilted. Platters slid. People scattered as Nyneve left the Hall at full gallop.

"That poor girl," murmured Arthur. Gwen glanced at him but said nothing.

The Round Table, revolving askew, jammed against the floor and stopped.

It was the mortal blow. The horses in the cellar, already thrown off-balance when the axlebox slid out of position, panicked as the jerk brought them to a sudden halt. They threw themselves against the harness, plunging and neighing. In the Great Hall the table made one rapid revolution, scattering gnomes, food, dogs, and the Sharan. In the cellar the axlebox skated across the floor, coming to rest against the wall with the axle tilted at an angle of forty-five degrees.

The sudden strain proved too much for the joists, and the floor collapsed with a series of sharp, splintering reports. The axle broke, and the Round Table, with its complement of diners and food, disappeared into the cellar with a crash heard by the children in Mara Zion village a mile away.

Arthur and Gwen sat stunned, staring into the yawning hole in the floor. The Sharan bolted for the forest, followed by the village dogs, including Bull's-eye.

Catching sight of Torre picking himself up, Arthur said, "Send Pellinore after that damned Nyneve and bring her to me. I'll deal with her, Avalona or no Avalona. And get Gawaine and a couple of others to help the gnomes catch the Sharan. And you, go and get that bloody dog of mine. I'm going to thrash him to within an inch of his life!"

There was a long silence. Gwen and Torre stared at each other.

"Get on with it!" shouted Arthur.

"Arthur," said Torre quietly, "you've fulfilled the prophesy."

"What you just said . . ." whispered Gwen. "It's *exactly* the way the story goes. You couldn't have known. You never heard the story."

"Bugger the story!" snapped Arthur, staring down into the cellar. Cries and groans rose out of the wreckage. "How bad is it down there?" he called.

"A few bruises," came the voice of Gawaine. "Gaheris seems to have a broken leg, and Kay's arm doesn't look too good. We need help down here. I can see somebody still trapped under the table. Bring some light, will you?"

Torches were lit and passed down through the wreckage. The horses were calmed and led away. Balks of timber were placed under the edge of the fallen table, and teams of men struggled to lever it off the trapped man.

Arthur and Gwen hurried down the cellar steps, arriving as the inert form was being dragged clear by the shoulders. The head hung at an unnatural and terrifying angle.

"It's the Baron!" Gwen exclaimed. "Is he badly hurt?"

Lancelot was kneeling beside the man, his ear pressed to the broad chest. When he looked up, his face was sad. "I think he's dead, Arthur," he said.

"He paid the penalty for sitting in the Hot Seat," said Merlin gloomily. "I warned him, but he wouldn't listen."

The word passed from mouth to mouth, and up in the Great Hall the sorrowing began.

11

THE ODYSSEY

"**I**T'S NIGHTS LIKE THIS," SAID FANG, "THAT MAKE you wonder why humans build their dwellings aboveground."

He was slumped comfortably before the fire with a mug of beer clasped in both hands. The Princess sat opposite, rocking the baby in its crib. Fang found himself smiling proudly. It was an instinctive reaction, the way his face fixed itself into a grin whenever he looked at baby Will. Now three weeks old, the funny little creature was beginning to assume a reassuringly gnomelike appearance.

"We'll never call him Willie," he said. "My father still calls me Willie sometimes. It's a stupid name. It discourages a gnome from doing anything with his life. You have to be careful with names. Look at the Miggot's cousin Hal. He started calling himself Hal o' the Moor and now he's stuck with living up there. Can you imagine what Pentor's like on a night like this?"

"Will sounds positive," said the Princess. "It's the opposite of Won't."

"Gnomes need something positive these days. I dropped by the new Disgusting this afternoon and Clubfoot was telling me things are bad for gnomes everywhere. It's the human influence. Gnomes are dying in accidents and there are new kinds of diseases. And the birthrate isn't fast enough to keep up with the losses. Our species is becoming extinct, Princess.''

''Not in this dwelling it isn't.''

''Well, we both know why *that* is.'' And overcome with a most ungnomelike lust, he leaned forward and gently squeezed the Princess's right breast. Female gnomes have large breasts at any time, but when nursing, they swell to gigantic proportions, ideal for fondling.

''Fang . . . ?''

''Yes?''

''I don't know quite how to say this, but . . . Don't you think it's time we got married?''

''Married?''

''Don't frown like that, Fang. Most gnomes who live together are married. It only needs Bison to say a few words and the thing's done.''

''I don't see the point, Princess. It doesn't *mean* anything. I can see it with *humans,* because they need to get the general consent of other humans to them indulging in filth every night. Marriage is a big and dirty step for humans. And it doesn't always work out for them, either. I hear there's all kinds of trouble at Castle Menheniot. Nyneve told me that Lady Guinevere's done nothing but complain for the last six months, ever since she and Arthur moved in. She says it doesn't measure up to Castle Camyliard. And she keeps asking when she'll be Queen of England.'' He chuckled. ''That's a hard question for any husband to answer!''

''You and I are not humans, Fang.''

Fang smiled expansively. ''Gnomes don't need ceremonies. Gnomes live together for companionship.''

''The Miggot and Elmera are married.''

''The Miggot's regretted it ever since.''

The Princess stared at him, aghast. ''Are you saying *you* might regret it, Fang?''

''Absolutely not, Princess,'' he said hastily. ''Absolutely not. Why, only yesterday I was saying to Bison—''

''So we'll get married, then.''

Fang took a deep breath. "Yes," he said.

And there came a pounding at the door. It was a second too late to save Fang from committing himself. For a moment he had a wild notion of sucking at the air to draw the word back. The Princess was smiling happily. It was not that Fang didn't want to be married. The problem was *getting* married. If he and the Princess had gotten married a year ago when he was leader of the gnomes, it would have been a great occasion and an opportunity for feasting.

But now, with Bison in charge and half gnomedom living at the beach under Drexel Poxy's rule, a wedding would be a sneaking affair, almost an admission of defeat. The Gooligog would ride in from Poxy's camp.

"Not before time, Willie, you filthy young swine," his father would say, brushing shyteshit from his shoulders.

It would be like admitting the Princess and he were wrong in their love of sex. And Fang was becoming convinced this was not the case—particularly since hearing the dire stories of plummeting population.

"Aren't you going to answer the door, Fang?"

"Oh, yes. Of course. I was thinking."

Fang flung open the door in welcoming gnomish fashion, to find the piercing eyes of the Miggot boring into his—a depressing sight on a comfortable evening.

"Fang."

"Miggot."

The Miggot hurried in, stamping snow off his boots. "You must come—"He broke off, staring at the crib. "What's that?"

"Little Will, of course."

"Yes. I'd forgotten. It's time you were married, Fang, you dirty young bugger. You'll never be leader while you two are living together in filth."

"Maybe I don't want to be leader."

"Bloody nonsense, you reveled in it before, and you could revel again. Think of the decisions you could make! Think of the power you would wield! And now all we have is Bison the broken reed," said the Miggot gloomily. "And half gnomedom living in the thrall of the abominable Poxy."

"At least my father's living in his thrall."

"Your father is a poisonous character," agreed the Miggot. "But then, who isn't? And yet there was a time when it seemed to me he mellowed. Just after he passed on the Memorizing ability to you. I always thought he was glad to be rid of the responsibility, but when I saw how quickly he joined up with Poxy, I wasn't so sure."

"Do we have to discuss such an unpleasant subject?"

The Miggot settled himself comfortably into Fang's chair. "I *like* discussing unpleasant subjects, Fang. And you're the host, so you must indulge me. It seemed to me the shytes were circling a little lower the last time I saw the Gooligog. He can't cheat death for ever. It seemed . . . Fang!" The Miggot's eyes, which had been half shut in contemplation, snapped open. "Why am I talking about your father? We have to get back to the Sharan!"

"The Sharan?"

"She's in labor! That's what I came here for! Get on your jacket and boots, it's a bloody awful night outside. We must attend to her."

Fang regarded the Princess, little Will, and the blazing fire unhappily. "Can't you and Pan attend to the Sharan?"

"I need you, Fang." The Miggot's glare was like twin thrusting swords. "The future of the gnomish species lies in your hands."

"And yours."

"True. But are you forgetting the purpose of this birth?"

"Of course not. The purpose of this birth is to . . ." Fang glanced at the Princess guiltily. Normally they kept no secrets from each other. ". . . is to safeguard the future of the gnomish species."

"Which lies in your hands," pursued the Miggot.

"And yours." Fang pulled on his boots, shrugged into his jacket, and kissed the Princess and little Will. "I won't be long," he said.

"You may be longer than you think," said the Miggot.

The snow was driving horizontally down the forest path, funneled by the trees. The rabbits, blinded, proceeded at a slow lope. Fang and the Miggot clung to their mounts' backs, eyes squeezed tight and trusting to the Miggot's rabbit's sense of direction. The journey seemed unending. The wind rose and the gnomes rode heads down, their caps deflecting the worst of the storm. Somewhere they heard a crash as a tree fell.

At last they reached the blasted oak and secured the rabbits in the lee of an exposed root. Then they made their way to a big chamber, hollowed by moles and supported above by arched roots. The Sharan lay panting in the light of a meager fire tended by Elmera. Pan sat beside the unicorn's head, playing his pipes softly and feeding her soothing thoughts. When the Sharan was in labor, a surprisingly sympathetic side of his nature always emerged.

"Not before time," snapped Elmera. "I suppose you called in at the Disgusting on your way. This isn't my job, you know. You're the Sharan's official guardian, Miggot!"

The Miggot ignored her. "How's she doing, Pan?"

"All right. She seems a bit frightened."

"Let's take a look at the rear end of her."

The Miggot and Pan commenced a close and expert inspection. Fang, embarrassed, tried to open up a conversation with Elmera.

"Bit of a storm outside," he ventured.

"You can look after the fire now. I'm going to bed." She stalked out of the chamber, thin for a female gnome, and trailing an aura of disapproval.

"Does she know?" Fang asked.

"Do you think I'd tell *her* anything?" By now the Miggot and Pan were sitting on the ground, their feet braced against the Sharan's rump, hauling on something about which Fang's mind refused to speculate. "Come and give us a hand, can you? You and Spector and me are the only ones who know about this. Let's keep it that way."

"And me," said Pan. "Don't forget me. I know."

"Yes, and you'd better keep your bloody mouth shut. If

word gets out, the three of us will be in deep manure. We'll be ostracized by gnomedom, and the giants will probably roast us on spits. Pull, you little runt. Pull!''

Fang, reluctantly approaching, was in time to see the Miggot and Pan fall onto their backs as the resistance suddenly ceased.

A human baby lay on the earthen floor.

''Success!'' shouted the Miggot.

''Oh, my,'' said Pan, awed, crawling to his feet and staring. ''Isn't it big!''

''It's a male,'' said Fang.

The Sharan twisted her head around and expertly bit through the umbilical. Then she began to lick the baby with a rough tongue. He uttered a cough, then filled the chamber with a hiccuping, squalling din.

The Miggot was hurrying from the corner of the chamber, trailing an armful of blankets. ''Where the hell has Elmera gone? You can always rely on her to run out in a gnome's hour of need. Go and get her, Fang!''

''Perhaps you ought to get her, Miggot.''

''Oh, for God's sake.'' Thrusting the blankets at Fang, the Miggot ran for the door. ''Wrap the baby up in those!'' he shouted over his shoulder.

The baby was immensely heavy and cumbersome. By spreading the blankets on the floor and pushing, Fang and Pan managed to get him rolled up in them like a gigantic chrysalis. Soon the Miggot and Elmera arrived, the latter wearing a thunderous expression that abated somewhat on seeing the baby.

''If he wasn't so big, he could almost be a new gnome,'' was her comment.

''So feed him,'' snapped the Miggot.

For one appalling moment Fang thought he meant Elmera to bare her scanty breasts; but she urged the Sharan to change position, then guided a teat into the baby's mouth. The baby clearly knew what this was all about and began to suck, waving tiny fists in appreciation. The chamber was suddenly quiet. Fang smiled at the Miggot and Elmera. The

Miggot returned a twisted grin. Pan, his job completed, lay down on a bed in the corner and went instantly to sleep.

"What now?" asked Elmera. "You can't keep that thing here."

"I realize that," said the Miggot.

"And you can't take him away. You'll be seen. You've got yourself into real trouble this time, Miggot. I always said you would, playing God like this!"

"We're moving the baby out tonight," the Miggot told Fang.

"Tonight? In this weather?"

"The weather is in our favor. Nobody will see us. Only a fool would be out on a night like this."

"I'm not a fool, Miggot!" Fang was annoyed. An hour ago he'd been comfortable at home and looking forward to cuddling the Princess in bed, and now he was facing a snowy journey and being called a fool into the bargain. "Bugger you, Miggot!" he snapped. "You can move the baby yourself!"

The Miggot frowned. Fang seemed determined to misunderstand him. "I meant the only people likely to be out tonight," he said carefully, "will be fools and two other people. We will be those two other people. We'll be in the cart, with the baby. The rabbits will pull the cart. Is that clear?"

"But suppose we run into a fool," said Fang worriedly. "Or even a band of fools. They might want to know what's in the cart!"

"Fools have no curiosity, Fang. That's one of their characteristics. Now, Elmera," said the Miggot quickly, before Fang could continue the discussion, "all I ask is that you help us get the baby into the rabbit cart. Then you can go to bed, and Fang and I will take it from there."

The baby, although no taller than a gnome, was immensely heavy, and all three of them were exhausted by the time he was loaded into a cart built specially for the purpose. Unlike the normal rabbit cart, this had four wheels and long shafts to dampen the effect of the rabbit's bounding motion. Both Gene, the Miggot's rabbit, and Thunderer were harnessed to the cart. The gnomes fortified themselves against the cold with beer and loaded several gourds of milk for the baby. Then they rigged a tentlike awning over hoops of hazel attached to the sides of the cart, so that the baby would stay dry.

Elmera watched silently. When they were finished, she said, "Keep him here for a few days at least."

"We can't take the chance. This isn't the kind of secret you can keep from gnomedom. And he gets any bigger, we won't be able to move him. It's now or never, Elmera."

"You're a cruel bastard, Miggot!" she stormed, eyes bright. Then she swung around and ran from the chamber.

The Miggot avoided Fang's eyes. "Elmera has always been a source of challenge to me," he muttered.

Fang said nothing. Silently they boarded the cart and urged the rabbits forward. Once they were outside, the force of the storm hit them, rocking the cart.

They took the beach path directly south from the blasted oak. The snow fell steadily, eddying around them. Drifts built up against the larger trees. They sensed rather than saw these by the way the cart would suddenly slow down. They sat side by side on the open front platform of the cart with the baby, warm and well fed, enclosed behind them. The rabbits plodded on miserably. They didn't like the weather any better than the gnomes did, although they were better dressed to deal with it. Progress was painfully slow. The wind seemed to cut through every crack in the gnomes' clothing. An hour went by, then another, and Fang judged it to be well past midnight. Tiredness overcame him. . . .

He slipped easily into a world a little different from the one he knew, but not much. It was a world he often visited in his dreams. Afterward, when he awakened, he would remember very little, just a vague impression of a human girl standing on the edge of a cliff and watching the sea gulls. . . .

She took off her blouse and laid it over a flaming yellow gorse bush. She stood still for a while, dressed only in a pair of white shorts, as the wind played with her hair. Her breasts were proportionately much smaller than a female gnome's, but they were neat and pink-tipped, and the sleeping Fang could appreciate their beauty. There was one part of the dream that had a nightmarish quality, however, and that came next.

The girl shrugged her shoulders with a gesture that was becoming familiar to Fang.

She spread her wings.

They were large and feathered white, at odds with the rest of her body, and terrifying because of it. She flapped them slowly, facing the sea.

"Oh, why can't I!" she shouted, a dreadful despair in her voice.

And then she was gone and Fang slept on. Different and more gnomelike creatures entered his dreams and brushed away the lingering images of the girl on the cliff. The new creatures were still frightening, however, and he groaned in his sleep.

He was awakened by the jerk as the cart stopped dead. The night was inky black.

"Go and see what the problem is, Fang." The Miggot spoke into his ear.

"But what if it's a fool?" He'd been dreaming of fools who prowled the forest on nights such as this: big gnomes, insane and hairy, with gnarled clubs and a total disregard for the Examples.

"What the hell are you talking about, Fang?"

"Never mind." The image was fading and he began to feel a little foolish himself. He jumped from the cart into the darkness—and found himself imprisoned in snow up to his chest. "Help! Miggot!" he cried.

"What?" He felt the Miggot's breath on his face. "What are you playing at now, Fang?"

"I'm stuck! Pull me out!"

Grumbling, the Miggot got his hands under Fang's armpits and tugged. Fang scrambled back onto the cart, panting. "Try your side," he suggested.

The Miggot peered into the blackness, then lowered a circumspect foot. "It's deep snow here too. You know what, Fang? We're stuck in a drift."

"Perhaps we can dig ourselves out," said Fang.

"How can we? The drift will get deeper the farther forward we go—and rabbits can't go backward; everybody knows that. We're doomed, Fang. The mission is a failure." He slumped back, defeated. "I should have listened to Elmera."

It was this last remark that told Fang how deeply into despair the Miggot had plunged. Cold, tiredness, and lack of nourishing beer had taken its toll.

"I'm going to take a look at the back," he said.

"How can you take a look? It's pitch-black!"

"I'll feel my way around," snapped Fang, losing patience. "I'm not going to sit here until I freeze. I suggest you have a drink of beer and pull yourself together." He crawled into the covered section of the cart. It was warmer here, and the baby seemed to be sleeping easily. He wormed his way past, ducked under the back awning, and stepped carefully to the ground. Here the snow came only to his knees. It would be possible to back the cart out if the rabbits were unhitched from the front and reattached to this end. But the task of unhitching the rabbits and getting them out of the drift would be insuperable. Up front, the snow would be well over his head. Fang sighed and leaned against the cart to consider the situation. The blackness pressed in on him, thick and impenetrable.

Or was it?

Wasn't that a light a little way back? A faint yellow chink, illuminating a thread of snowy ground?

Fang plodded toward it.

It was a door, set into a bank at the side of the path. Snow had been cleared from around it. He pounded on it, shouting. It opened.

Clubfoot Trimble stood there, showing no surprise. "Oh, it's you, Fang," he said in depressed tones. "At least someone had the courage to come out on a night like this. It's very bad for trade, this kind of weather, I can tell you."

"Clubfoot!"

"Who did you expect?"

"Well, nobody really. I hadn't thought about it." And Fang followed Clubfoot into the Disgusting Drinking Hole where a fire blazed merrily and benches stood empty, awaiting customers. "I didn't know you stayed open so late."

"What else is there to do?" Clubfoot's wife had been accidentally killed a year ago, stepped on by a giant whose identity only Fang knew. For a while he'd turned into a recluse and, like the Gooligog, had gone to live in the marshy land to the west. More recently he had been elected to take over from the late Tom Grog as host of the Disgusting. He was a good choice, being given to rambling monologues to which nobody felt obliged to listen and which provided a restful background to serious drinking.

"Clubfoot," said Fang seriously, "Miggot and I are on a mission of great importance. The very future of gnomedom hangs on the outcome of our odyssey. What do you think of that?"

"Odysseys are like life," said Clubfoot, who had ambitions of becoming gnomedom's resident philosopher. "They must be built on a solid foundation of beer."

That statement, made before a warm fire to a cold and discouraged gnome, seemed to embody all the wisdom of the ages. "I'll have a mug of your best dark," said Fang.

The beer was drinkable, but it was apparent that Clubfoot had not yet achieved the high brewing standards of his predecessor. The two gnomes settled at the fireside, feet stretched toward the flames. "Tell me about your odyssey," said Clubfoot. "Where are you bound?"

"Our destination is secret," said Fang, glancing over his shoulder. "And so is our cargo."

"That's good." Clubfoot nodded wisely, a response he'd been practicing lately. "That's good. It bodes well for the future of gnomedom that two distinguished gnomes should undertake a secret odyssey. And where is the Miggot now? Or is that secret too?''

"The Miggot is stuck in a drift," said Fang unhappily.

"Shouldn't you be digging him out?"

Fang eyed him speculatively, wondering how much he might safely reveal. "The Miggot is not personally stuck."

"But the cargo is?"

"The cargo is not personally stuck, either."

"Then what is personally stuck?"

"The cart."

"Oh." A great light dawned on Clubfoot's broad face. "I understand." He thought about it for a moment, then said, "No, I don't understand, Fang. It's probably no business of mine, but I've had experience with carts. And if they are hauled by rabbits, as they usually are, they don't get stuck in drifts."

"I can assure you our cart is stuck, Clubfoot."

"Then what are the rabbits doing?"

"Sleeping, I expect."

"Well, of course you're stuck, if your rabbits are asleep," cried Clubfoot. "You must wake them up. They've been fooling you. I expect they stopped pulling when they ran into the drift?"

"Instantly."

"Well, all you do, Fang, my friend," and Clubfoot rose to his feet and laid an arm around Fang's shoulders, "is to make them dig. Rabbits like lying in snowdrifts because they're out of the wind that way. They won't dig their way out unless they're forced into it. A good kick up the backside will usually improve their selfish attitude. And then they'll tunnel right through that drift, pulling the cart behind. Snow is soft, Fang. It's no obstacle to a rabbit with a determined gnome behind him."

Fang was already draining his mug and wiping the foam from his beard. "You're right, Clubfoot. If you've ever had the feeling I wasn't always listening to you, I'm sorry. It won't happen again. I must go. The odyssey must press on!''

And with these inspiring words he hurried into the snowy night.

He found the Miggot feeding the baby gloomily. "Oh, it's you, Fang. I thought you'd wandered off into the snow to die, not wishing to be a burden to me."

"The odyssey must press on!"

"What the devil are you talking about?"

"I have an idea, Miggot. Leave the baby for a moment and come and watch!"

Grumbling, the Miggot followed him forward. A faint hint of morning had lightened the sky, and now the drift could be dimly seen, rising before them like a pale mountain. From out of the drift poked the dark rumps of two rabbits.

Fang balanced himself on the dashboard and drove a vigorous boot into the right-hand rump.

"What did you kick Gene for?" cried the Miggot, outraged.

To even matters up, Fang kicked Thunderer with equal force.

The rumps stirred. Fang kicked them both again. They became galvanized into action, surging and bucking. Snow began to spray past the gnomes. The cart lurched and began to move forward. Soon the mountainous drift closed over them as they inched their way through a blizzard of snow from the rabbits' kicking paws.

"It's all a matter of understanding rabbits," said Fang a little later as they emerged from the far side of the drift.

By dawn the snow had ceased and the cart was skirting the beach, keeping close under the western cliff to avoid Drexel Poxy's settlement. The sea rolled toward them, choppy and clawed by the wind. They arrived at Pong's cave and reined the rabbits to a halt.

Pong's face peered fearfully out at them.

"Oh, it's you, Fang," he said, relieved. "And the Miggot. That crunching I heard, it must have been the wheels of your cart. For a moment I thought it was Something Else."

"Pong, we come on a mission of grave importance."

"Good. Come on in and have a drink of herb tea."

"Pong doesn't believe in beer," Fang explained to the Miggot.

"You mean the most important leg of our journey is in the hands of a crank?"

"It's the only thing Pong is crankish about. He has this theory that beer changes our behavior."

"Bloody nonsense. It *normalizes* our behavior."

"One has to keep one's wits about one," Pong explained. "Enemies are everywhere. I used to drink beer once, and it made me sleepy. When I'm sleepy, I'm at my most vulnerable."

Tiredness and cold had honed the edge of the Miggot's temper. "You're not talking about that bloody lopster again?" he snarled. "I thought we'd explained all that to you!"

"So you did, Miggot. So you did."

"How are things going in the Poxy camp?" Fang changed the subject hastily.

"Wonderfully well. I've been waiting to talk to you about that for some time." Pong glanced shiftily at them. "I hope you don't mind my . . ."

"Throwing your lot in with Drexel Poxy?"

"Well, yes. You and I have always been friends, Fang, and I wouldn't want this to come between us."

"Of course it comes between us," shouted the Miggot suddenly, voicing a pent-up grievance, "you silly little bugger! Poxy is a conniving swine! Poxy wants to sell us out to the humans!"

"The Great Poxy believes in cooperation, and that's what we're doing. And it's better for all of us. The giants supply us with food and stuff. The Lady Guinevere is a frequent visitor to the beach. She says she is our patron."

"And what do you do in return?"

"Nothing, Miggot. The Lady Guinevere feeds us out of the goodness of her heart."

"Why don't you gather your own damned food?"

"These are early days, and besides, it's winter. The humans have kindly offered to tide us over until the spring crops are available. And there's the Great Poxy's Grand Scheme, of course." He shut his mouth quickly, having said too much.

The Miggot was on to it in a flash. "Grand Scheme?"

"Nobody knows the details. But a whole new series of creatures will be produced, and the beach will flow with milk and honey."

"Listen to me, Pong." The Miggot's eyes were fierce in the light of the fire. "Your Great Bloody Poxy's talking nonsense. I'm the only gnome in Mara Zion who produces new creatures. I am the guardian of the Sharan, and that's the way things are staying!"

"Don't you think that's a little selfish, Miggot? If you persist in that kind of outlook, no wonder the Great Poxy talks about taking steps."

The Miggot stared at Pong, aghast. "Your mind has been warped! You're talking heresy!" With an effort he got himself under control. "You're questioning our whole society, Pong. The Guilds. One gnome, one job."

Pong said, "We're another society now, we beach gnomes. We have our leader and our Memorizer—your own father, Fang—and we need our Sharan. Or failing that, to use the words of the Great Poxy, *your* Sharan. We are new. Our needs are greater than yours."

"Fang, this is worse than I ever imagined! Look at his eyes! Those are the eyes of a fanatic!"

"They do look a little bright. But there's no point in arguing about it, Miggot. We have the journey to consider."

"Pong," said the Miggot, "forget what we've just been talking about. Put it out of your mind and listen to what I have to say. You must take us to Trevarron Isle again. Together with our cargo. The future of the gnomish race depends on it."

"But what about the winter storms!" cried the Intrepid One.

"Pong, look into my eyes. Deeper. Deeper. Think of

nothing at all, and repeat this after me: Bugger the winter storms.''

"Bugger the winter storms," said Pong woodenly.

"The winter storms are nothing to a sailor of my capabilities and genetic structure."

"The winter storms are nothing to a sailor of my capabilities and genetic structure."

"Miggot," whispered Fang, impressed. "How did you do that?"

"The power of the gnomish eye. We'll have no more trouble with him now. Pong! Let us provision the boat for our journey."

Pong stared at him. "We'd be crazy to go out there in this weather. Have you seen those waves?"

"But you said they were nothing to a sailor of your capabilities," Fang reminded him.

"Only because the Miggot wanted me to."

"Pong," said Fang, hating himself for what he was about to say, "do you remember your father? Now, what would people say—what would the Great Poxy say—if they knew that your timidity, and that alone, had doomed the gnomish species to extinction? They would say you were no better than Poop the Craven. The Miggot would make excuses for you, of course, being the kindly fellow that he is. He would say your genetic instability was no fault of your own. But no more would you be spoken of as Pong the Intrepid. Forevermore you would be Pong the Timorous, a victim of your father's genes. And your grandfather, Pew the Valiant, would become suspect too. In fairness to gnomish history, I would have to examine my memory to confirm the accuracy of the exploits that earned him his name.

"However," said Fang quickly, noticing a tear gathering in the corner of Pong's eye, "there is the other side of the coin. All gnomes must know fear in order to overcome it. That's where true courage lies. Do you know fear, Pong?"

"I know fear."

"Then you are a fortunate gnome, for—"

"Let's take the bloody boat and go without him, Fang. You're talking too much."

"For yours is the opportunity to redeem the failures of your father and his father before him, so that evermore the name Pong the Intrepid will be spoken with awe and wonder. Bear in mind that I am the Memorizer. I will remember your deeds this day—and through me, all gnomedom will remember forever!"

And now Pong's eyes were shining with pride.

By noon the wind had abated, but the seas were still restless with the memory of its strength, throwing themselves against the western rocks of Trevarron Isle and raising a spray that drifted inland like fog.

Elaine tasted the salt on her lips as she climbed the ridge. From the summit she could see her world, and a tiny world it was: a fragile land bounded by the white lace of wave against shore. A curtain of sleet hid the horizon so that she stood at the center of a gray sphere, all alone.

She walked slowly down the close-cropped hillside and came to a little cairn. She'd intended to bury the baby on the southern slope, so that he would get the winter sunshine and the early spring flowers. She found a suitable spot but was unable to drive the spade into the ground. Her arms wouldn't work for her. So she'd stood there crying, helpless, while the baby waited in the cottage for its resting place.

Eventually her feet had taken her over the ridge onto the northern slope, and this time the little grave had been dug. She'd fetched the baby, laid him in the bottom of the hole, and pulled the shawl over his face so the soil wouldn't dirty him. Then she'd filled the grave up. She'd cried again when the soil formed a baby-sized mound above ground level, and she piled a few granite rocks around it, to disguise it and yet to mark it.

The Norman warrior would never come back. Elaine knew that now. The death of the baby had severed the link. It was all for the good, because she now realized that the whole thing—the killing of her parents, the murderous warrior's

pretense of love, the pregnancy, the birth, and the death—
had driven her a little insane for a while. Now, a couple of
months later, surrounded by a severe winter that demanded
all her time, she could think more clearly. The Norman
wouldn't come back, and just as well. And the mound
caused by the baby's body had flattened out. Come spring
the grass would grow. Come spring she would take her boat
to Mara Zion and find herself a man.

She arrived at the beach and watched a sailboat reaching
in, regularly disappearing behind the backs of the eastbound
waves, appearing again a little closer. It was very small, a
gnomish boat.

Elaine wondered why the gnomes had come again.

12

SPRING TIDE

OVER THE NEXT FIVE YEARS KING ARTHUR FOLLOWED his legend across the land, spreading the word of chivalry as far as Badon in the east and Wroxeter in the north. The warlords of the hill forts were united, the dry stone walls were pulled down and used to enclose new fields, and roomy buildings were erected where once people had crouched in huts and roofed pits.

At Badon, Arthur and his forces met the Saxons, led by King Aelle.

Castle Badon stood on a singular hill rising from the rolling plains, guarding the junction of two ancient Roman ways: Ermine Street and the Great Ridgeway. It was an important strategic position. Both roads were in constant use, and for a while an uneasy truce existed; Saxon might meet Briton and nod a greeting or draw a knife as the mood took him. Generally, the closer he was to Castle Badon, the more likely he would be to draw the knife. Castle Badon was occupied by the Saxons.

Arthur and his Britons attacked. After three days of fierce battle the Saxons were defeated, with the loss of almost a thousand men. Arthur's forces occupied the castle. The Saxons retreated east reluctantly, burning villages as they went. Arthur paused and looked north.

Mara Zion was a long way behind him.

* * *

One day Fang visited the northeast corner of the forest to collect a pair of hinges from Scowl the Accursed. It was a fine spring morning and he sang in his gruff voice as he rode. On such a day, in such a pleasant part of the forest, the troubles of gnomedom seemed far away.

He saw the smoke of a furnace rising over the trees and soon found Scowl hammering vigorously at a flattened strip of iron. After a while he dipped it in a pot of water with a great sizzling. Finally he held it up and examined it. It seemed to be the blade of a knife.

"Oh, God, what have I done!" Scowl uttered the traditional Absolution.

Fang looked around at the trappings of evil: the furnaces, the bellows, the anvils, the hammers, the pots. It was a curiously empty scene.

"Where is everybody?"

"I'm everybody there is," said Scowl gloomily.

"What happened to the others?"

"They've gone. Or they've died. I don't know. They drifted away. And where does a gnome go when he drifts away from here, Fang? You tell me. Who would let an Accursed Gnome into his burrow and risk being struck by lightning? No, my guess is they've all died."

"But . . . why did they go?"

"They had no work. The giants can make all the things we used to make, and much better, too, because they're bigger and stronger. And they don't have to worry about breaking the Examples. It's a big strain on an Accursed Gnome; we break two of the three Examples every day. And even ordinary gnomes like you feel unhappy about what we do. So people have started getting their ironwork from the giants. It leaves their consciences cleaner."

The sun seemed to have lost its sparkle as Fang rode home, the hinges in his saddlebag. Another gnomish settlement was about to become extinct, and another piece of gnomish culture—although a reprehensible one—would be lost. What could be done?

He lay awake all that night, thinking about it, and by morning had come to an inescapable conclusion.

He put it to Nyneve on his way to the monthly Memorizing meeting. ''Nyneve, I think we gnomes are going to have to leave.''

''You don't mean join up with those stupid gnomes down by the beach, Fang? They're all mixed up with humans! That empty-headed Gwen's adopted them, ever since she came snooping around the forest because she got bored at home. That was five years ago, and she's caused all kinds of trouble since then.''

''We have heard stories,'' said Fang, ''although we try not to have contact with the abominable Poxy and his people.''

''And that unspeakable Palomides is tied up with them. And Lancelot. You think *he'd* have more sense.''

''I know all about Palomides,'' said Fang bitterly. ''He started the whole thing off by killing our rabbits—I saw him do it. And Poxy obviously knew all about it before we'd even told him, so he must be in on it too. Between them, they split gnomedom in half, and I think I know why. They want to get their hands on the Sharan. They've snooped around from time to time, but the Miggot's too clever for them. He keeps moving her from place to place.''

''I didn't know about that!''

''You've had enough problems of your own.''

''I'm sorry. I suppose I haven't been around much lately.''

''Well, anyway, we have no intention of joining Poxy's camp. We've held that little bugger off for five years, and we'll hold him off until the end.''

''Where will you go, then?''

''Back where we came from. Back to the spacebat.''

''Oh, Fang. Are things that bad? How would you get there?''

''I don't know. I've searched my memory lobe and found nothing. Somehow there must be a way for gnomes to get off Earth, and I have to find out what it is. Otherwise we'll die out. We'll become extinct.''

"Unless you all have more children. You've shown them it can be done. You've had three yourself."

Flushing, Fang hurried away to his Memorizing meeting. The Princess and he were inordinately proud of Will, Eve, and Lynette, but their pride was not shared by the rest of gnomedom.

In fact, gnomedom's disapproval of him seemed to have grown over the last five years. This was made quite clear at the official meetings, when Fang committed to memory anything important that had happened during the past month. Fang was indispensable for this purpose—otherwise, he thought gloomily, they would have dispensed with him long ago. Fang was the only gnome who knew the Memorizer's Apothegm, the lengthy saying that unlocked the hereditary memory lobe of the brain and allowed access to memories from the far-distant past. All gnomes accumulated the memories of their ancestors in the memory lobe, but only those who knew the Apothegm could recall them.

Gwen would have thought Fang a pessimist. To her simple mind it seemed everything was going well for gnomes. They were well fed, clothed, and housed; and they had proper jobs—which was something they'd never had before, according to that delightful little Drexel Poxy.

The beach gnomes had been appointed official jesters at Castle Menheniot. They sang and danced for her guests, and in return she had become their patron and protector.

It hadn't been easy to bring about the present situation. Arthur had objected strongly, for one. He'd said it was demeaning for gnomes to be so employed. He'd said they should be left alone to lead their own lives. But recently she'd been able to point to the results of such a policy in other gnomish settlements. Such settlements had simply died out. The gnomes—unable to compete with new animals, new diseases, and the heavy-footed presence of humans—had withered away.

But not her little colony at Mara Zion beach. They thrived. New gnomes were drifting in all the time and joining them. And Arthur spent so little time at Camelot (so convenient an abbreviation for Castle Menheniot that she'd begun to believe it really was the place referred to in the legends) that she had little difficulty in strengthening her relationship with the beach gnomes. Or with those excellent men, Lancelot and Palomides, either. Really, Arthur ought to spend a little less time fighting around the country and politicking in Cirencester, and more time with her. . . . A woman could find time hanging heavily on her hands, left alone in a drafty old castle all day.

Fortunately she was a woman who was interested in making the world a better place for humans and gnomes alike. And now, on this fine spring morning, she was riding south to visit her little protegés, with Lancelot at her side to protect her from bandits. A cart trundled behind, driven by Ned Palomides. Under any other regime Ned might well have *been* one of those bandits, but she had won him over to her cause by treating him like a responsible human being. The cart was loaded with all the things the gnomes needed but were unable to produce for themselves: shovels, knives, tiny metal cooking pots; hammers, nails, and saws for building (her beach gnomes were living in proper little cottages aboveground these days, instead of burrowing like animals). There was even some venison—the gnomes were developing human tastes in food, she was pleased to find.

"Hullo," said Lancelot suddenly. "What's that?" He reined to a halt and peered into the bushes. "I thought I saw something . . . there!" He pointed. "A gnome. Come on out, fellow, and we'll give you a ride south!"

But the creature that emerged was the strangest gnome Gwen had ever seen. He was excessively slender and fragile in appearance, and his face was triangular with tilting eyes. He wore clothes of a soft green fabric, and his cap was made of the same cloth, so that it drooped instead of rising to the usual jaunty point.

"I'm Pan," he said in answer to Gwen's query.

"I thought I knew the gnomes well. I've never seen you before."

The little creature drew himself up, affronted. "I am not a gnome. I'm Pan, as I told you."

"I'm sorry. I thought you meant Pan was your name."

"It's my name, but it's also what I am. I'm one of a kind. There is no other Pan in the forest."

"Impossible!" Palomides chuckled. "It takes two to breed."

"Perhaps your father and mother are dead?" suggested Gwen sympathetically.

"My father and mother are the Sharan."

"Is that so?" Palomides gazed at the little elf with growing interest. "Come and sit on the cart beside me, Pan. Where are you bound?"

"Anywhere away from the Miggot. South is fine. Drexel Poxy has a flourishing colony at the beach, I'm told. Perhaps they'll appreciate me there."

When they came in sight of the beach, however, it became clear that the flourishing colony was receiving a setback. A brisk gale was blowing in from the south, funneling between the headlands at the entrance to the cove and driving long rollers up the sand toward the cluster of tiny huts at the forest edge. To make matters worse, the wind was herding heavy clouds across an angry sky. The first drops of rain stung Gwen's face. She clutched her cloak around her.

A mounted gnome came bounding up, snatching his cap off as the wind was about to carry it away. She recognized him as Mold the Outrageous. "Lady Guinevere!" he cried. "We're going to be flooded out!"

Now she could see hurrying gnomes carrying tables, chairs, cooking pots, and anything else movable out of the houses and up the eastern hillside. Halfway up the rocky slope, a pile of possessions testified to their industry so far.

"But the sea's a long way from your houses," she said.

"High tide isn't till mid-afternoon, and the water's already as high as spring tides usually get! The southerly gale is pushing the sea toward us!"

By now her little friend Pong the Intrepid had arrived on

his rabbit. "The Great Poxy foretold this!" he cried. "But nobody would listen!"

"Sexual intercourse!" shouted Mold in disgust. It was exclamations like this that had earned him his name. Quite possibly, years ago they had been designed to shock the gnomes and to demonstrate his individuality, but now they had become automatic. "It was Poxy who persuaded us to build so close to the beach. 'We ride south!' he said. And when our rabbits began to get their feet wet, he said, 'We stop here!' And where is he now, when we need him most? Nowhere to be seen!"

By now more gnomes were arriving, shouting and gesticulating. It was quite flattering, thought Gwen, that they should be looking to the humans for help.

"Mold's right!" This from the Gooligog, arriving at a slower pace. "We were persuaded to build here by the Great Poxy. I committed the discussion to memory. Would you like me to repeat it verbatim?"

"Action!" cried Mold. "Why are we standing here arguing, when our very homes are in jeopardy? To the cottages, gnomes!" And he dragged ruthlessly at his rabbit's ears, swung him around, and rode for the settlement.

The other gnomes followed, the humans riding behind. Pong guided his rabbit beside Gwen. "There's been some question about the Great Poxy's leadership recently," he said.

"That's nothing new in gnomedom," grumbled Pan to Palomides. "King Bison is walking a tightrope too."

"And the Sharan?" asked Ned. "She's in good health, I hope?"

"I don't want to talk about the Sharan."

"The Great Poxy mentioned the Sharan only the other day, Pan," said Pong. "He felt it might be more appropriate for you and the Sharan to live here instead of in the forest. I don't agree, really," he added unhappily, "but that's what the Great Poxy is saying. I thought I ought to tell you."

"There's sense in that," said Palomides quickly. "This

is a thriving settlement. There must be three times as many gnomes here as in the forest.''

"Is the Sharan so important?" asked Gwen.

"She's the whole reason for gnomish existence," said Pong.

"Then certainly she should be here with our beach gnomes."

Pong sighed. "The Miggot would never come here."

"The Miggot is a cruel and heartless swine," said Pan. "I'm sure I could bring myself to serve another guardian, if one were officially appointed."

"That's settled, then," said Gwen, relieved. Transferring the Sharan made a lot of sense. Now that she came to think about it, Ned had proposed just such a relocation several times over the years. And the Sharan would be a unifying influence on the beach gnomes. It was rather worrying to find little Drexel's popularity slipping.

They arrived at the gnomish village. Over fifty small structures stood on a flat grassy area bounded by the forest to the north, the beach to the south, the rocky bluff to the east, and the brook to the west. Between the village and the beach ran a ribbon of flotsam: driftwood, dry seaweed, sea-gull bones, and empty crab shells, delineating the normal high-water mark. This bank of muck was now heaving as waves began to pass under it. Tongues of water crept across the grass toward the cottages.

Lancelot sprang from his horse and, seizing one of the cottages, tried to drag it toward the forest. Tiny by human standards, it was about four by four by three feet high. It resisted his efforts. "Come and give me a hand with this, Ned!" he shouted.

Somewhat reluctantly, Ned took hold of the building by the eaves. "This is pointless, Lance. We'll never get them all moved in time."

"We have to do *something*, Ned. We can't just stand around watching."

"I don't believe in empty gestures." Ned, still grasping the cottage, made no attempt to lift. "And anyway, it was the gnomes that got themselves into this mess. It's not our problem. Either they're self-sufficient or they're not.''

''For God's sake, Ned!'' snapped Gwen. ''Get on with it. The gnomes are depending on us!''

Grumbling, Ned lifted. Lancelot lifted. With a rending noise the cottage roof came away from the walls, revealing a gnome lying in bed, blinking the sleep from his eyes and regarding them in terror.

''The giants are attacking!''

The scream of warning alerted nearby gnomes to the situation, and they paused in their evacuation, possessions in their arms, worried expressions changing to fear.

''The giants are attacking!'' The word spread up the rocky bluff to the plateau where Bart o' Bodmin was supervising storage of the refugees' possessions. He looked up from his work and saw Lancelot and Palomides for the first time, apparently in the process of destroying the village.

There was not a moment to lose. ''To the dolmens, gnomes!'' he shouted.

He had waited two years for this moment.

The dolmens were Bart's invention. Two years previously, Drexel Poxy's grip on his little empire had begun to slip. A small team of gnomes, whose duties consisted of cleaning out the sewers at Camelot, refused to work. In the course of the endless meetings it became clear that a hard core of dissidents existed who objected quite strongly to many aspects of the gnomes' association with the humans.

''Poxy, you have sold us out!'' cried Bran the Restless.

Although Bran was never seen again—Bart reported seeing him riding west—the echo of his cry continued to reverberate through the village, gnomish memory being what it is. Until, one week later, Drexel Poxy uncovered a frightful situation that drove all else from the minds of the beach gnomes.

That evening as they sat around the village's central fire eating *meat*, a new and tasty food to which the humans had introduced them, Bart o' Bodmin rose to his feet. "The Great Poxy has an important announcement," he said.

Drexel Poxy stood, his eyes reflecting the glow from the fire. "The forest gnomes are preparing for war!" he boomed in a voice worthy of King Bison himself. "We must arm ourselves against the foe!"

There was an outburst of shouting in which could be distinguished the words "Buttocks!" from Mold the Outrageous, and "What foe?" from the majority. "What foe?" they cried, glancing nervously into the shadows.

"I just told you," shouted Poxy irritably. "The forest gnomes!"

"The forest gnomes can't be foes," said Pong. "They are gnomes. You must mean we should unite with the forest gnomes against the common foe!"

"Unite with the forest gnomes," cried the gnomes, relieved. They'd become increasingly unhappy about the rift between them and their inland friends. "Against the common foe!"

"It takes a common foe to make us see sense!" shouted Pong. "It's good to have a common foe again!"

There was a roar of assent. "We must send a message to Bison. We must meet and exchange views. We must make mutual decisions on how to deal with this terrible threat!" Buzzing with excitement, the gnomes began to discuss it among themselves. It would be good to see the forest gnomes again; dear old Bison, sensible young Fang, even the Miggot of One and Elmera. However, it slowly became apparent that their discussions lacked some essential element. There was a void that needed filling. Pong was the first to put it into words.

"Who is the common foe?" he asked.

By now Poxy realized he'd lost the day and must salvage what he could from the wreckage. He stared at the forest for inspiration; at the rocky bluffs, at Pong, at the sea. And suddenly he had a vision of a giant creature rising dripping from the sea on armored legs, pincers snapping.

"The lopster!" he told them. "The lopster is the common foe!"

They groaned with horror and followed his gaze. The sea surged darkly, breaking into threatening little waves near the beach. The lopster, they realized, could come at any moment. The matter was deadly serious.

"If the lopster is the common foe," asked the Gooligog shrilly, "what the hell are we doing living on the beach?"

"We will protect ourselves!" countered the Gnome from the North swiftly.

And so the dolmens came into being.

The dolmens stood on the rocky bluff, a row of great boulders precariously balanced. Bart o' Bodmin had directed the work. A group of Accursed Gnome refugees had dug away the soil and chipped away all extraneous granite from beneath certain big rocks chosen by Bart. When the work was complete, each boulder needed only the slightest push to send it bounding down the bluff toward the beach, and the common foe. The gnomes were all in favor of a trial run with one or more dolmens, to gauge their effectiveness and, of course, to see the splash when they hit the water. But Drexel Poxy would not allow it. "The day will come when we need them all," he'd said darkly.

And so the dolmens had remained poised above the village for two years, but the lopster had not attacked. Bart became a bitter and frustrated gnome. In due course the memory of the lopster faded and the main threat to the village became the dolmens themselves. On stormy nights the beach gnomes shivered in their tiny cottages, dreading each thunderclap, each gust of wind that might result in a dolmen breaking free and careering madly through the village, smashing cottages and gnomes alike. Bart came in for criticism. Poxy made the most of these occasions, however, leading the gnomes in a prayer to the Great Grasshopper, urging everybody to pull together and inveighing against malcontents. Bart, for the first time, experienced some resentment of Poxy's methods.

But now at last, the boulders would prove their worth.

"To the dolmens, gnomes!" shouted Bart o' Bodmin.

Gnomes took up their stations behind the dolmens, levers at the ready. Two years of training were about to pay off. The human peril would be smashed.

"Let go Dolmen Number One!" yelled Bart, lost in a haze of joy.

Three gnomes poked stout staffs under the boulder and leaned against them. The dolmen shifted, rocking. Timing their heave, they tilted the boulder beyond the point of balance. It moved away from them, slowly at first, noisily crushing stones in its path. Then it gathered speed, bounding, bouncing down the bluff.

Cries of alarm rose from below. Gnomes scattered, dropping household items as they ran. The dolmen's shape was irregular and it changed direction with each bounce. The humans heard the commotion but quickly realized they were out of its direct path. Lancelot apologized to the gnome in bed, who by now was frantically pulling on his boots, and replaced the roof. They watched with fascination as the dolmen, about four feet across, smashed its way through the cottages and, its momentum checked, rolled tamely into the sea.

"What the hell are you doing, Bart?" shouted Mold.

But Bart o' Bodmin was drunk with power. "Let go Dolmen Number Two!" he ordered, and yelled with delight as the next boulder sped on its destructive path. He saw the Great Poxy scuttling toward him, shouting. He saw the humans back away from their evil work, crestfallen and defeated. "Let go Dolmen Number Three!" he squealed, and his gnomes bent to their task with a will.

The Great Poxy appeared at his side, face contorted with emotion, reaching for him. He could only assume that his leader intended to embrace him; but now was not the right time. There was work to be done. Fighting off the Gnome from the North, he dispatched Dolmen Number Four.

This one cut a swath through the outlying dwellings and actually passed quite close to the giants. Bart had the satisfaction of seeing Lancelot jump back with a cry of alarm as a broken board spun past his face. It was the last satisfaction Bart had. Drexel Poxy and Mold the Outrageous wrestled him to the ground.

"You have some explaining to do, Bart!" shouted the Gnome from the North.

Meanwhile other gnomes had arrived and overpowered the remaining dolmen teams. The Gooligog came stumping out of the forest where he'd been contemplating his memories, hoping someone else would carry his possessions to safety. Hearing the sounds of destruction, he emerged to find his dwelling reduced to its components. "This day will live in infamy, Bart," he cried. "I'll make bloody sure of that. Your foul deed will echo through the annals of gnomish history."

Bart managed to twist his face out from a tussock of rank weed. "I was defending our village against the common foe! What's the matter with you all?"

The gnomes regarded the sea. Many of the houses were awash by now, but no monster rose from the deeps, no pincers reached for fleeing prey. "I see no common foe," growled Poxy.

"The giants are the common foe!"

"You have it wrong, Bart. We went through all this years ago. The lopster is the common foe."

Lancelot, Gwen, and Palomides arrived, mildly puzzled. "You smashed a lot of houses," said Lancelot. "Why did you do that?"

"Really, Bart," said Gwen, "it was too bad of you."

"I was misinformed," muttered Bart, beginning to understand. "I received poor intelligence. I acted in accordance with information received, and it's possible that a mistake was made somewhere."

"It was inevitable," said the Gooligog. "You perch a row of rocks above a village, and sooner or later someone's going to take a lever to them. If not on this happentrack, on the next. It's gnomish nature. Well, to hell with you all, that's what I say. I'm going to build myself a proper, sensible gnomish burrow at the edge of the forest where it won't get flooded out and where the trees are too thick for these bloody shytes to hover. I should never have been talked into building a cottage. Cottages are for humans, burrows are for gnomes. Good-bye.'' And he plodded back down the rocky road to the beach.

Bart, perhaps hoping to improve the Memorizer's final impression, called after him desperately, ''Have a nice day, Gooligog!''

It was a mistake. The Gooligog wheeled around furiously. ''Doesn't it ever occur to you people that I might not *want* to have a nice day?'' he shouted back.

It was late evening. The tide had receded and the gnomes had moved back into their homes, taking in refugees from the broken cottages until the damage could be repaired, lighting big fires to dry things out. The biggest fire of all roared in the center of the village, and around this sat Lancelot, Gwen, Palomides, various gnomes, and a dead deer.

Bart, striving to reassert himself, said, ''It looks as though we have some problems with our present location.''

Drexel Poxy replied testily, ''We don't have problems, Bart. We've never had problems. We have a few challenges, that's all. Today has been a good day. We've learned some useful lessons today. We've been through a testing time and we've emerged intact, our confidence in the future undiminished, our good friends the humans at our side.''

''And the dead deer,'' Mold pointed out, ''that's at our side too.''

''And the dead deer,'' agreed Poxy, giving it a mystified glance. Its eyes were open though dull, and its tongue lolled from its mouth. It lay slackly on the sand, fur matted. A flock of shytes, left over from the Gooligog's departure, eyed it covetously. ''Our challenge is to prevent a repetition of today's disaster. That will be simple. The remaining dolmens will be disarmed by packing soil and gravel around their bases.''

Pong the Intrepid said, ''I thought today's disaster was

that your houses got flooded out, like I said they would. You should have listened to me. I know all about tides. I've lived in that cave of mine for a hundred years, and my father before me.'' He shut his mouth quickly, flushing. The reference to Poop the Craven had slipped out accidentally, and he hoped nobody had noticed.

''We will build a dyke,'' said Drexel Poxy loftily.

''Why not just move back into the forest? Building a dyke is an awful lot of work.''

''I'm sure our friends the humans will help.''

''Of course,'' said Lancelot, in the process of butchering the deer. Entrails tumbled out at the thrust of a sword, and a dreadful stink arose. Taking his dagger, Lancelot began skillfully to skin the carcass.

''I wish you wouldn't do that here, Lancelot.'' Even Poxy's sensibilities were ruffled. ''Giantish rituals are not always acceptable to gnomes.''

''You want to eat, don't you?''

''Of course. We're all very hungry,'' said Poxy, who had been aware of mutterings of discontent from his followers for some time now. ''But we don't like to say anything.'' He glanced hopefully at the nearby cart. ''We've lost nearly all our food.''

''There was a misunderstanding,'' said Bart quickly, ''and several gnomes spent time carrying their personal possessions up the bluff instead of emptying out the community storehouse.''

''And then it was too late,'' said Poxy ruthlessly, ''because a dolmen smashed the storehouse to pieces and crushed the supplies. They just floated away.''

''On the tide,'' Bart pointed out, becoming annoyed. ''When recalling this day, I hope we will all remember that it was the tide that set in motion the sequence of events resulting in the accidental release of the dolmens. I'm sure none of us want to see gnomish history distorted.''

''You're too late, Bart,'' said Poxy with an unpleasant grin. ''The Gooligog's already made up his mind. You shouldn't have destroyed his house.''

Bart began to wonder if he'd done the right thing five years ago in Bodmin, when he'd thrown in his lot with Drexel Poxy. It had seemed a good idea at the time. But now they were at loggerheads over a simple misunderstanding, and Bart's status was in decline. Before long, thought Bart gloomily, he would be deposed as Poxy's second in command, and Mold the Outrageous would be appointed in his stead.

He must have sunk into gnomish contemplation, because when he next became aware of his surroundings, things had changed. A horrifying mass of flesh was searing on a hellish fire before him, and the gnomes were in an uproar.

"You can't expect us to eat that! That's a dead animal!"

"You've been eating dead animals for years!" A giantish protest.

"Rectums to that!" The voice of Mold making itself heard as usual. "Meat, yes. Meat you brought ready for the pot. Meat in bite-sized pieces that we cooked in our stews and didn't have to think about. Clean, civilized meat. Not this stuff. This is barbaric! The stink when you were cutting it up was bad enough, but now? A severed head on the beach. The eyes looking straight at me. Arms and legs and God knows what hanging there scorching over the fire. And what's that part hanging down there?—answer me that! Look at it all! It could be a huge gnome!"

"It's a deer. You saw it."

Another voice: "You should know we gnomes have a fear of being roasted on spits. It's probably a deep-seated memory of ancient giantish practices, glimpsed in the umbra. Can you honestly tell me you didn't feel queer when you stuck the spit up the bottom of that poor thing?"

Queen Guinevere's voice, tearful: "We didn't have time to cut it into little pieces. You really are the most hypocritical little swine! I've been feeding you and clothing you for five years now, and all I get in return is nastiness and mistrust!"

"We trust you, Queen Guinevere," said the Great Poxy smoothly.

''You trust me enough to jump to the conclusion that my friends are attacking you. You trust me enough to roll rocks down on me. Lance! Take me away from these ungrateful little beasts, before I kick them into the sea! I never want to see them again, ever!''

13

THE APOTHEGM

ONE MONTH LATER FANG PAID A VISIT TO JACK O' THE Warren to discuss the acquisition of a family rabbit, tractable and strong, suitable for carrying a female gnome and three small children. Rabbits being what they are, the depredations of Palomides and Bruiser had long ago been made good.

Mention of Fang's home life brought an envious gleam into Jack's eye. He began to wax maudlin about a gnome from the northwest corner of the forest, with whom he had formed a tentative liaison.

"I like her, Fang," he said. "I really *like* her. Bluebelle." He spoke the name with careful reverence, like a password.

"Well, that's good."

"I wish it was." Jack eyed Fang speculatively. "You're a gnome of the world. You've lived with a female for years. I'm speaking of the Princess of the Willow Tree."

"I'd hoped you were, Jack."

"And you're married. I attended the wedding."

Fang flushed. His wedding had been marred by a curious incident of which he would rather not be reminded.

It was a gnomish tradition that the bride's train should be carried by two children, representing the steady-state population, but at the time of Fang's wedding, the only gnome-child of suitable age was Fang's own son, Will. So the second child had to be carved from wood, mounted on wheels, and attached to the end of the train. Will was instructed in his duties, which included keeping an eye on the dummy rolling beside him.

Gnomish weddings include a parade around a ceremonial fire. This was symbolic of the lust, hopefully as short-lived as the fire itself, that the wedding was supposed to generate in the bride and groom. By the time the parade reached this point, however, little Will had lost concentration. He failed to notice the dummy had cut inward in circling the fire and rolled over some red-hot embers. The wheels burst into flame.

Will squealed, dropped his corner of the train, and ran. The guests panicked. Gnomes are peculiarly inept at dealing with fires, and Fang alone kept his head. Seeing flames quickly spreading up the train toward the Princess, and realizing that she would not have time to undress before they reached her, he threw her across Thunderer's back, jumped on, and urged the rabbit into headlong flight through the forest, the blazing dummy bouncing along behind.

The guests groaned and avoided one another's eyes. The symbolism was so complex that even Spector the Thinking Gnome was stricken into silence. There was no precedent by which to judge the event. However, every gnome present, watching the flight of bride, groom, and flaming effigy, felt in his bones that the portents were not good. It was the kind of incident one could blame crop failures on.

Fang and the Princess returned eventually, drenched, having ridden Thunderer into a pond. Oddly they seemed to think the whole affair was a huge joke. They were surprised to be greeted with awestruck horror, beard twirling, and head shaking. They were disappointed when many of the guests crept away quite early, probably to pray to the Great Grasshopper.

Jack o' the Warren had an anxious look. "What's it *like* living with a female, Fang? When you're with her all the time—day and night, if you get my meaning, Fang—there are bound to be embarrassing moments. Moments when the depths of existence are plumbed. Moments when the basic nature of life is forcibly brought home to you both. Do you understand what I'm referring to, Fang?''

"Moments when filth rears its ugly head?''

"Exactly,'' said Jack gratefully. "I knew you'd understand. No matter how careful you are, those moments will arise.''

"They will. Quite often. You learn to look forward to them.''

"But it's different for you!'' cried Jack. "As Spector once said, you're a gnome subject to uncontrollable lusts. You can shrug those moments off.''

"Spector wasn't talking about that kind of lust,'' said Fang irritably. "He was talking about blood lust. The Slaying of the Daggertooth.''

"Whatever. You can't deny you have three children. That tells me something.''

Fang was fairly sensitive on that subject. "What exactly brought this conversation about, Jack?'' he asked coldly.

"A tragic incident. Bluebelle and I happened to meet near the warren. We greeted each other in friendly fashion. We talked. I was thinking how nice it was to have a normal, intelligent conversation with a female gnome, free from any implications. A small flock of swallows were flitting around the treetops. The rabbits were basking in the sun. The wind—''

"I have to meet the Miggot shortly.''

"I was just setting the scene, Fang. I want you to picture in your mind's eye Bluebelle and me, the swallows and the rabbits.''

"And the wind?''

"Perhaps the wind is superfluous,'' Jack admitted. "And maybe the swallows are too. This is what happened. Just at the very moment we were laughing at some shared joke, two of those rabbits took it into their heads to indulge in filth. Right then and there, right in front of Bluebelle and me!'' He flushed a deep crimson at the recollection. "Clutching and vibrating—you know what rabbits are like.''

"Bad luck," said Fang. "How did you handle it?"

"Well, I tried to pass it off, of course. I babbled on and hoped Bluebelle wouldn't see them. But it was no good. The sight of those two rabbits triggered the others off, and soon they were all doing it, all over the compound! Well, Bluebelle couldn't help but notice what was going on. She went a funny color, muttered something, and ran. I haven't seen her since."

"She'll get over it, Jack. Females are resilient."

"Nobody will ever get over it, Fang. I'll carry that dreadful moment in my memory lobe all my life, and I'll pass it on to my children, if I ever have any, which is extremely unlikely; and they'll pass it on, and so on. The memory of my degradation will become a chapter in gnomish history!"

"But none of your descendants will ever actually recall that memory."

"They will if they happen to become Memorizers. Anybody could become a Memorizer, you once told me. It's just a knack."

It was probably at that moment that the great idea occurred to Fang. "That's right," he said slowly.

"Oh, my God!" wailed Jack. "What am I going to do? I wish I'd never resurrected the string. I never had this problem with the bogus rabbits!"

"The bogus rabbits?"

"A slip of the tongue, Fang."

Fang regarded him thoughtfully. "Doesn't it seem to you somehow *unnatural*, that this kind of thing should happen?"

"Unnatural?" Jack turned a tortured face to Fang. "Unnatural? Not at all. It was horribly natural."

"So why were you embarrassed?"

"Huh?"

Fang left Jack staring after him in bewilderment, and hurried to his meeting. He found the Miggot sitting on a charred root of the blasted oak, drinking beer and snarling at the hangdog, which sat at his feet. It was a dissolute and depressing sight. The sky seemed to have clouded over, and an unseasonably chilly wind rustled the trees, scattering a few leaves as though winter were around the corner.

"Miggot," said Fang, "pull yourself together and cast your mind back a few years. I want you to recall a conversation we had, just before I was deposed in that coup of Lady Duck's."

"There will be other coups, Fang, believe me. You'll be back!"

"Perhaps. Anyway, you'd criticized my urges and compared me to Bison. 'Bison's sexual urges are well under control,' you said. And then I'm afraid I lost my temper, and I said, 'Has it ever occurred to you, Miggot, that there might be something wrong with *your* urges?' And you said, 'Yes.' Do you remember that?"

The Miggot had not had Fang's practice as Memorizer, but he did have the photographic memory of gnomes. "I remember," he said. "And then I said, 'I'm accustomed to dealing with the Sharan and the business of birth and so on.' "

"So you did. But what did you say next, Miggot? Your exact words."

The Miggot closed his eyes. "I said, 'I ask myself questions.' I might say, 'What if . . . ?' And then I'll say, 'If that were so, then. . . .' And following that, 'But supposing . . . ?' And then suddenly I'll say, 'A-*ha!*' That's what I said."

"A-*ha!* What did you mean by 'A-*ha!*' Miggot?"

"It was a cry of discovery, similar to 'Eureka!' "

"And what had you discovered?"

"Nothing in particular. All I was saying was that I am in the habit of following my thoughts through and sometimes coming up with interesting answers."

"And you came up with an interesting answer about sex, didn't you?"

"Maybe I did, but this is hardly the time and place to discuss it."

"All right, we needn't discuss it. All I ask is that you listen to me and tell me what you think." Hearing no objection, Fang continued. "I was just talking to Jack o' the Warren, and it struck me how unnatural it is, the gnomish hatred of filth. We're the only creature in the world that feels like this. The Princess once said something interesting about that. She said it might be because the kikihuahuas created us with some kind of mental block, so we wouldn't fill the Earth with gnomes. We don't *need* to multiply, you see. All we need to do is maintain our population so we can do our job."

The Miggot displayed some interest. "A mental block? That makes sense. It could hardly be a physical incapability. That would be impractical, and our ancestors are very practical people."

"*I* don't have that mental block, Miggot. And neither does the Princess."

"But I have it, thank God." The Miggot's face creased in disgust. "Can you imagine how appalling it would be, to *want* to indulge in filth with Elmera?"

"But if you *wanted* to, it wouldn't be appalling."

"Logically you are correct, Fang. But in my bones I know it would be ghastly. It always has been, and it always will be. The struggling and the sweat and the horrible nakedness! A gnome can keep his boots and cap on for it, but not much else. Ugh!" He shuddered. "And yet . . . I don't deny I've sometimes wondered if we gnomes are really normal members of the animal world."

"Well, we're not, because we have the mental block. And if there is a block, there must be a key."

"No. It's locks that have keys, Fang, not blocks."

"Ask yourself, Miggot—what prevents you from becoming a Memorizer? And the answer is: There's a mental block that bars access to your memory lobe. I had that mental block, too, some years back. But when the shytes first started circling over my father, his duty compelled him to instruct me in the Memorizer's art. And he did this by unlocking the block. Or unblocking the lock," he said quickly, seeing an objection trembling on the Miggot's lips, "with a key."

"What was the key?"

"This is strictly between you and me, Miggot. It's a long poem thing called the Memorizer's Apothegm. Very long, and pretentious too. It starts off 'Out of the wombs of the Tin Mothers . . .' And it gets worse. If I didn't know better, I'd think my father invented it himself. You know what he's like. Anyway, it took a long time to learn. But when I'd mastered it—the very first time I was able to repeat it without a mistake—I could suddenly remember all kinds of things, going right back to the spacebat and the kikihuahuas!"

"So," said the Miggot, now thoroughly interested, "you're suggesting there might also be an apothegm for filth?"

"I prefer to think of it as a *sexual* apothegm, Miggot, because I've never really been able to think of sex as filth. To me filth is what gathers in the corners of the room, and under the bed, and on my father's shoulders."

"Well, that's exactly what sex is like. Sex and your father's shoulders have a lot in common. But I've always been an open-minded gnome, Fang, and I can see what you're talking about. I just have to make a very difficult mental switch, that's all." He screwed up his eyes and concentrated for a moment. "No. It's no good. I can't make it."

"But you will, when you've learned the sexual apothegm."

"Why should I want to learn the sexual apothegm?" asked the Miggot, surprised.

"If every gnome in the forest learned it, our race would be saved! We must multiply or die, Miggot!"

There was a long silence while the Miggot chewed thoughtfully on a lump of charcoal he'd picked from the root. At last he said, "Even if you knew it, Fang . . . you don't know it, do you?"

"No, but I intend to search my memory for it. It must be there somewhere."

"Even if you knew it, I wouldn't want to learn it. And neither would anyone else. Nobody could be persuaded to learn a poem that would open their minds to unbounded filth.''

"But suppose they didn't *know* it would open their minds to unbounded filth? Suppose they thought it was just a poem? Suppose the Memorizer's Apothegm doesn't need to be long? Suppose the essence is short, but generations of Memorizers expanded it with their love of ceremony. And to make sure someone didn't learn it by accident. The original sexual apothegm could be just a few simple words.''

"It might work. It just might work!" The Miggot rubbed his hands together in gathering glee. "Yes! It's a brilliant idea, Fang! You could make it into a poem yourself, and teach it to everyone at the next Memorizing meeting! Everyone except me, of course.''

"If I can find it in my memory to start with," said Fang, suddenly doubtful.

"Perhaps it's just not in there," said Fang, despairing, returning to the present after yet another exploration within his mind.

"You'll find it," said the Princess, leaning over and kissing him on the forehead. "You always succeed in the end. You're that kind of gnome, Fang.''

"I never found out how to get to the spacebat.''

"Perhaps you weren't intended to. If a poem can unlock secret memories, then other things could. The sight of a comet. A particular event. The key could be something that hasn't happened yet. But when it happens, suddenly we'll know what to do.''

"Perhaps the key to sex hasn't happened yet.''

"It has. It's in there somewhere. It must be, because your ancestors and mine discovered it—otherwise we wouldn't enjoy making love so much.''

"I never thought of that." He smiled briefly before sinking into gloom again. "No. It can't be right. You can't tell me the Gooligog ever enjoyed sex.''

"These things can skip a generation.''

"You're right!" He cheered up. "Pass me a beer, love,

and I'll try again. Just keep the children quiet for a while, please.''

Once again Fang dug into his memories.

The witch Avalona was everywhere. At one point in the distant past she had so terrified a gnomish Memorizer called Tremor that subsequent Memorizers had found it almost impossible to educe historical events before Tremor's time. Fang had conquered that particular fear long ago, however, and slipped easily past.

The events he explored were largely the result of formal Memorizing sessions, although many originated from past Memorizers' personal recollections. A Memorizer couldn't help but stamp his mark on gnomish history. The memories tended to be arranged in chains by subject matter. Since the chains naturally moved forward in time, Fang had to go back long before the chain arose, pick a promising subject, then follow it forward. Sometimes the chains simply petered out, leaving him in a void; and sometimes they divided off like happentracks, forcing him to make a choice. It was tedious work.

Occasionally he came upon familiar ground. One ancient Memorizer obviously fancied himself as a teacher, and in addition to Memorizing sessions, he held classes in history. *A group of young gnomes sitting on the ground, looking up attentively, appeared in Fang's mind's eye. He'd never seen so many gnome-children together before: it was a strange and moving sight. The teacher was relating the fable of the Bat and the Grasshopper, which Fang remembered hearing from his mother long ago.* For a while Fang followed the teacher's memory line; then abruptly it ceased.

He educed backward again. He paused during the short period when gnomes spoke the ancient kikihuahua tongue, and listened to Avalona teaching them English for her own purposes. No humans were visible in any of these memories. Their happentrack was far removed.

Then suddenly he found himself in the spacebat, and his memories were those of the kikihuahuas. He'd learned their language some years previously. Monkey-shaped creatures, gnome-sized, they trotted around busily in the dim interior of their huge organic ship. There was never a clue as to how they transported the gnomes to Earth, or how the gnomes were to be brought back. They chattered and worked their genetic miracles, while others slept the centuries away, lulled into hibernation with batmilk.

Impatient, Fang moved rapidly back to the early days of the spacebat. An incomprehensible number of centuries ago, he stepped onto the kikihuahuas' home planet.

One again he met the Tin Mothers.

Perfect robots, they were as intelligent as their masters the kikihuahuas, and they could reproduce themselves. The kikihuahuas lay around in luxury while the Tin Mothers looked after them. It was an idyllic existence; but, as always, there were malcontents.

Aoli was tired of machines. He began to experiment in a new field, watched benevolently by the Tin Mothers.

Genetic engineering. It's the only scientific field where some kind of machine is not the ultimate objective.

What is your ultimate objective, then?

To get rid of machines altogether.

And, lying on his deathbed, Aoli had enunciated the code that became known throughout the galaxy as the Kikihuahua Examples.

I'm not saying it's possible to live in accordance with these Examples at present, but they do represent an ideal for us to strive for. When we succeed, we will be qualified to teach others, all over the galaxy. We will be teaching harmony. We will be teaching the galaxy that its most precious natural resource is the genes of living cells. We will be teaching perfection.

And a thousand years later, a large number of kikihuahuas left their planet and began to roam the galaxy in spacebats with thousand-mile wingspans, leaving the Tin Mothers on the home planet, wondering where they had gone wrong.

Fang had educed it all before, but it was a fascinating study. He never tired of the interior of the spacebat and the life of the kikihuahuas; it was in his blood. Moving forward, he eavesdropped on another ancient conversation.

We must now select the characteristics of our initial colonization party.

It was a kikihuahua called Ou-Ou speaking. Fang snapped to attention so quickly that the Princess, watching him, put an arm around his shoulders and eased him into a more relaxed position.

First, the form our colonist will take. Obviously it should be a biped, like this. An apelike creature appeared in Fang's mind's eye. *Although it needn't be so big. A smaller form would be more economical. It will have an intelligence equal to our own. It must reproduce sexually in order to fit in with the current state of evolution on our new planet. Two sexes. Now, that should provide our designers with something to think about. Of course, the creature will need to be considerably more aggressive than we are.*

Aggressive?

There are frightful monsters down there. Our representative must be able to defend himself. To do this he must have certain innate characteristics.

Like what?

Like not submitting himself readily for slaughter when attacked. Like having the ability to make himself a few simple weapons, to beat off predators. Like kindling the Wrath of Agni occasionally, to frighten off night prowlers.

You're saying that our representative should contravene every single Example.

Or die.

The subsequent argument was heated by kikihuahua standards, and Fang followed it avidly, knowing he was coming close to his goal. An ancient Memorizer named Offo swayed the meeting by recalling several instances when the Examples had been broken in the name of colonization. The discussion became more specific.

A creature so powerful would be in danger of taking over the world. It would create a huge and intricate society, and we would suddenly find that our advance party had become colonists themselves, and would refuse to come back to the bat.

Only if they are allowed to breed freely.

But that's exactly what sexual creatures do.

Not if we inhibit them.

Then they would become extinct in a very short time.

Not if we make the sexual act a duty instead of a pleasure. Like all advance parties, their whole lives will be governed by a set of duties, one of which will be occasional reproduction.

That makes sense. But how shall we make sure the inhibition can be removed if their numbers fall dangerously low? It would be pointless if they became extinct down there, and there was nobody left to report back. We wouldn't know whether they had succeeded or failed.

It will be their duty to recognize such a situation. I suggest that they should also consciously recognize these elements before proceeding further:

- *that they are in real danger of extinction,*
- *that their physical form has proved satisfactory,*
- *that there is no shortage of habitable land for expansion,*
- *that the incentive to procreation is a last resort, and*
- *that having used it, they must return to the spacebat within fifteen Earth years, or die.*

That last element. That's a little drastic, isn't it?

If we did not insist on that, their population could recover exponentially, and we would be faced again with our original dilemma. All we want is that they should prepare the Earth for the eventual colonists, and report back to us when the job is done. Fifteen years of unlimited procreation will be long enough to restore a satisfactory memory pool. It should more than double their population, if I know sexual creatures.

Has it ever occurred to you how lucky we kikihuahuas

are, Afah, to have eliminated sexual reproduction from our genetic makeup?

Fang opened his eyes. "I think I've got it," he said. "It's just a question of knowing a collection of facts, and thinking about them all at the same time." The children, released from bondage, began to expend their surplus energy around the burrow. Fang watched them and the Princess for a moment, a deep sadness within him. "But if we go ahead with this, we'll have to leave Earth fifteen years from now. That'll mean leaving all this—our home, gnomedom, Nyneve, everything—and going to live in a huge, dark thing with walls made of flesh."

"But supposing we didn't? Supposing we refused to go?"

"Then I think there's some kind of metabolic switch in us that would just click off."

The Princess was silent for a long time. At last she said, "It's our duty, Fang."

"My father was a good gnome!" announced Fang.

"*Is* a good gnome, you mean," said Elmera. "He's not dead yet."

"I mean *was*," Fang explained, "in the sense that he is no longer our Memorizer. Or a member of our village."

"The bugger ran out on us!" shouted the Miggot. "Always remember that, Elmera!"

The regular Memorizing meeting was in session and, as usual, was getting offtrack. As a quarrel broke out between the Miggot and his wife, Fang tried again.

"I have the greatest respect for my father and his methods, but you will have noticed that I've made some changes to our Memorizing meetings over the years. Our proceedings are less formal. People can speak out more."

"Why don't you do the job properly?" Elmera asked.

"Properly?"

"Like your father used to. The robe. The incense. The wand and the mumbo jumbo. It was more of an occasion when your father did it. I like to see a bit of ceremony. A bit of respect for gnomish traditions."

"You should respect me for myself," said Fang.

There was a roar of gnomish laughter.

"Well, anyway," shouted Fang, becoming annoyed, "I'm making another change. I've given it a lot of thought, and I've come to the conclusion that a Memorizing session should be a two-way exchange. You will continue to give me your items for Memorizing but I, in return, will relate to you interesting events from the past. We all need to know more about our gnomish culture. It's something the beach gnomes seem to have forgotten entirely."

There was a buzz of interest.

"I was examining my memory only last night," said Fang, "and I came across a fascinating story that you may not know. Settle yourselves down, gnomes, and I'll tell it to you."

The gnomes relaxed happily against the roots of the blasted oak. They liked being told stories. It was much better than having to think. And so Fang had a receptive audience as he related the fable of the Bat and the Grasshopper.

It is remembered that there was a grasshopper who lived in a green meadow. The meadow sloped down to a winding stream overhung with willow trees. In the meadow it was always summer. It was a beautiful place in which to live, yet the grasshopper was not satisfied. He dozed through the sunny days when he should have been working, so that he could stay awake at night and gaze at the moon. "Oh, what a beautiful place that must be." He sighed. "See how silvery it shines. Oh, how I would love to live on the moon."

One day it occurred to him that if he could learn to jump high enough, he could reach the moon. It was only a matter of practice. So practice he did, every day, measuring his growing prowess against the willow trees until he could clear them with a single bound. And as is the way with fables, his perseverance was rewarded. The day came when he leapt so high that he escaped from Earth's gravitational field and found himself gliding through space.

"Whoopee!" he cried.

Soon he met a bat. "Where are you going, Grasshopper?" asked the bat.

"I am flying to the moon, which is the most beautiful place in the solar system, and where I will live my days in everlasting joy," replied the grasshopper.

"Stay with me," said the bat. "You may not like what you find on the moon."

"Who would want to live in empty space?" The grasshopper sneered and glided on by.

"More people than you can imagine!" the bat called after him. "It's not so bad, if you find a good home here!" But the grasshopper paid no attention.

Finally the grasshopper touched down on the moon and received a terrible disappointment. The moon was not silver, after all. That was a cruel deception perpetrated by the sun. The moon was covered with a fine, choking black dust. There was no food, no water, no willow trees. In fact, the whole place was thoroughly objectionable. The grasshopper tried to jump off the moon to get back to Earth, but he was belly-deep in dust and could get no leverage.

"Woe is me!" he cried, struggling. "Why did I ever leave my meadow?"

The bat heard his cries and swooped low. "I'll help you," he said, and he dragged the grasshopper out of the dust and flew with him into space.

"Mark my words," said the bat, "a world always looks more beautiful from the other side of the void. If you travel to strange places, you must allow for the possibility of disappointment. And you must always, *always* make sure you have a means of getting home again. Now take a look over there at Earth."

"That dull old place?"

"Just look," said the bat.

So the grasshopper looked, and to his amazement, Earth resembled a big, beautiful silver coin. "Go," said the bat, and gave him a push, and set him gliding home.

The grasshopper returned to his meadow and lived there happily, singing and hopping, but never hopping higher than the willow trees in case he should accidentally leave Earth's gravity again and not be able to get back. He hadn't yet worked out a way to travel safely, and another time the bat might not be around to help him. But he thought about what the bat had told him, and toward the end of his days he did discover a safe way to travel. That, however, is another story. . . .

"That, however, is another story," concluded Fang.

"That bat is too smug," said Lady Duck. "He reminds me of my mother, telling me I should be satisfied with my lot." She looked proudly at King Bison. "I wouldn't be where I am now, if I'd followed her advice. Come now, Bison. We have work to do. We don't have time to listen to stories." And she left, Bison following with some reluctance.

"I think . . ." said Fang slowly, "I think the story is intended to tell gnomes not to leave Earth until the right time. It was the first fable ever told. It just possibly might have been told by the kikihuahua to the first Mara Zion Memorizer. The bat could have been the spacebat."

"And the grasshopper?"

"Well, gnomedom, of course. But it could also refer to our route off Earth. You see, there's the end of the fable: 'Toward the end of his days he did discover a safe way to travel.' "

"I thought it referred to him dying and going to heaven. . . ." Wal the Bottle's voice trailed away.

"What is it?"

"I'm not sure. Just an odd thought. Have you ever wondered why people swear by the Great Grasshopper? It's just a saying, but could there be a connection?"

"The Great Grasshopper . . ." Fang repeated thoughtfully. That evening he tried to track down the origin of the phrase, but without success. It seemed the gnomes had always sworn by the Great Grasshopper. He translated the words into the ancient gnomish tongue, but it didn't make any difference.

That afternoon, however, the gnomes soon tired of speculation. Flasks were passed around, and a few eyes closed in contemplation. "Tell us another story!" shouted Clubfoot.

"Another story!" The gnomes took up the cry.

Fang eyed them, a sinking feeling in his stomach. This was it. This was the crucial moment. And they all looked so happy and relaxed, drinking beer with little thought for the future and the terrible unknown. If he went ahead with what he planned, he might well save the race from extinction, but he would be committing these gnomes to finding a route off Earth within the next fifteen years. If they didn't find it, they would die.

And yet he had no alternative.

He forced his face into an ingratiating expression. "It's a little poem," he said. "It comes right from the earliest days of gnomedom, when Avalona first taught us this language. It's probably translated from the language before that," he continued, improvising.

"A poem!" they cried happily. Poems were fun. They didn't take a gnome long to learn. "What's the poem about, Fang?"

"It's about gnomes." And taking a deep breath, Fang recited a poem composed by the Princess.

> *The shape of a gnome is a wonderful thing,*
> *Two eyes and two elbows and two everything.*
> *This island that we and the animals share,*
> *Has room for us all and there's plenty to spare.*
> *It's sad that we gnomes get more scarce every day,*
> *It seems that our species will soon fade away.*
> *So lend us the will to conceive and beget,*
> *In fifteen more summers we'll honor our debt!*

"And that's it," he said. "It's not much, but it's a piece of gnomish culture."

"It sounds a little suspect to me," said Spector.

But the gnomes were busy muttering. He heard snatches

of the poem, then they fell silent. It was safely in their memory lobes.

"The Memorizing session will now begin," he said. "Bring me your memories."

He noticed Jack o' the Warren smiling at Bluebelle but was unable to decide whether the smile contained any element of lust. The other gnomes watched one another, waiting for the first memory to be suggested so they could dispute its validity in time-honored fashion. The Memorizing session commenced.

At one point Fang fancied that Elmera leered at him, but he hoped it was his imagination.

14

THE FALL OF DREXEL POXY

ARTHUR CAME TO CAMELOT IN LATE JUNE. IT WAS midnight when he arrived, but his bedchamber was kept ready for such occasions. After making sure the rest of his small party was taken care of, he retired for the night.

"Shall I tell Queen Guinevere you're here, Sire?" asked the chambermaid.

"No. She'll be asleep. I'll see her in the morning."

He lay back in bed staring at the vaulted ceiling, his head pillowed on his hands. Strange, how a man could be afraid of meeting his own wife. But it was almost two years since he'd last seen Gwen; two years of fighting and peacemaking around England. It was over now, for the time being. But within months someone would be plotting against him, and he'd have to go to Cirencester.

Cirencester . . . What a stinking hole it was. Crowded streets, people everywhere, the river a veritable sewer. How good it was to be back in Cornwall! The journey had taken over a fortnight because of the various calls he'd been obliged to make on the way: to pacify a ruffled Baron here, to settle a boundary dispute there.

But gradually, as he rode, the countryside had changed in character. The sandstone Cotswold hills had given way to the rolling hills of Devon until, quite suddenly, he was riding across the moors. The very air smelled different. The sun shone more brightly, the wind blew more keenly. He felt the most extraordinary tightness in his throat when the massive outcrop of Pentor came into view. Then he topped a rise and saw the familiar river with Camelot tucked under its elbow. He was home.

Nyneve. . .

Better not to think of Nyneve. Better to think of Gwen and the good times they were going to have that summer. They would take a boat on the river and sail down to the sea. They would climb to the top of Pentor and drink wine. They would walk the forest paths to Mara Zion village and see the people there; those who hadn't moved to Camelot when Torre and Governayle and the others moved. There were many happy days ahead for Gwen and him. He'd earned these days, and so had she. This was the reward.

So why was he frightened to meet her?

Two years was a long time. A woman could change her mind about a man in two years. There had been signs that she was becoming dissatisfied before his last departure. She'd complained of the loneliness, but then she'd always been a complainer. It didn't necessarily mean anything. And she'd found other interests to occupy herself: praiseworthy interests like championing the cause of the gnomes.

Lancelot supported her in that. Lancelot, whose name was so often connected with Gwen's. It seemed he'd heard little else in Cirencester. "Why didn't you bring Sir Lancelot du Lac with you, Sire?" And from the more powerful nobles: "I'm surprised you've left Lancelot and Guinevere back at Camelot together, Arthur."

The legend had spread as far as Wroxeter and farther. It had distorted people's view of the present, and it had aroused all kinds of unreasonable expectations of the future. He felt like the son of a famous father. The legend was impossible to live up to—and yet it had made things easier in some ways. It was so familiar to people that if he deliberately followed its course, he got very little opposition. On the other hand, if he acted contrary to the legend, he was met with outrage.

The legend said that Gwen and Lance were lovers, and

so people believed it. They wanted to believe it. The truest of his friends regarded him with sympathy, the most insincere with contempt.

Nobody felt the way he did about the pair. Lancelot, although a good friend and ally, was a prude. And Gwen, although reasonably beautiful and quite intelligent, was somewhat frigid. Furthermore, she enjoyed being queen and would not want to risk losing that status.

What unhappy reasons for being sure of one's wife!

Pondering on this, Arthur fell asleep at last. . . .

"Hello, darling!" She was kissing him lightly on the forehead, the sunlight gilding her hair as it cascaded past her face. "You should have woken me up."

"Let me look at you." He held her at arm's length. She looked back at him, clear-eyed. Yes, she was pretty. He hugged her to him and kissed her properly and was pleased to feel a definite stirring of affection within himself; and perhaps a little lust too. He laughed as the worries of the night began to fade. She hugged him back and climbed into bed beside him—whether out of a sense of duty or love, he didn't know. And just for a few minutes it didn't matter.

Afterward they sat drinking a local tea that he hadn't tasted since leaving Camelot, while the sunlight lanced through the tall windows and specks of drifting dust looked like their personal stars.

"Tell me the news," he said.

"There isn't much to tell. While Torre was away fighting, Governayle looked after things and did a good job. He may not be much of a soldier, but he has a good head on him. The village of Mara Zion thrives. The Irish came twice, but they made no trouble, and brought some useful goods for barter. The gnomes have been making themselves useful, and they really seem to have settled down well at the beach. There was a slight problem with a high tide in the spring but we sorted that out. Ned Palomides has been keeping an eye on them recently, after I had a little disagreement with them."

"Palomides? But isn't he a bit of a rogue?"

"Probably, but he always treats me with respect. And he seems to have the gnomes' interests at heart." She smiled at him. "And that's about all the news from Camelot."

"What about Lancelot?"

"Oh, him? He got all miserable and left, after my little dispute with the gnomes. I'm sorry, Arthur. I know you thought a lot of him, but I can't stand people with long faces around me. And Lance was like that—always disapproving of this or that. Never satisfied. I don't think I ever saw him laugh."

"So where is he now?"

"I heard a rumor he went over to Trevarron Isle. A strange woman called Elaine lives there—she has a son, too, I believe. I expect Lance is living with her. She sounds the kind of woman he'd take pity on."

"I'll have to find time to visit him while I'm here."

"Well, don't worry about it now, darling. I've organized a welcoming party for you tonight. It's short notice, but all Menheniot will be here, and I'm hoping some of your old friends from Mara Zion will be able to come too. I've invited the gnomes to entertain us, as a goodwill gesture."

"It would have been nice to have had a quiet evening alone."

"Nonsense, darling! People will be glad to see you back. You must give them a chance to celebrate a little. After all, you're something of a stranger these days. . . ."

Alas for idealism. There was no Round Table in the Great Hall of Camelot. The tragedy of Mara Zion had been taken as a warning not to fly in the face of the natural order. And the natural order dictated that the leaders should be at the head table and the followers elsewhere. So the long tables were arranged in ranks; and Arthur, Gwen, Torre, Governayle, and a handful of other favorites sat at a table at right angles to the others.

To the west was a raised platform, and on this stood a miniature table. Gnomes sat in a row along the far side of this table, facing the guests. They had discarded their traditional conical caps and now wore forked hats with a tiny silver bell at each tip.

Arthur asked, "Are those your beach gnomes, Gwen?"

"Yes. Don't they look nice?" She smiled at them in a proprietary manner and waved to Drexel Poxy, who waved back. "I'm so glad they came. I don't like to be bad friends with anyone." A faint cry came from one of the other gnomes.

Arthur frowned. "What did he say?"

"Oh, don't worry about him. That's just Mold. He often shouts things like that, just to shock people."

"Well, I didn't catch what he said, so I wasn't shocked. And in any case, I don't shock easily."

He was shocked, however, at midnight when Gwen clapped her hands for silence and announced the entertainment for the evening.

"First the gnomes will dance for you," she said, "and then we have something really special. Something you've never seen before."

A minstrel began to pluck at his lute, and the gnomes climbed onto their table. Then began one of the most embarrassing performances it had been Arthur's misfortune to witness. Gnomes are more thickset than humans, and their dance was clumsy and pathetic, with much foot stamping and hand clapping, ducking and bowing. There were more males than females, which gave an unbalanced look to an already awkward performance. They were clearly self-conscious about the whole thing. This was aggravated by Mold, who kept slapping the others on the buttocks, and by Poxy himself, who kept hitting them over the head with a bladder on a stick.

"Are they enjoying it?" asked Arthur.

"Of course they are. It's one of their traditional dances. And our guests love them!"

Apparently they did. The Great Hall reverberated with rhythmic clapping as the guests encouraged the dismal performance. This prompted the gnomes to exaggerate their movements further, and to caper in a most ungnomelike fashion. Poxy started to utter gnomish shouts of bogus enthusiasm—which was a mistake because the others began to do likewise. Seditious shouts of "Away, Thunderer" roared from gnomish throats, intermingled with lone cries of "Anal passages!"

"This is just terrible, Gwen," muttered Arthur. "They're debasing themselves."

"All entertainers debase themselves to amuse their audience. It's their side of the deal. And they're being paid well, believe me."

"Yes, but gnomes . . . ?"

"You've always said we should treat them the same as humans. So now they're being treated the same as human jesters and tumblers." She regarded him critically. "Perhaps you'll like the next part better. It's a little more intellectual."

Eventually the gnomes finished their bitter dance and resumed their seats, with the exception of Drexel Poxy and the Gooligog. A stool was handed up and the Gooligog sat on it, looking glum. Poxy held up a hand for silence.

"We are flattered by the human interest in gnomish customs," he shouted, "and tonight we have a real treat for you all. Tonight you will witness a gnomish ceremony never before performed for a human audience. Tonight you will be afforded a glimpse into the far-distant past. Tonight"—he paused impressively—"we give you the gnomish Memorizing rites!"

There was a roar of applause and some laughter, drowning the Gooligog's testy response. "It's not a bloody rite. We never call it a bloody rite. It's a meeting at which I preside, that's what it is. You make us sound like some kind of weird cult!"

He sat staring mutinously at the Gnome from the North.

"Do we have a question?" Poxy asked the gnomes brightly.

"That's not the way it starts," snapped the Gooligog. "That's the kind of stupid thing my son Willie says. He's degraded the whole process. Now get down off the bloody table and let me handle it my way!''

The audience chuckled, thinking this was all part of the act. Poxy stepped down with a furious glance at the Gooligog.

The Gooligog straightened his ceremonial robe. Then he rose and spread his arms so that the robe hung from them like wings. In a tall human his attitude might have inspired awe; but he was a chunky little old gnome, and it looked comical. There were a few stifled chuckles.

"Bring me your memories!" he chanted.

And as often happened on these occasions, there were no takers. The Gooligog sat in a growing silence, and the human audience became restless.

The Gnome from the North stood. "I have a memory!"

"I hear you, Great Poxy. State your memory for consideration."

"I submit the following incident," said Poxy slowly, his mind frantically seeking an event worthy of note. His gaze fell on Gwen and gave him inspiration. "The spring tides were unusually high this year, and threatened our village. If it hadn't been for the help of the humans, we would have become homeless. Many deeds of heroism were done. However"—a shadow crossed his face—"due to the stupidity of certain fools, some of us *did* become homeless, and our food stores were lost."

"You didn't exactly distinguish yourself, Poxy!" shouted Bart. Since the episode of the flood, his relationship with his leader had deteriorated further.

"At least I didn't wipe out half the village by rolling rocks on it!"

"Silence!" yelled the Gooligog, jumping to his feet. "A Memorizing meeting is a time for responsible deliberation, not mindless quarreling. It's a time for agreement between gnomes as to what the true course of history is. And in any case, Poxy's topic is invalid. It was committed to memory weeks ago."

"I don't remember you committing it to memory, Gooligog," said Bart.

"The Great Poxy convened a special meeting, and I committed it then."

"Then it must have been a secret meeting."

"Well, it was," admitted the Gooligog.

"But that's against the rules!"

"I make the rules, Bart o' Bodmin. Now sit down and let us continue."

"I demand to know why the meeting was secret!"

Since there were signs of disorder and Mold was beginning to shout obscenities, the Gooligog deemed it wise to reply. "The Great Poxy decided on this course. The circumstances were exceptional. In the excitement of the event, memories had become unreliable. Mental images of life-threatening moments had obscured the overall sweep and pattern of the situation."

"Nipples!"

Mold's shout of skepticism carried clearly around the Great Hall, which had become deathly silent. The entertainment was far more absorbing than even the most optimistic had expected.

"Are you calling me a liar, Mold?" asked the Gooligog incredulously.

"Absolutely. I'm saying that you and Drexel Poxy cooked up a fake memory between you, because the real memory would reflect upon the leadership of our settlement."

The human audience was forgotten now. A wholly unselfconscious and typically gnomish dispute was in progress. The Gooligog, having already sprung to his feet, had little left in the way of dramatic gestures. So he climbed onto his chair and, teetering, shouted, "I have never cooked up a memory in four hundred years of Memorizing! I was in the forest when the affair of the spring tides began, and it was practically over by the time I got back. So I relied on the word of our great leader, and why not? Your accusation reflects on the heritage of every gnome here!"

"It doesn't reflect on me!" yelled Bart, climbing onto the table.

"Nor me!" yelled Mold, joining him.

They began to shake the Gooligog's chair.

"I demand to know your memories concerning the affair of the spring tides!" shouted Bart.

Drexel Poxy climbed onto the table. "That is restricted information!"

"No memories are restricted!" The remaining gnomes, horrified at this breach of gnomish custom, climbed up too. They stood in a tight and quarrelsome group, the Gooligog on his chair protruding above them. "What do you mean, restricted?" they demanded.

"Privy to the Gooligog and I!" cried Poxy desperately.

"No, I can't have that, Drexel." The Gooligog had his arms around the shoulders of Bart and Mold to steady himself, and possibly this had induced a feeling of brotherhood toward them. "No memories are restricted."

"So recall, Gooligog!" ordered Bart. "Do your duty. Recall your memories of the Affair of the Spring Tides."

"The Affair of the Spring Tides!" insisted the others, in whose minds the event had acquired capital letters like a mystery novel. "Recall, Gooligog!"

"Don't be intimidated, Gooligog!" cried Poxy.

"Stifle the Great Poxy!" somebody shouted, and two gnomes grappled Poxy to the ground and sat on his head— an act of open violence that never would have occurred in legitimate gnomish society. "Recall, Gooligog!" they said.

"Back off, then," snapped the Gooligog irritably. "Give me space."

They helped him down and he sat on his chair, arranging his robes in dignified folds. He brought his hands together in front of his face, closed his eyes, and bowed his head.

"Cut the crap, Gooligog!" said Mold impatiently. "We're not asking you to recall events on the Home Planet. The Affair of the Spring Tides only happened a few weeks ago."

Sighing, the Gooligog said, "That day the tides were unusually high, as the Great Poxy had forecast, and they threatened the village. It was apparent that the village had been built too close to the water, despite the advice of the Great Poxy. Fortunately he was able to alert the gnomes, and had the forethought to enlist the help of the humans Guinevere, Lancelot, and Palomides."

"That's all lies!" shouted Mold. "I gave the warning! Poxy was nowhere to be seen!"

"I merely repeat what the Great Poxy instructed me to memorize." The Gooligog closed his eyes again. "The evacuation was proceeding satisfactorily, and it seemed all would be well because the Great Poxy had designed the cottages to withstand the natural elements. Unfortunately he had not foreseen the actions of the gnome Bart o' Bodmin. Bart, who had been drinking, was deceived by a combination of strong sunlight and alcoholic hallucination into believing that a monster was rising from the deeps and advancing on the village. So he ordered the release of—"

"Lies!" screamed Bart. "I hadn't touched a drop! I let the dolmens go because people told me the giants were attacking! And I could see them down there, ripping the roof off a cottage!"

A muffled objection came from Poxy. "Nobody said the giants were attacking."

The gnomes regarded one another. "I seem to remember people saying that," said someone. "I remember thinking it was a despicable thing to do, attacking us in our hour of distress."

Now the human audience began to respond with murmurs of sympathy. "What wretch attacked the gnomes, Gwen?" asked Arthur. "You were there."

"Nobody attacked them. Ned and Lance were trying to move one of their cottages to safe ground, and the roof came off in their hands. Lance told me all about it. It seems there was a gnome in bed at the time, and he placed the wrong construction on things. It was he who panicked and thought he was being attacked, and then he began to shout. The others took up his cry. They didn't know any different."

"Ah." Arthur looked relieved. "So the gnome in bed was the problem. Our people were blameless."

"Absolutely, darling. We were trying to help."

On the table, the gnomes were absorbing this intelligence. One question loomed above all others.

"Who was the Gnome in Bed, Gooligog?" asked Bart.

"The Gnome in Bed was not identified."

"I can identify the Gnome in Bed!" cried Mold. "The truth must be told! The Gnome in Bed was Drexel Poxy himself! After I sounded the alarm I couldn't find him anywhere, so I went to his cottage. He'd overslept, the idle bugger. I heard him screaming when the roof came off. I knew bloody well the giants weren't attacking because I'd just been talking to them, but other gnomes didn't. They believed Poxy and they spread the word. Who can blame them? He was their leader."

There was a long silence. The gnomes got off Poxy's head and he stood, weeping.

"Poxy," thundered the Gooligog, "you have betrayed the trust."

"This is a sorry moment for gnomedom," said Bart. "And under the circumstances I'd like to ease my conscience," he added, shooting Poxy a look of sly triumph.

"No!" cried the Gnome from the North. "You'll destroy us both!"

"Yes, but they'll forgive me, because I'm the one who's going to rat on you."

"Ease your conscience, Bart!" yelled Mold, interested. "It's your sacred duty!"

Bart took a deep breath and faced the gnomes. "I'd like to tell you about a conversation six years ago," he said quietly.

The gnomes, sensing this would be a long story, settled back.

"I want you to imagine a low drinking hole in Bodmin, lower even than Clubfoot's hole," Bart began. "And I want you to imagine two gnomes sitting in there: one cunning and unscrupulous, one friendly and gullible. The unscrupulous one was Poxy," he said, in case there should be any misunderstanding, "and the gullible one was me."

"Have you ever dreamed of an empire, Bart?" Poxy's face was demonic in the lamplight. "Have you ever lain awake at night wondering what it would be like to be in charge of Bodmin, and to issue orders and have gnomes jump to obey you? And to receive intelligence from outlying areas, and to send task forces to deal with things? And to conclude alliances with your neighbors and then, when they least expect it, slip in your own people as their leaders? And see your empire expand by your own cleverness, until your sphere of influence is bounded only by the sea? And then to build boats capable of holding a hundred gnomes, or maybe a thousand?"

"No," said Bart.

"All right. Suppose I told you all this could come to pass. And then supposing it *did*, just the way I said it would. What would you think then, Bart?"

"I'd think you were a very remarkable gnome, Drexel."

"The difference between the ordinary gnome and the remarkable gnome is that the remarkable gnome *plans*, Bart. He is always one step ahead. Which brings me to prophesies."

"Prophesies, Drexel?"

"Gnomes love a prophesy," Poxy had said, his face getting alarmingly closer. "There's a bunch of stupid gnomes down in Mara Zion who dye their caps red, if you can believe it. And there's some kind of giant down there who can step out of the umbra, who pretends she can foretell the future. The Mara Zion gnomes are enormously impressed by this. Added to which the forest of Mara Zion is prime gnome country, much too good for the gnomes who live there. It all adds up, doesn't it?"

"I'm sure it does, Drexel."

"Here's my plan. You go down to Mara Zion and start prophesying about a legendary gnome called, say, the Gnome from the North. Tell them he'll lead them out of their sorrow and tribulation—gnomes always want to be led out of that. Impress it on them; get their Memorizer to memorize it, until the name of the Gnome from the North becomes as familiar as their own navels. And then, in their darkest hour, I'll arrive and fulfill the prophesy."

"But what's the point?" Bart had asked.

"They'll be amazed and respectful gnomes, Bart. They'll hang on our very words, and without them realizing what's happened, we'll be in charge. We'll hold them in the palm of our hands. Our fame will spread throughout the land. We'll build a gnomish empire, you and I. Think of the power!"

And Poxy's eyes had blazed into Bart's, and something of Poxy's vision had seeped through into Bart's brain.

The power!

"We'll do it, Drexel, you and I!"

"We ride," Poxy had said quietly, "at dawn."

"And that is the absolute truth," said Bart, placing a hand on his stomach. "I swear it by the Great Grasshopper."

"Is it true?" the Gooligog asked Poxy.

And the shrunken figure raised a tearstained face and whispered, "Yes."

"You are no longer fit to be our leader, Poxy."

The Gnome from the North mumbled something brokenly. It sounded like reluctant agreement.

"In which case," said Bart, with hardly a glance at the stooped and retreating figure of his ex-chief, "we shall need a new leader. I propose Mold!"

"I accept!" cried the Outrageous one.

"Mold! Mold!"

"Breasts!" yelled the new champion triumphantly as they hoisted him shoulder-high.

Gwen turned to Arthur. "This is a great privilege for us, Arthur. We're witnessing the election of a new gnomish leader! I shall remember this evening all my life!"

"So shall I," said the king unhappily.

Annoyed by his lack of enthusiasm, Gwen began to circulate among her guests and, as the music began, found herself cornered by Ned Palomides.

"How did you allow that to happen?" he asked harshly.

Surprised, she said, "Well, naturally I feel sorry for little Drexel, but—"

"Guinevere, you are a bloody fool!"

Outraged, she stared at him. "I am your queen! Take that back, Ned, or I'll have Arthur deal with you!"

Palomides was beyond caring. "Arthur wouldn't be too pleased with your performance, either!"

"I don't know what you're talking about."

"Don't act so bloody innocent. This is *me* you're talking to. Ned Palomides. We both know what the Sharan can do." They were standing against a heavy tapestry, and Gwen found she was gripping the fabric tightly, as though to cling to some kind of reality. The other guests had gathered at the other end of the hall where brandy and mulled ale was being served. Suddenly Ned seemed grotesquely threatening, his face close to hers, exuding a powerful smell of wine. "If Arthur had that animal, he could rule the land! He could create soldiers so strong, no enemy could kill them! He could build an army of giants and conquer France! You know that as well as I do!"

"I . . . I'd never thought of it."

"Don't talk like a fool." His hand gripped her arm, hurting. "Of course you thought of it. Why else did you befriend that poisonous little Poxy? Why have you been bribing the beach gnomes with food and stuff all this time? Why did you agree that the Sharan should be kept at the beach?"

She stared at him. The room seemed to be spinning, the others an impossible way off. "Ned, it was Drexel who said the Sharan ought to be turned over to his people."

"You knew he would suggest it sooner or later."

"No!"

"And we could have done it too. We were *that* close"— he shoved a finger and thumb under her nose, a fraction apart—"*that* bloody close to getting control of the Sharan through Poxy. And now Poxy's finished and we have to start all over again." Suddenly his manner changed. "How could you let it happen? I've been on your side all through it, helping you."

"Ned, there's been a terrible mistake."

"You're damned right there's been a mistake!" His temper flared up again. "And I made it! I've wasted five years buggering around with you and Lancelot and those bloody gnomes!"

"You never said anything," she said wearily.

"Of course not. You don't talk about that kind of thing with Sir Perfect prancing around you all the time. It was understood. You were always saying how you wished you could be more help to Arthur. And you were always talking about the Sharan, ever since she showed up at your wedding. And you had Poxy in your pocket. Oh, yes. It was understood, all right."

She said slowly, "There's something else I understand."

"What?"

"If all that was true, did you really intend to build an army for Arthur? Are you loyal enough to do that, Ned, working away quietly in the forest for a few years? Or would you have built the army for yourself? Is that why you're so angry?"

"I can't believe you're so stupid not to see the value of an animal like that." He was deflating, his expression becoming sulky.

"It wouldn't have worked, Ned. You're not a leader. You remind me of the Miggot. He's clever, but he can't even lead his own wife. So he used the Sharan to create a hangdog that he could boss around. And that's what you'd do. If you had the Sharan, you wouldn't create an army to conquer the world. You'd create a hangdog and never leave the forest!"

"To hell with you all!" He turned his back on her and walked away.

"Ned!" He turned around but didn't meet her eyes.

''You've insulted your queen. You've called me stupid, and maybe I am. But I'm clever enough to know you're a danger to Arthur and me. So don't let me see you anywhere near Camelot or Mara Zion, ever again. Go to France. Go to Ireland. Go anywhere away from here. I don't trust you.''

The evening had fallen apart on Gwen. She rejoined the drinkers and the dancers but found no consolation. Arthur was taciturn and poor company, and the other men were merely drunk. When at last they went to bed, Arthur turned his back to her. Puzzled and hurt, Gwen lay awake beside him, and near dawn she heard him murmuring a name that was not hers.

15
TRANSFORMATIONS IN MARA ZION

AFTER MUCH SOUL-SEARCHING, FANG EXPLAINED THE significance of his poem to Spector. His choice of Spector had not been made without misgivings.

"Oh," said the Thinking Gnome when he'd finished. "Oh, I see. Well, that explains it, of course. A lesser gnome—Jack o' the Warren, for example—would have not paused to analyze the unusual sensations with which I've been plagued. He would have allowed his baser instincts full rein, and hang the consequences. But I function on a more intellectual plane, I'm happy to say. I transform my instincts into manageable symbols. Symbols never got a gnome into trouble," he concluded loftily.

"Perhaps you ought to explain all that to the others."

Spector needed little persuading. The notion of addressing a meeting of gnomes on the subject of sex fired his imagination. The possibilities for involved discussion and probing analysis were almost infinite. A few cogent topics had already occurred to him. He smiled gently.

"The red dragon of lust has breathed fire into the loins of gnomes!" Spector proclaimed in portentous tones.

A couple of gnomes sniggered. Others flushed and examined various blameless parts of their bodies, such as their fingernails. Lady Duck uttered an outraged shout. ''I invoke Hayle!''

King Bison said, ''What red dragon is that?''

''The red dragon that was foretold.''

''I don't remember any red dragon,'' said Bison, puzzled.

''And neither do I,'' shouted Lady Duck. ''I believe it's a filthy invention of the Miggot's! There's certainly no fire in my loins, I'm very pleased to say!''

''It could be Fang's idea,'' said Bison to his wife quietly. ''He was telling me some strange theory of his the other day. It had to do with''—he lowered his voice—''loins.''

''Well, Fang can keep his loins to himself! We all know the trouble Fang's loins have gotten him into. Why should he drag the rest of us down into his pit of perversion?''

Clubfoot Trimble observed, ''Funny, it doesn't feel like a pit of perversion anymore. In fact, it feels pretty damned good.'' And he leered at a young female gnome sitting on the other side of the circle. She leered back.

''Where *is* this red dragon, Spector?'' asked Bison. ''We're not talking about another Morble, are we? I don't think I could stand another Morble loose in the forest.''

''I was speaking metaphorically. The red dragon represents our desire to perpetuate the gnomish species.''

''Is that all? Why a red dragon, for Agni's sake? Why not a red rabbit? That would be more appropriate surely?''

''Whoever heard of a red rabbit?'' asked Spector, annoyed.

''Whoever heard of a red dragon?''

''It's not a *real* red dragon, you damned fool.'' The Miggot entered the argument. ''It's a *symbolic* red dragon.''

''Sometimes,'' said Jack o' the Warren thoughtfully, ''I think rabbits have the right idea. They have no sense of guilt. No sense of shame. They just go ahead and do it.''

''So it could just as easily be a symbolic red rabbit.'' Bison pursued his point, ignoring Jack. ''You could easily have said, 'The red rabbit of l-lust' ''—and here Bison flushed, stumbling over the words—'' 'has breathed fire into the l-loins of gnomes.' But you didn't. You said 'dragon.' Why?''

"Bison's hit the nail on the head, as usual!" cried Lady Duck. "The dragon was meant to intimidate us. It was a cheap trick!''

Spector, uncharacteristically, lost patience. "I had no intention of intimidating anyone!" he shouted. "All I wanted to do was sum up the situation as I saw it! It didn't have to be *me*, but I didn't see anyone else stepping forward. So I volunteered, out of the goodness of my heart. The situation needed summing up, so I bloody well summed it up. If I'd known it would lead to this, I'd have kept my mouth shut. And then where would we be? Answer me that!''

"But why talk in riddles, you fool?" asked Lady Duck.

"You want it straight? Then you can have it straight. The fact is that after millennia of near celibacy, some gnomes are feeling the stirrings of filth!''

"A-*ha!*" exclaimed Bison, scrutinizing the audience for signs of guilt. "So that's what it's all about, is it? Of course," he added hastily, being a fair-minded leader, "I'm quite sure that filth has its place in the scheme of things.''

Lady Duck swung around on her husband. "What's gotten into you, Bison? Do you feel any stirrings of filth? You'd better not, or it'll be the worse for you! I did my duty long ago!''

"I feel no stirrings of filth," Bison reassured her.

Lady Duck turned to Elmera. "Do you feel any stirrings of filth?''

"Well . . ." Elmera avoided her eyes. "I . . . it doesn't strike me as being filth anymore, Elmera. It strikes me as somehow . . . normal. Pleasurable, almost.''

"Pleasurable?" trumpeted Lady Duck. "What in hell is pleasurable about grappling all night with that bloody Miggot?''

"Who said anything about the Miggot?''

Lady Duck snorted with outrage. "What's gotten into everybody?" She stared around at the gathering. Everybody looked sheepishly at everybody else. "Bison, are you and I the only sane ones here?"

He regarded her helplessly. "That seems against all the odds, my dear." His eyes roamed among the crowd, seeking an ally; or failing that, at least a buttress of common sense. His eyes found Fang. "Fang will have an explanation," he said confidently. "Spector could be wrong. Where are the signs of these stirrings, anyway? If there really were stirrings, everyone would be lying around together, groping and struggling like the giants do. But this is a very decorous gathering, I'm happy to say." He smiled at the audience. "A typically gnomish gathering. I'm proud of you all."

Nobody smiled back, however. The gnomes wore oddly intense expressions. The Miggot said mildly, "You're right, Bison."

"It's a decorous gathering?"

"No. Fang might have an explanation."

"Fang? Fang?" roared Lady Duck. "Fang's the worst of the bloody lot! Fang and that Princess of his never think of anything else! Every morning they bear the scars of the night's filth. The sunken eyes. The trembling hands. The nasty, sniggering chuckle. Their brains are corroded with lust and their bodies are going the same way. They spend their lives in mutual degradation, surrounded by the spawn of their evil doings!"

"I say, that's putting it a bit strongly, isn't it?" Bison's eyes returned to where Fang and the Princess stood holding hands.

"They're thinking about it right now. You can tell just by looking at them!"

"Yes, but so's everyone else. It's the current topic of conversation."

"Well, *I'm* certainly not thinking about it. It's the farthest thing from my mind, I can assure you!"

"I don't see how it can be, my dear."

"Are you contradicting me, Bison? Has the red rabbit gotten you too?"

"Absolutely not. You need have no fear of that. I'm with

you all the way, Lady. This thing has to be nipped in the bud.''

''Then nip it in the bud, Bison.''

Bison's unhappiness was such that even this phrase seemed to have sexual overtones. Flustered, he faced the gnomes. ''There is a suggestion—only a suggestion, mind—that a handful of gnomes among us have become afflicted with, um, um, *giantish* tendencies in the area of, um, um, repro— Well, *you* know what I mean. That's the way it seems to me.''

''That's just what I said,'' observed Spector coldly. ''Except that I said it a damned sight more elegantly.''

''Yes, but you don't catch Bison using a word like *loins,*'' retorted Lady Duck.

''We're wasting time!'' cried Clubfoot Trimble, who had established meaningful eye contact with the female gnome opposite. ''We've gone full circle! Let's put it to the vote!''

''Put what to the vote?'' asked Lady Duck.

''The issue!''

Somewhat taken aback by the incisiveness of the normally bumbling Clubfoot, Lady Duck said, ''What issue?''

''Filth!'' called somebody.

''Don't be ridiculous! How can we vote on filth?''

''Just like any other vote. Whether we're for it or against it!''

And there was a roar of agreement.

''You must refuse to put it to the meeting, Bison,'' said Lady Duck. ''These gnomes have become inflamed. I can't answer for the consequences.''

''A vote! A vote!'' shouted the gnomes.

''The democratic process, Bison,'' called Spector.

''Don't do it, Bison,'' warned Lady Duck. ''It would be political suicide.''

''I won't do it!'' roared Bison.

But for once even Bison's powerful voice was lost in the outcry. ''Shame!'' yelled the gnomes. ''Resign!''

''Resign?'' said Bison, puzzled.

''They're challenging your leadership, Bison,'' Lady

Duck explained. "This is nothing less than an attempted coup. It's Drexel Poxy all over again!"

"A coup?" Bison considered the notion. The gnomes surged around the platform, yelling. "A coup?" The idea began to have its attractions. As he gazed at his milling followers he was struck by the unsavory resemblance they all bore to the Miggot; the furious little eyes, the thrusting beards. And in the case of the females, the thrusting breasts. It was the horror of this last image that decided him. "We will put it to the vote!" he bellowed.

"You fool, Bison. You have forfeited your kingdom."

"Have I?" he said, feeling no sense of loss. The gnomes were all smiling now. "Who proposes the motion?" he asked. "You, Miggot?"

The Miggot's expression was crafty. He was well aware that he was the most unpopular gnome present, with the possible exception of the Gooligog. "Not me. Fang proposes the motion."

"Fang! Fang! Slayer of the Daggertooth!" cried the gnomes.

"You have feet of clay, Bison," said Lady Duck quietly. "The situation calls for a strong hand. I will speak on your behalf." She stepped forward. The crowd fell politely silent. "Now listen to me, gnomes of Mara Zion," she said. "This is a crossroads in the history of gnomedom. If ever a happentrack branched, then a happentrack will branch now. We are deciding the whole future of gnomehood, and if we decide wrongly, we will be casting away our history as though it had never happened. Let us not get carried away by the heat of the moment. Let us consider the Kikihuahua Examples, and the legacy that our great creators bequeathed us. Let us vote for Bison, who represents honesty and virtue and clean living. Let us vote for everything that is good; everything the word *gnome* stands for.

"On the other hand," she thundered, her expression stern, "we can vote for Fang and the degradation of the flesh, for the stuffing of every corner of the Earth with our kind so that our very children get trampled underfoot, for the perversion of unbridled, nightly filth. Bison is a fair-minded gnome and he offers you that choice. So vote, gnomes. Those who wish to walk the slippery slope to corruption, raise your hands—if you dare! Crawl out of your stinking holes and show yourselves, you scum!''

A forest of gnomish hands shot skyward.

"Well, that wasn't too bad," observed Bison. "I think Old Crotchet is on our side."

"Crotchet has arthritis, Bison," Lady Duck explained quietly. "He can't raise his arm above his shoulder. But never mind." The battle lost, she smiled. "You can take a well-earned holiday from the cares of office. The fate of gnomedom rests in younger hands."

"Fang! Fang!" roared the gnomes, hoisting their hero shoulder-high.

And an echoing cry came from the forest: "Fang! Fang!"

Startled, the gnomes nearly dropped the Slayer of the Daggertooth. "Who's that?" Fang shouted, quickly assuming his role as spokesman for the forest gnomes.

"It's us."

"That sounds like Mold," said the Miggot. "What the hell does he want?" A small flock of shytes could be seen circling above the treetops. "And the Gooligog. This looks like an official visit."

"A resumption of diplomatic relations," suggested Jack o' the Warren. "That often happens on a change of leadership."

"The news of the coup hasn't had time to reach them yet, you fool," snapped Lady Duck. "The truth is, they've come to resume diplomatic relations with King Bison. I only hope their disappointment won't change their minds."

"Are we sure we want diplomatic relations with Poxy?" asked Bison doubtfully.

"No!" cried the Miggot. "We bloody well don't!" He faced the forest. "If there are any followers of Poxy in there, you can bugger off back to the beach right now! We have nothing to say to you!"

"We're not followers of Poxy," said Mold, entering the clearing on foot with the Gooligog, Pong the Intrepid, Bart o' Bodmin, and various other beach gnomes. "Poxy is a mere memory in the Gooligog's mind, a sad chapter in gnomish history. Poxy was deposed last night, and I am the new leader of the beach gnomes. I intend to uphold the Kikihuahua Examples," he assured them, "so far as is feasible."

"That's good news, Mold," said Fang.

"I'll go further. I believe the beach is an unsuitable place for gnomes to live. We've been dupes of the abominable Poxy for five years, but we are dupes no more. Our eyes were opened at Camelot." He went on to describe Poxy's perfidy, concluding, "And so Poxy rode north, back to where he came from, and his disciples, shamed, departed in all directions. We came back here where we belong."

"How many of you?" asked the Miggot.

"A few. Twenty. Most of those who left five years ago. We were never Poxy's gnomes, really. Our hearts were always here in the forest."

"I moved back into the forest long ago," explained the Gooligog.

"I never left my cave at the other end of the beach," said Pong.

"And I only stayed in the village," said Mold, "in order to gather evidence of Poxy's wrongdoings."

"And what about you, Bart?" asked the Miggot. "What's your excuse?"

"I was one of Poxy's dupes," admitted Bart, glancing unhappily from gnome to gnome. "I throw myself on your mercy."

"Begone!" shouted the Miggot. "Back to Bodmin where you belong!"

"I can't go back to Bodmin. Poxy's gone there."

"Then go somewhere else, but never enter the forest of Mara Zion again!"

"I say, Miggot," said Fang, "that's a bit drastic, isn't it?"

"He's an untrustworthy gnome, Fang. He tricked us from the start. He cost us six years of anger and despair!"

Elmera, faced with the difficult choice of siding with her husband or Fang, chose Fang. "Balderdash, Miggot! The last six years have been no different from any other! Your whole life has consisted of anger and despair!"

Miggot, staring at her furiously, became aware that her breasts jiggled in a fascinating manner when she was annoyed. It seemed to put a different complexion on things. His fury abated. "You're right, Elmera," he muttered. "I must watch myself."

Amazed, she said, "I'm used to it." Really, he was quite a handsome gnome when he was aroused, with the most arresting eyes. And he was probably the cleverest gnome there. People listened to him when he shouted. That was something to be proud of.

More was to come. There was a commotion in the forest: the sound of yelling and snapping twigs.

"That's the remainder of our group," said Mold. "They didn't want to show themselves until our situation was resolved. They are proud gnomes."

The noises approached, and suddenly the proud gnomes burst from the undergrowth in a solid phalanx, shouting excitedly.

"Welcome back," said Fang.

"Speech!" shouted Lady Duck. "You must address your new empire in the proper manner, Fang. This is the occasion for a rousing speech!" She smiled at him broadly. She was always loyal to whoever was the gnomes' leader, and she was incapable of bearing a grudge.

"A rousing speech!" chorused the gnomes, lifting Fang and setting him on a stump.

Fang regarded his people. "It's good to see everybody together again," he began. "And being the kind of gnomes we are, we'll forget the past and treat the newcomers with understanding. We will set the moles to use and get the new dwellings built right away, and meanwhile I'm sure each of us will take a guest into his own home."

He surveyed the ex-beach gnomes. "A lot has happened in the past few years. We've had to adapt to the joining of happentracks and the arrival of giants. The giants are our friends, but that doesn't mean gnomes must become humanized—as I'm sure the newcomers now realize. New customs have arisen to meet the changing circumstances. At Memorizing sessions, for instance, we've been taking more of an interest in our gnomish heritage.

"We've been hearing gnomish fables from the past, and learning gnomish poems. Perhaps I should take this opportunity to recite one of our favorites now. It's short and easy to learn—and quite rewarding too."

"A poem!" cried the newcomers happily. If Fang was going to teach them a poem, it meant they were accepted.

And, smiling at them blandly, Fang began:

> *The shape of a gnome is a wonderful thing,*
> *Two eyes and two elbows and two everything. . . .*

"Arthur's back at Camelot," said Nyneve. "He arrived the night before last from Cirencester. He didn't sleep with Gwen. But then last night they were going to have a party for him."

"So he probably got boozed up and slept with her last night," said Merlin. "Too bad, Nyneve. Isn't it about time you forgot about him? You haven't seen him for years."

"I'll never forget about him."

"You're twenty-one now. You're a grown woman, Nyneve."

"You've been telling me I'm a grown woman ever since I was thirteen years old, Merlin, you dirty old bugger. Jesus! I wish you were a cold fish like Avalona." Nyneve appealed to her stepmother. "Why is it that you have no emotions, Avalona, and yet Merlin's . . . Well, you know what *he's* like."

"I am a Dedo and Merlin is a Paragon."

"But you're both Fingers of Starquin."

"I am a Finger. Merlin is a mutation. An error. A chance male. They have their uses." She regarded Nyneve thoughtfully. "The time has come to make certain adjustments to you, in order to get a correct balance of ifalong possibilities."

"Stay away from me! I'm not so scared of you these days, Avalona!"

"I realize that, which is why I am going to point out the advantages of what I am going to do. Up to now you have merely been my handmaiden. But as of today, you will be a Dedo like myself."

Nyneve felt her stomach knot up with horror. "But I don't want to be a Dedo! I'm an ordinary girl and I want to stay that way!"

"When you are a Dedo, you will not age by human standards. As the years go by, you will still look like a girl of twenty-one. Arthur, being a human male, will appreciate that."

"No!" Nyneve was crying with terror. "Dedos have no feelings! *You* have no feelings! What's the point of living if I can't love Arthur?"

"Listen to me, Nyneve. In less than one and a half millennia the human population of Earth will explode. Mara Zion will become a city as big as Cirencester. England will have hundreds of cities that size, and many others so big that you simply cannot imagine them. Humans will be everywhere, and forests like Mara Zion will be rare. In order for a Dedo to pass for a human, she will have to act like a human in every way.

"She will need human emotions. She will possess all the Dedos' other characteristics, such as our sense of duty, and if necessary, these will override her human traits. But in all other respects she will, in effect, be a human. She will think like a human and feel like a human.

"An in human terms, she will be immortal. That is what the Dedo of the future will be. That is what I am offering you. There is a precedent. Morgan le Fay possesses such human emotions as suits her."

There was a long silence. "So I will still love Arthur?" said Nyneve at last.

"For the rest of your life," said Avalona.

Nyneve walked; Avalona and Merlin rode the mule. They saw nobody as they made their way north through the forest twilight; no humans, no gnomes, no forest creatures. *It's just as though we have a whole happentrack to ourselves,* thought Nyneve. She would not have put it past Avalona to arrange it that way, to make sure nothing went wrong on the journey.

Night had fallen by the time they reached the forest edge. The looming breast of Pentor rose before them, silvered by the full moon. Nyneve regarded the moon intently and saw, faintly, another orb overlapping. They *were* on a different happentrack. There were no humans on this world, no animals, nothing animate that might divert them from their course of action by causing happentracks to branch. They were riding to Pentor and nothing could stop them.

Avalona's powers were immense and frightful, yet she looked like a little old lady perched ridiculously on the rump of a mule.

And soon, thought Nyneve, *I will have powers like hers.* The realization shook her. She was quite certain she wouldn't be able to handle it and that she would accidentally destroy the world, including Arthur and herself.

They leaned into the slope and plodded upward. The mule drew close and Avalona turned toward Nyneve, a pale face against the darkness. "With the change comes the power to deal with the responsibility," she said, anticipating Nyneve's thoughts as usual. "That is the difference between you and Merlin. If you remember, the last time we visited the Rock, Merlin failed to fulfill his responsibility, and he left it unguarded. That is the kind of behavior you will learn to expect from a Paragon. You remember the story of Siang the Paragon and the Thing-he-did? He mated with an ape and the result was the human race. That tells you everything you need to know about Paragons."

They halted beneath the granite cliff of Pentor Rock and dismounted. Avalona said, "This time you will remain here, Merlin; otherwise I will be forced to assume you are totally useless and will have to dispose of you."

"Why are you talking to me like that? I've done nothing wrong!"

"But you may, Merlin. I have scanned the ifalong briefly and observed that on a measurable percentage of happentracks you will fall asleep. By threatening you I have reduced that percentage of happentracks to a more acceptable level. Keep standing, keep watching the Moon Rock, and if a facet starts to glow, you know what to do. Don't you?"

"Place my hand against the facet, accept the essence of the traveler, and send him on his way through the greataway," recited the old Paragon sulkily. "And to my certain knowledge," he added with weak defiance, "travelers use this Rock once every 3,265 years on average. So you're making a big production out of nothing at all, Avalona."

"You hear the Paragonic attitude toward our Duty, Nyneve?" commented Avalona. "Now take my hand and stand close to me."

Avalona's hand had a reptilian dryness, but that was not why Nyneve was shuddering. She'd been on this route before, many years ago when Avalona had taken her to meet Starquin the Five-in-One. It had been a disorienting, terrifying experience for a practical girl who liked to keep her feet on the ground. She watched while Avalona placed her free hand on that strange, warm part of the Pentor outcropping the locals called the Moon Rock, and she shuddered violently and wished she'd had the forethought to relieve herself before undertaking this outlandish journey.

Then she was in the greataway.

There was weightlessness, and there were stars beneath her feet and all around her. She and Avalona were encased in an invisible capsule, the wall of which felt like soft flesh. If she pushed herself away from this wall, she would soon reach the wall opposite. There was nothing to be afraid of, nothing. She was *not* going to fall into the stars that Avalona said were really suns, she was *not* going to throw up, she was *not* going to wet herself. Everything was under control. She'd done it before and she could do it again.

Taking a deep breath, she scanned the greataway around her.

There were stars, but there was Time, too, and there were Alternatives. She could sense them all, and they filled her with so much wonder that she forgot her physical entity and its limitations. She was a part of the greataway, and it was a part of her. Certain of Avalona's words floated into her mind. When she'd first heard them, she'd confused them with religion, because she'd been young and inexperienced. Now she knew them as truth: "In the beginning there was only one happentrack. Multiple happentracks began when the first animal was wise enough to make the first decision."

It was a comforting thought. She was not at the mercy of the greataway. Instead, the greataway was at her mercy, and at the mercy of all creatures like her.

Simple words came to her.

She looked at the immensity and said, "I love you."

"I know what you mean," said Avalona, her voice echoing oddly.

"You really do, don't you?"

"We have little in common, you and I. But we do have this."

"I'm not frightened anymore."

"There is a stage of awareness when fear has no meaning. You have reached that stage, Nyneve."

"How long did it take me?"

"1,295,498 Earth years. That's fast by human standards. You have adapted well, and you are very suitable."

"Are you pleased?" And for once it was not a stupid question to ask a Dedo.

"I am pleased," said Avalona.

"Have you found Starquin?"

"We are traveling on his psetic line now."

"How long has it taken us?"

"Two million years."

"But what about Earth?"

"Earth is still as we left it. It will be the same when you get back."

"I don't understand."

"Soon you will understand everything. Open your mind the way I taught you, Nyneve."

"Is he here?"

"He is here."

It was like an old memory revived, as Starquin touched Nyneve for the second time.

Then Starquin spoke. And as he spoke, Nyneve grew stronger, as though his words fed her body. Avalona was forgotten. Merlin and Arthur were forgotten. The ifalong was everything, and the ifalong was hers to shape.

Aeons later, when she knew everything there was to know, Starquin said, *"We are our consciousness. I have given you my consciousness. You are me, and one day you will save my life."*

Nyneve turned and rode the invisible ship back, and a few million years earlier she arrived beside the Moon Rock.

"Where's Avalona?" asked Merlin, still awake.

"In Starquin."

He thought about it. "Thank God for that," he said at last. "So it's just you and I, Nyneve?"

As he moved closer she said, "Avalona is in me too."

16

THE LAST GREAT BATTLE

FIFTEEN YEARS PASSED.

One misty autumn evening there was a knock at the cottage door. Nyneve was engrossed in the far-off ifalong and didn't hear, but Merlin opened an eye. "Come in," he croaked. They never bolted the door these days. Nyneve was well able to defend both herself and Merlin against intruders.

"Arthur!" exclaimed Merlin as the tall figure entered.

The years had treated the king well. He'd filled out physically and gained an indefinable dignity. He possessed, Merlin had to admit, a kingly bearing despite his obvious tiredness.

Nyneve stirred and stretched, yawning. Her breasts rose beneath the cream fabric of her shift. Arthur watched her in sad appreciation.

"By God, you don't get any less pretty, Nyneve. You don't look a day older than when I first met you."

Her eyes snapped open. "Arthur, it's you!"

He smiled. "Didn't you expect me? I thought you could foretell the ifalong."

She flushed. "I don't spy on people, Arthur. Nothing is so important that I have to keep an eye on everybody's movements."

"Avalona thought it was," said Merlin. "She spent days anticipating everything. She said you never know when a happentrack might branch. She was a clever Dedo, Avalona was.''

''It so happens I don't see things the same way,'' said Nyneve. ''I believe a lot of happentracks tend to average out. So I didn't know you were coming, Arthur. It's a pleasure to see you. What brings you here?''

He sat down, glanced at her, then away. ''Tomorrow I ride for Camlann. The Saxons are massing there. We've suffered a lot of defeats lately, Nyneve. The old days seem a long time ago. Everything is falling apart, and we lost half the country last year. Most of the original Round Table knights are dead: Torre, Pellinore, Gawaine. . . .''

''I'd heard. I'm sorry.''

''What was it all for?'' His eyes looked tired. She hadn't seen him for two years, and she noticed new lines on his face; the vertical lines that come from tension and defeat. ''I thought we were going to change the world with the Round Table and our principles of chivalry. Everything was so new and so right, and so *good* when we started out. And yet the more victories we won, the more we seemed to lose. People simply wouldn't see sense.'' The frustration was twisting in him like a rage. ''Why not? We were *right*. Everybody knew that. Your stories proved that; we heard them wherever we went. People loved them. But they didn't love us. They fought us every inch of the way, and once we were out of sight they would return to their old ways: up with the gentry, down with the peasants, bring out the instruments of torture. Why?''

''The stories were an ideal, Arthur. Reality is another thing. Reality is hungry soldiers who haven't seen a woman for days. Reality is sweat and dirty pants.''

''And reality is that people would rather make up their own minds. That was where we made our mistake. We tried to shove chivalry down their throats like religion. They threw it up into our faces. In the end I began to think we were no better than them. Most of the time we were the aggressors, Nyneve. We kicked those Saxons all over England. Did they really want to fight? Did they really want to learn our ways? Even our allies didn't want to be our allies—I realize that now. They joined us because we were powerful. Reality is that people are stupid and selfish and cowardly without exception, and that includes the Knights of the Round Table.''

"So why did you come here, Arthur?''

"Tomorrow I ride to Camlann,'' he said again. "Will that be the end?''

"The stories said it was the end.''

"So what was it all *for?*''

Nyneve wanted to cry. "It was for Starquin. Perhaps it was for humans as well. People will always remember you, Arthur.''

He sat silent for a moment, his jaw clamped tight and the lines very apparent. Eventually he said, "I don't think I know anything anymore.''

"You know why you came here tonight.''

"So do you.''

"No, I don't. I told you I don't spy.''

He was silent.

There was always a temptation to peep into the ifalong. Merlin had probably already done it; he sat there grinning like a pleased dog. Nyneve resisted the temptation and allowed her human side to guess. " 'Camlann, where the last dim, weird battle of the west is fought,' '' she said, quoting from the story. "I can tell you how to win, Arthur. I can predict every move of the Saxon forces. Is that why you came?''

He said, "It would be wrong to win. I've learned that.''

"Then what?''

"The story says that there will be an inscription on my tomb. It will say 'Here lies Arthur: once and future king.' Is that right?''

"That's what the story says.''

"I have to ask you this, Nyneve. Why *future?*''

"It was a story, nothing more.''

He regarded her closely, then said, "It doesn't matter.

I'm going to die at Camlann. I came here to tell you something, not to ask you anything."

"Please tell me, then."

"It's my last chance, Nyneve. I have to tell you that I love you. I've loved you from the moment I saw you in the boat at Avalon. I've loved you every time I saw you in the forest, and I've loved you when I didn't see you. I've loved you through every battle I've fought, and I'll love you when I die at Camlann. I've loved you every single moment of my life. Forgive me. I had to tell you."

She was crying openly now, and suddenly she stood and pulled the shift over her head and threw it aside. She stood naked in the firelight, black hair tousled. As she looked at Arthur, wondering if she was possessed by human or godlike impulses, the tears turned to laughter. Nothing had any importance at all when set beside love. She turned to Merlin, sitting pop-eyed in his chair, and said, "In the words of Avalona, you are superfluous, Merlin. Get out of here before I disincorporate you, and don't come back until morning."

Then she reached for Arthur.

The woman was tall and beautiful. She didn't look old enough for the young man at her side to be her son.

The young man at her side . . . Gwen studied him covertly as they sipped herb tea. He was broad-shouldered and handsome, with wiry auburn hair that reminded her of Arthur. His face was square, with a broad, smiling mouth and bright blue eyes. Lady Jane had said he was twenty-one, but he seemed older and more experienced. He had a way of looking at her that made a pulse in her neck throb. And she was getting toward forty. . . . Shakily she put her cup down.

"It's good to have company," she said. "I wish you could stay longer than one night. With Arthur away so much, Camelot is a lonely place."

"I'm sure it is." Lady Jane wasn't listening, Gwen realized. Since she and Harry had arrived that afternoon, there had been several occasions when she'd gone off into a kind of trance. "Don't you have anything stronger than this stuff?" asked Lady Jane abruptly, putting down her cup with a grimace.

She was certainly outspoken, thought Gwen. That was to be admired. "Wine, perhaps?"

"Yes." Lady Jane was gazing with open curiosity around the room.

Gwen was quite proud of her furniture. "Most of it's from France," she found herself saying, "but the tapestries are from the East."

"Doesn't King Arthur bring back stuff from his wars?"

"He doesn't believe in looting." Gwen couldn't keep the regret out of her voice.

"What a pity. What's the point in fighting if you don't loot? King Arthur must learn to please his troops. It's rape and pillage that knits a rabble into a fighting unit," said Lady Jane with relish. "Rape and pillage. The men must have something to look forward to, or they'll have no stomach for the battle."

"Things haven't been going too well lately," admitted Gwen.

"They say the Saxons are gathering at Camlann."

"So Arthur tells me. He's riding there tomorrow."

"I may take a look myself," said Lady Jane. "I enjoy a good battle."

"Oh." Nonplussed, Gwen turned to Harry. "Are you fighting at Camlann?"

"I see myself more as a tactician. I've made a study of all the famous battles. It's a fascinating subject, military strategy."

"Harry's officer material," said Lady Jane proudly. "You don't waste a man like Harry on the battlefield."

"That was a wonderful victory of King Arthur's at Badon fifteen years ago," said Harry. "The flanking movement under cover of the ridge; it was classic. I wish I'd been there to see it. Of course, I was only a child at the time, but King Arthur's always been my hero. Somehow I can identify with him." He'd moved closer in his enthusiasm; their knees almost touched.

"It was a famous victory," she said weakly.

Lady Jane stood. "I'll go to bed if you don't mind, Gwen. I'll have a long journey tomorrow if I want to get to Camlann. I'll take a goblet of wine to bed. Sometimes I don't sleep very well in a strange castle." Smiling, she left.

"Tell me about Badon," said Harry, his brilliant eyes fixed on Gwen's.

"Well, I don't really know very much. . . ."

"Of course you do. Arthur must have told you all about it."

"I can't think what's happened to Arthur. I expected him home before this."

"He's probably spending the night in Mara Zion. I expect he's met some of his old cronies and they're discussing tactics for Camlann."

"Tactics? I doubt it. His knights were all here yesterday, discussing Camlann until—" She was about to say "until I wanted to scream" but stopped herself. This young man and his mother were clearly very knowledgeable about military matters. "It was very interesting," she finished lamely.

"Will he be using similar tactics to Badon?"

"I believe so." Somewhat ashamed of the lack of interest she'd displayed during the strategic discussion, she said, "They were talking about a broad front in the valley, and a diversion at the ford. Meanwhile Arthur would take an out-flanking force through the forest to the north."

"He'd have to cross the open ground between the river and the forest to do that."

"Yes." Gwen felt well informed and clever. "But it seems there's a tributary flowing down from the forest. It crosses that ground in a deep gully. Arthur says it looks like just a strip of reeds from level ground. That's the way the outflanking force will go, in single file through the gully. It'll take time, but in the space of two hours we'll have a thousand men in the forest without the Anglo-Saxons knowing a thing."

"What a fine strategy." His eyes were shining.

Their knees were touching. Gwen felt a surge of desire. He'd started moving things about on the low table now, hitching his chair even closer so they could see a model battle from the same position. "I . . . I . . ." She was not sure what she wanted to say. She wanted to say something intelligent and perceptive. She hoped Arthur wasn't coming back tonight.

"Let's say this salt shaker is Arthur's outflanking force," said Harry. . . .

A light drizzle was falling as the young man and his mother rode away from Camelot the following morning.

"Did you get enough out of her?" asked Morgan le Fay.

"Enough to ensure the destruction of Arthur and every Briton in the west of England," said Mordred.

They gathered on the plains to the west of the river at Camlann. The last of the knights were addressed by Governayle. King Lodegrance had brought a small army from the far west, and Bedivere had raised another six hundred in the north. Gareth brought men from Wales. Arthur rode up with four hundred men from the southwest, to join the main body camped beside the river.

"How does it look?" he asked Governayle.

"We've had better days." Twenty years had left their mark on Governayle; he was no longer the carefree youth of Mara Zion. Time had not dulled his wit, however; and it was he who had suggested the outflanking movement by which Arthur hoped to surprise the Saxons. "We're outnumbered about three to one," he said.

The Saxon tents covered the southern hillside of Camlann and extended over the ridge and out of sight, giving the impression of limitless forces. Dull clouds hung low over the hills, and a light drizzle fell, matting the horses' coats and dampening the spirits of the squires who were preparing them for battle.

Arthur took Governayle aside. "I talked to Nyneve the night before last," he said.

"Did she give us any hope?"

"As much as she could. Not a lot. This is our last battle, Governayle. You know that, don't you?"

"We've had some good times. We'll go down fighting."

Arthur hesitated. "We . . . we could call it off, you know. We could send every man home. We could save a lot of lives that way. Is there any point in fighting a battle we can't win?"

"You certainly know how to depress a fellow, Arthur. What's gotten into you?"

"I slept with Nyneve the other night. I've been going through hell ever since. My God, if Gwen ever found out! I've betrayed her, Governayle, and I'll never forgive myself."

"Don't feel so bad about it. What about her and Lancelot?"

"I don't believe anything ever happened between them. Neither of them are the type, somehow. . . ." Arthur was gazing southward. "There's another army coming. Will they be on our side, or with the Anglo-Saxons? Who is leading our enemy, by the way?"

"I heard an odd thing from a messenger we captured. It seems one of their leaders is called Mordred. Rumor has it that he's the son of Morgan le Fay from the west. By rights he should be on our side, but Morgan's thrown in her lot with the enemy, I don't know why. You remember her, Arthur? She was that good-looking woman at Baron Menheniot's tournament, when the archers peppered Sir Mador de la Porte." Governayle chuckled. "That's one of the best memories."

"I have another memory of that day," said Arthur slowly. "I was seduced by Morgan le Fay."

"You certainly get around."

"How old is Mordred?"

"Early twenties, I believe. Why?"

"He might be my son."

"And he might not." Governayle regarded his leader

worriedly. Arthur seemed to have all kinds of problems on his mind; not a good omen for the battle to come.

Fortunately the arrival of the men from the south put all that from their minds. The leader was an old acquaintance.

"Lancelot!" cried Arthur. "I never expected to see you again."

Smiling magnificently, the perfect knight dismounted. "It's good to see you, Arthur. And this is Galahad." He introduced a tall, handsome knight in silver armor similar to his own. "Son of Elaine of Trevarron Isle."

Governayle's mouth had dropped open. "Galahad?" he said. "The last time I saw you was twenty years ago in Tristan's time. You haven't aged a bit."

Now Galahad looked puzzled. "I'm only twenty years old, sir. I've lived all my life on Trevarron Isle with my mother and Sir Lancelot."

"Time has played us some queer tricks over the years," said Arthur. "Nyneve would be able to explain it." Her lively face and black hair had dwelt in his mind's eye for two days.

"That's right," said Governayle. "I remember now. It was Nyneve who brought you to the Great Hall."

"It must have been a different man," said Galahad. "I met Nyneve for the first time today."

"Today?" exclaimed Arthur. "Where was this?"

Galahad pointed. "Near that hill. . . ."

Dumden Hill sat on the plain like a bun on a table, two miles south. The lower slopes were fuzzed with bushes, but the soil was thin and no trees grew. The top was bare rock, with grass in the creases. Nyneve reached the top at about noon and sat down with her arms around her knees. The clouds hung close above her head, and a light, cold wind ruffled her hair. The armies were spread across the land beneath her, toy soldiers with their tiny toy spears and bows. Arthur's forces were nearest, separated from the Anglo-Saxons by the wandering silver thread of the river.

"You're going to lose."

The voice came from behind. Nyneve turned to see Morgan le Fay smiling at her coldly.

"I know. But in the end we'll both win. Starquin will be saved."

"Let's hope so." Morgan sat beside her; a little taller, a little older-looking, but centuries older in years. Not evil, not good; just another Dedo.

Nyneve hated her more than anyone on Earth. "We could work together."

"Not when you're so wrong. But perhaps it doesn't matter. Every able-bodied man in England will be here." They had come from the farthest corners of the land, and they were still coming in the thousands; armies, groups, lone figures straggling across the fields to Camlann.

The quicker she wins, thought Nyneve, the less men will be killed. "Where's Mordred?" she asked.

"You know about Mordred? Of course you do. Mordred's in there, planning. He's born to it, of course. Just imagine it, Nyneve! The son of Arthur and me, down there. The capabilities of the boy! He won't stop at victory, of course. Once Arthur's beaten, he'll divide the Saxons and get them fighting among one another. He's a master tactician, is Mordred. The Saxons are just a rabble of tribes—they'll be happy to kill each other off. Then perhaps we'll move to France and stir things up. All this is just practice, of course. I don't pretend we can eliminate the human race this easily."

"The Saxons are attacking." Clear trumpet notes rode the wind.

"No, humans will become more sophisticated," continued Morgan. "Communications will improve and tribes will get bigger. They'll come back to Pentor one day, and they'll have machines to kill one another with by then."

"Arthur's holding them at the river. It looks as though your people have broken through to the north. Oh, why do they have to fight like this? Haven't they learned anything from the gnomes?"

"The direction of progress is clear. In due course humans will have weapons that can destroy Earth."

"In that case they'll destroy the Rocks with it. Isn't that what we're trying to prevent?"

"You have too much human in you, Nyneve. You have a sentimental attachment to this world. It doesn't matter a damn whether Earth and the Rocks are destroyed, provided it doesn't happen at the exact instant when Starquin is on the psetic line leading to your Rock at Pentor. And right now my reading of the ifalong tells me we're still heading for that unfortunate coincidence."

"I agree. Look, that's Lancelot down there. I recognize his colors. He's fording the river. They're mounting an offensive." Nyneve couldn't keep a certain pride out of her voice. "They're hopelessly outnumbered, but they're attacking! Don't you see something praiseworthy in that kind of spirit, Morgan?"

"Very much so. Racial suicide is just what we want."

Time went by. The battle ebbed and flowed. Deeds of heroism were done and legends were born. Many men died. The Saxons grew confident and moved their headquarters forward. By early evening a cluster of tents had been set up in a crook of the plain at the edge of the forested hills.

"Arthur's moving men into the forest above that glen," said Nyneve.

"Of course he is," replied Morgan.

Arthur led the task force himself. Perhaps it was bravado, or perhaps it was an unwillingness to send his men unled into a hopeless position. The battle was lost; it had been lost months before. The great outflanking move planned at Camelot was now just a dream; he had insufficient men to carry it through. There was, however, a slight chance that he could assemble a force in the forest and make a direct attack on the enemy headquarters. It was their last chance.

Arthur crawled along the ditch against a rush of chilly water. Rain had swollen the flow. Fifty men crawled behind him; a thousand would not have been enough. Behind them, fires were being lit and the battle was winding down for the night. No ground had been yielded; the adversaries still faced one another across the river. Casualties had been heavy, and much the same for both sides—which meant that Arthur's smaller forces had lost the day. Another day's fighting and it would all be over, unless a single, crippling blow could be delivered under cover of darkness. . . .

"We'll take the north side of the ridge," Arthur murmured to Governayle, immediately behind him. "We'll work our way east and then climb over the top. The tents will be below us."

"I thought I was going to drown in that bloody river. There was a pit in the bed, and my armor took me down. What a way to die!"

"Quiet. We're nearly there."

Arthur lifted his head and peered through the reeds. He jerked down again. Soldiers stood a few feet from the ditch. The trees were twenty feet farther. He crawled on, and soon overhanging bushes provided better cover.

"All right. This is far enough." He climbed out of the ditch. Trees were all around him; spreading oaks and chestnuts. Not the best of cover because the trunks were few and far between, but the leafy canopy cut down the fading daylight. He grasped Governayle's hand and hauled him from the ditch. Others followed. An owl hooted like a woodwind.

"Hurry!" Governayle whispered urgently into the gloom of the ditch. Fifteen men gathered. Sixteen.

Arthur said, "I heard something." It was a stealthy sound; a faint chink of armor, as though somebody had begun to move, then thought better of it. Everything was still again. Across the river, men and horses could be seen moving. Occasionally someone would shout an order, but there was no sound of fighting; no screaming or clashing of metal on metal. The battle was over for the night. Somewhere a minstrel plucked at his lute and began to sing a slow Welsh song.

Some twenty-five men stood shivering in the woods.

"Now!"

It was more of a scream than a shout; a frenzied and

triumphant scream from the south. A mob of soldiers ran yelling from the nearby forest and ranged themselves along the ditch, stabbing downward with pikes. Another group spread through the trees to the north, cutting off Arthur's retreat. A third force moved from behind the trees to the east and began to advance slowly down the forested slopes.

"Arthur!" Another shout, and a young man ran into view, laughing insanely. Arthur didn't recognize him in the dim light, but there was something familiar about his appearance. He carried a sword, but he didn't approach any closer. "You've lost, Arthur!" cried the youth. "Do you know who's beaten you?"

Arthur said to his men, "I'm going to fight. You do as you like, but I think they'll kill us whatever we do. Who's that laughing fool, by the way?"

"I think it must be Mordred," said Governayle.

"We'll stand in a circle," said Arthur. "We'll be broken up in the end, but at least it'll protect our backs for a while."

"Yield!" cried Mordred.

"How's Excalibur working these days, Arthur?" asked Governayle.

"Good enough. Here they come!"

The attackers rushed them from all sides. Outnumbered ten to one, the little circle contracted. Yelling, two soldiers attacked Arthur simultaneously. Excalibur flickered twice, and they staggered away, swords drooping, clutching their wounds. Governayle fought beside Arthur like a man inspired, and the rest of the force gave ground only grudgingly. But for every man they beat off, several more arrived to take his place. Gradually Arthur's force dwindled, fighting tiredly now, the circle contracting further as men fell.

On the other side of the river, Gareth said to Lancelot, "Arthur's fighting over there. I can hear him. They've been caught on the edge of the forest." He peered into the gathering dusk. "We'd better get over there quickly!"

"We can do no good."

"We can save Arthur!"

Lancelot shook his head violently; not in disagreement,

but to silence an imp of a voice speaking in his mind. "They're expecting us to do that. We'll lose an army trying to ford the river. Their archers are in position."

"You don't know that!" Gareth was outraged. "You're a bloody coward, Lancelot!"

Lancelot shut his eyes, hearing the voice in his mind, wondering what was happening to him. He shook his head again. "I'm going mad," he muttered. "I'm possessed!"

Keep your men out of the river, said the voice again. *The river is certain death for them all.*

"I will go alone," he said. "One man can cross the river without being seen. A thousand can't."

"You don't have to do that." Gareth was contrite. "I spoke without thinking."

"I don't intend to mount a one-man frontal attack," said Lancelot sarcastically, "but at least I can scout out the situation. They won't kill Arthur. He's more use to them as a captive—a symbol of our defeat. I may have a chance to get him out of there. I can try."

"I'm coming with you, Father," said Galahad.

"May God be with you both," said Gareth.

"If we don't come back," said Lancelot, "you must yield to the Saxons. There's been enough killing."

"Are you conceding?" asked Morgan, surprised.

"This is just one battle. The war will last thirty thousand years, and I'll be fighting you all the way."

"But why are you sacrificing your key figures? You've lost Arthur and Governayle. Why send Lancelot and Galahad after them?"

"To bring the battle to a quick end," said Nyneve. "The Britons can't fight without leaders."

Morgan was puzzled and mistrustful. "But the Saxons will massacre your people."

"We'll see. And remember, Morgan, the Britons are no more my people than the Saxons are. I'm on the side of the human race."

"Mordred is going to have a wonderful time. He likes his enemies weak."

"Mordred is half human. He may let you down."

"And what about Arthur? When you were human, I got the impression you were attached to him."

"I'm prepared to make sacrifices."

"He's good in bed."

"I know. What's Mordred like?"

"That's a strange question to ask."

"You're a strange person, Morgan. But just keep quiet for a moment, will you? I have one last move to make down there."

It was the one thing Arthur hadn't expected. As he raised Excalibur to parry the blow, he felt the power go out of the sword. Only half deflected, the enemy's thrust entered him. "Governayle!" he cried.

There was no reply. He stole a quick glance to his left. Governayle lay motionless on the ground.

"That's enough!" came a scream from Mordred. "They've lost. I want Arthur alive!"

Arthur found himself on his knees. A terrible weakness swept through him, and he felt warm blood washing down his belly and thighs. He dropped Excalibur and felt himself. His hand was wet and dark in the twilight.

"You're finished, Arthur," said Mordred.

Ignoring him, Arthur turned to Governayle. He saw the eyelids flicker, and the eyes shone momentarily as one of Mordred's men swung a lantern close.

"Well, now, it hasn't been a bad life," whispered Governayle.

"We've done more than most men."

"Whatever they may say about us in the ifalong, it's been worth it." Governayle began to cough weakly.

"Mordred," said Arthur, "be good enough to bring a priest for my friend."

A bubbling sound came from Governayle. He seemed to be laughing. "I can handle it myself, thanks," he said at last. "I have a nodding acquaintance with the Almighty." Then his eyes closed and he sighed the last of his breath away.

"And how about you, Arthur?" asked Mordred. "Are you going to live long enough for me to parade you through the streets of Cirencester?"

"I don't think so."

"What!" Mordred dropped to his knees. "Hold that lantern close, soldier!" He examined the fallen king and saw the wound. "God damn you, Arthur!" he cried. "What the hell happened to the legend?" He picked up Excalibur. "In the end this wasn't much use, either."

There was a commotion nearby, then a group of soldiers appeared, holding two men pinned by the arms. "We caught them trying to creep through our lines, Sir Mordred."

"You're not wearing armor, Sir Lancelot," said Mordred. "What were you hoping to achieve?"

"We have come for the body of our king," said Lancelot. "If there is any humanity in you, Mordred, you will let us take him."

"And give you a figurehead? Why should I do that?"

"Because he is your father. You must allow him the dignity of a proper burial in Mara Zion."

"He's my father? Where did you get an idea like that?"

"Look at him. Look at yourself. Can't you see the resemblance?"

"Coincidence."

"What has your mother told you about your conception?"

A flicker of doubt. "She said my father was a warrior who took her by force."

"You mother is Morgan le Fay, Mordred. Would she allow any man to take her by force?"

"Are you calling my mother a liar?"

Lancelot smiled. "I said she was Morgan le Fay. You know her better than any man alive. What do you think?"

Mordred was silent, thinking. Eventually he said, "It's really not relevant. What matters is that Arthur is here and he is dying. He is little use to me dead. Perhaps we have the makings of a bargain.''

''We could save a lot of lives.''

''A simple truce does not interest me, Lancelot. The lives of soldiers are immaterial.''

Lancelot said, ''Exchange me for Arthur.''

''You? But I could kill you right now.''

''I will be a living emblem of your victory. You will be able to haul me through Cirencester in a cage, if that's what you want.''

''That, and surrender of your forces?''

''Yes. Remember, Mordred, the more men who live through this battle, the more men will be your subjects in the years to come. With me as your captive and a famous victory to your credit, there is little doubt that you will become King of England in Arthur's place.''

''That is certainly possible.'' The idea began to shape up pleasantly in Mordred's mind. ''The cage will not be necessary if you're prepared to be cooperative, Lancelot. You are a respected man in Cornwall, and that could be useful. In time I might even grant you lands.''

''As you please, Sir Mordred.''

Mordred glanced at Arthur, now motionless on the ground. ''You take him back to your lines, you . . . what's your name?''

''Galahad, Sire.''

''Take him away, Galahad.''

On Dumden Hill, Morgan le Fay said, ''You bloody fool, Mordred!''

''He was human, after all,'' said Nyneve. ''There aren't many humans who would refuse a kingdom. And there's not much point in a kingdom if you don't have any subjects. And now that he's thinking of being King of England, you can see what his next step will be, can't you, Morgan?''

''I don't have your affinity for the human race, Nyneve.''

''Well, he'll be needing a queen, won't he? And there's one ready-made for him, waiting there at Camelot. Marriage to her will go a long way toward legitimizing his claim to the throne, in the eyes of a lot of people.''

"That sniveling little shrew? Surely he could do better than her!''

"I'm sure he could, and I'm sure he will. But just for the sake of appearances, he could do worse than have Guinevere at his side.''

Unexpectedly Morgan laughed. "You cunning little wretch, Nyneve. You've made a fine Dedo. It's a pity we have this stupid disagreement about the human race. But when Mordred is king, he'll be in a position to do all kinds of damage. And I have thirty thousand years to play with. I'll win in the end, you'll see if I don't.''

"You're supposed to say, 'Where am I?' '' said Nyneve.

Arthur stared at her. "I was wounded. I thought I was dying.''

"Well, I can take care of little problems like that. Don't you remember how Avalona healed Lancelot's finger? A mortal wound is nothing to a Dedo.''

He looked around. "This is your cottage. How did I get here?''

"Galahad and I brought you. You lost a lot of blood and you've been unconscious for two days. I couldn't do anything about that, and I thought it best not to try.''

He tried to sit up. "I'm as weak as a kitten. What's been happening—''

"Don't even think about all that stuff. Things have changed a lot, Arthur. Don't worry about it.''

"Who is leading our forces?'' he asked in a tone that allowed no evasion.

"We have no forces, Arthur.''

"You mean we're beaten?''

"Not exactly. We've disbanded. Some of our people have gone north with the Saxons to throw the Picts out of Northumbria.''

"Please stop dodging the issue, Nyneve. Who's in charge of England?''

She said, "Mordred and the Saxons. And before you start complaining, Arthur, remember this: You were fighting for a united England. Well, now we've got it. Isn't that worth something?"

"But what about Cornwall? We'll never survive under Saxon rule."

"Mordred and Lancelot came to terms, and Lancelot is ruling the west from Camelot, subject only to Mordred as England's king."

Dissatisfied, Arthur was trying to struggle out of bed. "I must go to Gwen."

"She's with Mordred," said Nyneve.

He stiffened. "With Mordred? Do you mean held hostage by Mordred? Or do you mean in bed with Mordred, for Christ's sake?"

"The latter."

"By God!" exploded Arthur. "The young swine defeats me in battle and now he has to disgrace me. And Gwen's old enough to be his mother. This is a question of honor, Nyneve. Bring me Excalibur!"

"I'm afraid he has Excalibur too."

"Bring me my horse!"

"And the horse."

"The dog?"

"He doesn't have the dog."

"Faithful old Bull's-eye."

"Bull's-eye took a fancy to Gareth. They're in Wales somewhere."

"What a flock of shytes! Don't I have anything left at all?"

"You have me."

He eyed her gloomily. "It's no good, Nyneve. Gwen is my wife. What you and I did was wrong. That's probably what cost me the battle. I committed adultery in the sight of the Lord, and he visited retribution on me."

"Arthur, you are the most irritating man, and I can't think why I love you. You have the most amazing capacity for getting everything wrong. Firstly, the Lord wasn't looking when you and I made love; I can tell you that for a fact. And secondly, it was Gwen who cost you the battle when she blabbed your strategy to Mordred. And thirdly, it wasn't adultery. You and Gwen were never married.''

A methodical man, he worked his way steadily through Nyneve's points, nodding as he found himself able to swallow them. The final point stuck in his craw, however.

"What was that last one again?''

"You and Gwen were never married.''

"Of course we were married. The Baron brought the Archbishop all the way from Canterbury.''

"That's what I thought too. But Governayle came to me before he rode for Camlann. Something had been bothering him for years, and he felt he had to tell someone in case he didn't survive the battle. It seemed that the Archbishop never did get through, after all. The Baron was at his wit's end, because he'd promised you and Gwen a fine wedding. Well, you know what Governayle's like. He volunteered to play the part of the Archbishop to avoid having to cancel everything and send people home. The idea was that the Baron would tell you later, and you could have a secret wedding to legalize things. But then the Baron died at the feast, and Governayle decided he might as well keep his mouth shut. So''—she smiled happily—''you never were married to Gwen, Arthur.''

His face was dark with fury. "And you expect me to fall into your arms?''

"Yes.''

"Bring me my clothes!'' he shouted. "Or did Mordred take those too?''

"Merlin took them. He's washing them.''

"Well, then . . . !'' he cried, looking around for something at which to vent his temper.

"Well then, what?'' Nyneve slid a hand under the blanket and began to twiddle the hairs on his chest.

He looked at her. "Oh, I don't know,'' he said more quietly. The look lengthened. "Perhaps you'd better get into bed with me, Nyneve. I seem to be at a loss.''

"You're in no shape, my love."

"I'll be the judge of that."

Nyneve turned her head away for a moment. When she looked at him again, she was smiling. "Love me now, Arthur," she said. "I need a memory I can keep for a long time."

17
THE DAY OF ASCENSION

FANG WAS MORE UNHAPPY THAN HE'D EVER BEEN. Head down, he stumbled along the forest path, burdened by a fear and a guilt so powerful that he could hardly think. The words of the kikihuahuas kept coming back to haunt him: ". . . that the incentive to procreation is a last resort, and that having used it, the gnomes must return to the spacebat within fifteen years or die."

And tomorrow was exactly fifteen years from the day he'd removed the sexual block from the minds of the Mara Zion gnomes.

Arriving at the blasted oak, he was surprised to find the weekly market in progress. He paused at the edge of the trees and, unnoticed, watched the bustling scene for a while. These were the amiable folk who had been put on Earth to fulfill the gentle wishes of the kikihuahuas. These were the creators of life, the harmonizers of the forests and moors. Their children played around their feet. There were almost as many youngsters as adults these days. All living together in the forest. These were his people, the gnomes.

"You bastard!" the Miggot of One was yelling. "You cheated me and you know it. You'll suffer for this, Spector. I should have stuck with Clubfoot. When he sells a flask of beer, you get beer, not vinegar."

"Let the buyer beware," said Spector, keeping calm. "Isn't that so, Bison?"

315

He'd picked the wrong man. Bison had a grievance too. ''Wal o' the Bottle sold me a potion that was supposed to make me grow bigger. 'A giant in a month or your money back,' he said. And now look at me. I'll swear I'm smaller than ever.''

''Why would you want to be big, Bison?''

The ex-chief's gaze roamed over the gathering. ''There's not a gnome here who wouldn't like to be as big as a giant. Think of the things you could do!''

''Listen,'' the Miggot said with a snarl, losing patience and seizing Spector by the lapels, ''what are you going to do about it, you bugger?''

Scorning the reasoned reply, Spector drove his fist into the Miggot's nose. Grappling, the gnomes fell across a table loaded with artifacts for the tourist trade. The table collapsed and the gnomes fell to the ground, rolling among tiny carvings and seashells. Yelling with excitement, the crowd formed a circle. The Miggot and Spector grimly pounded away at each other.

Fang forced his way through and pulled the adversaries apart. ''What do you think you're doing?'' he cried, outraged. ''You're behaving like giants!''

Spector rose to his feet, unabashed. ''I feel good. I've wanted to punch the Miggot on his stupid pointed nose for two hundred years, and now I've bloody well done it. It's a catharsis. I feel a cleaner gnome.''

''Violence never solved anything!'' Fang was sick with horror. Since the sexual block had been removed fifteen years ago, the gnomes' behavior had gradually become more giantish. Perhaps this was why they all had to die—because they were no longer gnomes, and no longer able to fulfill their function on Earth. Certainly their numbers had increased, but now they were failing in a different way. ''And why have you taken to brewing beer, Spector?''

''Clubfoot charges too much. I'm undercutting him. Give me a year and I'll starve the bastard out of business.''

Fang was appalled. The very concept of money had been unknown in gnomedom fifteen years ago. It had only come into being as a convenient medium of exchange until things settled down again and the refugee beach gnomes found their feet. Barter, and the obligation to return a favor, had been the gnomes' way in the past. Now it had all changed, and money—the giantish coin—had become an end in itself. It had happened so gradually that nobody had noticed.

"But Clubfoot is a member of the Brewer's Guild! There's only supposed to be one brewer in each settlement! The secrets are shared among guild members only!"

There was an unpleasant smile on Spector's face. "Secrets can be unsecreted. I've unsecreted Clubfoot's brew."

Now Clubfoot joined in. "You've been snooping around my cellars!"

"The forest is free for all," said Spector airily, "and guilds have outlived their usefulness. They stifle trade. In these difficult times, competition is the name of the game, Fang. And always remember this—it was the Miggot who first usurped Broyle the Blaze by lighting his own fires. Gnomes must be free to pursue whatever trade they wish. Otherwise, what are all our children going to do when they grow up? Wander off into the bush to be eaten by wolves?"

"But what does all that have to do with punching the Miggot on the nose?"

"It was a visual symbol of the new freedom we gnomes have found," said Spector. "It was an uplifting experience, and I am now a more rounded and complete gnome. Given similar circumstances"—he stared at the gathering with glittering eyes—"I'd do it again."

And astonishingly someone shouted, "The Miggot had it coming."

There was a roar of agreement. "Spector! Spector!" they shouted.

"A simple act of violence," said the Thinking Gnome, "has freed us from the bonds of the Miggot's unspeakable personality. Actions speak louder than words, gnomes!"

"Do you realize what you're doing, Spector?" said Fang urgently, as the gnomes cast around for something to act on. "You're changing the whole structure of gnomedom!

Nobody will respect anyone for their intelligence anymore! Our leaders will be the gnomes with the strongest arms!''

But Spector's eyes were glazed and fervid. "I happen to have a good right cross." He climbed onto a stump. "Gnomes!" he shouted.

As the Thinking Gnome began a powerful and impassioned speech, the Princess joined Fang. Putting her arms around Fang's neck, she whispered in his ear, "I think you ought to tell the Miggot."

"Tell him?"

"He's your best friend."

"The Miggot is?" The emptiness of his social life came sharply home to Fang. "I suppose he is, really," he said, amazed and depressed. At some point in his life, he thought, he would have liked to make a real friend, a companionable and compatible friend to whom he would reveal his hopes and dreams and innermost thoughts. He and the friend, thought Fang, would sit side by side with their backs against the bole of a giant elm, warmed by the summer sun, drinking beer and exchanging views on gnomedom, talking slowly and nodding wisely in agreement from time to time. The friend would never interrupt him. The friend would be about his size, and similar in general build. His beard, perhaps, would be a little bushier, and his eyes would gleam with trustworthiness. That was what a friend was. Instead he had the Miggot.

He took the Miggot by the arm. The Miggot looked at his hand suspiciously. "Miggot," he said, "you and I have been friends for a long time."

"Friends?"

"We're going to take a long walk, and we're going to talk. I have very important things to tell you."

A glimmer of interest showed in the Miggot's piggy little eyes. "Things that have a considerable impact on the future of gnomedom as we know it?" he asked hopefully.

"You could say that, Miggot."

* * *

"Move to Camelot?" said Elaine. She walked to the cottage door and looked out over the gray sea of autumn, whipped into spikes by the east wind.

"It won't be so lonely. There's lots of servants in the castle, and a village around it." Galahad became aware that he was pleading. "Lancelot wants you."

"Leave Trevarron Isle? I've lived here all my life."

"So have I. There are other places in the world just as pleasant. Camelot is one."

She was still doubtful. "What exactly would my status be?"

"Well, the same as here, of course."

She laughed bitterly. "You're still only a child, Galahad. It would *not* be the same at Camelot, because there would be a lot of people watching me and trying to work out exactly where I fitted in. Lance would never marry me, you know that."

"Surely he would."

"You've known him as long as I have, my dear, and you know he's peculiar in some ways. He sees himself as a complete and perfect individual. If he was married, he would have to share. That would make him less than complete."

"He's a good man. He's treated me like a son all these years."

There was a long silence. A gull landed on a nearby fence post and watched them with a yellow and hungry eye. At last Elaine said, "That's because he's your father."

"What!"

"Lance didn't live with us because he loved me, you know. He came on a whim, and he stayed when I told him who you are."

He found his knees were trembling, and hoped it was the cold of the east wind. He was a soldier, not a weakling. "You told him who I am?" he repeated steadily. "I thought I was your son. My father was a Norman soldier who didn't come back. I've always despised him."

"My son died. I buried him up on the ridge. Soon afterward the gnomes brought you to me. You were just a baby, and about the same age.''

''The gnomes?'' He was incredulous.

''They explained. It was difficult for me to understand—they have some strange ways. They said you were the son of Lancelot. And I wasn't in a state to ask questions—I wanted a baby so much. When I told Lance, he seemed to understand what the gnomes had done. He knows them better than I do. I wish I knew who your mother was, though. Often I've suspected it might be Queen Guinevere.''

He put an arm around her. ''I'd rather think it was you.''

''And that's another reason I could never live at Camelot with Lance. Queen Guinevere wouldn't like it. Whenever I visited Mara Zion, I used to hear about her and Lance, and they tell me she can be quite vindictive. I'm safer here, Galahad.''

''Guinevere's gone to London with Sir Mordred, Mother.''

She stared at him, astonished. ''With Arthur hardly cold?''

''There have been a lot of changes since the battle.''

Suddenly Elaine laughed. ''There have been no changes here on Trevarron Isle, Galahad. The land and the sea will always be here. Saxon, Briton, Norman, Celt—it's all the same to my pasture and my sheep. That's the real reason I'm staying here.''

Galahad sighed. ''I know what you mean. It's going to take me a long time to get used to Saxon rule.''

When he arrived back at the mainland, even the beach looked alien to his prejudiced eye. The pebbles seemed sharper, and there was a lanky, dead albatross at the high-water mark. The forest looked somehow sinister, as though foreign animals might lurk there. He found himself remembering things people had told him, about how there used to be three moons in the sky, and how strange it was when the happentracks joined.

He walked north, along the forest path.

The ghosts of chivalry seemed to be everywhere. He heard

phantom armies clashing, Irish shouting. The woodland birds squeaked like armor, and somewhere an animal cried like a wounded man. He walked on, wondering, and came to an open place where the grass was worn with frequent footsteps. Around a large rectangular rock there was no grass at all. He found a slot in the top of the rock, and the rusting remains of an anvil bearing the words:

WHOSO PULLETH OUTE THIS SWERD OF THIS STONE AND ANVYLD IS RIGHTWYS KYNGE BORNE OF ALL BRETAGNE.

And for a while he regarded it, and pictured the scene of long ago. There were no performing bears in his imaginings, and all the knights looked like Lancelot. Then he walked on.

He came at last to a large building with the roof half fallen in, and moss growing on the aging timbers. The doorway was now an arch open to the sky, and grass grew through cracks in the floor. In the center of the floor was a pit that had been a cellar until the joists collapsed. He stood on the edge of the pit and looked down. Seeing a huge circular table down there, he descended a flight of steps to get a closer look. The ghosts of the past seemed very strong here.

He sat at the bench that surrounded the table.

For a while he rested and wondered what life was going to be like under the Saxons and King Mordred.

His eyes must have closed, because he suddenly had the feeling that time had passed, and the afternoon was turning into evening. He ought to be getting on. He would spend the night in Mara Zion, collect his horse, and be in Camelot by noon tomorrow. How would Lancelot react to Elaine's decision?

"A lot of things started here."

The voice was so tiny that for a moment he thought it had spoken in his mind like that strange voice Lancelot and he had heard during the battle of Camlann. Then he became aware that he was not alone. Two small figures stood above him, looking down into the cellar. They started with alarm when they saw him, so he waved a reassuring hand.

"Hello."

"Oh, it's only a giant," said Fang.

"Come on down."

Fang and the Miggot descended the cellar steps and climbed onto the table. They both looked exceptionally gloomy and well attuned to Galahad's own mood.

"Can't you read?" said the Miggot sharply.

"What?" Galahad regarded the gnome, surprised.

"Look where you're sitting."

"What about it?"

"That's the Hot Seat," said the Miggot reprovingly, pointing to the carved letters that Galahad hadn't noticed. "This all happened before your time, of course. But when this table was built, Merlin said that seat was reserved for a perfect knight. If anyone else sat there, he would die a grim and horrible death." There was no mistaking the gusto in the Miggot's voice. "And the prophesy came true. Baron Menheniot died in that seat."

Galahad smiled. "But perhaps I'm a perfect knight."

"Who are you, anyway?"

"My name is Galahad. Who are you?"

But they were regarding him in surprise. "Galahad from Trevarron Isle? Galahad who's Lancelot's son? That Galahad?"

"I don't know of any other."

Fang and the Miggot exchanged significant glances. *That* Galahad," said the Miggot.

"Well, he can't help us now," said Fang. "The situation's gotten beyond Galahad, I'm afraid."

"What situation?" They looked so despondent standing there that Galahad felt an overwhelming desire to help.

Fang explained everything.

It took a long time. When he'd finished, Galahad said, "But it might not happen. Tomorrow might simply go by like any other day, and you'll all still be alive. I don't see any reason why you should die."

"There's no doubt," said Fang sadly. "You have to be part kikihuahua to understand, but there's really no doubt, Galahad. I can feel it in my very cells."

"Fang," said the Miggot quietly, "he *is* part kikihuahua. He has the Princess's genes."

"Oh, yes. It had slipped my mind."

"There's something else that's slipped your mind. Just try recalling what Merlin said at Arthur's wedding feast, about the Hot Seat."

Fang closed his eyes. "It's reserved for a knight who hasn't yet been born. He will shine like the rising sun above all other knights, and he will champion the oppressed."

"And remember, Fang, Galahad hadn't been born at that time. Now, what did Merlin say next?"

"He will champion the gnomes, and will have the knowledge to lead them from the brink of disaster into a place of milk and honey."

"Would you describe this day as the brink of disaster, Fang?"

"Of course I would. It's as brinkish as you can get. Would you please stop asking me questions and get to the point?"

The Miggot turned to Galahad. "You are the perfect knight. You must lead us from the brink of disaster."

Galahad looked perplexed. "I wish I knew how."

"You have the knowledge," said the Miggot firmly.

"Do I?"

Fang belatedly realized what the Miggot was getting at. "Have you ever tried to remember things about gnomish history?"

"No. How could I do that?"

"I'll tell you how."

And Fang explained the technique. The Miggot dozed off within an hour, which meant he never did learn the Memorizer's Apothegm. But as the sacred words became established in Galahad's mind, it was like a curtain being drawn aside. He searched his newfound memories. Not even a Memorizer's memories are perfect, and he discovered things that Fang had forgotten, or perhaps never had known.

By nightfall he knew what he had to do.

The sun lifted over the rim of the sea, tipping the jagged waves with crimson. The Mara Zion gnomes, tired after their night's journey, lay on the sand. Pan, awed by the occasion into showing some sense of responsibility, kept a careful watch over the Sharan. Nyneve and Galahad stood with Fang, the Miggot, and Pong, watching the sun wash the cliff's face with light.

"This is about the right time," said Fang, swallowing his fear. "If we leave it too long, we may be too late." His glance strayed to the gnomes. They were still alive, snoring and smacking their lips over dream meals.

The tide was out and the breeze smelled of drying seaweed. The little group of gnomes and humans set off, sloughed through the sand, clambered over rocks past the cave of Pong the Intrepid, on to a place where he'd been too scared to go, ever.

"Th—there." Pong stammered, pointing. The opening was a black mouth in the brightening cliff. "I think that's where he comes from."

Fang and Galahad went on alone. Galahad was unafraid, but Fang entered the cave with a scampering heart. The interior was dark and smelled of fishy dead things. Pale crawling things sat on ledges, waving feelers. Stealthy scratching sounds were amplified by the echoing cavern.

A huge creature hopped out from a dark corner and landed with a thud before them.

It was almost as tall as Galahad. Fang jumped back with a squeal of fright, clutching at Galahad's legs. The human, inexperienced in what this beast should or should not look like, accepted it at face value.

"It's—" Fang gulped. "It's the lopster! There really *is* a lopster. I wish there wasn't."

"That's what your friend Pong calls it, but it's quite harmless, really. You would call it the Great Grasshopper."

"The Great Grasshopper?"

"You remember the story of the Bat and the Grasshopper? You must do, if I do: 'He thought about what the bat had told him, and toward the end of his days he did discover a safe way to travel. That, however, is another story,' " quoted Galahad.

"It's not hungry, is it?" asked Fang unhappily. "What's it doing here?"

"It's waiting for you. It's been waiting for thousands of years." Galahad laid a hand on the head of the creature. Words sprang into his mind, triggered by the effect of the sight of the Grasshopper on his memory lobe. He spoke them.

"Deheldh ab acrhib. Te shuma."

The Grasshopper stilted out of the cave, its horny feet clicking against the pebbles. It ignored the scream of fright from Pong the Intrepid, crossed the beach to the water's edge, and waited. Galahad and Fang followed. After a moment Nyneve, the Miggot, and Pong joined them.

"Come over here!" Galahad called to the rest of the gnomes. He laid a hand lightly on Fang's shoulder, then walked away, his purpose fulfilled.

He found himself a rocky knoll overlooking the beach, and sat down to watch. The sun was higher now, clear of the horizon, and it was going to be a fine day. A sudden feeling of loneliness overcame him, and he longed to run down the beach and join the gnomes, but he resisted the temptation. His place was here with people his own size.

Down on the beach, the Great Grasshopper was puffing itself up. Its structure was loosening. Molecules were receding from one another like miniature galaxies so that the Grasshopper appeared to be swelling, although it was no heavier than before, and its feet sank no farther into the sand.

"We gave you to Elaine because we didn't want anything to spoil your childhood," Fang had told Galahad. "You see, being part gnome makes you rather defenseless, and giantish children can be cruel and elemental. Nyneve told us Elaine would look after you, and that Lancelot would look after her, so you were quite safe. But now you're adult, and you can't rely on them anymore. Just stay out of trouble, and the giants will come to appreciate you for being a good man. Go to Nyneve if things get too bad.''

The Great Grasshopper was huge now, towering above the cliff so that Galahad was looking at its underside. There, suspended in an insubstantial pouch, lay the gnomes, Pan, and the Sharan. They, too, grew insubstantial as the Grasshopper's aura began to affect them. He saw a tiny arm wave and heard a faint cry of *"Away, Thunderer!"* He waved back.

Nyneve was walking toward him. She was crying.

The Great Grasshopper was hovering clear of the sand. Its hind legs were far out to sea. Galahad was beginning to have difficulty in discerning where it began and ended. Then suddenly the wall of its foreleg rushed toward him, through him, and past him, leaving a faint ozone smell. The Grasshopper and its passengers were gone.

Lighter than air, they would be rising through the Earth's atmosphere, expanding until their constituent atoms were as far apart as the atoms between the planets, and the Grasshopper itself was larger than the spacebat with its thousand-kilometer wingspan. Then, engulfing the spacebat, the Grasshopper would shrink, passing through the bat's very cells and finally coming to rest in one of the bat's mighty chambers. It would deposit its passengers, normal-sized again, on the fleshy floor. It would then suck batmilk and hibernate until its next assignment.

That was the way the kikihauhuas had defeated the Tin Mothers and escaped from their Home Planet. Without the use of machinery, how else could it have been done?

Galahad looked at the sky and thought of the Princess, whom he'd only known for a few hours yet whose genes patterned a part of his being.

"Good-bye, little mother," he said.

Nyneve stood before him. Her face was wet with tears.

"It's just not worth it, being part human," she said. "The pain is too bloody much."

Galahad put a strong arm around her shoulders and they stood close for a while, two very different creatures but both with human emotions.

18
RETURN TO EARTH

"**W**HAT DO YOU MEAN?" ASKED FANG. "THERE'S absolutely no way I'm sucking batmilk until I die of old age. And what about all the other gnomes? I'm responsible for them."

"You will not die for many millennia," Afah assured him. "Batmilk slows the metabolism almost to a standstill. You will die quietly and naturally, long in the distant future, and your tissues will be absorbed by the bat. That is the honorable way. Thus will the temporary race of gnomes cease to exist. You have done your work and we are thankful for it, even though it was in vain."

"What do you mean, in vain? We've brought back lobesful of data!"

"Your data reveals many factors that render Earth unsuitable for colonization. The joining of happentracks brought another intelligent race into your world. Kikihuahuas cannot coexist with other intelligent races. Conflict is inevitable, and we are not equipped to deal with conflict. If we had known the happentracks were going to merge, we never would have sent you down to Earth in the first place. It was a rare and unfortunate event that has invalidated the whole project."

"Send us back!" cried Fang. "We'll take our chances. It's better than sleeping to death! I have young children. My wife, the Princess, is preg—I mean, pregnant." Fang tried appealing to the kikihuahua's sentimental instincts. "How can you deny my children the chance of a full gnomish life?"

"Such is the fate of the obsolete life-form."

"Well, anyway, there's no way we're putting those tits in our mouths."

"You have no alternative." Afah was puzzled and a little disgusted by this lack of acceptance of fate. He'd always mistrusted the gnomes. Their genes contained some nasty traits. Necessary for survival on Earth, but nasty. He sighed, eyeing the squat, aggressive little creature. The main problem was sex. It warped the mind. Why should Fang be so concerned about a dormant fetus in his sleeping partner's womb? Why should he be concerned about anything at all? He'd performed splendidly, and because of his warning, gnomes had been retrieved from all other regions of Earth. And even though their data were superfluous, their tissue was invaluable. Now was the time for them all to go into an honorable retirement. "I can't understand your attitude," he said worriedly.

"You'll understand quickly enough if the gnomes are forced to take over the bat. We're experienced in coups, Afah."

"You can't take over the bat! By the Sword of Agni, you'd tear it apart within one generation! You'd kill us all!"

"We're going to die, anyway."

"But *we're* not. Where's your pride in your species, Fang?"

"Perhaps you should listen to our proposal," said Fang more calmly.

So Afah listened, and when he understood the proposal, he discussed it with Phu and Ou-Ou; then finally they awakened a host of kikihuahuas and put it to them in a general meeting. And with some misgivings they agreed.

"After all," Afah said as their emotions of guarded consent colored his mind, "what difference do a few millennia make? We will sleep for a while, and then, when the time is ripe, we will act."

"If the time is ever ripe," said Phu gloomily.

"We will give them thirty Earth millennia, as they requested."

"I always said those gnomes would be nothing but trouble."

A short while after the decision had been made, Fang came to Afah's chamber. The kikihuahua leader was Memorizing recent events before composing himself for a period of hibernation.

"Wake up, Afah!" said Fang cheerfully.

"It is you, Fang. What can I do for you?"

"I have a little problem with my gnomes."

"That hardly surprises me."

"They're not happy about all going to sleep and leaving you kikihuahuas in charge of this bat."

Afah blinked. "We've always been in charge of this bat. And you are a kikihuahua just as much as I. Why this divisive attitude, Fang, my friend? I don't understand what you're talking about."

"The gnomes don't trust you, Afah. They think you might allow us to oversleep, if you get my meaning."

A great sadness filled Afah. Trust was implicit in the kikihuahua philosophy. They were mutual emotes, so it was almost impossible for one kikihuahua to conceal anything from another; almost impossible to lie. What kind of monsters had they created? "I am truly sorry," he murmured.

Fang was abashed. Afah's sincerity was obvious. "I'm sorry, too, Afah," he said. "But the gnomes have led a rough life down there on Earth, and it's made us careful. All we're saying is this: We want a joint watch to be kept for the next thirty thousand years, so that at any given time there are both kikihuahuas and gnomes awake in the bat."

"That can be arranged."

"Thank you. Please don't take it badly, Afah."

Afah regarded him. "I won't take it any way, Fang. You see, you gnomes are more powerful than we are. You are aggressive and resourceful. So long as you are aboard this bat, you will be a problem for us—even more so than the hordes of Yub, presently asleep in a remote chamber. We can only hope your vigil will be successful, and the time will come when you can return to Earth. You are not suited to life in the bat.''

Fang said sadly, ''You can't imagine how wonderful it was, living on Earth. Every morning you'd see the sun, or else the rain. And you'd look out and sniff the air and wonder what the day would bring. You'd get dressed and put your cap on, and mount your rabbit. Then you'd go visiting. You'd see the Miggot, who'd be grumbling about something. Then around noon you'd drop in on Clubfoot at the Disgusting and have a beer and a chat with people. The trees would be high above you and the animals would be all around, so that sometimes you'd have to be careful. Maybe in the afternoon you'd go to sleep. And in the evenings there'd be singing and dancing and eating and drinking. . . . And all those times there'd be the Princess, and the children. . . .''

''You love Earth very much.''

''It's so hard here, not being able to go *outside*.'' Fang regarded the walls of the chamber with distaste. ''And you don't realize how this bat stinks, like a giant's battlefield. And it's so dark, with just that blue glow. We've been used to sunlight all our lives. I realize,'' Fang said hastily, ''that you feel at home in the bat, and I really don't mean any offense, but . . .''

''I understand. After all, we created you in order that you would feel at home on Earth. It seems we succeeded.''

''I just hope we can go back. The sooner the better. Nyneve was always talking about thirty thousand years. It seems a long time.''

''You said the giants are a violent and bloodthirsty race.'' Afah made the kikihuahua equivalent of a smile. ''Their civilization may run its course quickly. Fast-growing societies often don't last long.''

The years passed, and the centuries, and the millennia. The watches went by, kikihuahua and gnome observing

Earth through the spacebat's telescopic eyes. They saw Mankind's first timid paddle in space, and they watched a few probes skitter by, heading into the greataway. Then there was a pause and some signs of minor conflict, which the kikihuahuas later found were caused by the Consumer Wars of the Fifty-fourth Millennium. The first giant domes were built. The kikihuahuas traced the spread of the Great Ice Age and the start of the Age of Regression. For a while Earth seemed to sleep.

"Are they all dead?" a gnome asked eagerly. "Is it time?"

"No," replied a kikihuahua. "We still see a ship occasionally. The giants are probably in those domes. It's a well-known part of the civilization cycle; a society gets scared and careful and lazy, goes indoors, lies down, and becomes almost totally dependent on machines for food and entertainment. It's happened to many races we've visited. It happened to us."

"What can be so good, inside a dome?" asked the gnome.

"Often the people live a communal dream, with adventures and killing and love, all without danger to themselves. But there are always a few who don't want to live that way, and sooner or later they persuade the dreamers to wake up and go outside. No, the situation is deceptive on Earth right now. They are sleeping but they could awaken. We've seen it all before. So long as an occasional ship comes and goes, intelligent life is there. . . ."

Fang awakened a few thousand years later. In the dim luminescence he recognized Afah bending over him. He shook his head, trying to clear the effects of the milk. Then he drank from the gourd Afah offered him.

"It's our watch again, is it?" he asked. Somehow the idea of another year spent wandering around the bat's fleshy tunnels, killing time, didn't appeal. Millennia of batmilk had sapped his initiative. Afah's next words snapped him into full wakefulness, however.

"It's been many centuries since the last ship was observed. There's a good chance the human race has run its course.''

As they made their way toward the observer's chamber Fang said, ''They weren't all bad, you know. There was a very nice giant called Nyneve, who was even quite pretty. And we created a giant ourselves, to look after our interests when things got tough. In the end we hardly had time to use him. He was kind and good and one hell of a bore, but you'd have liked him, Afah. We called him Galahad.''

''I'm sure he was a masterpiece,'' said Afah dryly. The tunnels had narrowed, and some time later they were crawling through passages where the bat's gravity had diminished, and Fang had to be careful not to bump his head on bony overhangs. ''We are now inside the bat's skull,'' explained Afah. He squeezed through a narrow opening and Fang followed with difficulty. Now they were in a small chamber occupied by another kikihuahua, or something that looked very much like one. ''Hello, Elahi,'' said Afah.

Fang shivered as the observer turned their way. Elahi's eyes were pale and empty, devoid of expression, apparently blind. Emerging from each temple, a glistening strand dangled between Elahi and the wall of the chamber. In some unpleasant way Elahi was plugged into the bat. He'd heard Fang and Afah, but he couldn't see them. His brain was receiving images of the solar system. The strands were the bat's optic nerves. ''By the Sword of Agni!'' Fang muttered in horror.

Elahi reached up and pulled the strands free, leaving small pink orifices in his temples. Simultaneously life returned to his eyes, and he focused on his visitors. Except for his bare temples, he now looked like a normal kikihuahua.

''Afah,'' he said. ''How can I help you?''

''Nothing is happening on Earth?''

''Nothing has happened for a long time.''

''No ships have come or gone?''

''Nothing at all. The planet seems to be dead.''

''There were no destructive wars of any kind? Earth is still inhabitable, so far as you can tell?''

"Yes."

"Let's saddle up the Great Grasshopper!" cried Fang in delight.

"You are still willing to take your chances down there, Fang? I believe that a large proportion of gnomes are now happy where they are. Some of them become quite resentful when awakened to stand their watch. Some have refused."

"You always get some rotten apples."

"Kikihuahuas don't get rotten apples."

"I can believe it. We'll take the gnomes who want to come. The rest can stay here, if that's all right with you. First we must send down an exploration party. Just a handful of us, to scout out the situation. The Miggot, perhaps; and myself; and the Princess, of course. . . ."

"And I," said Afah.

"You?"

"It is my duty. What we are proposing amounts to a colonization of Earth by the kikihuahua race, and I am the leader on this bat. I will go to Earth with you, and return to the bat when I'm satisfied everything is in order, and that the main body can be sent down."

"That sounds fine to me." Fang was already halfway out of the optic chamber. "I'll go and wake the others." Bouncing in the low gravity, singing a gnomish song of joy, he hurried to the hibernation pouch.

Sally was building a simple trap. She'd found the ideal spot the previous day when she'd been strolling the cliff path watching the gulls. She'd come across a recent rockfall where the cliff had crumbled, taking a bite out of the path so that she had to detour inland for a few meters. The pebbles still rattled down.

Bushes stood nearby, carved into cowering shapes by the wind. She broke off the longest sticks and laid them across the narrow gully. Then she gathered twigs and placed them crosswise. Finally, by late afternoon, she'd patted moss into place and scattered leaves over the hole until the deception was perfect.

Finished, she straightened up, watched the soaring gulls for a few moments, then did a curious thing.

She unbuttoned her long-sleeved dress and pushed it off her shoulders so that it dropped and hung in folds around her waist. Her breasts were small and perfect, but there was nothing unusual in that, for a girl of her type. What *was* unusual were her arms. She stretched them out horizontally as though embracing the sea.

She had only four fingers on each hand.

The fifth, the thumb, was bent back and elongated as far as the shoulder. It held a pale bundle against her arm. At first glance this made her arms look unnaturally thick.

Sally shrugged her shoulders, her breasts rose, the thumbs sprang away from her arms, and her wings unfurled—large, white, the membrane covered with down, the larger feathers down-curved into an aerofoil. They were big and beautiful wings of which a swan might have been proud; but they were not big enough to carry Sally into the air.

She flapped them nevertheless; great, slow sweeps as she watched the gulls circling an incoming fishing boat. Then she held them extended and motionless. She felt the wind lift some of the weight from her feet, making her feel lighter but not light enough.

"I wish . . ." she sighed. "Oh, God how I wish that . . ." And she did not put her wish into words but allowed the tears to trickle down her cheeks as she watched the gulls in their effortless soaring. She dipped and curved her wings in imitation of the birds, her mind out there over the water, her eyes seeing the surface far below. . . .

"Sally!"

She stepped quickly back from the edge. She felt the wind on her breasts and looked down at herself. The human in her reasserted itself as she furled her wings and pulled her dress up, glancing around guiltily.

Marc was running along the path toward her, red-faced and excited. "Come and look at what I've found!" he shouted before he reached her.

Whatever it was, he obviously thought it was more interesting than her bare chest and bird envy. She followed him down toward the beach.

He was taller than she, a year older, and quite different in build. His shoulders were broad and his arms long and extremely muscular, which had the effect of making his legs appear stumpy. He was dark-haired and handsome in a Cornish way. Sally found him attractive, which caused her parents some concern.

"He's just an ape-boy," her mother had said on more than one occasion. "Why can't you hang around with boys of your own kind?"

Sally had tried, and failed, to explain that it was not the body of Marc that attracted her, powerful though it was. It was something about the way his mind worked. He always seemed to be in tune with her own thoughts. They both felt there were some questions somebody ought to be answering. Questions about the world beyond Mara Zion . . .

The path broadened at the beach. Marc took her hand and led her along a forest path. "This thing I found, it's weird. And I mean really *weird*, Sally. You remember the savior that blew up? It was walking along, then suddenly it just exploded? Well, that's nothing compared to what I've found."

It was not far. Marc pushed his way through a clump of dense bush against a rocky face.

"A cave!" cried Sally in delight. "I've never seen this one before. How did you find it?"

"I was following Blackberry Nan one day, and I saw her go in here. After she'd left, I took a look."

"But this isn't weird. It's quite exciting."

"Wait till you've seen what's inside."

She followed him, ducking her head. Once inside, she could straighten up again; the cave was roomy. Soon her eyes became accustomed to the dim light.

"Over here," said Marc.

He rolled aside a few stones, exposing the foot of the rock wall. "Look at that."

Sally knelt and stared at the rock. "It's . . . transparent. There's something behind it."

"Feel the rock."

She did. "It's cold. It's like ice, isn't it? But it's not wet. Ice would have melted away. It must be something else."

"Look closely inside there."

Sally peered at the rock. There was a dark patch near the surface of the transparent area. Beyond was a pale bump, but she couldn't see farther than that. "What is it?"

His voice was husky. "It's a man."

"What!" And suddenly the dark patch sprang into focus. It was the top of a head, and the bump was a nose. Beyond that, a beard showed. Sally backed away hastily. She imagined she saw the head move. "Oh, God," she said, scrambling for the daylight at the cave's entrance. "What did you bring me here for?"

"I *did* warn you."

"Yes, but there's weird and there's *weird*. This is as weird as you can get. What's he doing there? How did he get there?"

They began to walk back toward Mara Zion village.

"I wondered if this was the end of a glacier. I remember learning that things come out of the end of glaciers, millions of years later, perfectly preserved. But there are no glaciers in these parts. He must be somebody from a previous civilization who got stuck in there somehow. But that doesn't explain the cold rock."

"We could ask a savior. Saviors know a lot."

"Probably, but they don't always tell."

"This savior will. We'll torture it until it does!"

He smiled indulgently. "Which savior is that?"

"The one that's going to fall into my trap. The evening cliff patrol."

"Oh, shit." He regarded her in dismay. "What have you been doing now, Sally?"

"Well," she said defensively, "why the bloody hell not? I'm really getting tired of the saviors running our lives for us. Do they think we're stupid or something? And now the moors are off-limits.''

"What?''

''Yes, didn't you know? They've put up sentry posts and they're stopping people from going up there. If we want to visit the wild humans at Meniot we have to go a roundabout way. And as usual, they won't tell us why they've done it. 'It is for your own good,'' she mimicked in a tinny voice. "Well, I'm going to get the truth out of the evening savior. The truth about the moors and quite a number of other things. Some questions need answering, Marc!''

"Oh, shit,'' he said again, helplessly. He knew better than to try to deter Sally from a course of action.

The Swingers' village came into view. A group of children were playing kick-up, racing around the clearing and scampering up and down the trees in pursuit of a huge, hydrogen-filled ball. A knot of elders stood outside the schoolroom with their elbows resting on the window ledges, looking in at a teaching savior's screen. A few dedicated athletes practiced for the Cornish Games, flinging themselves around their apparatus with confident abandon. Nobody worked. Nobody dug, planted or harvested, sewed or cooked. The saviors looked after that side of things.

"I'd better go, Marc,'' said Sally. "I'll meet you on the cliff path this evening. Be there.'' She frowned at him, then ran off in the direction of the Wingers' settlement.

Marc watched her go with some foreboding, then the screaming of a child caught his attention. She had fallen from a high branch. A savior appeared from nowhere, scooped her up, and examined her for broken bones. Apparently deciding she needed a more thorough examination, it set off at a run in the direction of the hospital, several kilometers away. The anxious parents unhitched their horses, climbed into the safety cages, and galloped off in pursuit. The game resumed more circumspectly.

Marc approached his father. "They'll be banning kick-up now,'' he said.

Adam smiled. "If they'd intended to ban the game, they'd

have done so long ago. They've calculated the odds on injuries and decided the benefits to our health outweigh the risk. They know there will be an injury every seventy days or whatever, and Katie is just a statistic bearing out their projection."

"Poor Katie."

"The saviors do their best. That's what machines are for."

"And they know what we're going to do. They've got it all calculated."

"More or less. They have an ancient word for it. The ifalong."

"I just wish we could surprise them," said Marc. He thought of Sally the way he'd sometimes seen her, when she hadn't known he was looking. Standing on the cliff watching the sea gulls with naked longing in her eyes. Unfurling those pretty wings and waving them in imitation. "Sally says the saviors locked a whole bunch of people in the dome." The dome was huge, looming into the sky north of Pentor like a silver sunrise.

"They went in of their own accord, as your friend Sally knows very well, if she's watched her history lessons. They have dreams in there that are just like real life, but much safer. You've heard people speak of Dream Earth, Marc. It suits the dreamers and it suits the saviors. There's nothing sinister about it."

"And yet *we* can't go into the dome."

"The dome is for true humans."

Marc and Sally watched in breathless silence from the cover of a bush. The savior came thudding along the cliff path in the twilight, head jerking this way and that as it checked that nobody was lying injured anywhere, that no child was lost or frightened, that the weather forecast had been correct, that the gulls were maintaining their population, and that everything else in the district of Mara Zion was in order. Meanwhile it hummed a merry little tune so that nobody would be startled by its approach. Thump . . . thump . . . thump . . . tootle, tootle, tootle.

Then the watchers heard a snapping of branches, a scrabbling sound, and a rattling cascade of stones. The happy tune continued, but faintly, almost lost in the thud and splash of waves.

"We've got it!"

"Quiet, Sally. It may still be mobile. Wait here a bit longer."

She shook herself free from his restraining hand. "Marc—it's only a savior! It's not a parent or anything. It doesn't matter whether it's mobile or not. It's not going to blame us for anything." She hurried to the rockfall and stared down into the gloom where the waves burst in frothy luminescence against the rocks at the foot of the cliff. "There it is, see? It's not getting up. That's a good sign."

Spray was drifting over the twisted, humanlike figure. "So what do we do now?"

"We go down there and confront it, of course. We question it. We interrogate it. If necessary, we apply pressure."

"It's pretty steep for you, Sally. Shouldn't we wait until morning? It'll still be there."

"The tide will rust it, you fool. You know they can't stand seawater."

"Listen, if you want any help from me, you'd better stop calling me a fool. Just tell me how you think you're going to get down there."

"With the rope, of course. I came prepared."

They descended to a platform of large boulders, all that remained of ancient falls after the tides had swept the small stuff away. The savior lay twisted, humming pleasantly to itself. Its right leg was broken. The skin had split and a mess of parts had spilled out.

"Hello," it said. "I'm damaged and I haven't been able to notify anybody. Will you be kind enough to carry a message back to Mara Zion?"

"No, we won't," said Sally, chuckling triumphantly.

"You're going to stay here until you tell us what we want to know."

"Of course. What can I tell you?"

Its readiness took Sally by surprise and she hesitated. Marc said, "Why did the true humans go into the dome?"

"Because it's much better for them in there." The savior's tones were quiet and reasonable. "The dome was built long before we came on the scene. The humans were already in there, their minds living in a place they call Dream Earth. They'd already discovered mental activity is much safer than physical. Not to mention the increased life span resulting from a perfect diet, administered intravenously. You humans are delicate creatures, like all organic life-forms. You must be protected."

"Suppose we don't want to be protected?" asked Sally.

"It's for your own good."

"Why won't you let wild humans into the dome if it's so good for people?" asked Marc, glancing at Sally's wings. "I'm sure there are people outside who would like to try dreaming."

"The domes are for true humans. That is the way. True humans are inside and wild humans are outside. I thought you didn't want to be protected, anyway," said the savior cunningly.

"We're getting nowhere," said Marc.

Sally was flushed with frustration. "Why don't you allow my people to go out in fishing boats?"

"We do not prevent you. Your own physique prevents you. You Wingers cannot swim. The young man with you belongs to a different race. His kind can swim, so they can go out fishing. Our duty is to protect you from yourselves. Humans are not always completely rational."

"Why can't I swim? Why am I different from him?"

"You were born different. Your parents' genes are different from his parents' genes."

"*Why* are our genes different from True Humans?"

"It is not in your best interests to know that."

"Marc, get a rock. Bash it till it talks."

"Good idea," said Marc. He picked up a large rock and poised it over the savior's good leg.

Sally leaned forward, staring into the savior's flat eyes. *"Who are we?"* she asked quietly.

"It is not in your best interests to know that."

"Bash him, Marc!"

Marc hesitated, the rock held high. The savior's eyes met his blandly. The savior's face was well made. It was convincingly human—with skin, underlying bones, and a complex musculature allowing an extensive range of facial expressions. Now it twisted its features into a pleading look.

"I can't do it," said Marc at last.

"Give me the rock! I'll do it! I'll smash it straight through the chest screen!"

"The rock's too heavy for you, Sally."

"Oh, shit!" Sally cried. "What a bloody fiasco! These bastards have got us by the short hairs, Marc. We've *got* to make him talk. We'll never get a chance like this again. We'll get the truth out of him if we have to pound him to a pulp. We'll—"

"Quiet! Somebody's coming. I heard voices."

"You're just saying that to shut me up. You know what, Marc? You're a bloody weakling!"

"I just can't see the point in smashing up this savior when we both know it's programmed to keep its mouth shut."

"We have nothing to lose. It must have some instincts of self-preservation. When that kicks in, it'll tell us everything. It'll crack suddenly, and scream for mercy. It'll—"

"Somebody's coming down the rope!"

A cascade of pebbles rattled onto the boulders. They peered up, but it was too dark to make out details on the cliff face. "Bloody hell," muttered Sally. "I bet it's my dad."

"Or mine."

The rope twitched. 'Who's that?" shouted Sally. "Tell us who you are or we'll bash your head in! We're ready for you!"

The reply was one they would remember for the rest of

their lives. The accent was strange and the voice tiny, as though a foreign mouse had spoken.

It said, "We come in peace."

It was Fang who spoke.

The words would have been more appropriate if addressed to a formal gathering of Earth's leaders. It takes time to find a leader in an underpopulated region, however, and the exploratory party had landed only a couple of hours ago. Walking toward Mara Zion in the gathering darkness, they had headed for the first human voices they heard.

They assumed these would be the lonely and frightened survivors of an almost extinct race, who would be grateful for help and guidance during their final years.

Instead it seemed their heads were in danger of being bashed in.

"We've made a mistake," muttered Fang, reversing direction and bumping into the hairy buttocks of Afah. "Back up the rope, gnomes!"

Afah began to climb, but the Miggot, above him, accidentally grasped the Princess's ankle instead of the rope. She lost her grip and fell onto him. With a wail of fright he crashed onto Afah. In an instant the four members of the exploration party were rolling down the steep slope. They arrived in a heap at the feet of Sally and Marc.

"Bash them, Marc!" In the twilight the scrabbling figures looked like gigantic spiders.

"They said they come in peace."

"They don't look like things that come in peace. They look like things that bite!"

However, when the small creatures picked themselves up, they looked reassuringly bipedal, although one had a tail.

"We are kikihuahuas," said Afah. "We come from another world."

"Where's your ship?" asked Sally suspiciously.

"We don't actually use *ships*," explained Fang eagerly. "We use bats. We—"

"That's the stupidest thing I ever heard! And why aren't

you gobbling and twittering? Things from other worlds gobble and twitter. They don't have normal vocal cords. But you even speak our language. You know what I think? I think you evolved in a sewer somewhere. Given time, almost anything can evolve in a sewer, so I was told.''

"We used to live on Earth, long ago," said Fang, before Afah could launch into a long-winded explanation.

"Prove it!"

"This place is called Mara Zion." Fang began to give a detailed description of the topography, but Sally cut him short.

"We know all that stuff. Tell us something we don't know."

"Then you wouldn't believe me."

"Why are you different from him?" asked Sally, pointing to Afah. "Why does he have a tail? And he's covered with fur, but you three wear clothes. You can't all be Wawas, or whatever the hell you call yourselves.''

Afah was appalled at the turn events had taken. There was a certain protocol attached to historic encounters between intelligent races. Leaders met and exchanged expressions of mutual esteem. There were usually tall buildings involved, and well-disciplined crowds and speeches. And above all, there was a deep respect for kikihuahua achievements in genetic engineering.

Notably absent from such occasions were belligerent interrogations, accusations of lying, and blinding clouds of salt spray.

He said quietly, "Let me handle this, Fang." Then, drawing himself up to his full height—an act that went unnoticed by the humans—he said, "Take us to your leader."

"No," said Sally.

"I am a member of the most numerous form of kikihuahua," he explained, maintaining his dignity. "The other three are of a temporary form that we created for the specific purpose of exploratory work on the planet Earth. In your language they are called gnomes."

"Gnomes?" Sally uttered a shriek of incredulous laughter. "Gnomes are funny little people in children's stories. They live in burrows and wear pointy red hats."

The Miggot spoke for the first time. Picking up his cap and wiping the moisture from it, he held it out. "What the hell do you think this is?" he said with a snarl.

There was a pause while the two factions regarded each other in frustration. There seemed to be nothing useful this encounter could achieve. It would have been better if it had never happened.

At that moment the situation was further complicated by the savior. Unnoticed by the others, it had gradually struggled to a sitting position, its eyes easily coping with the dim light as it stared at Afah. It registered his height, his weight, his general physique, his fur, his tail. Meanwhile other sensors noted his body temperature, his odor, and his vocal characteristics.

Finally satisfied, it raised an arm and pointed a long finger unerringly at the kikihuahua.

"Master," it said.

Sally whirled around in a fury. "My God!" she cried. "Don't we have enough problems without that crap? Is the spray getting to you?"

But Afah had been going through his own tortuous process of recognition.

Something in the appearance of the sitting figure had touched a chord in his memory lobe. He began to explore it, tracing it back through generations of inherited memories with nothing to guide him but the shape of the savior and a spill of parts from an injured joint. He went further back, until he was revisiting the earliest kikihuahua explorations without having identified the elusive recollection.

Finally he reached the images of the Home Planet, the world from which the kikihuahuas had fled aeons ago, driven into the greataway by the suffocating presence of one of their own creations: the last electromechanical device ever constructed by Afah's race. . . .

"By the Sword of Agni," he whispered, "it's a Tin Mother!"

19

MEETINGS IN MARA ZION

"**A**FTER ALL THIS TIME," MURMURED AFAH, "WE still haven't been able to shake them off. They've been searching for us ever since we left the Home Planet. And now we've inflicted them on someone else. Isn't it possible for us ever to escape the consequences of our own actions? Was the Exodus all a mistake?"

Fang had also been searching his memory lobe. "It seems to me we developed a way of life that wasn't compatible with the Tin Mothers, and we made the choice to go a different route. We weren't running away. The Exodus was a glorious adventure."

Fortunately it was too dark for Fang to see the look of irritation that Afah shot in his direction. "Agni alone knows how many worlds they've contaminated; how many intelligent life-forms have fallen victim to their stranglehold!"

"It's not that bad, really." Marc broke into the conversation, as it was going rapidly downhill. "The saviors have never done anyone any harm. Our history lessons tell us they arrived peacefully and immediately set about helping people. Unfortunately we sold out to them in exchange for an easy life."

"You see, Fang?" said Afah. "We must get back to the spacehopper and report our shame to the bat."

Fang decided it was time to make a stand. "You can if you like. I'm staying, and so is the Princess. And I'm sure the Miggot will. I refuse to set foot on that bat again. I've wasted thirty thousand years of my life in there. You can go back and send our children down, and anyone else who wants to come.''

Afah said, ''You cannot remain on a planet already inhabited by an intelligent life-form. Such is our code, Fang.''

''Bugger the code!'' shouted the Miggot.

The Princess said, ''We're *not* going.''

''Shut up, all of you!'' shouted Sally. ''Stop arguing, or I'll stamp on you—and then none of you will be going anywhere!'' Fang watched in horror as she snatched Afah up. ''Let's talk about something useful for a change. You say your people built the saviors, or Tin Mothers, or whatever the hell they are. All right. So get this Mother to explain where Marc's people and mine came from, and why our racial history was edited out of their lessons!''

Afah had begun to kick, but it soon occurred to him that this was even more undignified than not kicking. Motionless and rigid, he said, ''It is the least I can do, when I think of the trouble my people have brought to your world. Please put me down.''

Sally complied. The moon chose that moment to emerge from behind a heavy bank of clouds, casting a silvery glow over the sea. Fang began to fidget with impatience. He was sure the history of Sally's people was very important to them, but it had little relationship to the gnomes and their problems. She was waiting for Afah to speak, impatient herself, waggling her arms in a curious way. The two giants were quite different in build. Sally was slender, with queer arms; whereas Marc was built like a huge gnome, squat and muscular. Fang regarded Sally's arms.

He could see feathers there.

His heart thudding, he looked again at her face. Now, in the moonlight, he could see her features more clearly, and he recognized them.

She was the creature of his dreams. The girl with wings. Fascinated, he stared openly. Perhaps she *was* important, after all. He wished Nyneve was there; then suddenly, in a moment of deep sorrow, remembered that thirty thousand years had passed.

"Miggot," he whispered.

But the Miggot's attention was elsewhere. "The moon," he whispered back.

"What?"

"Look."

Fang looked. There, to the right of the hard-edged disc, was another outline, fainter but unmistakable. . . .

Misty Moon was back.

"Miggot!" he squeaked.

"Don't say anything. That may come in useful."

Fang turned his attention to Afah, who was staring down into the face of the Tin Mother. "Our people haven't met for a long time," said the kikihuahua. "The first thing you can do, is explain the origin of these humanoid creatures."

"It is not in their best interests to know."

"But I say it is, and I am your master."

"Of course. During an age of human exploration of space," began the Tin Mother unhesitatingly, "Mankind felt it necessary to create adaptations of his own form for use on worlds with special characteristics. When we arrived here, there were two new races still awaiting shipment, known colloquially as the Swingers and the Wingers.

"We were duty-bound to discourage further space exploration—the dangers are too well known for me to go into that. The new races were not particularly well designed for life on Earth, so we separated them from normal humans, whose life spans we had prolonged indefinitely. The kindest course of action was to place the Swingers and Wingers on reservations until they became extinct. This we did."

There was a long silence. Sally finally asked in a small voice, "What world was I designed for?"

"A low-gravity planet."

"Would I have been able to fly?"

"Yes. You understand why we could not tell you all this without direct orders. It would have been demoralizing for your people."

"Well," said Marc shakily, "now that we know, what shall we do?"

"Command the Tin Mothers to send us to the worlds we were designed for, of course."

"The technology is not readily available," said the Tin Mother. "The True Humans have lost interest in science. They have become pure minds. Their machines decayed long ago. It would take much more than your expected life span to regain the ability to leave Earth's gravitational field."

Sally said to Afah, "You can take us in *your* ship."

"I'm afraid not. Our genetic structure is designed to withstand the molecular expansion necessary to leave Earth on the spacehopper. Yours is not. You would die."

"Oh, God!" cried Sally. "What the hell are we going to do?"

Marc watched her sadly. He could see no end to her despair. "The kikihuahuas must help us get rid of the Tin Mothers," he said. "It's the least they can do. And then we must all help the True Humans do the same thing. And then we must all start rebuilding our civilization. If we can't go to the worlds we were designed for, at least our descendants will be able to."

There was a long silence while Afah digested this. To the gnomes, the reply was obvious. But Afah had to take many other considerations into account, particularly the suggestion that the humans would redevelop powered space travel.

In the end he sighed and said, "Yes, we will help you."

Sally uttered a scream of delight, bent down, and hugged him. "You may look like a monkey, Afah, but your heart's in the right place. And these other three are just like little humans. You really *are* gnomes, aren't you! Isn't this fun, Marc? I can't wait to tell my people!"

"An awful lot of people *like* the Tin Mothers," Marc warned her. "And nearly all the True Humans do, or they wouldn't stay in the dome. This isn't going to be easy, Sally."

Optimism reigned elsewhere, however, and the group began to climb the rope back to the cliff top. "First we should show them the man in the rock," said Sally. "It's on the way home. If the gnomes really were here long ago, they might have some ideas about him."

Amazed and scared, they stared at the rock in the flickering light of a torch.

"He's gone," said Marc. "He was right there, and now he's not. This looks just like ordinary rock now."

"He woke up and broke out," said Sally. "He broke out and now he's roaming the forest, neither alive nor dead, bellowing with despair."

"We'd have heard him," said Marc. "And he'd have left a hole in the rock."

"Perhaps he was a prince under a spell," suggested Sally. "Dreaming in there like True Humans dream in the dome. Waiting to be awakened by the gaze of a beautiful woman. And when I looked at him, he took his place in his magic kingdom."

"Perhaps it was all a trick of the light," ventured the Princess. "It *is* difficult to see in here."

"He was there," Sally insisted. "I saw him."

"For God's sake, stop gawking at that rock like a crowd of idiots," snapped the Miggot, "and let's get out of here. Caves are unsavory places. They can turn a gnome weird. My Cousin Hal used to live in a cave."

Fang was silent. He'd been suffering the most aching nostalgia. There had been the climb down from the cliff to the beach and into the forest, where nothing seemed to have changed. The animal noises were the same, and the smell of leaf mold awakened familiar memories. The general direction of the paths had not changed over thirty thousand years. A couple of times he'd caught the Princess's eyes, and they had been shiny with unshed tears. She felt the same as he. And then, shortly after they left the cave—

"This is the Stone from which King Arthur pulled the sword," said Sally. "You wouldn't know about that because it was a human thing, the most wonderful thing that ever happened. Arthur found the Stone by accident and pulled out the Sword, but they wouldn't believe him. So masses of nobles gathered, and knights and ladies, and he did it again, and they knelt before him and called him King of all England. And the sun came out at that moment and shone on the Sword and all the diamonds in it, and on Arthur's hair. His hair was red, by the way.''

''What happened next?'' asked Fang.

''Everything was wonderful, and everybody stopped fighting because Arthur was such a good king. And he married Guinevere, the most beautiful woman in the world. Sir Lancelot fell in love with her, and she loved him, too, but she didn't say anything because she was a good queen. Some people said they were caught in bed together, but I don't believe that for one moment.''

''I'm sure it never happened,'' said the Miggot. ''What about Mordred?''

''I don't remember a Mordred.''

''And Nyneve?'' asked Fang.

''She was jealous of Guinevere. She was a nasty piece of work. How do you know about Nyneve?''

''Oh. . . I must have heard the story myself, when I was here last. Do they tell the story often?''

Marc laughed. ''All the time. And it seems to grow with the telling. My father says it's just our reaction to the saviors. He says they protect us so much that our imaginations rebel. The more blood and fighting in the Arthur stories, the better people like them. And there's another good thing about them—they happened before the saviors came, or even the computers. So they're human things, and the saviors can't do anything about them.''

There was a certain nostalgia about their arrival at the village of the Swingers too. It was located on the site of old Mara Zion. The giantish creatures gathered around, amazed, pointing and prodding.

Marc's father, Adam, was the village chief, and after the initial commotion he was able to get people to stand back. He took Fang and his companions to the schoolroom and set them on a desk.

"Don't make so much noise," he told the Swingers, who were yelling with excitement. "My son tells me our guests have an unusual relationship with the saviors. We don't want to attract attention until we hear what these little fellows have to say."

People took their seats, "Are they gnomes?" somebody called, unable to contain his impatience. "*Real* gnomes, like in the Arthur stories?"

"We three are," Fang piped back, pleased that their fame spanned thirty millennia.

"What about the monkey? Is he your pet?"

"I am not!" Afah squeaked, outraged. "The gnomes were created by my people."

There was a murmur of excitement. They were obviously amazed that Afah could talk. Adam said to his son, "Tell us all about it, Marc."

"I'll tell you what I know." Nervously, unaccustomed to being in a position of such eminence, Marc addressed the Swingers. Sally stood beside him, nudging him from time to time when she felt he hadn't gotten it quite right but managing to refrain from interrupting. She, too, was over-awed by the size of their audience. Her own people were not so gregarious, and the Wingers' village was a scattering of ramshackle tree houses.

Marc described the savior's tumble, which he attributed to carelessness; the arrival of the kikihuahuas and their identification of the Tin Mother; and the Tin Mother's equally astonishing revelation of the origins of the Swingers and the Wingers. At this point the audience began to mutter.

"You mean they're waiting for us to die off? We're just a nuisance to them?"

"The savior says we're not well suited to Earth."

"And perhaps it was right," said Adam. "After all, the Swinger population is down to a few dozen hereabouts, and the Wingers are fewer than that."

"So what do we do?"

"We rebel!" Sally yelled back unexpectedly. "We fight our way through to the True Humans and we stir them up, and we dismantle every last savior, and we fire up the star-ships and take off for our real homes!''

The simplicity appealed to the wilder element in the audience, and there was a spontaneous burst of applause.

"There's more than one group of True Humans in the world, and the saviors are everywhere," Adam pointed out.

"So we start here. And listen," continued Sally, "we should stop calling those bastards saviors, because that's just what they're not. The kikihuahua has a good name for them—he calls them the Tin Mothers. That's what his people named them when they realized what a load of trouble they'd built for themselves. So what we're going to do, is wipe out those Mothers!"

This time the applause was even more sustained.

When he could make himself heard, Adam said, "You're right, Tin Mothers they are. But we need something to shake up the True Humans. Something to make it worth their while shutting off their dreams and facing the real world."

"Tell them aliens have landed," somebody suggested.

"Switch off their life-support systems!" This from Sally.

The meeting became a general discussion after that, with the schemes for enlisting the support of the True Humans becoming progressively wilder. Drink began to flow, and an impromptu party developed, during which the objective of the gathering was somehow forgotten. Toasts were drunk to the gnomes and to Marc and Sally, without the proposers quite remembering why these central figures had become, in some way, heroes. By dawn the forest clearing was littered with snoring bodies.

"They're no different from the giants we knew years ago," observed Fang in disgust. He and his companions had remained sober and dozed whenever possible. They felt the need to keep their wits about them. Now, as the new sunlight began to tip the treetops with crimson, they were in reasonably good shape.

"By the time they awaken, all impetus will have been lost," observed Afah.

"Perhaps not," said Adam, who had remained protectively near the little people all night. "Nobody likes to be told their only purpose in life is to become extinct. This is the start of something new, and tomorrow the news will be carried all over the forest."

Fang's eyelids felt sandy, and the great scheme for saving the human race was losing its appeal. "I'm going for a walk. I'd like to take a look at things again, in daylight." He'd been surrounded by huge and powerful creatures for too long. He needed to get away from the danger of being trodden on, and into the world he knew and loved. He needed to revisit a few old haunts.

"I'll come with you, Fang," said the Princess.

"Cheer up, Fang," said the Princess.

They walked hand in hand down leaf-carpeted paths. The scenery was familiar enough, yet unsettling, as the path kept taking unexpected twists. Fang found himself thinking about old times, remembering old faces now sleeping a million kilometers away. He remembered ancient events that seemed to have happened so recently that it was a shock to realize that even the trees had passed through countless generations since then.

"We've done the right thing, haven't we, Princess?" he asked.

"Of course we have. We don't want to rot away in the bat."

"I didn't think we wanted to," said Fang doubtfully. "But now I'm beginning to wonder. Everything's different."

"You and I are the same."

He tried to smile. "You'll never change. But me? I don't feel like the same gnome. I feel as though all the stuffing's been knocked out of me." He gestured at the forest. "What do we do now? Where do we start? And how did we get caught up in this rebellion against the Tin Mothers?"

"It's our duty, Fang. Afah said so."

He straightened up. "It's not just a matter of duty. We don't have any choice." The moment of uncertainty over, he brightened and strode forward.

"Away, Thunderer," said the Princess mischievously.

"They still think I'm a hero because of the Slaying of the Daggertooth—which never happened, really. Not the way people think it did. What do *you* think, Princess?"

"I think you're a very brave gnome who rid the forest of a horrible creature."

"The daggertooth chased me home, and I slammed the door so hard that a rock fell from the cave roof onto its head. Certainly I shouted, 'Away, Thunderer!' But that was to make the bloody rabbit hop around a bit, and divert the daggertooth's attention from me. I'm no hero, Princess. There's no such thing as a hero, really. A hero is just an ordinary gnome on a happentrack that doesn't have any branches. Other people can make what they like of it, but *he* knows he has no choice."

"You did some thinking in the bat?"

"There wasn't much else to do. Aren't you disgusted, now that you know the truth about the daggertooth? You know, I cringe whenever they shout, 'Away, Thunderer!' It embarrasses me to say the words."

"It's a stirring cry and it does the gnomes a lot of good. They're going to need a lot of good memories to build on. We've got a big job in front of us, Fang."

"Last night, did you notice? Misty Moon is coming back."

They arrived at a broad clearing where rock lay close to the surface and showed through in places. Fang sat, drawing the Princess down beside him. The morning sun slanted through the trees, sparkling on the dew-tipped grass. Fang fell silent, staring around.

"It's beautiful here," said the Princess quietly.

"It's . . . it's more than that." Excitedly Fang squeezed her hand. "It's part of the old gnomedom, Princess!"

Then she recognized it too. "Only the trees come and go. The land stays the same. It's still our home, Fang."

And it was. The flat, smooth granite bore familiar markings: ancient glacial furrows that spanned a million happentracks, and *here*—Fang pulled away moss and tightly rooted grass clumps—yes, *here* was the old insect racetrack, the little rocky knob marking the starting line. And *there* was the mound where the starter stood. . . .

The sound of cheering gnomes echoed through Fang's memory lobe.

"Remember Jumbo John?" asked the Princess, and Fang smiled.

It had been a busy meeting with gnomes from all over the forest attending, and the insect racing had been fast and exciting. Vast quantities of hazelnuts had been won and lost. Bitter disputes had erupted, to be forgotten within minutes. Much beer had been drunk.

Finally it was time for the last race of the day, which by tradition was the most prestigious. The rubber joes were the cream of the crop. Some of them had never raced before but had been bred and trained in secret, brought to a peak for this one race, after which they would probably go to stud.

The crowd fell silent. All bets had been placed. The owners stood at the starting line. They carried boxes containing their rubber joes, and thorn-tipped hawthorn twigs as goads. Now was the moment when the sleekest, speediest insects of the season would be revealed.

The marshals cleared the track, paying special attention to Clubfoot Trimble, who had once stepped on a speeding joe inches before the finishing line. Although he maintained it was an accident, investigation by the Race Committee uncovered a large quantity of hazelnuts wagered by Clubfoot on the subsequent winner, which up to the time of the accident had been running a poor second.

The six proud owners held their boxes in their left hands, their goads in their right. Arriving late came a seventh, the Miggot of One, striding through the crowd bearing his box in both hands, an unpleasant smile on his pointed features.

The starter gave the traditional cry: "Display your steeds!"

The owners tipped out the contents of their boxes. Six mettlesome joes fell to the forest floor and began to run in impatient circles, guided by their owners' goads. The Miggot, who knew how to time an entrance, tipped his box last. His smile intensified into a leer of triumph. The seventh joe fell to the ground. The crowd gasped in awe.

The Miggot's steed was the most monstrous rubber joe ever known to gnome or man. It stood tall on innumerable powerful legs. Its size has since been compared to the nine-banded armadillo. Its feelers resembled the antlers of an elk. Although humans know the rubber joe as a mere wood louse or sow bug, in kikihuahua legend the Miggot's insect stands alone as a superb example of a much-maligned species.

It did, however, strain the gnomes' credulity. There were shouts of suspicion. King Bison was called upon to adjudicate.

"That is no more a genuine joe," said a contestant, "than my rabbit, Loppy. It's a creation of the Sharan. The Miggot has abused his trust. I demand this creature be disqualified and that the Miggot be censured!"

The Miggot had been growing steadily pinker with outrage. This was not the first time such an accusation had been made. Clubfoot once, on the official occasion of a Memorizing meeting, had alleged that another member of the Miggot's stable, Strider, was an offspring of the Sharan's womb. If it hadn't been for the Miggot's love of winning, he would long ago have quit the racing game in disgust.

With a squeal of fury he flung himself at the complainant and began to batter at him with his fists. This happened a week after the gnomes had learned Fang's sexual apothegm, when the side effects had not been fully realized. Violence was still regarded as aberrant behavior, and the Miggot's opponent fled, convinced he'd been attacked by an insane gnome.

The Miggot stood foursquare over his rubber joe. "I give my word," he said breathlessly, "that this joe is genuine, bred by myself from a strain I discovered west of the tidal flats. Jumbo John has never known the Sharan's womb. To suggest otherwise is to deny everything we gnomes stand for!''

With this patriotic, if somewhat baffling, statement, he knelt and applied his goad experimentally to the rear of Jumbo John. The joe broke into a sprint.

Amid mutters of apology from all concerned, the starter cried, ''Apply your goads!'' Caught unawares, the Miggot's opponents stabbed belatedly at their steeds. The race was in progress.

Jumbo John strode powerfully away from his adversaries, opening a widening gap. The smaller joes trailed behind, prodded mercilessly by their owners. The spectators yelled encouragement. After the initial confusion, much of the wealth of Mara Zion had quickly been placed on the broad back of Jumbo John. The Miggot's joe moved well ahead of the field and seemed to have the race in his pocket.

Then the unexpected occurred. Jumbo John stopped and looked around thoughtfully, waving his feelers. The Miggot applied the goad. Jumbo John assumed a crouching attitude. He seemed to be trying to sit down, so far as it is possible for a wood louse to do so. The crowd screamed. The Miggot invoked the Sword of Agni. Jumbo John stayed put, and the rest of the field closed the gap.

Then a stream of tiny rubber joes emerged from beneath Jumbo John, who began to list like a sinking ship. Reddening with temper, the Miggot attacked Jumbo John's rear end with the goad. Certain members of the audience, to whom motherhood was sacrosanct, fell upon the Miggot. A tide of tiny joes spread across the racecourse. The other runners, reaching them, stopped dead.

''Abandon the race!'' somebody shouted, and others took up the cry. The situation was embarrassing and shameful. Jumbo John lay on his side, twitching, a few of his legs still making token running gestures. Tiny joes continued to emerge. He must have been full of them. It was an indictment of the whole sport of rubber-joe racing. The Miggot, abashed, stepped back, the hands of the spectators still upon him.

Then a murmur of excitement from a section of the crowd signaled a new development. The first wave of Jumbo John's young was approaching the finishing line. Jumbo John himself rolled over on his back, an empty shell with legs around the edge. All movement ceased. The Miggot, mentally assembling rules and precedents, watched in growing triumph as Jumbo John's offspring swarmed over the line.

The crowd was in an uproar. Eventually the marshals restored some semblance of order, and the gnomes waited for King Bison, Chairman of the Race Committee, to give a ruling.

Bison, however, had prudently crept off home. . . .

Fang shook his head, dispelling the memory of a clearing crowded with gnomes, and the happy days he'd known.

"Whatever did happen in the end?" asked the Princess. "I took the children home because of the foul language. People were still arguing when I left."

"Oh, they ran the race again. They ruled that although a part of Jumbo John had crossed the line first, the rest of him hadn't. A joe has to be completely over the line to win. Somebody from the other end of the forest won, I think. The Miggot was furious. He sold his stud to Wal o' the Bottle on the spot and swore never to race again."

They got to their feet and walked across the clearing in silence, but it was no longer the silence of despair. Gnomedom was still all around them, sleeping, just waiting to be awakened. "All it needs is gnomes," said Fang at last. "And they're the same gnomes as they used to be. Lady Duck, Bison, Clubfoot Trimble, Pong, and all our friends. Just think, Princess, our bodies have only aged two years in the bat. All the Mara Zion gnomes can come here, and gnomedom can be as good as it ever was!"

He burst into a gnomish song of joy that sent the birds skittering from the trees and caused the forest animals to stop dead in their tracks and look around fearfully, thinking they heard the roaring of a new and terrible predator.

The boat slid toward the blackness of the distant shore, and the rowers bent to their oars in unison; a rhythm like a lullaby. She was sleepy and cold, but there was no discomfort in the cold. He lay beside her as the dark shore approached.

"Nyneve."

She opened her eyes. The black shore receded and there was brightness all around. Morgan le Fay watched her impassively.

"Wake up, Nyneve. We have work to do. The time is near. The ifalong has dwindled to a thread. We're together now, Nyneve, working toward a common goal."

"What you're trying to say is you were wrong."

"I'm saying that a single happentrack now stretches from us to the crucial event. I see no possibility of a branching. We cannot fail, but have identical objectives and identical methods of approach."

"And you were bloody well wrong."

"It now appears," agreed Morgan coldly, "that there would have been little point in eliminating the humans. The Tin Mothers have done it for us."

"As I foretold they would."

"It was an inspired projection."

"Actually," admitted Nyneve with a grin, "it was Avalona's inspired projection. She knew the Tin Mothers were inevitable, and she knew the gnomes were the only people who could handle them."

"It's good to have Avalona out of the way. She was a real pain. Much better to have a Dedo who speaks my language in Mara Zion. You have drinks in this place?"

"Mead," said Nyneve, fetching a bottle and two glasses.

"And I expect you had wheat germ and goat's milk for breakfast," said Morgan sarcastically. "Ah, well, a glass of mead is better than nothing. What are you doing for a man these days?"

"Oh, you know, this and that." Nyneve had important work to do, and she would rather Morgan wasn't around when she did it. She waited with ill-concealed impatience for the Dedo to finish her drink. Once the door closed behind her visitor, she ran to the corner of the room and pulled aside a curtain.

He was still asleep, his breathing deep and slow, his arms folded across his chest. The color had returned to his face. She bent and kissed his lips, and found them warm.

He opened his eyes.

His eyes regarded her without surprise. "How did the battle go?" he asked.

"That's all in the past now. It doesn't matter."

He winced at a memory. "I was wounded. I thought I was going to die. You nursed me. Of course. I remember now."

"Just lie still for a while. You've been asleep for a long time."

"Guinevere." A look of real sorrow came over his face. "She went off with Mordred. How could she do that?"

"I think she was under a spell."

"Perhaps if I went to see her. . . ?"

"Forget her." Annoyed, Nyneve said brutally, "She's been dead for thirty thousand years. There! You had to know sometime."

"I don't understand."

"That's because I lied to you when I put you to sleep. A long, long time has gone by. You'll find out."

"Well, hello!" The voice of Morgan came from behind. "So *this* is what you do for a man! The kingly fellow who tupped me at the tournament, no less. Well, here's a little wake-up gift for him!"

And, laughing, she tossed Excalibur onto the bed.

"King Arthur?" said Adam wonderingly. "*The* King Arthur? Of the Round Table and all that?"

"That's right," said Arthur, a little bemused himself,

still trying to come to terms with the passage of years and the apelike humans that surrounded him.

"Look at Excalibur," said Fang. "See, it has the name on the blade." It had been one of the happiest moments of Fang's life when Nyneve and Arthur had walked into the village. He couldn't understand why Nyneve still looked so young but was sure she would explain everything in time.

"All those legends . . ." murmured Adam. "The Tin Mothers often use their screens to show us human history. They even show us stuff that happened before they came— they say they copied it from a computer called the Rainbow, in the dome. But they never show us anything about the Age of Chivalry. They say it's not in our best interests to watch violence."

"So how do you know the stories?" asked Fang.

"Oh, traveling storytellers. Word of mouth, handed down over generations. They say the True Humans spread the first stories, from ancient history they got from the Rainbow. But the Tin Mothers suppress all that, just like they suppressed the truth about our origins. . . ." He looked at Arthur closely, then smiled. "You're fooling us, aren't you? You can't be Arthur. He was supposed to have been killed at Camlann, thousands of years ago."

"Wounded," said Nyneve. "I nursed him, and then put him to sleep."

"For all that time?"

"It wasn't any different from what happens to the True Humans in the dome."

"Cryogenics," said Adam. "We've heard of it. But it wasn't invented in those days."

The human and the Dedo fought a brief battle in Nyneve, and the human won. "I invented cryogenics," she said boldly. "I have certain powers." Surely there's no harm in telling them that much. After all, she reasoned, according to the most likely ifalong, these people won't be around much longer. . . .

Adam was still smiling. "If you say so."

"Nyneve used to travel around with Merlin," Fang said,

feeling the need to defend Nyneve's credibility, "telling people stories about the Age of Chivalry."

"Merlin? Merlin wasn't real, surely?"

"Of course he was," said Nyneve. "His sister, Avalona, was my foster mother. I lived in the forest with them both."

"The only True Human in the forest now is a weird woman the children talk about called Blackberry Nan. I've never seen her, but they swear she exists."

Nyneve laughed. "That sounds like me in one of my disguises. I'm not a True Human, though. There is a difference."

"You'll have to forgive us. This all sounds unlikely. All the same"—Adam's gaze returned to the convincing figure of Arthur: tall, obviously True Human, red-haired, with Excalibur at his hip—"they must have been wonderful times."

Arthur merely smiled.

"Can you tell us about them?" asked Marc, more willing to believe than his father. There were enthusiastic cries of encouragement from the younger Swingers.

"Nyneve is the storyteller," said Fang. "She can put pictures into your head."

"If you like," said Nyneve.

For an hour she held the Swingers in an enchanted state while they relived the glorious Age of Chivalry, the battles and the tournaments, the clash of swords and the thunder of hooves, bright banners, bright metal and bright blood, yells of triumph and of agony, the smell of feasting and of death. The Swingers sat in the trees, on the grass, on the roof of the schoolhouse, experiencing it with all their senses.

Arthur smiled quietly to himself, remembering what it was really like.

Afah left after a few moments and walked quietly away into the forest, sick to his stomach. Fang, the Princess, and the Miggot stayed until Nyneve had finished; a little horrified, a little disgusted, but very much aware of the effect of the story on its human audience.

When it was all over, Adam said quietly, "Perhaps now we have our means of stirring up the True Humans."

20

THE DOME AT CAMELOT

THE TASK FORCE SET OFF AT DAWN.

They had decided to travel in the guise of itinerant performers, keeping the identity of the kikihuahuas as a trump card to be revealed if needed. They took one packhorse on which the gnomes and Afah sat, ready to slip into the saddlebags at a moment's notice. Adam and Marc took turns leading the horse, and Nyneve, Arthur, Morgan le Fay, and Sally walked ahead. The sky was clear, the last stars fading.

"I smell disaster," said the Miggot, nursing a pounding headache due to overindulgence in cider the previous night.

"Everything's fine!" said the Princess gaily. The gnomes carried packets of bread and cheese, with small flasks of beer hung from their belts. Fang was already eating. By the time they reached the fringes of the forest, the sun was brightening the ground in little patches as though an artist had flicked his brush around, and even the Miggot began to cheer up. It was good to be back on Earth.

The feeling did not last long. "Look!" said Adam. "The bastards meant what they said about closing off the moor."

A Tin Mother stood motionless and erect on the open ground before them.

"It's standing guard," said the Princess. "It's guarding the moors against trespassers like us."

"It's our servant, remember," Fang pointed out.

The Miggot's gloom returned as he scanned the landscape. "The moors look different," he said. "It's all changed." He pointed to an immense silver crescent cutting into the sky. "That must be the dome they talk about. And look, they've built rock walls all over the moor. In my day a gnome could run for miles and never see a sign of giantish habitation."

"They're very old walls, Miggot," said Fang. "Most of them have fallen down."

"It'll never be the same. Nothing ever is. My Cousin Hal used to have a saying: 'Things get worse.' He called it Hal's Law. He said it was a universal truth, like entropy."

"We'll be able to see Pentor soon," said the Princess brightly. "That'll be nice. It'll bring back happy memories of Hal for you, Miggot."

"I have no happy memories of Hal."

"Better slip into the saddlebags now," Nyneve warned them. "We don't want that Tin Mother to see you. There's no point in revealing our hand yet."

The robot gave no acknowledgment of their presence, however. Sally tapped it but it stared woodenly over her head, not moving. She kicked it. Nothing happened.

The Princess's head popped out of her saddlebag. "Perhaps it's dead," she suggested. "Perhaps it's all rusted away inside there."

"I've never seen one like this before," said Adam. He stepped close and stared into the Tin Mother's eyes. No telltale lights burned in their depths. The chest screen was blank. The Mother was either switched off or derelict.

"Perhaps the whole race has run its course," said the Miggot hopefully. "Races do. It's even happened to races the Sharan created." Remembering something, he scanned the moors nervously. "I hope it happened to the fogdogs," he said.

They left the robot standing there, and climbed onto the moors. As the great Rock of Pentor came into view it became clear that the Tin Mothers had not, after all, run their course. Several could be seen on the exposed moorland, some of them rigid and motionless, but others busily pacing around. At least twenty stood around a huge tracked vehicle about a kilometer away. This vehicle was rectangular and featureless except for a tracery rising above its flat top, sustained by two towers and resembling a spiderweb on a dewy morning.

"What on Earth is that?" asked Fang. The hairs on his head prickled as though he were in the presence of some unimaginable evil.

A Tin Mother came striding from behind a rock before the gnomes could hide themselves. "This is a restricted area," it said. "I am surprised that you were not told. I regret that you must leave."

Fang had to play his trump sooner than he'd wanted to. "We're kikihuahuas, and the humans are our friends. Let us pass."

The Mother regarded him calculatingly. "You do not look like a kikihuahua."

"What about him?" Fang pointed to Afah.

"He looks like a kikihuahua." The Tin Mother inhaled noisily. "He smells like a kikihuahua." There was a pause, then: "He *is* a kikihuahua. We received word from the coast that a kikihuahua had arrived. You must be it."

Fang had been hoping for a display of subservience. At the very least, the Mother should have addressed Afah as "Master." At best, the robot would have sunk to its knees and pledged undying loyalty. Neither of these things happened, nor any of the wide range of possibilities in between. The Mother grunted and fell silent, presumably discussing the situation with its colleagues. Fang had the unhappy feeling that he was being outthought.

"My hair feels funny," said the Princess. "It's prickling."

"You may pass through," said the Tin Mother at last, "but you must not approach Pentor Rock. This is for your own good, and should not be taken to indicate any lack of respect on our part."

The Rock stood about a kilometer away; an irregular outline against the vast curve of the dome. There was a curious glow in the air like evening sunshine after rain, and a faint odor of ozone. The Rock itself seemed to be shimmering, but Fang had the feeling that the phenomenon was centered on that great machine. He could almost see lines of force converging on it.

The Tin Mother explained, "Pentor Rock is to be converted to hydrogen atoms."

Fang glanced at Nyneve, remembering odd remarks she and Avalona had made in the past. So this was the moment she'd been working to prevent, all these thousands of years. He felt a deep awe, and a sense of wonder, that he was in some way involved in such an historic occasion.

Morgan felt no such respect for the occasion. "If the Mothers didn't blow it up, the humans would, for some reason or other. It's an inevitable happentrack."

"Yes," said Nyneve. "But I *knew* it wouldn't be the humans."

"Avalona knew, you mean," admitted Morgan grudgingly. "The old bat."

"How are you going to do it?" Adam asked the robot with some skepticism.

The Tin Mother became quite talkative. "All systems will be shut down while the conversion takes place. The converter—that machine over there—will draw energy from the entire country. Even priming the converter absorbs great amounts of energy. Priming has been taking place for two days already. The converter," continued the Mother in a burst of confidence, "has possibly the greatest capacity for doing good of any machine in the galaxy. Admittedly this is an unusual situation and we have not been able to erect the solar generator field from which the machine would normally derive its power. But when properly set up on the surface of a planet, the converter can produce a balanced atmosphere by fractional disintegration and subsequent molecular reconstruction of the rocks around it, thus creating a world suitable for organic habitation."

"But there's no shortage of air around here," said Sally. "Why are you doing this?"

"Unfortunately our purpose on this occasion is destruction, pure and simple," said the Tin Mother, and Fang fancied he detected a hint of relish in its tone. "We do this for the benefit of the human race—and now, for the kikihuahuas too. Pentor Rock is similar to rocks on other worlds we visited. Such rocks are used for an unusual and dangerous form of space travel. Only organic species are capable of using it. And organic species are irrational, headstrong, and fragile."

"So you want to prevent travelers from using the Rock?" asked Morgan.

"And to prevent hostile aliens from attacking."

Meanwhile the Miggot had been muttering to himself and had reached a worrisome conclusion. "The True Humans," he said, "what about them?"

"Well, what about them?" asked Adam.

"Their minds are plugged into a computer in the dome, aren't they?"

"That is approximately correct," said the Tin Mother.

"Well, what happens when you fire off that converter and they lose their power? You did say all systems would shut down."

"Regrettably there will be loss of life. The human bodies may live for a while, but their minds will not survive the temporary loss of power. The organic mind is a delicate thing when compared to the electronic mind and cannot be switched on and off at will."

"So you'll kill them!"

"Their deaths will be only a temporary setback for the human race. Ample breeding stock still exists in pockets outside the domes and in the dome caretakers. We are ensuring their safety. The future of the race as a whole is more important than a few dreamers. And now we have you kikihuahuas to consider too."

The task force exchanged frightened glances. "When does disintegration take place?" asked Adam.

"At noon today."

''So the True Humans die at noon?'' Adam's voice shook. ''Why don't you delay the countdown and get them all out?''

''There are severe logistics problems in releasing several hundred thousand frail humans into a primitive environment. I'm sure you can appreciate that. Many of them would die from starvation within a few weeks, and there would be untold savagery. We have considered the problem at some length and we have decided they are happier where they are. It would not be a kindness to jerk them back to reality and then death.''

''We'll have to think about this,'' muttered Adam, drawing the others away from the Tin Mother. Once out of earshot, he said quietly, ''I think they *want* to kill the True Humans.''

''Why?'' asked Fang. ''I thought they were your saviors.''

''Yes, but now you kikihuahuas have arrived. The Tin Mothers' first duty is to you. Humans are much bigger and stronger than you, and they see us as a threat to you. So now they have two objectives that they can accomplish at the same time: They can wipe out large numbers of humans, and they can destroy Pentor Rock. . . . I still don't understand what they've got against that Rock.''

''It's a very long story,'' said Nyneve. ''We don't have time to talk about it now. We only have three hours to get the True Humans out of the dome.''

''Did you expect this development?'' asked Morgan curiously.

''No,'' Nyneve admitted. ''Too many random factors have popped up. The ifalong's all twisted. We'll have to play this by ear, like normal human beings.''

''I wish I knew what you two were talking about,'' said Arthur. ''Come on, for God's sake. The gnomes must stay here and try to hold the Tin Mothers off until we get back. Afah must come with us because the Tin Mothers will obey him. Fang—we'll see you later.''

Events seemed to be moving very quickly.

"Good-bye, Fang," said Nyneve, bending forward and kissing him on the cheek.

"Do you have a plan?" he asked hopefully. She'd always seemed so sure of things before.

"I have a plan, but I don't know if it'll work. And I don't have time to analyze the ifalong."

Fang, the Princess, and the Miggot watched the others hurry away over the brow of the moor.

Matthew, the caretaker, made a point of walking on the moors every day. Although the dome was immense, a person could still feel claustrophobic in there. Sounds echoed, there was a pervasive medicinal smell, and above all, there was the presence of thousands of comatose humans, dreaming their lives away.

As he emerged from the air lock he saw scenes of unaccustomed activity on the moor, and a huge tracked vehicle.

"I'm sorry, sir. Access to the moor is restricted today."

"Oh." He turned back without questioning Gentle Jim. No doubt the saviors had very good reasons. Gentle Jim took him by the arm and guided him back into the air lock. He found himself irritated once again by the way the saviors insisted in pairing off with the humans, so that a person had a robot at his elbow every minute of the day. The majority of the dome staff didn't seem to mind because the saviors were only too ready to help with the less pleasant chores, such as the dreamers' personal hygiene.

Now Gentle Jim escorted Matthew to the Rainbow Room.

"Once again I must request that composite reality be adjusted to remove undesirable elements from the current dream," said the savior.

The Rainbow Room was half a kilometer wide and a full kilometer long. At present it displayed a ghostly pastoral scene. People played beside a placid lake in a forested valley. A silver transporter trundled slowly toward them, bringing fruit. The people, laughing, ran to meet it. A golden bird was painting a picture in the sky. A furry water rat traced a wake across the river. It was a pleasant, peaceful fantasy.

"I can't see anything objectionable about that scene," said Matthew. "But then, I can't see anything objectionable about anything the dreamers do. If they want to spend their lives picking flowers, that's their problem, not yours."

"What you see is intended to provide a contrast to the real purpose of the dream," said Gentle Jim.

Now the sky-painting bird folded its wings and dropped like a stone. Talons open, claws downward-pointing, it hit the water rat squarely on the back with an audible thud. The dreamers cheered. The bird began to flap heavily away, the animal struggling in its talons, trailing an arc of bright blood.

"You see, Matthew?" said Gentle Jim.

"I see a recreation of a common event in nature. I do not see what is wrong."

"The scene was obviously enacted to indulge a perverted lust for violence."

"It's just a communal *dream*, for God's sake. Neither of those creatures were real. They're just images created by the dreamers, for fun."

"I'm seriously concerned, Matthew. We prevented the dreamers from indulging in war scenarios because the violence was unwholesome. We managed to steer them away from overly competitive sports. We eradicated sexual peculiarities. And now we're getting this kind of thing. I must recommend that we adjust the composite reality again."

"If you continue like this, they'll be totally unsuited for real life when they leave the dome."

"I was making the recommendation as a matter of principle," said Gentle Jim, eyes flickering as he received input from elsewhere. "Both that and your comment are irrelevant, in the present circumstances."

There was something sinister about this last statement. Matthew glanced at Gentle Jim sharply. "What do you mean, irrelevant?"

"We will dismiss the subject now, because we have visitors. They are being escorted through the air lock at this moment.''

"We'll dismiss the subject when I'm good and ready!" snapped Matthew. "Who the hell do you think you are, telling me what I can and cannot talk about?"

"You are overwrought," said Gentle Jim solicitously. "Perhaps you would care for a sedative." Like a conjurer, he produced a hypodermic.

"And perhaps you would care for a kick in the teeth!" shouted Matthew, out of control. "Come any closer with that needle and you'll get one!"

So it was that the seven arrivals were greeted by the regrettable sight of the head caretaker, beside himself with rage, hopping around the Rainbow Room kicking at a robot, who dodged after him with hypodermic outthrust.

"What's going on here?" exclaimed Adam.

"Who in hell are you?" asked Matthew. "And what do you mean by letting them in?" he asked the savior who had accompanied them. "You know damned well we don't allow visitors in the dome. Particularly Wild Humans and their pets. The dreamers are extremely susceptible to infection.''

The savior said, "They commanded me."

Sally pointed to Afah. "His people built the robots, so they have to obey him."

Matthew was furious enough to have ignored this statement, had it not been delivered in tones of calm conviction. He scrutinized Afah more closely, realized that he was not a howler monkey as he'd first assumed, and calmed down somewhat. "That takes some believing," he said.

"Somebody must have built these robots, so why not Afah's people?" Sally retorted. "He's a kikihuahua from another world. He calls the saviors 'Tin Mothers.' His people escaped from the Tin Mothers long ago, and the Tin Mothers have been following them ever since!"

Matthew appealed to Arthur, being the person who looked most like a True Human. "Is she telling the truth?"

"She is, but we don't have time to talk about it. The Tin

Mothers are going to cut off the power to the dome in about two and a half hours.''

"But that will kill the dreamers!"

"Exactly. We're going to have to snap them out of their dream. Wake them up, or whatever you call it.''

"Reincorporation. But the saviors are in charge of bulk reincorporation.''

"Seize control from the Tin Mothers, Afah,'' urged Sally. "You're supposed to be their master.''

"That is true,'' said Afah. "And individual Tin Mothers may give the impression of obeying me. But as a group they will always find reasons to procrastinate. Once they are convinced of the rightness of their actions, it is a waste of time to try to persuade them otherwise. So if the dreamers are to awaken, they must do it of their own volition. Is that possible, Matthew?''

The caretaker looked doubtful. "In theory, yes. They've always had the option of waking up to the real world. But they've never done it, not in a thousand years. Why should they? If they want the appearance of reality, they can have it in their communal dream. They can have anything they want: love, adventure, magic, space travel, even ordinary office jobs.'' He frowned. "That's not quite true. The saviors impose a degree of censorship. It's cleverly done, though, and the dreamers aren't aware of the limitations of their dreams.''

"So what they really have is freedom.'' Nyneve spoke for the first time. "Even though we might think their minds are trapped in the Rainbow. Even though their bodies are locked in the dome. They believe they have the freedom to do whatever they like without fear of consequences, for as long as they want to do it. They won't want to give all that up.''

There was a thoughtful silence.

"Let's take it away from them,'' said Morgan.

The gnomes had not enjoyed being left behind. They found a flat rock and sat on it, watching the activity around

Pentor and wondering what they should do if the others failed to return by noon. They were getting hungrier by the minute. They'd eaten their bread and cheese and drunk their beer long ago. Gnomes have high metabolic rates, and Fang's stomach was an aching void.

"Perhaps we should slip down into the forest and forage around," suggested the Miggot. "It wouldn't take long."

"Anything might happen while we're away," said Fang. The sun was high. "And anyway, it must be getting horribly close to noon."

"Those Mothers are supposed to be our servants," the Miggot reminded him. "Hey, you!" he shouted.

The robot swiveled its head. By now they had learned that gnomes and kikihuahuas were interchangeable as beings to be obeyed. "Yes, Master?"

"Go down to the forest and bring us some food. Mushrooms and beechnuts. Maybe some hazelnuts if you can find any."

"And milk," said the Princess. "See if you can find a goat."

"Beer," said Fang hopefully. "You never know when you might come across some beer. Or cider."

"No cider," said the Miggot.

"Beer, then."

The Tin Mother, who had been listening with robotic patience, said, "I regret that I must refuse your request."

"It's your duty to obey!"

"Under normal circumstances I would obey gladly. Unfortunately I am about to be switched off to conserve energy."

"Well, get one of the others, then!"

"We shall all be switched off in four minutes and thirteen seconds, in order to fulfill total energy demand by the converter."

There was a moment's shocked silence. "So soon?" said the Princess.

"So what is your decision, Fang?" asked the Miggot sharply.

"Decision about what?"

"About this situation. You are our leader. You must make a decision."

This seemed unfair somehow. "Would Bison have made a decision?"

"Bison is not here, Fang."

Fang gazed around the moors desperately. The shadow cast by Pentor Rock was terrifyingly short. The structure on top of the converter was glowing in pulses, like a black-smith's furnace. "How soon did you say?" he croaked.

"In two minutes and forty-three seconds. Forty-two. Forty-one."

There was an air of defeat in the dome.

"Don't they realize what time it is?" asked Adam.

"They only have two minutes left," said Sally.

"It's not enough."

The Rainbow Room displayed a peaceful scene: a large number of people sitting quietly in a grassy meadow beside a deep, slow river. Behind them, a fairy-tale castle rose into the clouds. Before them sat a pretty girl with black hair, an older woman with a face of unearthly perfection, and a man, red-haired and rugged.

"What are they doing?" asked Gentle Jim for the tenth time in the last hour.

"You can see what they're doing," snapped Matthew, his nerves ragged. "They're listening to Nyneve. You remember Nyneve, don't you, you stupid bugger?"

"Of course I remember Nyneve, Matthew. Nyneve has disincorporated her mind and entered the dream, together with her friends Morgan and Arthur. But how can they be listening if she is not talking?"

"She was talking a little while ago."

"But now she's projecting images directly into the dream-ers' minds!" cried Sally triumphantly. "Just like when she told the chivalry stories!"

The Tin Mother was silent for a while. "That is not in the best interests of the human race," it said eventually.

"Twenty-one. Twenty. Nineteen," said Marc, watching the clock.

"Oh, God," said Sally.

"How do you know it's not in our best interests, if you can't hear what she's saying?" asked Matthew.

"We rely on you to monitor the dreams, Matthew, because you possess human judgment. If Nyneve is speaking directly into people's minds, you cannot monitor. Neither can we. We are faced with a dream within a dream—one that we know nothing about, and one in which anything could go wrong. She could be portraying scenes of dreadful violence."

"It's only a dream."

"I would rather see them walking around and doing things. This passive imagining is not good."

"The whole of Dream Earth is passive imagining, you fool!"

"Gentle Jim has a sneaky look," said Sally.

"One. Zero. Now. Oh, God. Now. Now. I don't hear anything."

"The wall of the dome is thick."

Nyneve sat with her eyes closed. The dreamers were lying down now. One of them moved, kicking a leg.

"Everything would be gone if the power was off. The Rainbow Room would be empty of images. The lights would be out."

"So they haven't fired off the converter."

Sally asked the Tin Mother, "Why haven't they fired off the converter?"

The robot did not reply. Its eyes flickered.

"We'll go and see for ourselves!" shouted Marc, running to the door.

They hurried down the corridor and crowded into the air lock. The door hissed shut behind them. "Just supposing the power goes out now?" said Sally. "Right at this moment?"

"Shut up."

The outside door opened and sunlight flooded in. They stood at the catwalk rail.

"The Rock's still there."

"So's the converter. It's glowing—look!"

"So what's going on?"

"There's somebody coming. It's a gnome. It looks like the Miggot!"

The tiny figure came scurrying over the breast of the moor and raced for the dome. "I'll fetch him," said Adam. He clattered down the steps and ran to meet the Miggot, ignoring the outstretched arm of a nearby Tin Mother.

They saw him scoop the Miggot up and carry him back. By the time he reached the catwalk again, Adam was too winded to speak. The Miggot, however, had recovered his breath.

"Fang and the Princess!" he shouted. "They're in terrible danger!"

"Calm down, Miggot," said Marc. "They're well clear of the danger zone."

"They're not! They're not! They're sitting right on top of the Rock!"

"What!"

"It was the only way we could stop the Mothers from firing off the converter!"

"Well . . ." Adam thought for a moment, panting, while the Miggot pranced around his feet in impatience. "Perhaps they should stay there until Nyneve and Morgan have finished with the dreamers."

"No, they can't." The Miggot glanced over his shoulder. Satisfied that no electronic creatures were present, he said quietly, "The Tin Mothers wanted to demolish the rock in spite of Fang and the Princess. They said the death of two obsolete gnomes was a small price to pay for the safety of Afah, their true master. But Fang pointed out that without the Sharan, he and the Princess are the only kikihuahua breeding stock on Earth." He chuckled despite himself. "Only Fang would think of that."

"Good. So as long as they stay up there, everything's all right."

"No, because it didn't take the Tin Mothers long to realize there's plenty of kikihuahua breeding stock in the ship."

"So what did you say to that?"

"We said, 'What ship?' but they knew there had to be some kind of ship, and they said they'd start their radio telescopes searching right away. The bat's not far away, and too slow to escape. The Mothers could start building a ship today and still have time to catch up to it before it leaves the solar system. My guess is, they're searching space with their instruments right now! And as soon as they detect the bat, they'll blast the Rock, and Fang and the Princess with it!"

"What can we do?" said Adam. "I don't know how long Nyneve intends to stay in Dream Earth."

"You'll have to get her out of there right away, because Fang won't come down from the Rock until you do! He seems to feel some weird kind of loyalty to Nyneve."

Adam said, "And Nyneve knows it. That's why she's still in there. She must have predicted what Fang would do."

"Get her out!" cried the Miggot.

"But what about the dreamers? We can't just let them die."

"They'll die in any case, when the Mothers blast the Rock! At least let's save our own people. We've lost, you silly buggers! Can't you get that into your thick heads?"

Adam made a quick decision. "Matthew! Take us to Nyneve's body, quickly!"

They ran down endless corridors. Eventually they reached the storage regions where a door opened onto a catwalk. Involuntarily they stopped dead.

The room was so vast that they could not see the ceiling; neither could they see the floor. All they could see were people, thousands upon thousands of them, lying naked on soft transparent shelves in endless rows and endless tiers. A misty rain fell, bathing them constantly. Each human being was connected by colored wires to a box on each shelf. Cables, tubes, and catwalks were strung around the whole area in an infinite three-dimensional web. A deep hum throbbed almost below the level of human hearing, and the humid air held a thick stink of body wastes and antiseptic. It was an awesome, horrifying sight.

"Oh, my God," whispered Sally.

"Your people are across there and down two tiers," said Matthew, pointing. "The transporter will be here in a few minutes."

"We don't have time for that," said Adam. "Can we get there on foot?"

"Yes." Matthew ran out across the catwalk. The others hurried behind. The catwalk swayed and clattered. They passed pale, naked bodies, one after another. Tubes hung from above, feeding the bodies, and tubes hung below, draining them. Sally gulped as she ran, fearful she might be sick. Averting her eyes from the bodies beside the catwalk, she saw bodies through the transparent shelves above, their buttocks flattened. Sex had never meant so little. Bodies stretched into the distance, as far as the eye could see. In Sally's mind they became meat, no different from slaughtered and skinned deer. She wondered if they were worth saving.

They reached the row where Nyneve, Morgan, and Arthur lay. Matthew turned left and the others followed, clattering along the catwalk. Some of the shelves were swinging slightly. In the distance stood a figure, bending forward as though inspecting something. It was a Tin Mother.

Sally's eyes were not human eyes. The genes of a sea eagle were in her, and she could see details the others could not. Far away, the Tin Mother raised a knife above a clothed body on a shelf.

"Stop!" screamed Sally. "I command you to stop!"

The runners halted, misunderstanding.

"That Mother's got a knife!" she cried. "It's going to kill Nyneve!"

The Mother was too far away; they could never reach it

in time. It paused, however, turning toward the sound of Sally's shout. It felt the need to explain. "This is necessary for the benefit of the kikihuahuas!" it roared across the vastness. "Two humans must die so that the kikihuahuas may live on in peace and gentleness!"

"You can't do this!" Matthew shouted back. "Are you in communication with the Rainbow? The Rainbow would never allow this!"

"There are times when a small unit in possession of all the facts is a more appropriate decision maker than the greatest of computers," boomed the Tin Mother.

So saying, it plunged the knife down.

When two knights collided, the dreamers could feel the earth shake beneath them; and when they bled, the blood was warm and salty. It was a rough and violent world Nyneve was showing them, yet more fun, somehow, than any of their own dream worlds.

It had an indefinable glory.

The world was simple and there was no need to explain why the Britons were good and the Saxons bad; those facts alone were enough. The code of chivalry existed only among the Britons. The Saxons, Morgan's contribution, were blackguards to a man, and so were the Picts and the Celts. Arthur defeated these forces again and again, defending all of England against his attackers until he was betrayed from within.

The rumor swept across Dream Earth: Something exciting and different was happening at Camelot. More dreamers arrived, deserting their dull old haunts for a world constructed by people who knew how. Forlorn inventions were left behind: bartenders, waiters, ships, and unicorns; all purpose gone, gradually fading away.

Nyneve told her story as never before, assisted by Morgan, who proved an able replacement for Merlin. Arthur sat watching the openmouthed dreamers, smiling, awaiting the time when he would play his part.

Finally Nyneve secured England's borders against the

marauders and turned her attention to internal matters; to feasts and tournaments, loving and living. The dreamers settled back, entranced, relaxing. The period of danger was over. This fine new world was safely established. It hadn't mysteriously disappeared, like so many of their other more stimulating inventions. Nyneve soothed their minds with scenes of domesticity, a little excitement here and there, a few quests, a damsel rescued from a fearful fate. All was well with Camelot. It was a bright and perfect world, perfect and good, and astonishingly realistic.

Morgan took her cue.

Mordred crept away from Camelot, evil surrounding him in a palpable cloud, and set a course for destruction. The dreamers shifted nervously.

Mordred did not go to the Saxons, or to the Picts or the Celts. Helped by a spell cast by Morgan le Fay, he rode into the future on a coal-black horse in search of his ally: the worst enemy Mankind would ever know. He lived through the frenzied era when fossil fuel ran out and Earth was shaken by the Consumer Wars. He shivered through the Great Ice Age, which caused most of Mankind to retreat to the domes. He searched through that peculiar era when Earth's magnetic field reversed and mutants were everywhere—but even in that strange time he could not find the perfect enemy for Arthur, his hated father. He watched the Age of Resurgence begin. The starships left Earth and distributed Mankind into a thousand different worlds—and then, when it seemed that humans were too strong ever to have a serious enemy, he found what he wanted. . . .

Timing the plan to perfection, Morgan le Fay finished her story.

Ten thousand dreamers took over for themselves, rapidly building on Nyneve's world. Camelot became massive and beautiful, spread over a hundred acres. Men clad themselves in armor and created themselves horses and weapons; women generated fine clothes and filled the castle halls with beautiful furniture and tapestries. Battles were fought and enemies were vanquished in a hail of arrows. Camelot's boundaries were extended. Arthur took his place as a leader of armies.

Across the great plain lumbered the Tin Mothers, led by Mordred. They regarded Camelot with dull, mechanical revulsion. A tournament was in progress. A lance lifted a knight from his horse and dumped him bleeding to the ground. The dreamers cheered. The Tin Mothers strode onto the sward.

"You'll hurt themselves!" they boomed.

Annoyed, the humans shouted back, "Get out of the way!"

"We cannot allow you to endanger yourselves like this!"

"We are not endangered. Nothing is real!"

"Your minds are endangered. You are becoming dehumanized by exposure to violent sights. You are beginning to regard them as commonplace. As a result, you will become violent and antisocial yourselves! If you don't stop, we shall be forced to destroy this scenario!"

Now Nyneve took Arthur's thoughts and gave them voice, and projected them into the scene.

"The scenario is not yours to destroy," he told the Tin Mothers. "And perhaps you should consider this: You were brought here by Mordred, who is possibly the most evil person on Earth. He's using you for his own ends. He wants the world of chivalry destroyed because there's no place in it for himself!"

Nyneve smiled as she relayed Arthur's words. Somehow he could not fail but do and say the right thing. In any other man that would have been a remarkably dull attribute, but in Arthur it was fitting.

The Tin Mother said, "Evil is not a significant factor in our considerations. It is a human concept unrelated to what is, or is not, expedient. It is expedient for us to destroy this scenario to save you from yourselves, and this we will do!"

So saying, the Tin Mother snatched the sword from the hand of a knight and broke it over his knee.

Another knight, riding past, caught the Tin Mother full in the chest with his lance, and the robot fell backward, torn open, circuits melting and dripping. A second Tin Mother stepped forward, seized the knight by the foot, and swung him to the ground. The Tin Mother knelt over him. The few dreamers who still had memories of the real world expected it to tend to the injured man.

It took him into its arms and broke his neck.

A howl of rage arose. "What are you doing?" shouted a dreamer in the guise of Uther Pendragon. "Who do you think you are?"

"That was not a man. That was an image," said the Tin Mother. "I committed no crime. I am here to serve you. Now stand back while we destroy the rest of this perverted scenario. Wish yourselves elsewhere."

Arthur stood tall on a grassy knoll. "They are the forces of evil!" he roared. Drawing Excalibur, he dragged a struggling figure from behind a tree. "This is Mordred, my bastard son. He leads the Tin Mothers against us!" Mordred, dark and saturnine, glared at the dreamers with fierce and cunning eyes. "Look at him! He is evil incarnate!"

"Mordred . . ." The name passed among the dreamers. "Kill him, Arthur!" shouted somebody.

"He is my son," said Arthur. "I cannot kill him." He flung Mordred aside and plunged Excalibur into the nearest Tin Mother. It sank to the ground, hissing. "Help me rid the world of these villains," Arthur shouted. "They would reduce us to a race of weaklings unfit to live in the real world!"

The Tin Mothers, guided by Morgan, had begun to destroy Camelot. With fearsome strength they were pulling the chiseled rocks apart and throwing them to the ground. In minutes they were undoing the work of ten thousand dreamers' wishes. Yelling their outrage, a vast crowd of dreamers attacked with swords, crossbows, and spears.

Nyneve and Morgan withdrew to a distant hilltop.

"Don't make it too easy for Arthur," said Nyneve.

"Too easy? Hell, I have a vested interest in Mordred," replied Morgan, grinning.

They watched the most unusual battle Dream Earth had

ever known, when Britons fought robots. Led by King Arthur; inspired by the visions of chivalry and glory Nyneve had planted in their minds; cheered on by a multitude of queens, ladies, damsels, and wenches—a thousand knights flung themselves at the Tin Mothers.

Mordred climbed to the topmost tower of Camelot and screeched orders to his forces from there; Arthur, however, fought in the thick of the battle, Excalibur flashing like fire. The Tin Mothers fell back, driven into the ruins of a keep.

"Hold your line!" screamed Mordred. "You'll be trapped, you fools!"

Strangely, he seemed to have gained some measure of support from the dreamers. "We love you, Mordred!" called a group of damsels.

On her hilltop, Nyneve asked, "What the hell is going on?"

"It's a good sign," said Morgan. "They're beginning to appreciate the importance of evil."

"I suppose so. But *Mordred* . . . ?"

"One of my finer creations. I'll be sorry to see him go."

Nyneve thought for a moment. "Perhaps we should keep him around, after all. Just as a symbol, you understand. No big thing. Just to give people something to get worked up about from time to time."

Morgan grinned. "Keeps them on their toes."

Now the Tin Mothers were surrounded, and one by one they fell. The knights moved into close quarters, slashing and thrusting, and the acrid stink of burning insulation wafted across the plain. With a great cry of despair Mordred conceded defeat, swung apelike down the ruins of his tower, leapt astride his black horse, and galloped from sight. The battle was over and the field of Camelot was littered with crumpled Tin Mothers. The victors began to converge on the castle gate.

A lone figure appeared on the ramparts, blood seeping from many cuts, brandishing a sword that flashed like no other.

"My noble knights!" shouted Arthur. "My friends! To

all of you I give my thanks. This day we have fought long and hard against the forces of evil, and we have triumphed. And yet my joy is mingled with sadness, for it was my own son, Mordred, who assembled the evil machines and sent them against us. Machines that pretend to be on the side of the righteous, with their sly words, with their appearance of caring—while slowly they turn the human race into a world of effete dreamers frightened to face reality.

"Yes, frightened! We're all frightened, cowering here in Dream Earth because we don't have the guts to go out into the wind and the rain and live like real people. Frightened to get out and compete against one another, to till the soil and earn a living by honest work. Frightened of the heat and the cold against our soft bodies. Frightened of pain, of childbirth, of death. And encouraged in this fear by the robots that Nyneve calls the Tin Mothers. It's not our fault; they are a powerful enemy and they caught the human race at a vulnerable moment.

"The Tin Mothers are like a vise, crushing the human spirit. They are like a pillow suffocating human endeavor. When they came to real Earth, we let them conquer us without raising so much as a sword against them. But now, here in Camelot, we've shown ourselves what can be done, when we have the will to do it. The Tin Mothers saw the danger to themselves, and look what they did! Camelot was beautiful, so they tried to destroy it. It was exciting, so they tried to suppress it. But this time they met their match. The spirit of Camelot was too strong for them—too *human* for them. So we beat them. They were defeated in this last stronghold of the human race.

"But they still rule real Earth! They still walk the lanes and the moors, discouraging people from adventure, wrapping them in protective cocoons. They're out in real Earth, thousands of them, and now they've shown their true colors. They've realized they can't keep you locked in Dream Earth forever, so they're plotting to destroy you!"

There was a murmur of alarm from his audience. "I know!" shouted Arthur. "I've just arrived from real Earth myself! The Tin Mothers plan to drain all the power from the dome! You know what that means. Your minds will die. True, your bodies will survive, but they will be zombies with no free will, obedient to the commands of the Tin Mothers. Your minds—the real *you*—will be snuffed out here in Dream Earth like candles at bedtime!''

"What can we do?" someone yelled. "Tell us what to do, Arthur!"

"There's only one thing to do," Arthur shouted back. "It just takes a little determination, that's all. Reincorporate! Get out into the real world, smash the Tin Mothers, and build a new Camelot, one that will endure forever! Reincorporate!''

Nyneve lay down on the grass and closed her eyes.

She thought, she wished. *Reincorporate.* . . .

She opened her eyes to find herself back in the vast hibernation chamber of the dome. A great dark blur hovered over her like a thundercloud. She blinked and focused. The cloud became a Tin Mother. As she wondered drowsily what it was doing, it raised a knife and shouted words that made no sense at all.

"There are times when a small unit in possession of all the facts is a more appropriate decision maker than the greatest of computers!"

"What?" she said.

The Tin Mother had apparently made its point. It plunged the knife toward her heart.

Nyneve reacted sluggishly, rolling aside. It was probably this slowness that saved her life, because it did not give the Tin Mother time for a second try. The knife grazed her back and thudded onto the shelf. The Tin Mother, caught off-balance, grabbed at the shelf to save itself. The shelf swung away. The Tin Mother, fingers scrabbling at the smooth surface, fell between the shelf and the catwalk, crashed to the railing of the next catwalk below, bounced off it, and fell through level after level of the chamber until all sounds ceased.

Nyneve found strong hands steadying her shelf. Eyes stared at her anxiously. Beside her was the nose of the Miggot of One. Incredibly, there were tears in the eyes of that irascible little gnome.

"Oh, Nyneve," said the Miggot, "I'm so glad you're safe!"

All around them, the dreamers began to stir.

21
STARQUIN LIVES!

THE SUN WAS A CRIMSON MEMORY IN THE WEST AND blackness was slipping in from the east, but the upper curve of the dome still gleamed. Rosy clouds brushed its surface, and the moor glowed with a pink reflected light. Fang and the Princess watched the day end from their perch atop Pentor.

"I'm so cold," said the Princess. "And hungry. Do you suppose the Miggot got through, Fang?"

"Of course he did."

"Unless the Tin Mothers stopped him."

"He would have ordered them out of the way. The Miggot stands no nonsense."

"Let's huddle together a bit closer, Fang. For mutual warmth. In a way," said the Princess, "it's quite exciting to be looked on as breeding stock. Don't you think so, Fang?"

"As long as they keep looking on us that way. It won't take them forever to find the bat. And once they do, they'll have breeding stock to spare."

"But not such *enthusiastic* breeding stock," said the Princess hopefully, cuddling close. "Shall I tell them I'm pregnant?"

"Not unless we have to. . . . What are you doing, Princess?"

"Well, we have to do something, and this is the best thing

388

I can think of. Besides," she said sadly, "it might be the last time."

"Everything's going to be all right," said Fang. "Nyneve will be here soon, and she'll put things right. But just in case . . ." He began to fumble with his clothes.

And so the gnomes consoled themselves while the converter aimed its destructive network of filaments at them, and the Tin Mothers scrutinized the greataway. Nothing had happened all afternoon. Most of the Tin Mothers were immobile, conserving power. The penetrating hum of the converter was constantly in the ears of the gnomes.

Later the Princess said, "Something's happened."

The Tin Mothers began to move again, as one, like a battalion given a command. The hum of the converter deepened. Two Mothers detached themselves from the group around the giant machine and began to pace toward the Rock.

"I don't like the look of this," said Fang.

"I'm scared, Fang."

"That makes two of us. Hold my hand, Princess." They crept to the edge of the rock, keeping the approaching robots in view. "What are the bastards up to now?"

The Tin Mothers halted, looking up. "Come down!" one called.

The gnomes did not answer. They had been through this before.

"Very well. We shall come up and get you. We have considered the matter at some length and have decided that we are justified in using force."

"But we are your masters!" shouted the Princess. "And mistresses!" she added as an afterthought, with some vague notion that it might strengthen their case.

"That is true," replied the Tin Mother, beginning to climb. "It is because we hold you in such high regard that we are taking this unprecedented step. Your value as breeding stock has been reduced to near zero since we located your organic ship six minutes ago. However, it is not in our power to destroy even two kikihuahuas. We will try to avoid damaging you as we remove you from danger.''

"Suppose we jump?'' asked Fang, moving to the very brink of the drop.

"That would be a pointless thing to do,'' said the Mother, gaining the summit and advancing toward them. "But we will not deny you the right.''

"I didn't mean it like that,'' said Fang desperately. "I meant if we jump, you will be responsible for killing us. How can you justify that?''

"We do not understand your logic,'' said the Mother, grasping him by the arm. The other Mother, following up, took hold of the Princess. "But it is no longer a point worth debating.'' Picking the gnomes up, the robots carried them back across the summit of Pentor.

"We tried, Princess,'' said Fang.

"There was nothing more we could have done, was there?'' The Princess was crying.

"I expect there were all kinds of things on all kinds of happentracks. But we're not like Nyneve. We don't know how it's all going to work out. Don't cry, Princess. It's not our fault.''

"I just keep thinking of Nyneve dying in that dome.''

But Fang was staring north.

"I don't think she's going to die in there,'' he said, a sudden exultation in his voice. "I think she's done what she set out to do. Look, Princess!'' High in the Mother's arms, he could see over the rim of the moor.

Advancing through the twilight toward Pentor came an immense body of people. They surged across the valley, out of sight of the Tin Mothers around the converter but clearly visible from the top of the rock. They all wore white like avenging angels, although the mundane fact was that white robes were standard dome issue for ambulatory inmates. However, it was an inspiring sight, and the gnomes quickly drew the Mothers' attention to it.

"They're coming to get you, you bastards,'' said Fang.

The robots considered the oncoming hordes and communicated with their fellows. After a moment of frozen immobility, one of them spoke.

"It seems more likely that they have come to witness the conversion. Humans enjoy a spectacle."

In the distance, the multitude reached a sentinel Mother and flowed over it as though it did not exist. Fang's Mother said, "They attacked that savior. Communication ceased almost instantly. Please explain that, Fang."

"I told you. They're going to get every last one of you."

"But why?"

"You've outlived your usefulness on Earth," said Fang.

The main body of people moved toward the converter. A small group broke off, running toward Pentor. Their shouts carried clearly to the top of the rock against the background roar of ten thousand voices.

"Fang! Hold on!"

"We will save both kikihuahuas and the humans," said the Tin Mother, "at the expense of the few." The hum stopped and the filament glowed suddenly white, lighting up the moor and reflecting from the Mothers like actors on a floodlit stage.

The rock began to hum. Fang saw Nyneve and Arthur arrive at the base, glancing up at them. Nyneve flung herself against the smaller part of Pentor known as the Moon Rock, pressing the palms of her hands to the indentations while Arthur began to climb. The rock began to vibrate with a deep resonance that passed through the Tin Mother's body to Fang, shaking him to his very cells. He felt, rather than saw, a ribbon of force extending into the sky and away into some unknowable corner of the greataway. He felt a surge of joy and love that transcended his terror. It was a total love, extending from that instant into his past and future, so that he would never be the same gnome again.

Arthur came scrambling over the lip of the rock. "Turn that thing off!" he shouted.

"Too late," said the Mother.

There was a sound like the cracking of a gigantic whip. Afterward Fang found it difficult to describe exactly what he'd seen. It seemed that a bolt of light shot from the converter toward the rock. Just as he closed his eyes he caught an image of Arthur facing the converter, Excalibur held high. He heard a clashing, metallic reverberation. The Mother trembled as the rock shook beneath its feet. A sulfurous whiff caught at his nostrils. As he opened his eyes, smoke was drifting away on the breeze.

"What happened?" he asked shakily.

Arthur was still standing there. Excalibur glowed with unimaginable heat.

Nyneve came crawling onto the top of the rock and collapsed there, pale, shaking, yet smiling. "It's all right now," she said. "Starquin's passed through. He's safe. Thank you, Arthur." She caught sight of the gnomes, still in the grasp of the Mothers. "Starquin thanks you, too, Fang. And you, Princess. I'm sorry I took longer than expected in the dome, but I knew you wouldn't let me down."

Arthur was regarding her curiously, Excalibur still at the ready. "What was it like, helping Starquin on his way?"

She chuckled. "Like nothing on Earth. Even you couldn't match it, Arthur. It's an incentive given to us Dedos, to make sure we do our duty at all times."

He smiled ruefully. "I'll try to do better."

"Where's Morgan le Fay?" asked the Princess.

"She's gone home. There was nothing more for her to do here. She played her part very well. In fact," said Nyneve thoughtfully, "I'm not sure she was playing a part."

Fang shouted suddenly, "They're turning the converter on the humans!"

"It seems this rock is defended," said the Tin Mother. "But there are other ways. A substantial charge remains."

Down below, the Tin Mothers had swung the converter to face the oncoming humans. The scene was set for the most appalling carnage.

"Everything is fine with us and the humans now," said Fang desperately into the ear of the Tin Mother as the converter's hum deepened. "Machines are useful for a while, then they become obsolete. It's the way of all things. No criticism is intended.''

"But we are perfect."

"You were perfect up to the time we kikihuahuas left the Home Planet. But you should have stayed where you were. We left because we'd invented something better.''

"We saw no sign of improved versions. There was no development program, no prototypes.''

The human tide surged on. The Tin Mothers held their fire, listening to Fang.

"Your statement is puzzling. Explain why we didn't recognize the prototypes.''

"Because they were not machines."

"You are referring to your genetic-engineering program. We fail to see how its products could replace us. Our functions are different.''

"We can create life-forms that do everything you once did for us—and do it better. We can breed creatures to carry us over land, to take us on water or through space; to clothe us, to feed us. . . . Haven't you heard of the Kikihuahua Examples? True kikihuahuas never kill, or work metal, or light fires. Those are wasteful processes. Although,'' Fang said wistfully, "a good blaze can be a lot of fun. But we don't need machines anymore. We fled from you, don't you understand? We fled from our mistakes.''

After a long pause the robot said, "You fled into worse danger. Space travelers have been known to disappear without trace. We followed, ready to help. And along the way we helped other races. Finally we reached Earth and helped the people here. Such is our duty. Such is the way you built us.''

People were climbing over the converter, attacking the delicate filaments with rocks and clubs. The Princess said quietly, "Oh, Fang. We're safe.''

"We befriended humans," said the Tin Mother, "and now they are destroying us and our creations. This is not the first time we have been rejected by those we try to help. It makes us doubt the purpose of our existence. All over

Earth, humans are leaving their domes in pursuit of some illogical dream they call chivalry. We don't understand why the first objective of chivalry is to destroy us. We have many millennia of useful life. But so be it. We must accept that what you say is correct, Fang. We will shut down.''

So saying, the Tin Mothers knelt and put Fang and the Princess down, gently, on the summit of Pentor Rock. They remained kneeling.

The Princess, feeling unaccountably sad, placed her hand on the nearest Mother's leg. ''It's not your fault. It's ours, for not thinking things through when we created you. We're not so perfect as you are.''

''She can't hear you, Princess. They've all switched themselves off.''

All over the moor, the Tin Mothers stood motionless. The humans had gradually ceased their activity too. The converter had fallen silent.

''She . . .'' said the Princess. ''You called the Mother 'she,' Fang.''

''Or 'he.' It doesn't matter. Anything's better than 'it.' They meant well.''

They heard a scrabbling on the rock. More people were climbing up. Adam arrived, followed by Marc, Sally, the Miggot, and Afah.

''We won!'' shouted Sally exultantly. ''We beat the bastards! Look at them, all over the place, despondent. Beaten. Now we should dismantle every last one of them, starting with these two here!''

''Please don't,'' said the Princess.

The Tin Mothers knelt, with heads bowed, on top of Pentor Rock. A full moon had risen, silvering their masklike faces. The glow behind their eyes had died, and their chest screens were blank.

''Leave these two as a reminder,'' said Afah.

And there the two Mothers stayed for a thousand years until the combined forces of wind, rain, and snow toppled them and they fell into a crevice behind the smooth rock with the strange warm facets. There they disintegrated and were forgotten by everybody except the Rainbow.

A roaring came from the moor, deep and vibrant, swelling until it seemed to reverberate from the very stars.

"What's that?" asked Marc.

"It's all those people," said Sally. "They're cheering us." She waved, spreading her wings.

"All those people . . ." murmured Adam. "How are we going to feed them? Where are they going to live?"

"Oh, don't be such an old misery!" cried Sally. "Come on, let's go down there and behave like heroes for a while. I need to boast and gloat!"

Nyneve and the humans left the kikihuahuas standing on top of the rock. Once on the ground, Adam said, "I'm going back to the village. I'll need time to prepare our people for what happens next. We'll have to start building shelter and organizing food supplies. It would be a tragedy if those people died of starvation and exposure now that we've got them out of the dome." Nodding to them briefly, he hurried southward down the moorland path to Mara Zion.

"Old worry-guts," said Sally.

"He's not a bad fellow," Marc said, defending his father.

Nyneve had been regarding Sally and Marc thoughtfully. "I've got an idea," she said. "Are you willing to trust me for a while?"

"Another adventure?" asked Sally eagerly.

"The biggest you'll ever have."

"That sounds good to me," said Marc.

Nyneve took a deep breath. "Well . . ." she said. "I just might know a way to get you two people to the worlds you were created for. The journey won't be like anything you expect, but if you trust me you'll find it worthwhile."

"But . . ." Now Marc was hesitant. "We'll need time to organize things, won't we? I'll have to notify the village, and we'll need some food and clothes and—"

"You can tell whose son he is, can't you?" said Sally disgustedly.

"We'll be back before you know it, Marc," Nyneve assured him. "This isn't your usual kind of space travel."

"Oh . . . all right, then."

"Coming, Arthur?"

"Not this time." The tall man smiled. "Those people will need a leader, particularly over the next couple of days. I can't leave them now." He kissed Nyneve and hurried away. "See you soon!" he called.

"He's another one," said Sally. "The world is full of them."

Nyneve said, "Join hands and stand with me beside the Moon Rock." She placed a hand in one of the indentations. Concentrating, she used the technique taught her by Avalona long ago.

"Oh!" cried Sally, as they lay suspended in their invisible capsule, watching the stars drift by. "Now this is *really* flying."

Two days later the remnants of the revelers around Pentor Rock were startled by the sudden fiery materialization of three people, who in the meantime had traveled to many worlds and found an ideal one, where the gravity was less than half of Earth's, and slender trees reached to an orange sky. This world was equally suitable for Swingers and Wingers.

One month later Adam led a mass exodus from Earth.

A curious thing happened to Nyneve shortly after they left Earth on that first occasion. She became aware of an immense presence drifting along the same psetic line as herself. For a while she and her companions were engulfed by this presence, although only she was aware of it. It was a presence she'd met before: huge and wise and almost immortal—and certainly inevitable. It *glanced* at her as it passed, and filled her mind with one simple remark.

"Thank you," said Starquin, as he passed by.

"Isn't this exciting!" cried Sally. "I never want to go back to Earth!"

* * *

After a moment Afah said, "You're going to stay here?"

"Of course," said Fang. "You can send the other gnomes down as soon as you like. We'll set up gnomedom again in Mara Zion."

"It's not going to be easy. You'll be living on the same—what do you call it?—happentrack as the humans."

"Arthur and Nyneve will see we come to no harm. Things are going to be a lot better from now on. And anyway . . ." Fang glanced at the sky. Was it his imagination, or did Misty Moon look a little more distinct? "Happentracks can do funny things. What about you, Afah?"

The furry kikihuahua looked down at the dark mass of the moor. People were lighting fires, and figures could be seen dancing. "When we looked into Dream Earth," he said, "we found a gentle people living gentle lives that harmed nobody, full of pleasant imaginings and kindness. Then, in defiance of all we kikihuahuas stand for, we helped to teach them once again about fighting and killing and evil. We've turned them back into the savages they used to be, thirty thousand years ago."

"We had to free them from the Tin Mothers. It was the only way."

"We had to free them from our own careless invention, which we ourselves had outgrown. We've visited all kinds of unhappiness on these poor humans, and there will be more to come. They've tasted blood and they've remembered what it used to be like to be human. Now they'll have to adapt to life outside the domes, and they'll use their new-found aggression to do it. They'll be fighting one another for food and living space. They'll pull all their old weapons out of the cupboard. They'll fire up their spaceships. Everything they do will be against the Kikihuahua Examples—yet it is we who triggered them off."

"I found Nyneve's stories rather fun, myself."

"That's because you have some human genes in you."

"Come on, Afah. You're taking it too hard. There's nothing you can do about it now. What's done is done."

"There is something we can do, and I'm going to make

sure we do it. We can stay around until the humans recover from the first flush of their new vitality, and then we can guide them in the ways of the Examples.''

''You may have to stay around for a long time.''

''Time is of no consequence to a kikihuahua asleep in a bat.''

A month later the Mara Zion gnomes returned to Earth.

With the Princess at his side, Fang ruled wisely and well for two hundred and thirty-six years. In the fortieth year of his leadership the happentracks diverged and the gnomes found themselves once again in a world free of humans. Nyneve visited them often, but Arthur and his subjects were visible only in the umbra, gradually becoming less distinct.

The Princess bore Fang twelve more children, and the conception of each was enjoyed to the full by this unusually virile couple. Despite their own changed views on sex, the other Mara Zion gnomes never quite got used to such un-ashamed fecundity.

''Where will it all end?'' asked the Miggot when Fang announced the onset of the eighth—or it may have been the ninth—pregnancy. ''Is there no limit to this perversion?''

It ended many years later, one cool autumn evening when the Princess was seen walking slowly through the forest with the aid of a gnarled stick. She sat on a stump in a small clearing where mushrooms grew in a circle, and waited. The humanoid woman who materialized there saw her tear-stained face and nodded. She accompanied the Princess back to her dwelling, picked up the wrapped bundle, and together they walked to a mist-enshrouded lake.

The Princess watched without surprise as a narrow black boat appeared around a headland with a number of black-cowled human figures at the oars. Her companion, also dressed in black, stepped aboard and laid the bundle on a bench in the center of the boat. The Princess took her place beside the bench, and the woman returned to the shore.

''Thank you, Nyneve,'' said the Princess as the oars-women bent to their task.

"Thank you," the Dedo called back. "Thank you both."

The Princess watched as Nyneve turned and walked slowly back into the forest of Mara Zion, head down, until the mists hid her from view.